ALSO BY DAVID THOMSON

Warren Beatty and Desert Eyes

Suspects

Overexposures

Scott's Men

America in the Dark

A Biographical Dictionary of Film

Wild Excursions: The Life and Fiction of Laurence Sterne

A Bowl of Eggs

Hungry as Hunters

Movie Man

SILVER LIGHT

David Thomson

SILVER LIGHT

ALFRED A. KNOPF

New York   1990

THIS IS A BORZOI BOOK
PUBLISHED BY ALFRED A. KNOPF, INC.

Published in the United States by Alfred A. Knopf, Inc., New York,
and simultaneously in Canada by Random House of Canada Limited, Toronto.
Distributed by Random House, Inc., New York.

Grateful acknowledgment is made to Theodore Presser Company for permission to
reprint an excerpt from "Three Places in New England" by Charles Ives. Copyright
1935, 1976 by Mercury Music Corporation. Used by permission of the publisher. Sole
representative, Theodore Presser Company.

Library of Congress Cataloging-in-Publication Data
Thomson, David.
Silver light : a novel / by David Thomson.
p.   cm.
ISBN 0-394-55622-4
I. Title.
PR6070.H678S55   1990
823'.914—dc20   89-15448   CIP

Manufactured in the United States of America
First Edition

For Kate

". . . that was the first night I was ever really on the mesa at all—the first night that all of me was there. This was the first time I ever saw it as a whole. It all came together in my understanding, as a series of experiments do when you begin to see where they are leading. Something had happened in me that made it possible for me to co-ordinate and simplify, and that process, going on in my mind, brought with it great happiness. It was possession."

—Willa Cather, *The Professor's House* (1925)

"You fit a lot of descriptions."

—Captain Reverend Samuel Johnson Clayton to Ethan Edwards in *The Searchers* (1956)

Prospectors

Matthew Garth, who, it is said, in 1865 led the first great cattle drive from Texas to Kansas; who, in the same year, was reconciled with his adoptive father, met a woman to marry and was about to begin the rest of his life

Susan Garth, his daughter, born in 1870

Bark Blaylock, her friend from childhood, born in 1875 or '76 (that doubt is not the half of it)

Nora Stoddard, the daughter of Senator Ransom Stoddard, born in 1921

James Averill II, born in 1900, an Easterner of wealth and position, yet much drawn to the idea of the West

February 18, 1950

As dusk fell on her eightieth birthday, with only the wood fire for light, Susan Garth, alone in her silent house in a wild part of Arizona, read the two cards she had had that day. The one from Bark declared "we have come through together." And the one from Jubal—who would have expected that?—told her the light and teacher she was for him, how she had inspired him to make something of himself. She vowed she was not impressed, not touched, no not even lonely, and she could be rougher with herself than ever she was with others.

Yes, Bark, she said, as she put the cards on her mother's old chest, we have come through, and don't dare think it isn't still our story. As for Jubal, she told him—she did populate her house with conversational spirits—that her best light for him would be when he was too far away to see it.

The cards looked decent on the top of the chest, the beaten leather black once but so pale now, like moonlight, and still with her mother's initials—T. M.—outlined in vanished gold. Susan Garth did consider whether to get her gun and shoot the lock away, open the beast, at last. Didn't eighty merit some celebration? Some shock?

But she decided against it. Whatever that trunk held—the bones of her father, or the most lovely picture of the West—opening it would be a disappointment. If there were ghosts for company in the house, wasn't it the prospect of the trunk being opened that intrigued them?

PART ONE

Where They Are Leading

Contacts

She had been so busy writing this letter in her head, she no longer questioned whether she should write at all. Others, she would have admitted, could not have dared or dreamed. But there was something in Nora Stoddard—some fear of fear itself—that could not resist those thunderclouds if ever they loomed on her horizon.

Why not? she demanded. Why not drive headlong into them?

It was no deterrent to her to be told she was a woman, a member of a responsible class, the daughter of a senator; nor even that James Averill was married already, tied down, in place. Without any thought of harming his wife, without even being led on by the persistent reports that Averill did act as a free agent, still Nora doubted anyone was ever tied down. Those who noticed bonds needed them. Those most secure were at liberty. Not that Nora was complacent in this state, or would have denied charges of arrogance. She loved explosions, but she was of the opinion that nothing was ever lost or destroyed. Today's debris was just tomorrow's new dust.

She had lived part of her life in desert places, and while she was a glowing physical specimen—a fine and lovely woman, it was said—still, she understood the lonely severity of the eagle or the Gila monster.

So she had prospects of James Averill, a wish to meet him, a readiness to have him; yet, for all that, the certainty that he was free, untouchable, as lonely as herself.

Santa Fe, N.M.
May 16, 1950

My dear James Averill (Is that forward? This is our first warm
evening, a blessing, and I am honoring it with a *rosé d'Anjou*).

It is all priceless—which means there likely will be a very
impressive tag on these pictures in twenty years. (Can we wait?
We must. We have to.) I suspect these old visions are rising
slowly in the American imagination. Perhaps since the war we
have more need of them.

Her name is Susan Garth. She owns up to eighty, but she
might be older, she has lived so long in the sun and the desert.
It is harder in the West, estimating age. Youth goes quicker, and
then a face deepens into its own leathery scrutiny.

She is out-of-the-ordinary, old-fashioned but unsentimental,
small, rather cantankerous, and somewhere between forgetful
and grab-your-eyes shrewd. She resides now in northeast Arizona, near a place called Canyon de Chelly (which I haven't
penetrated yet—she prefers to visit me, and drives down, driving herself). She is the daughter of one Mathew or Matthew
Garth, who was a Texas rancher, and of Tess Millais (French,
n'est-ce pas?). They would have been two of all those who came
west/West looking, searching and wondering, but ready, I suppose, if they found nothing, to pretend to be just dreamy souls
full of the land and the space, etc.

It makes me sad, thinking of this. Am I drunk, or is there
something of me in their story? I never know if I count as a
Westerner.

Her pictures are amazing. I have seen just a few, and she
claims there are five thousand. (Yet she also seems to convey
that photography isn't her only work.) I imagine she keeps them
in boxes—there are plates, too—wrapped tenderly in old dresses
or nightgowns. She has taken pictures for over sixty years, print-
ing them herself. It is hard to imagine a darkroom out here in
all the light. That dark is a modern invention.

I think she might be what we're looking for, someone in the
line of Solomon Burke or William Jackson—the *real* thing. And
she's a dear, quaint soul.

One fly in the ointment—I don't know how considerable. She
says, if we show, then the first patron has to be an old friend
of hers—a "Bart" or "Bark" Blaylock. I'm not sure I heard that

name right, but I couldn't ask again—she can be a bit intimidating. Some old-timer, I suppose. I hope you won't be put off.

Nora

She left this letter overnight, to cool or dry, and in the morning it
did seem too loaded with untidy openness—a little corny, a touch
creepy. So the woman, not quite young now, but unprepared for
anything else yet, sat down at the pine table with the morning sunlight and the cold wine bottle, and tried again. She was clear and
matter-of-fact about the improvement; she was so well aware of her
recklessness, the quality that London, England, and Smith College
had not tamed. But could she rein it in? She hoped there might be
maturity possible, a way of learning without loss, in a more cautious,
judicious observing of things, and it pleased her to overcome a little
of her wildness. She wrote this second letter and sent it to Boston.

Santa Fe
May 17, 1950

Dear Mr. Averill,

There is an old woman I have discovered, who moves me
greatly. She does seem to be a natural camera genius and she
has not shown anywhere before.

Her name is Susan Garth. She is eighty, yet apparently in
sturdy health. She lives out in remote country, with Navajo for
neighbors. I had seen her a few times in the museum, and I got
talking to her because she stood in front of one of our Edward
Curtis photographs. Stock-still. For half an hour. So I spoke to
her, and said, wasn't it fine? And so it is. I stopped to look at
it with her, really *look* at it, rather than assess it. She waited so
long, she left me with no other choice. And she said she lived
near the site of the picture: the Canyon de Chelly, in northeast
Arizona. Do you know it? She said *she* had pictures, too. At first,
I thought she meant she collected. But, no, these are *her* pictures.
And she waited still, so I felt I should ask to see them. But I
don't believe she had had any such design. For she looked at
me with great intensity and suspicion—she is bird-like, but as
wizened and as dark as an old Apache.

She said, "Could you *see* them?" It made me feel perched on a ledge—exposed. But then she nodded to herself and two weeks later she brought in seven—deserted views, huge landscapes and prospects. I cannot easily say why they are so special. Perhaps it is just that I can believe I have found them. But they are crystal-clear and strong. It is as if the stones had taken the pictures.

There are thousands, she says, and she makes it seem no more startling than there being thousands of some otherwise rare flower in a remote valley. She does impress me. Though I'm uneasy saying that—for there is something beaten into her frail figure so that I am not sure I'm fit to be impressed by her. You don't feel you can understand her. She is entirely direct, but there is a mysteriousness about her. She may not often converse with people and so has got into some habit of deadly, straightforward thinking. Does she know how to let anyone like her?

I believe there is a show in Susan Garth. And it might interest you: I think you will love the photographs and want to assist them. However, I must tell you that as soon as I mentioned the faintest likelihood of a show, she brought up this old friend, his name is Bart Blaylock, who would help. I got the impression that he has been her patron, and maybe more. Could the Averill Foundation share with him?

Sincerely,
Nora Stoddard

Boston
May 20, 1950

Dear Nora (I hope I may use your name now),

Your letter filled me with wonder and excitement. And with questions.

I am touched by the impression left on you by this Miss Susan Garth (she did sound like a spinster, albeit one with old flames to light up your gallery). Indeed, as I found myself liking her, I felt the more admiring of you. For I could not grasp her without following the shifts in your appreciation, or seeing you in her glass.

As you may surmise, I am eager to see the photographs and meet Miss Garth. She sounds like a considerable undertaking. On the quality of her views, I have no doubt; it would be impudent of me to compete with your taste and trained eye. As to the Canyon de Chelly, however, I will speak up. It is an authentic wonder of the world—I do not just mean America's world either. I was there in 1906 when my father took me on a tour of the West—it was the heavenly summer of my young life: for I observed the same sort of bond between my father and the country we saw then, as I feel between you and Miss Garth.

Therefore, I have a notion to bring my son out to see you, the canyons and the photographs this summer. He is ten, a little older than I was in '06, and undoubtedly ready for the experience. (I would like him to think on more marvels than Sugar Ray and Jake La Motta!) I will let you know, but we could not be with you much before the end of June. I thought we might fly to Albuquerque and then motor.

But now—"Bart" Blaylock! Can it be? I bet it is—but it is "Bark" Blaylock. Why, he is nearly famous in his funny way. He was a writer and publisher of *Wild West Tales* for years, and *he managed Jack Chance*, the noblest middleweight of my youth. I may be wrong about this, but I have a fancy that if you mentioned the name to your mother—or if I had, to my father—I think they would have waxed a little anecdotal over him. Everyone knew everyone in those days. There were probably only a few thousand people between the Pecos and the Colorado rivers. So I would be honored to "share" with him—whatever that entails. I assumed he was dead. He seemed to have a corner on the dangerous life.

With all good wishes,
James Averill

Written in a journal he was keeping for his son:

And so, at the next weekend this no longer quite young lady drove from Santa Fe to Shinbone (you can believe that name is made up, if that's how the raw sound strikes you), which is in Lincoln County, and where her mother had elected to live since the death of her husband, Ransom Stoddard (you know *he* is real). And I see now that my letter gave her no inkling of a need for caution, or delicacy; and she was not anyway likely to be restrained, for she thought her life was working out at last. So she strode up to her mother—watering the cactus rose, perhaps—and let us suppose she said, straight out in the ebbing light, "James Averill says I'm to ask you about Bark Blaylock," laughing at the name, as if it belonged to a character in a comic book, never foreseeing that it could be gathered in a soft part of her mother's memory.

Well, James Averill III, you might be surprised, but not astonished, to hear that her mother broke down on the spot with weeping. God knows how or why! I had made the suggestion casually. But in all that time and space, who knows what tender moments have gone unseen? You know now that a child must sometimes see a parent in tears—should do so—and be ready to help without that parent feeling hopelessly ashamed or compromised. I am telling you this whole story because I want you to know how your father was moved by love for this breezy Nora Stoddard, out there in the West where large things felt suddenly possible. And as easy as driving two hundred miles after work, before dark. On those dead straight roads in northeast New Mexico. The key has something to do with those confident roads and wondering if you will ever arrive. It is a kind of dream. That may be how they live so long out there in the unimpeded air.

The page then torn out and burned.

On a homemade postcard, sent from Chinle, Arizona, to a post-office box in Beatty, Nevada, dated May 1950. The message was in thin, upright black ink.

> Maybe they *will* show me. My "dreadful" photographs. The girl is Nora Stoddard. We owe the Stoddards something. Are we old-timers in for revival? You should write your life. Invent what you can't recall. It will easily pass for fiction what with all your Wyatt Earps. Do you remember her on the other side? Put her in!

And on the picture side of the card, there is a black-and-white photograph of a dark-haired girl in a white dress, worse for wear, in the desert, about 1885, staring into the camera, daring it to take her, getting ready to punch out its touching, innocent eye.

The Wilderness, 1864

On a night a few nights before the Wilderness, in the treed meadows west of Fredericksburg, where a Texas regiment was bivouacked, this quiet talk between two men silently reckoning the odds on their own death or glory in the days to come. Neither one of them had had liquor in weeks, yet they were drunk on their low, murmuring colloquy. Not as anyone passing by would have remarked on, not as either of them knew. But still they were drunk with the reputation of strong men passing the night in small talk instead of crying out for help or deliverance. And the two men were Matthew Garth from the Big Bend part of Texas, and another man, old enough maybe to be his father, yet unnamed in the dark.

This Garth had been not quite awake, half counting off the night, so slow, so cold, half dreaming of the warm spaces of Presidio, when the other fellow had come up to him like a blanket or cloak, a heavy scent of tobacco and hard times in the darkness, without any asking or explaining. This odor had taken up a place close to Matthew, as if for the night. And it had shortly thereafter lit up a pipe: Garth saw the flare of a long, exhausted face in the match, and then the crimson breathing of the pipe. It might have been miles away, a fire consuming a city.

The pipe had at first supplied a sweet, aromatic Virginian flavor to the air: it woke Matthew up properly and he was charmed by it. But as time went by, so the other fellow's supply lessened, or else his smoking reached down to the pit, the chancre, in the pipe. There was something foul in it, unrelieved, putrid, waves slipping over Matthew's face. He flinched, he tried to time his own breathing to the ebb and flow of this factory, the pipe. Then it was the dead being smoked, their limbs piled into the bowl, like the leftover parts of meats being submitted to a grinder. In the night, more removed from reason or calm, Matthew began to consider if this wasn't some ghost sent to him to draw him into the pipe. The pipe was as big as a canyon. He wondered if he might die if the battle did come on the next day, but he was not bitter or aggrieved at this specter of a man picking on him. If it was part of some design . . .

"So you're rich," this older man decided, with a sneer such as could not have been forgiven in daylight. It did not follow from what they had said before, but it told Matthew this unseen companion had been putting things together in his own dogged, blind way.

Matthew laughed. "How do you measure that?"

"This Dunson has the ranch? A big ranch? About as large as Dunson wants it to be?"

That *did* explain the history of Thomas Dunson.

"And he has no heir but you?"

"Not that he ever mentioned."

"You're damn rich. No doubt about it."

Matthew laughed again, but now it was another kind of laugh, one in which he saw the dark humor for the first time. "I don't have a thing but what I have here," he explained. "And some clothes and books in the house in Texas."

"You've never wanted for one thing." There was triumph in the older man's voice. "If only because that Dunson is clever enough to keep you out of the way of wanting and thinking—"

"No such thing," said Matthew Garth.

"You'll go back to ease and revelry, living on the beef of Texas. What Dunson got, that's your wealth, your patrimony."

"Well, maybe you're right," said Matthew—it was a dreamy voice now, and it was hard to determine whether it was patient or dangerous. But the line of talk had made him see Dunson's eyes, and that desperate look of wanting, without ever knowing what the wanted thing might be. Always looking away at the distance and desire. But he said, agreeably, "I likely will get it by inheritance, without all the woes and worry."

"Sell it and build yourself a palace!" Now the other man laughed, a choking noise, full of his pipe's rot and hard accretion, "Like a star on the bare land."

"It's a strange thing," said Matthew, "but I see a change in our times."

"Change? Nothing changes."

"Our land, it was Mexican when we got there. In '51. Not that there was anyone there to notice. We came south to it, five weeks it took by wagon, and we saw not one soul until the day Dunson liked the land."

"He liked it wide and empty, I daresay," the older man nagged away. It was the sort of voice gets itself shot.

Matthew remembered. "He's one with a feel for the ground. I believe he smelled the water. I can see him now that day, looking out over the grassland and leaning over to one side just to grab up a piece of grass or earth. I can see that sort of swoop he made, to his right it was, but never stopping going forward, his hand like an ape's skimming the ground. You could see how happy he was to know this was the place. He was from out of New York, you see, and something in him had always expected the openness. And he said, 'This is it.' "

"Tall man?" asked the older man.

"Most say so."

"I can see that, too."

"No, sir, you can't," said Matthew, full of good-humored surety.

"You think a man has to be rich to feel the wonder in land that's his? You that kind of fool?"

"Well, I hope not. I can see it would be possible."

"Oh yes," said the other man, with a disturbing reverence hidden in the dark. "It's a possibility. What did Dunson do then?"

"Killed the Mexican."

"He did!"

"Yes, sir. Mexicans came riding up, two of them. Said the land was owned by some grandee way away to the south. And Dunson asked how did he get it, hadn't he taken it from the Indians? And the Mexican—he was an amiable man—he smiled and said it was likely so. Then Dunson said, well, he was taking it away, and he had to kill the Mexican."

"Had to?"

"Dunson leaned into him. The Mexican didn't have a choice. There he was, one minute, riding along on the sweet land, singing—"

"You heard him?"

"I mean, he might have been, free as could be. Then the next he knew he was going to have to die for no cause of his own. The suddenness, man! Don't you see it? The progress!"

"I could admire your Dunson," said the older man.

"But that taking's over," said Matthew Garth. "Dunson's got him a lawyer now, an educated drunk in Fort Stockton. You couldn't have the land now without the paper."

"Your Dunson read?"

"Enough."

And then there was silence as the two men thought about the story. The light was beginning to creep over the fields. There were noises in the camp, the clots of blue-gray smoke from the first fires, and grumblings before duty and the day.

"What's your name, sir?" asked Matthew Garth.

"Edwards," said the older man. "Ethan Edwards."

"From Texas?"

"I don't have a fixed, reliable home. My brother has a place there, only a small place. Desert nearly. Comanche country."

"They killed my folks," said Matthew Garth, matter-of-fact. "In a wagon train."

"So Dunson's your adoptive father?"

"He took me in."

"Christian action?"

"Just collected me out of the wilderness," Matthew agreed.

"What were you doing there?"

Here it was: that first story, the one that always made Matthew writhe. The wagon train, the Indian attack—and Matthew had run, pretending to be going after a stray cow when he was really losing himself, leaving his parents. The first great panic.

"I got separated," said Garth. "Looking for my cow. What could I do then but walk?" He looked for an answer. "Till I came upon Dunson and his man, Groot."

"Invented you for his own boy he did—that'd be the point."

It was light enough now for Matthew to see this other man's face was more hostile than he had imagined. There was no ghostliness, though, in the features; no, the face was hard and solid as a butt, and about as lean and purposeful.

"Sir?" asked Garth. "You believe we will die here?"

That butt of a face turned on him, and it grinned. There was a boy's face beneath the roughness of the campaign. There was inventiveness and fun in it still, and the cold moonlight of hope.

"Hereabouts, I daresay," said Edwards, and he started a chuckle that brought courage even to Matthew Garth.

Bark Blaylock, 1885

"What you gonna be?" the girl asked him out there in the desert, where they used to be together, day after day, no one seeming to care that she was five years the older and altogether more knowing of the things that inspire a boy of ten in a girl of fifteen, even if she was so tiny a thing, and so scrawny. Together, year after year, always fisticuffs and arguing so that he, at least, didn't notice the dependency. How is a child going to know that a first friend—especially a mettlesome, perverse, punitive one—is the best he'll ever have? When he finds her such a trial, such a load, his daily ordeal, he thinks of her . . . he was going to say as an "enemy," but opponent is more like it. And an opponent always beating hell out of him which only made him wilder, so he cried and cried. And who else was there to console him but his torturer? They lived, you see, on the edge of Death Valley, before that place acquired glamour or society!

"I said, 'Who you gonna be?' " the girl insisted; there was a will-fulness to her like an iron brace or corset, barring that womanhood which her body felt so close. Nor would she let the heat and the slows of afternoon have their way with this whiny boy. Wouldn't let him dream or read in the shade; and likely would use the heavy, bound book to throw at his head. She had to lift up the rock and examine the dream, the way she would always want to study a rattlesnake or a Gila monster, whatever he said, with him yards away, fearful and angry, stamping his foot, telling her to come off, and crying again. "Where d'you keep all them tears then?" she asked, scorning the true feeling he believed in. And she'd turn round to watch his tears, for they amazed her more than the reptiles, and seemed more alien. The grin on her dark-burned face was like some-thing she'd borrowed from the monster, exultant at his tears and her power. He wanted the Gila to bite her. He did. And cut the monster away, leaving the bite in her skin forever.

Still, he answered, though he was battered already in his hopes. "Wyatt Earp," he said. Everyone then thought of being an Earp.

"You can't, worm. Uncle Ethan's always Earp. He really *is* Earp, if you want to know."

"Then Charles Dickens."

"Be another author," she said, so sly.

"Which one?" If only she would talk of books to him.

"Yourself, of course, snake!" She was laughing at him, always scheming fresh ways.

"Writing's soft," he said, to deter her.

"You like Mr. Dickens."

He did, but what was the problem? "I never find anyone else who reads him." The set of Dickens Edwards had, all in blue with gold lettering on the cloth, were like boxes that only he opened.

"I don't know that's the point," said the girl, watching him very closely.

Then the boy's heart lifted in another sweet direction, "I could be heavyweight champ!"

"You'll never be big enough," said wiry, black-eyed Susie Garth. She dared him to answer, but he still hoped he might miss the beating. Oh, but she was cunning. "Know what I want to be?" she asked. Her bare foot poked at the ground in some wheedling show of shyness.

"What?" He was helpless and feeble.

"Your husband." It was the trap closing, and she made kissing shapes at him with her stained mouth.

He couldn't help it; he never could. "Piss on that!" he roared. Just like he imagined John L. Sullivan might do. He hadn't seen so much as a picture of John L. then, in 1885, but he had heard men talking in Tonopah about him, as if they knew him, and the one took up a fighting stance to show the others how awesome John L. was, with the fists up, and the backs of the arms towards the opponent. It was a way fighters can only stand for the camera, the pose holding the body still for the picture's delay. You could get pulped fighting like that. Which he was about to, again.

"What'd you say?" she demanded.

"You know!" he yelled, furious with himself.

"Did I hear you say, 'Piss on that!'?"

"Yes you did!"

"That," she said, "is an insulting remark of the kind that grown men might have to die for."

He groaned. He wanted to fly away, or vanish. She was going to powder him. Why did he have to hear the words, too, her entire little scene?

"In Dodge, and Tombstone, that would be a challenge, wouldn't you say?"

He nodded. He hated her; he longed for John L. to knock her off her awful bare feet. Just to hear her bony bum bump on the ground, and see the surprise on her face.

"Well," she decided, "seeing as you are no more than a boy, I will content myself with Queensberry justice. On your feet, picklehead."

He was as tall as her when he stood up, and he'd think maybe magically this time a boy's natural strength will be there for him, and maybe he can gull her. What he'll do, he'll circle right, away from that chopper hand of hers. Get her moving so her skirts might tire and slow her. And he did, the boy did, and he kept his head bent over, watching her right fist, and he edged away from it so he never saw or heard her left come in below till he heard his own ribs squeak and knew he couldn't breathe. It had gone in right under the bottom rib, hooking up. And he was lifted off his feet by it, his already powerless feet that wouldn't hold flat on the ground when they came down. How did that little spring know how to hit so hard? It wasn't force; it had to be knowing. He saw the mark of it on her face as she watched him go down, such a grim, serene smile with the cracked lips clamped shut, too proud to speak. And then the right, forgotten and only waiting, slamming into the side of his face—when he was down, too!—so he felt it swell straightaway.

And she did speak then. "Damn," she muttered, as if she'd forgotten somewhere she had to be. And her right fist swung loose like a ball on a string.

The kid, Barclay, was curled up on the hot ground, snorting and gasping and trying to weep, but it's hard if you can't cry for lack of air, and wanting to vomit but having no command of his stomach, and thinking he was bound to die, believing he was a fish, twitching, never to regain his proper element.

Susie had her right arm against her side, but it didn't stop her getting astride him. He could see one of her bare feet, with little hairs on the toe knuckles, and the toenails rough and torn. He heard her skirts billowing up above him, and it was cool all of a sudden, like a tent had gone up. He could look up and see the white walls of her dress and the legs arching like trees. He saw the dark where they met up there, so far away, like the peak of a mountain. And then he heard the clatter on his face before he saw the twinkling golden fall of her piss and heard her chuckling, judging the aim out there outside her skirts, and getting him, dead shot, no matter how he tried to turn, with the warm bitter stuff filling his gaping mouth. He *would* kill her one day! How could he know she might be his best and only friend?

She walked off a bit after she had emptied herself, and he saw her up on a rock looking at her hand—he was forgotten! If you have never had a girl destroy you in a fight and then soak your head with her carefully stored-up piss, when there is no one else there to send her off to prison, and you have just got to find a way of talking to her afterwards with dignity, then you don't know the fortitude of the human imagination. But even he needed ways and time to explain to himself that, really, nothing much had happened and he wasn't a slave, or trash, if he gave this girl the time of day again.

One way was crying. It brought her back to him with a sort of amused, considering look on her triumphant face. And it allowed her to be a new comfort to him, without having to apologize or make the promises that she would never do it again. If he cried, she could come back as another person, not the defiler and the annihilator, but a kind of mother to him. Such ease, so hard come by.

She kneeled down beside him and watched his hair dry.

"What's the matter?" she said; she said it cooing, like he was her baby. "Tell Sue-Sue."

He dared not answer. It was his only chance of having his wretchedness overlooked—he became speechless.

"What's the matter, little Bark?" And Susie sighed to herself at the thought of all his small distress. She stroked and soothed him, and she said, "There, there," all the time, talking to herself, and sometimes she tickled and he giggled like bacon popping in the pan, and she pretended to be surprised that he was still alive. And he thought he was in wicked heaven—if only the way there was less arduous. She could be so kind, so soft and so restoring. And he was always ready for what came next, mute and resigned, and because he was so docile he began to see it was not so bad either.

Her small hand—her left one now, a touch slower, so it was graver and lovelier—would undo his pants and bring his thing out in the light, and she'd always say "Oh!" like a grumpy old lady and it was the last thing she dreamed of seeing. And she'd murmur as she inspected it, and that quiet sound made it grow. She'd look at him as if he was really her own child, and made her so content. Then she'd dip her head and it was as if he was ill and she was saving him, sucking out the poison. But he felt diminished, as you might if you were sick.

It was so quick in the desert, and so quiet. She made no noise but he just felt the slow, mercurial rising, and he couldn't quite be pleased with it, no matter that it took away the hurt and the shame. And it was so warm. Then she sat up and spat away a gray gob of him. Could she spit! And she'd only spit the once, out of honor.

"There you are, sparrow Bark," she'd say.

And the two of them looked up, children without a doubt, the boy scurrying with his buttons, as a tall man in a black suit appeared over the rise. He wasn't looking for them as much as roaming.

"Uncle Ethan!" the girl called out. "I must have broke my hand."

And the tall, gloomy figure turned towards them and said, "That'll be the day."

James Averill, 1950

Written in the journal he was keeping for his son:

How stirring it was, this reappearance in my circle of awareness of Bark Blaylock; it was as if he had returned from the dead,
or one of those large, obscure tracts of America that were known
as "the Territory of . . ." before they clamored for statehood,
before they traded in their wildness for the package. You must
realize, Jim, that it is an emotional thing for a Southerner or for
one of that persuasion to go West. If the South had been the
Southwest—those territories—I believe there would be two
Americas now. You see, the West was another place.

I kept thinking about Bark Blaylock—the little I knew, or remembered, and the many gaps I found myself trying to fill. Had
there been such truly empty areas in his existence? What I knew
of him was all so lit up with the air of ingenious, bold piracy.
You see, I had not met him yet; and so I could not conceive of
Bark Blaylock having empty, quiet days, or falling asleep in the
afternoon sun. I was blind to him being anything but a
"Character"—a twentieth-century cowboy, dry as the desert and
as odd as cactus, a romancer, reckless but taciturn, someone
who had weathered in history's wind. The absurd thing is that
once I heard he was alive still, I assumed he must be a rugged
monument of hardiness—like a mesa in Monument Valley. Very
old, yet never elderly. I did not realize that he might feel frail,
worried or a failure.

Well, you have met him now. He was your friend, your old
"uncle" for a day or so, and he took you to that movie and sat
through it quietly, for your sake, not peppering the screen with
his six-gun out of wrath or despair, but observing that you loved
the film and listening to your pleasure. I know the two of you
talked about it, and I'm sure the conversation would not have
been possible with me, or anyone else, there. It's nice for me to
imagine it, and to marvel at his grace in letting you watch *Red
River* in your own way. That crusty old-timer of fancy might
have told you not to believe in such pipe-dream stuff. Yet maybe

he is old or wise enough to know we will never stop the wonderful lies. Or sad enough.

You see, he had a role in that industry himself. I went back
through your grandfather's things—I went over to Cambridge
to Houghton and had them get out some of the boxes—apparently, no one has touched them. There are 117 boxes of James
Averill papers and no one has yet looked at them. The people
at the library were not even apologetic about it: I expect they
have whole buildings of such unexamined treasure. Maybe fifty
years from now there will come some young historian who
"unearths" amazing richness. And he may find some note of
your grandfather's admitting he was bored by me, alas, or that
he had just been with a dancer in Havana—stuff I'd sooner leave
there. After all, he took pains never to show me if I bored him.

As I was saying, I put a few things about Blaylock together.
I was sure grandfather had known him. It seems that in the '20s,
when my father was encouraging research in the West, he was
in touch with Bark Blaylock. There was an *Encyclopedia of Western
Authors* that father paid for; it was published in 1926, with an
entry on Bark Blaylock as follows:

'Bark' (Barclay or Bartholomew) Blaylock. Writer, editor, publisher
and adviser to the motion pictures. Born probably in 1875 or '6,
Blaylock was a boy in the Old West who lived on the Nevada edge
of Death Valley. He is the author of many short stories and narratives with Western themes, some of which were put out by his
own company, the Tombstone Press—notably *Roy Bean Remembers, I Rode With the Clantons, The Death of John Q.* and *Bride of the
Comanche*. Though short romances, full of spirit and adventure,
his works show an unexpected sense of historical detail and accuracy. He has traveled all over the West, and is familiar with the
Yukon and Mexico. He was in Los Angeles from around 1914, and
he was often employed on Western motion pictures as an adviser
on costumes, lore and general authenticity. He was present at the
Death Valley filming of *Greed*. While known to his many friends
as a convivial talker, Mr. Blaylock is reticent about biographical
details. He was married to, and divorced by, a Constance Miller.
It is intriguing to reflect on the rumor that he was the son of Celia
Ann Blaylock, an early wife of Wyatt Earp.

Very intriguing! I thought—there it was, at the end of the
entry in this old, out-of-print book, composed of the careers of
Western writers you will never hear of again. Just think how

many there were, so busy, so illustrious for a moment, able to
order fresh oysters by the dozen, and how many of their "book-
lets" with engravings on the covers of cowboys like statues of
heroic energy, their mustaches dragging down their brave faces,
so they always look sad or humorless. (I believe some must have
been deadpan jokers! I hope so, anyway.) I had a bundle of their
books when I was your age—and I may have read some of
Blaylock's tales. My father had a poor view of such literature,
which only fired my curiosity. He said they were rubbish, and
mostly the work of men (he sometimes implied women in New
Jersey sweatshops!) who had never been, and had no intention
of going, an inch west of Chicago.

But my father did know Blaylock, and was "intrigued" by
him. Now, it may be that he took a fancy to Blaylock because
old "Bark" was in the boxing business. You see, your grandfather admired pugilism and what it represented. Though we
were not permitted to talk about it in front of your grandmother,
he went to the fights and had an interest in some boxers. I mean,
he owned a piece of them. Perhaps Jack Chance, who was actually managed by "Bark." Chance was a middleweight who
was supposed to be a quarter Indian, and he was good enough
to fight for the title, but he never got that fight because . . . well,
maybe because "Bark" wouldn't deal with the fellows who ran
the business. I know this: your grandfather was very proud of
a picture of himself sparring with Chance. Of course, it was
another pose. Your grandfather must have been sixty. He's in
a suit, with Chance smiling at him and their raised fists entwined. Grandfather had that picture framed; and he kept it
carefully when there were many other things he let go.

All of which suggests he took "Bark" Blaylock seriously. I wish
we could ask the old man about this. I haven't time now to go
through all the boxes in the library, and I wouldn't want to
burden you with the task. (I'd like to think of you doing it one
day, but not as a duty.) Who knows what's there? Soon, no one
will care—and later no one will know it exists.

Still, I have been thinking about Blaylock, and I have found
out this much. Wyatt Earp did live with a woman named Blaylock. They may have been married: I suspect out there in those
days marriage and such other formalities were not always bothered with, or were entered into and forgotten as the mood
changed.

Earp had been married, in January 1870, in Lamar, Missouri,

to a Urilla Sutherland. But she died in the same year, in labor, and the baby died too. Earp then was twenty-two. He had been a farmer, and he had helped his family move from Iowa to California—it seems he drove a wagon on that journey. Think of that! Well, now, wait for this—they all got bored with San Bernardino (I can't think why) and went back east to Missouri. Such huge enterprises, so seemingly casual. Think of the energy. And the aimlessness. Wyatt then worked for the railroad and was himself a bit of a boxer! You can begin to get drawn into this, young man—don't blame your father if the Averill fortune collapses while he starts his detective work.

Well, some time after 1870, somewhere, Earp met Celia Blaylock. They were together when he arrived in Tombstone, in the Territory of Arizona, in—as far as I can tell—1879. By then, Wyatt Earp had been a lawman in Wichita and Dodge City, both in Kansas. Do you begin to see the possibility? Wyatt Earp was in Wichita in 1875 and Dodge in '76, apparently with Celia Blaylock. Our "Bark" may have been Wyatt Earp's boy! But then why, in heaven's name, would a Western author, a character, not boast about that the rest of his life? Because the parents were not properly married? Because this Celia was no better than she should have been?

Or is the answer something to do with this: at some time, in or around 1881, Wyatt Earp apparently discarded Celia Blaylock in favor of a younger woman, some sort of actress, named Josephine Marcus, whom he married, and with whom he lived the rest of his life—Wyatt Earp died only in 1929, when he was over eighty. And what happened to Celia Blaylock? What might become of an abandoned woman then in Tombstone, which is a small place now and was then only what it was because there was silver in the ground, and a rush to get it out in which there was no time or courtesy for life's victims? I cannot find a word more in the histories of that woman or of any child she had.

Susan Garth

Nora Stoddard: Miss Garth, this is a tape recorder. I expect you've
heard of them.

Susan Garth: Expect I have.

NS: It will record our conversation and . . .

SG: We're going to have a conversation?

NS: I certainly hope so.

SG: I thought you were going to ask me questions.

NS: Well, yes, that's so, I am.

SG: I don't see that as a conversation.

NS: Well, I take your point, but I hope we're going to be friendly
about it.

SG: What's that got to do with it?

NS: Think of me as your granddaughter, perhaps. Someone who
wants to hear about the old days.

SG: I don't know. I don't know if we'll get along.

NS: We *are* getting along. Aren't we?

SG: I don't know what's in your head. Nor whether I should go out
of my way to please you.

NS: This is not done to please me.

SG: It's not? Why are you doing it then?

NS: The history of photography is my area—my responsibility.

SG: You don't look the responsible type.

NS: I don't?

SG: Doesn't trouble me. I'd just as soon see that wicked smile of
yours.

NS: Wicked?

SG: Eager. Ambitious, awake. I've said the wrong thing?

NS: I think we should just try, and maybe not try too hard, don't
you think?

SG: It's your business. I don't know what it's for.

NS: It's for the New Mexico Oral History Project.

SG: I don't live in New Mexico.

NS: I know that. But it's not relevant. You see, the tape recorder
belongs to New Mexico—like this office.

SG: Oral history?

NS: That's right.

SG: I'm not deaf, you know. Not a bit.

NS: No, I realize you're not. I'm sorry. Oral history is when you have people talking in their own voices about what they have seen and done in their lives. So others who come later will know. I mean, wouldn't you want to hear the words of the people who came out West in wagon trains, and the Indians? Your parents?

SG: All of them?

NS: Why no, not all of them, Miss Garth. Just some of them.

SG: Who says which ones?

NS: No one says. It's up to the researchers—those they think are interesting. Those alive still.

SG: I don't expect as many of them would be. My father wouldn't have said a word, if you'd put a gun to his head.

NS: Well, no, I daresay. But you see, in oral history, we value the ordinary people. They don't have to be President Lincoln or Wyatt Earp.

SG: That one was a downright tedious man. No one ever wanted to listen to him talk.

NS: Oh really? Did you know him?

SG: Heard, I only heard it.

NS: Well, that's interesting, isn't it? It's what people heard others say that contributes to history.

SG: They could be liars. We all could be.

NS: But you heard he was tedious.

SG: That's interesting?

NS: I think so. It serves as a corrective to legend, you see.

SG: Is that right?

NS: Because the legend makes us think that Wyatt Earp must have been a rather dashing fellow. You see, it may be that the legend is wrong. It's only what people wanted to believe.

SG: That's all people know how to believe.

NS: But if you say you heard that Earp was boring . . .

SG: Earp burps.

NS: I beg your pardon.

SG: What we used to say—Earp burps. We used to sing that.

NS: That was commonly said?

SG: *We* said it. Friend and me.

NS: Well, there you are, Miss Garth. I never heard that before, and you see later ages may be very glad to know that people said that about him. If Wyatt Earp had indigestion, that can help us understand him.

SG: Yeah?

NS: I think so. After all, you never know what small illnesses or failings the famous people had. I mean, he may have been bad-tempered because of it. That could be quite significant.

SG: Or because he heard it.

NS: What?

SG: 'Cause he heard kids saying "Earp burps." That would rile him.

NS: You're absolutely right. Did little children do that, do you think?

SG: I don't know. He'd probably shoot 'em if they did.

NS: He would? Children?

SG: With his temper?

NS: You're teasing me.

SG: I thought you were teasing me.

NS: No, I wasn't.

SG: I'm sorry, then.

NS: You think this is foolish?

SG: Well, I don't know. I think I did. But it's started me looking back already.

NS: It has?

SG: I knew a little boy and he used to play at being Wyatt Earp. He was serious about that.

NS: You knew him well?

SG: I don't know about well. I knew him a long time.

NS: He's passed on now?

SG: He has?

NS: No, I was asking you.

SG: I don't think so. I hope not.

NS: You're friends still.

SG: He's the one.

NS: Which one?

SG: Bark Blaylock, the one I was telling you about.

NS: Oh really, where is he now?

SG: Nevada.

NS: Las Vegas?

SG: No. Near it. But not Las Vegas.

NS: I see.

SG: You don't.

NS: You were fond of him?

SG: Earp burps.

NS: What?

SG: It's like that.

NS: I don't understand.

SG: Well, like we don't know if Earp had indigestion made him angry, or if he was mad from kids singing out "Earp burps." Same with was I fond of Bark.

NS: Miss Garth, I'm going to turn the machine off.

SG: Why's that? Isn't it working?

NS: I don't even know if it is. To tell you the truth, I spent all of last night———

Santa Fe
May 23, 1950

Dear James,

The enclosed tape will show you that I am possibly the greatest menace that oral history has yet faced. It would have been a mercy if the machine *had* failed me, and there had been nothing there. Instead, I sound like one of those idiot interviewers on television—I am scarlet. My only hope is the bleakness I saw in Susan Garth's terrifying eyes: that "oral history" is just so many spools of tape on library shelves beginning their steady million-year progress towards being tombs. Have you ever thought that those fossil spirals we find in rock may not be shells but the tapes of some earlier, utterly forgotten civilization?

I *will* try again; I learned a lot. And when I listen to the tape—which took a day, I had to take it in very short doses, like medicine, I was so ashamed of it—I could hear that our Miss Garth is not just a good talker. She is in her strange way ready to talk. I turned the tape off, I thought, because she was moved by her recollection of "Bark" Blaylock. But I realized, in listening, that I was protecting myself and my own failure to grasp exactly what she meant by the "Earp burps" remark. I still don't know—I don't think. But I knew then that she was showing me—very quickly, and aloofly, so that it all depended on whether I wanted to see—something very dark about human affection, and the mysteries that chance or point of view could make of it. And, of course, I wasn't ready. But I will not let the witch get the better of me.

I told her we would do more, and she said, "I suppose so," in a calm, indifferent way. Please don't conclude that she put on an "act" to daunt me or the machine. She was herself, only more so—that is why I sound so dreadful: I didn't find her level. I thought it could be conversation, and she was right—it almost had to be theater, a ritual.

This is for your eyes only—not for the Averill Foundation and its very earnest and humane belief in oral history and the preservation of old photographs. Somehow I hope you will not mind my being an ass—though I know you will expect me to improve.

One last thing. I took her to lunch afterwards. She didn't know what to do with "lunch." She drank two double Jack Daniel's and nibbled at the bread. I urged her to eat, but she seemed to find it . . . impossible. So I gave up, and we talked, and she said, out of the blue, "Jim Averill?"

I said, yes, did she know him? meaning you.

She thought and said it must have been your father. In Wyoming. She had never met him but a friend of hers had been his associate. She said it in a very definite, rather discreet way, as if I was to gather that the friendship had been warm. I pushed her, but she was very grim about it; perhaps she needs the machine, now. But she said her friend had written to her in those days, from Sweetwater, Wyoming, and Jim Averill had been much in her mind. So . . . ?

I cannot wait to see you here—and your son. Perhaps we can go to the Canyon de Chelly together, unless you find that inconvenient.

Sincerely,
Nora S.

James Averill

Charlottesville
May 28, 1950

Dear Nora,

How our correspondence is getting afoot—though perhaps the good Miss Garth would tell us, "That is not a correspondence."

Whatever, it *is* a communication; a connection, call it. I was entertained by the tape—it would make the dead warm again; but I was more touched by the manner with which you sent it —indeed, even that you sent it at all. I can easily imagine people wishing to impress the Averill Foundation quietly burning the tape, or doing whatever one has to do to destroy them. Wiping, I suppose. But I think the real cautious careerists would have needed to vanquish the tape entirely. You didn't, and, for what it's worth, you have impressed this Averill mightily.

Of course, this Averill feels he has no great foundation, and does not know why anyone relies on his Trust. I hope I am not being pompous, or sentimental, but the letterhead is not me. Many people write to me, or solicit, assuming that it is. But the business never convinces me. That's why I'm answering you from my old home, here in Virginia, which, through neglect and sleepy indifference, I have turned into a cozy, untidy, rather forlorn place for living in. Still, it is where all the earlier Averills have lived, and I hope my son will live here, too. So perhaps I delude myself, though my wife has given the place up. It is too humid in summer for her; and too dull in winter. And she is right on both counts.

I want more of these tapes. If you insist on devoting them to the detailed history of photography in the West—so be it. I will not complain too much. But what I really *want* is much more of the radio play in which the wise old crone and her Margaret Sullavan–voiced interrogator do the fox-trot of faking each other out. I know you were frustrated, but I think you must be if the comedy is to work so well. I may be sorry—I don't know you or Miss Garth—but I think she will lead you. You don't need to be afraid of what she will say, or where her wandering will take you. Be frustrated; have your plan, and let her ambush you every time. But don't be wretched or guilty afterwards. I think she has decided to tell you her story, and that means she has made up her mind you are fit for it. That is a very sensible estimate of you—of your honesty and sentiment, not to mention your professional abilities. It is also, I think, her guess that the story will work if it falls upon the ears of someone who doesn't quite *see* the path that is being taken. I don't know how I know that, or *if*. But I think I heard it in the tape. It was as if she was writing the cross-talk, silently urging you into your part.

Of course, I have not seen her. I have just seen a few of her pictures; I have read about her; and I have heard the voice— clear, parched, dry, lapidary and dreaming. So I probably ideal-

ize her as a Sybil. I expect she has many real ailments to make
up for the deafness she doesn't have! I'm sure she isn't the
perfect old woman I hear, like the Old Woman Who Lived in a
Shoe. You can fall in love with a voice—the purity can be so cut
off from all those qualities in life that vex us, or bore us. It is
music. But I think she is very wise and understanding. You can
trust her—I know that. The Garth Trust.

For instance, she is on the mark with my father. He did go
West, after he had graduated Harvard in 1870. I think there was
a common feeling in those years for young people to get away
from the East, to enlarge America. I suspect there was an un-
conscious desire to remove oneself from memory of the Civil
War battlefields. My father was a Southerner, and he had a
Yankee education which began in the immediate aftermath of
the war. There was bitterness, and the West's fresh air may have
been sought as a cure or as a way of saying this land is so large
even the war's pain can be absorbed by it.

My father, in addition, flinched from the family business and
its fortune. I do not mean he disowned it, or cut himself adrift.
He wanted to make his own life; he did try. I don't know every
detail, but in the early 1870s he went out to Texas, to your part
of the world and to California. He rode horseback over the Sierras; it must have been barely mapped then. And he took it all
in, doing nothing in particular. That much was the sign of a rich
man, I suppose, though maybe then in the West it was not easy
to tell the rich from the ordinary. I like to think so.

He did end up in Wyoming. He had a business for a while,
designing and dealing in carriages. I don't quite know how, but
he became a lawman in Wyoming—a county sheriff, I believe,
but I'm not sure. It's not always clear the differences between
the various degrees and ranks of frontier lawmen. Some jobs
were more real than others. Some were heartfelt positions,
meant to preserve order and decency. Others were licenses to
settle conflicts of interest and power.

But my father served in Wyoming. He got caught up in the
Johnson County War, one of those disputes between old cattle-
men and the new farmers. He took the side of the new and the
less privileged, which I could have predicted, and which probably made him a traitor to his class—which I'm sure he had
wanted all along. Some are born to betray but can't betray unless
they're born to it first.

So, if he had a sweetheart in Sweetwater, I wouldn't argue—

and I don't mean to make light of her either. He didn't talk about it to me—but fathers probably don't discuss old friendships with their sons. They just sit at the head of the table, patient and enduring, and hope the sons will believe all is well. They *should* talk more.

The funny thing is that I do have a photograph that could well be circa 1890, when my father was in Wyoming. It is a picture of a young woman. I don't know if I can quite describe it to you. The woman is not undressed, but there is an air about her that her chemise, or whatever it is, has been slipped on quickly. She is probably only eighteen, or thereabouts, very pretty, with long hair and no smile, but a very level, fresh look into the camera and one hand at the knot holding her chemise together. There is light falling on her hair and one shoulder from a window, and the other side of her face is darker. You feel a sadness threatening her. Who is she? I wonder. Could it even be that Susan Garth took her picture? Somehow, I think not. I think she is looking at a man.

My father, perhaps. But the picture is too good for an amateur. And if my father could take that one picture, why didn't he take more? Do you believe that fondness can make anyone a good photographer for a moment?

Anyway, my father came back east, after Johnson County— there were massacres there, I think. And he married my mother, and he moved into the high state of being an Averill. He did the rounds—Charlottesville, New York, Newport. He oversaw the business and he set up the Foundation.

I don't know that he was ever happy. He became a quiet man, rather reined in, guarded. It may be that my mother noticed no solitariness in him, but I think in memory I feel it. He had a smile for many occasions, a way of letting things slide past him. Some people may have thought he drank, but he didn't really. One day when I was ten or so, I saw him in his room, sitting at his desk, and he uttered a very deep, faraway groan. It was as if the house had slipped on its footings. The noise seemed to come from everywhere, not from one man. And it was full of pity and loss, as if this man had realized everything about his life was wrong and there had been a moment when he had started to take a wrong course, which, at the time, had been imperceptible, but which, by then, had opened up a chasm only despair and solitude could fill. Some venture he had not followed?

And if I look at the girl's face in Sweetwater, it could be that she has seen the moment, and is brave enough not to cry.

James

Bark Blaylock

This was early on in the summer of the terrible and tumultuous year of 1881—yet I was so unaware of, and unconcerned by, all that famous to-do that I have to look up the dates in books of record, and I must suppose that it was late May or early June. For me, it was the heat of the day and the raw, jelly-like condition of being only five or six. Which is to say that I am not sure how much of this I *know*—I mean remember—or how much came from what others told me afterwards. When you are that young, that open but unappreciative, you know every aroma of coffee, bacon, and molasses, but not the year. Nevertheless, the things I felt or perceived—visions and impressions that will not shake free of me—they fit, more or less, with what the world now knows of that year, 1881, a year that looks like a great drama, but which passed then, as slowly as the heat went away in any late afternoon in Tombstone.

We had a shack behind the Bird Cage Theater, on Allen Street, between Fifth and Sixth. I know that for I sat on the stoop in the evenings and heard the music from the theater, and because in the afternoons the girls would sit out on the bare ground talking and laughing, telling stories and watching their clothes dry on the lines they had strung up. My mother was determined that none of those lines would ever make use of our shack—though it was handy and there were nails in it that must have been used for it. I was told not to talk to the girls, in that we would not be there long—in our shack. It was a small inconvenience along the way. But I could not tell what was or might become long. So I waited at the stoop, attempting to ignore whatever remarks the girls made and guarding the vacant and appealing nails.

There was a huge old girl, who was new at the Bird Cage, Big Minnie Bignon, and she was bigger than men. She was sitting out in the sun, and the pink of her was so glaring, I could not look at her without my eyes tearing.

"Oh, come on over here, Bark," she would call. "Let Big Min give you a cuddle. You'll think you're wrestling with a sugar bear. You can suck on one of my pretty titties, if you want." She laughed, and rolls and trills went through her body; there were all those folds, hills and such balloons of flesh—I could have imagined she had as many dugs as an animal, all brimming with that sugary pink milk of hers.

"You will not notice the vulgarity." It was my mother's voice, from behind me, inside the shack. For she was lying in there, on the bed, shivering and shaking with a fever and her misery. I daresay that what she said was meant as instruction to me. But it was a strange thing, with her inside the shack and me outside, her voice somehow like that of a storyteller, understanding my story but not seeing it. And though I have seen horrible things, far worse than Big Minnie, I have the unaccountable sense that I have not been marked or spoiled by the vulgarity. Maybe it would have been simpler if I had been, if I had known how to go along with it. But if it hurts, I say, it does not take possession of you: this is the Blaylock principle of worthy pain and self-respect—if you are a beaten man you have come through intact! And those happy, prosperous and altogether cheerful fellows, with smiles like Big Min's fat, they are assuredly doomed. It is some trick, if you can make it work for you, but the West is the proper place for that magic.

This shack we had was always putting me in mind of a conjuring show I had seen at the Oriental Saloon. It involved one of the girls —it must have been Lizette, for she was the only one small enough to curl up inside the basket with the lid closed—and then the man thrust Mexican sabers all through the basket. The points stuck out on the far side. And the audience went silent, and people looked for blood coming out of the basket. So the fellow took out the swords and held up the lid of the basket. He looked in, and I swear he began to appear aghast, but then Lizette stood up, one hand above her head and the other poised on her hip, unmarked, with not so much as a small rip in her golden costume. I would have wept my heart out if she had been hurt—she was the first lovely girl I saw, though I believe in later years she got to being a whore, too, after she had floated in the air above the throng at the Bird Cage, hanging on wires, and pretending to swim up there so that the gentlemen could properly inspect how slender she was. And she was. But, as I say, she came down to earth.

Anyway, I am drifting. What I meant to say was that our shack might have been run through with a dozen Mexican or Toledo blades, there were so many cracks and slits where the light came in. There were always boards falling out of the shack, and nailing up to do. And inside the shack you could walk in and out of these shafts and leaves of light, playing with them. And wherever you looked there was gloom and these bright shreds all in the one view: it was upsetting to the eye, and I know I believed it was a cause of my mother's fever.

Or else the leaving. For we had been living in a fine hotel, and the marshal came to call on us there, and took his sort of care of us. He would often make my mother laugh, until the times when she would not stop crying, and then she got too much for him. I do not know how we found the shack, and I do not recall then noticing that it was so much inferior to the hotel. I liked it better because in the hotel there had always been all manner of people in and out of the rooms. Night and day, it was like a meeting place, with card games, and men gathering to discuss matters of great weight. I was hurried from one room to another, with different men patting my head and telling me stories and seeming to believe that I knew them. It was unsettling for a boy, though the grown-ups were very pleased with themselves. I did prefer the shack, which was restful and secure but for the slivers of light that moved through it as the day passed. Even if my mother was sick, still now she was mine to look after.

Then, that afternoon, a tall man came through the Bird Cage—for that was the means to and from the street—stepped between the girls without any acknowledgment of them and came up to me. He carried a bottle of whiskey that flashed in the sun, and though it was a hot day he had a soldier's cloak.

"Blaylock?" he asked.

"Yes, sir," I said. I stood up.

"Mother inside?"

"He's to come in," my mother called out, so weak, the calling hurt me.

"You know me?" the tall man asked of me.

I shook my head, for I did not recall I had ever seen this sad-faced man before.

"*He's* your father," said my mother's voice, so determined. She sounded like a lady trying to pick out her nicest hat. And the man went past me, handling the door of the shack as if it was a page in a book. And it wasn't much stronger. "Let me talk with him," my mother said, but if that request began for me, so it seemed to close, more passively, looking up at his strict eyes and at the bottle which could have lain in his arm in some stray arrow of light.

The girls were talking and laughing again; the man's coming had stilled and interested them. One of them called out to me, "Your mama's catching on, kid." And I saw pretty, curly heads nodding. They had a bottle of their own, and I took it for some ladies' companionship in refreshment on roasting afternoons. They forgot me soon. They were getting ready to take down their clothes: the cottons were hot and clean, and the girls waved the garments to cool them. I heard a piano in the Bird Cage being tuned. A girl began to sing, and the others joined in softly, like cows lowing to be milked.

I looked at the shack. There were so many slits of vantage to choose from. I could see the blob of my head shadowed on the latticed back of the tall man. He moved and the bars of light stirred with his motion. He was kneeling by my mother's cot, putting the bottle to her mouth. I heard her giggle. Then the man took a swig himself and he climbed on the bed to keep my mother warm.

I heard him talking to her, some plaintive, asking tone in his voice. It did not seem appropriate, if he was nursing her. Somehow it made him sound as if *he* expected help and comfort. But my mother did not protest or differ. I only heard her weary sighs of understanding as she took in his story and all the upsets it had left him.

I could not hear or understand all he said; he was speaking so closely into her. And I did not wish to be discovered, or left out there all night. There were fights at the back of the Bird Cage after dark, and miners who threw up their rotten dinners there. So I tried to wedge myself in one of the cracks in the body of the shack, neither quite inside or outside, yet attempting to hold the tattered shell of our home together.

He told her a story about a man who had come home from the war, and who was hardly home when his family's house was destroyed by savages. One child, a girl, was taken by these Indians, and so the man, because he was her kin and had nothing else to do, went in search of the girl. It was a quest that lasted many years and took him from the summers of Mexico to the snowy heights of Colorado. For these Indians were a wandering tribe, or else they knew he was following. The man grew older in the search, and he was surprised to find at last that the girl had grown into a woman. It changed the intent he had kept all along to mercifully kill her when he found her—for she had been defiled by the savages. Instead he brought her back to other kin, who took her in. And he went up to the door of their house, to see the fearful young woman safely inside, then turned away as if he could hardly live beneath a roof again or know what to do with himself.

It seemed to me a strange story, but it must have amazed my mother, or she was sleeping from it. She seemed to be at peace beneath the man, who was exhausted from telling the story.

By now it was very close to night. All the girls had gone inside when a man came out of the Bird Cage. I knew it was Bill Brocius from his crumpled top hat, and I got ready for him with a smile. For he liked to make me laugh.

"Hello there, my boy," says he. And he gave me a paper bag of hard candies. "How's your ma?"

"I think she's sleeping, Bill."

"Ah," he says, and then the tall man came out of the shack, and Bill stepped back to examine him. "Aha," he said again.

"What does that mean?" said the tall man.

"Means, Ethan," said Bill, "that I was enquiring as to whether Bark here would fancy a little trip, to Fort Sumner, to see a pal o' mine. It would give the lad a break, don't you see? Away from this hellhole."

The tall man grunted, and I wasn't sure that he and Bill might not have a fight. So, to make friends between them, I said to Bill, "Mother says this is my father."

"There you are then," laughed Bill.

And so it worked out as agreed that I could go with Bill. With a pony to ride, and Bill to tell jokes all the way there and back. So Mother could get well again. And we went immediately, as if there was hurry or Mother was very ill.

Nora Stoddard

In that summer of 1950, Nora Stoddard was twenty-nine. She had never married, yet she was consistently described as a knockout, eligible and a Yank in London in those heartless mid-1930s when dangerous young viability was so prized, in Washington and at Smith, to say nothing of Santa Fe. Indeed, in New Mexico, she was one of the talked-about young women in the state, not only for her own attributes and her allegedly brazen disregard for what people said, but for being the daughter of the late Senator Ransom Stoddard. In other words, in her own way, Nora Stoddard had achieved some aspects of living legend.

On this evening, a young, scrupulous historian of the new documentary school had driven from his faculty office in Albuquerque to dine with her, working on the three-quarter-likely assumption that he might stay over. He had taken care to have no classes or meetings the next day, and he had come with roses from his own garden (jammed in a compress of soaked tissue into a sponge-filled pot), a bottle of French rosé and a packet of rubbers.

There is no need to name him, he is a momentary figure in this story and of published reputation elsewhere; he will reach his proper eminence at the university, even without Miss Stoddard; he will go on, to the East and research chairs that will fill his life. Miraculously, this young historian was restored, deflated, to his own apartment— minus wine, flowers and rubbers—by midnight. He had been a welcome enough guest, but he had been laughed at for his failure to handle the defective plumbing. As he drove back, he told himself that there had been an eerie edge of instability in Nora Stoddard's laughter, not at all senatorial or collegial. It was a shocking laugh, one that revealed disturbance and wildness. He doubted she could be a reliable scholar, and he made a note to beware of the museum in Santa Fe, so much more interested in dramatic atmosphere and publicity coups than in the solid, important work.

Of course, she had been a little drunk by then, or else willfully acting drunk. But the history professor had not been averse to any tendency that might aid his romantic design. If this woman couldn't take care of herself, was it his duty? Yet he had been nettled when he arrived by the suspicion that Nora Stoddard had already been drinking.

"There you are," she had said, and there had been a grin on her sunburned rosy face, half a lurch in her step, that were altogether too inviting or precipitate. He wondered if she was going to fall, and whether then it would be in order to go straight down on her, like a doctor in an emergency. The professor knew that his wooing had to work: he had planned it out, in the way of one of his big lectures. Not that he had notes or anything; no, he prided himself on speaking freely, extemporaneously, but with an effortless and complete command of the facts. It made history seem closer to religion, one student had told him. And he had a special reputation already for arousing the spirit of history in young people.

"I thought you weren't coming." And she laughed out loud again, as if at a private joke. The historian smiled forgivingly, hoping to show Nora Stoddard the value in taking her lead from him.

"I don't believe I'm late," he reasoned. He had timed it exactly. "I didn't want to throw your cooking out."

"Oh, it's Mexican," she said. "It's endlessly patient."

"Mexican?"

"Don't you like it?" She was being personal so much too soon. "I bet you don't like it."

"I don't often eat it. It'll be refreshing." She was ready to laugh again, but she controlled herself. She gazed upon him, and he could certainly smell bourbon now, not too much, but it was at odds with the delicacy of her neck and the hard line of her jaw. She was very noble there. He enjoyed studying her, and he knew he would like it when she was asleep and he had time to let his scrutiny pore over her neck.

"Are we expecting to do it?" She winked when she said this—it was as if she wanted to make both of them ridiculous. He could not credit this asking, but he felt the challenge in it, and he laughed back at her, cringing when he sounded shrill in the small apartment.

"One never knows," he replied.

"No, one doesn't, does one? Would you like a drink? I would."

"We should put those roses in fresh water," the professor reminded her.

"Oh." It hadn't occurred to her. Why not just tear the roses to pieces—after all, weren't they tribute for her? "Can you do that? I think there's a pot or something up there. I'll make drinks." She took two steps away, stopped and came back to him. "The roses are very sweet," she said contritely, and dabbed a kiss on his mouth. Her breath, he thought, could do with some of the roses.

"I'm told I have one of the best rose gardens in New Mexico," he told her.

"Really?" She was shuffling ice, like a barman. "Are they rare?"

"Roses," he announced, "are not native New Mexico. Except the cactus rose. No, roses were brought here, and like all beautiful things they need great care."

"They make me think of England," said Nora Stoddard. "They're bread and butter there."

"You have been spoiled," said the historian lightly.

"Ruined," she said, without remorse or rebuke, and gave him a large bourbon on the rocks. She had not even asked what he wanted.

Nora Stoddard just sat him down with a drink—silent, dramatic compulsion, he noted: her mania?—and put a large black-and-white

photograph before him. It was a picture of the desert with mountains
far off, shining in the evening light, sepia or gun-metal. The light
was like flesh. In the foreground was a woman, dark, about forty,
unimpressive and not yielding to the camera, but seemingly driven
to the limit of her being by the need to stand up straight and still in
front of it. She looked as if she might be biting herself to keep from
moving. Here and there at the edges of her dress, where some wind
had stirred, the picture was smeared as if moths were attached to
her, or as if her world was gnawing at her fabric.

The professor smiled in recognition. "That austere frontier existence," he surmised.

"You like it?"

He did not enjoy being on any spot he couldn't describe or measure
in advance. He wanted data, context, circumstantial grounding—he
was the sort of historian who could quickly start to explain once
those elements were furnished. Without them, he felt embarrassed
by the woman's resolute stare from the picture.

"Who did it? About 1890, is it? It doesn't quite look like New
Mexico."

"Eighteen-eighty-sevenish," she allowed. "It's called *The Suicide*."

The title did fit; the picture slipped into place. One could not
fail to grasp the woman's reticence because of it. But the title was
problematic. "Did the photographer know that in advance?" he
asked her.

"You think he might have saved her?"

"The title's very blunt, and rather incriminating. You wonder."

"One does." There was something in her voice that made him look
at her, rather than at the picture. Her zeal shocked him. He had been
settling into some secure sadness, but she had the rapt attention for
the picture of someone at a cockfight waiting to see which creature
perished. It did not make the professor comfortable.

"Perhaps," he said, "he could have talked to her more and composed a little less." The professor had a good line in urbane irony
over excess or melodrama—he needed it with students.

"The photographer was a woman."

"You surprise me."

"You don't think a woman could be so withdrawn, just to watch?"

"There's a firmness in the picture. A resolve. I wouldn't have
guessed a woman."

"That austere frontier life," said Nora Stoddard, but the professor
never caught the echo.

"We were harder then," he agreed.

"Have we changed so quickly?"

"Rapid change *is* one of our specialties."

"Or was the frontier a racket?" She looked nervous about his judgment.

"There were surely crooks and liars," he admitted.

"Was 'frontier' a word for tidying up the mess?"

He took stock. "I think the frontier remains a useful concept. For it *was* a physical reality. A moment when intelligence beheld an absolute wildness."

"And took it apart."

"The one modern thing in your picture is the fact of picturing, the camera as a machine." He realized he had found a line of attack against her.

"I doubt a woman could have been there . . . fifty years before, in the 1830s. It's Nevada, I believe, where there was nothing."

He nodded. "I'm always a little suspicious of those exquisite panoramas of wilderness. Those untouched prospects. Doesn't the camera tame it—turn it into picture postcards?"

"But do you like it?"

"Well," he conceded, "I like talking about it."

She shifted in her chair, tucking her legs beneath her. "What is your work, your research?" She seemed sober now.

"It's a long haul. I'm looking at how families extended, broke up, re-formed—all the variants—in New Mexico in the era of statehood. The Stoddard era." He smiled for her, loyal, but to what?

"How do you do that?"

"There are diaries in the library. I collect letters. Postcards, too," he smiled demurely, "though I concentrate on their messages. They're often illuminating. And quite poignant. People didn't bother to lie in postcards. Huge sentiments in short sentences."

"And you can still talk to people?"

"People?"

"They're still alive. There are so many who were there. But not for long. I have an old lady I'm recording. We have a grand time together."

"I'm not sure of them."

"Why?" Her eyes widened. It was as if Nora Stoddard had an infinite love for people. It amazed her, this sincere invention.

"They want to please you. They make it up. They don't remember, so they lie. I find the documents much more . . . sacred, if you know what I mean."

"But if people can *tell* you what happened?"

"I'm afraid they are less than impartial. Accuracy is not their interest."

"They're concerned—that's all! Is the truth accurate?"

"Ah, philosophy! It may simply be that I'm not good with people. I do feel more at peace with the papers. I can study them, and fathom them out. But the people . . ."

"They look at you and demand response."

The professor felt bitter, cornered and defensive. She knew she was unfair to him, but there was a blood lust that would not stop.

"It makes them feel important, too," he said. "And I am more concerned with people who were not important, not known. The ordinary ones who came and went."

Nora Stoddard stood up—she was no loyal friend to the famous, yet she resisted an alliance with this humdrum clerk.

"Are you hungry?" she demanded. Food, the silencer of broken talk.

They went to the pine table by the window. She had not laid it before he arrived, but abruptly now she filled it with a hot chicken stew, with blue-corn polenta, salad and refried beans. She sketched the dishes for him, advised him on how to eat them and alluded to the fire in the orange chile sauce she had made. He agreed that beer was the better drink to have with the meal.

"It does smell very good," he said, stirring at the pieces of chorizo in the chicken dish. She watched him take his first few mouthfuls, and she lowered her head, so as to catch the violent discoveries in his eyes.

"I like it," he assured her.

"Not too hot?"

"Not at all."

"It comes up on you," she said, feeling like Geronimo, master of a childish trap.

So it did. In a few moments, he had asked if he might hang his jacket on the back of the chair. There was that laugh of hers again, the sound of wonder that a man with so controlled and judicious a mind should be so timid. He looked very slender and young without his jacket; she saw there was not much flesh on him. Did he starve and dwindle in libraries as he amassed his data? His suspenders were chosen so as to match the thin blue stripe of his shirt—and the shirt was still crisp from some careful ironing, his own, she guessed, not that quick, brutal job laundries do. He had been as studious as a wife.

"More beer?" She was on to his needs, worrying for him.

"I see what you mean." He was red-faced now and his small bald spot—as if a tennis ball had bounced there—was awash with sweat. "Good Lord."

"Did you like the picture?"

"Well, what would 'like' mean?"

"Did it move you?"

The professor sighed at the raw directness of the question. It was his steady discovery, daily confirmed, that education was a matter of guiding people to ask the correct questions. "I don't know if I know enough for that."

"What else would you need?"

"Photography, it seems to me, wears its heart on its sleeve. It is facile; it moves us so easily. Shouldn't we be wary?"

"I know the woman who took the picture," said Nora Stoddard. That settled the matter for her.

"Ah," said the professor: he was having to argue with downright possessiveness. "I wonder, could I use your facilities?"

"Sure," she said, not bothering now to nag him on the name, the word, for that function.

He was some time there, and she measured how surprised or apologetic she should be when he returned.

"Look," he said. His face was damp, and he kept the bathroom door decisively shut. "Your flush isn't working."

"Oh, right," she agreed, without conciliation. She knew it.

"You should have said." He wanted to hit her.

"Yeah? I should. But I didn't."

"You need to get someone in to see to it. Your meal was rather too much for me. I had a small ulcer at Princeton."

"Oh!" She gave him at least the benefit of a joke. She chuckled politely. "You mean it's . . . filled?"

He nodded briefly. "I'll try again," he said. He was sweating now with labor as well as the sudden, plunging opening of his bowels. Like the trap door splitting beneath a man left to hang.

The professor went back to the bathroom. He closed the door again. Nora Stoddard reached across the table and felt in the inside pocket of his jacket. She came away with the envelope of rubbers, examined it, and then put it inside her copy of *Across the River and into the Trees.* As a bookmark. The tip peeping over the pages like a spotter.

"I feel such a fool," he was back again. "Mending those things isn't my forte."

"Not to worry." She did not get up. She watched him put on his jacket.

"I'll go in the bath," she murmured. "If I need to."

He took it in, that solution, but it plainly struck him as another kind of problem.

"You'll forgive me if I leave?" he asked her.

"You're not feeling good?"

"Not a hundred percent."

"Can you drive?"

"Oh, you bet. It's a straight road."

"Well . . . I'm sorry," she said, slowly, with a hint of moody carnal regret to taunt him. "You've got everything?"

"You must come down to Albuquerque," he said. A small laugh. "We should start again."

"It's a good policy," she said.

She watched him go from the window, and then she got out her wine, the rosé. She went to the bathroom, opened the door, and let the stink come out into the apartment.

After a while, on the sofa, reading the Hemingway and methodically drinking the wine, carrying the bookmark on with her, page by page, as she read, Nora recalled the name Susan Garth had given her. For they had talked of cisterns and pipes earlier and Susan had said there was a young man in town who fixed things. Nora found the piece of paper in her bag. There was a number and a name, "Jubal."

It was nearly eleven o'clock, but she picked up the phone and dialed. It rang for a minute, and Nora smiled as she waited. Then at the other end the phone was picked up, fumbled, and a thick voice said, "Yeah?", dragged out of dreams or some clotted slime. She inhaled the smell from the bathroom and began to talk.

Matthew Garth

He had been asking himself for a year to be more cheerful, to talk to people; so he may have read a natural benevolence into the letter that was not warranted. Or he may have been so little accustomed to men and their messages that he missed its boisterous note of

unfounded bonhomie. The letter reached him in Texas in the fall of
1878, and it neither warned nor alarmed him. Yet hadn't Tess cried
out at him about the things he did not notice—as if she still hoped
to be rescued from what she was intending?

My dear Mr. Garth,

Here I am, sir, on a sweet and extensive spread of buffalo
grass in the Missouri Breaks part of Montana. I have a mind to
amplify my herd with the very best Texas half-bred longhorns.
I believe that I could handle two thousand head, with at least
one hundred of your bulls. And I mean to pay you top prices
as pertaining at the time, for I cannot find anyone of repute who
does not, in the end, admit that yours are the best animals in
Texas.

So I am wondering if I might coax you into making once more
the historic drive you undertook a dozen years ago.

[A banner-tailed rat made a weaving run across the room,
claws skittering on the boards. Garth flung a corkscrew at it,
missed—the screw quivering in the wall]

You might then take the Union Pacific from Abilene to, let us
say, Cheyenne, timing it so that you could bring the herd on
over the Wyoming grasslands, coming into Montana at the Bighorn. But, of course, you know your business best. I write as
an armchair rancher, never having made these great adventures
in person.

It seemed to me the out-of-doors romance of such a journey
might appeal to you, Mr. Garth. But I would run to another $2
a head for travel expenses as inducement.

I surely hope you will come. This is fine but lonesome country
and my wife, Frances, and I would promise to entertain you.
One day this country of ours will be dependent on men like
ourselves reaching out in association and concerted influence. I
know we will be friends and I would dearly like to take you on
a tour of my library.

Very cordially,
David Braxton

P.S. I am enclosing a map with various lines of route that you
might choose from. It was done roughly in my own hand, but
I think you can appreciate the possibilities.

Now, if you consider this nothing but my fanciful idea, why just ignore the whole thing and leave me in the peace and obscurity of this particular dead end of the still wild West.

The map was neither impressive nor coherent, just a pattern of lines, like the exploring system of waterways in the breaks country, weird, whimsical but lively. Matthew Garth could feel this Braxton's uncontrolled exuberance in the flourish of his penmanship. So he put the map aside and gazed out of the window, for reasoning, knowing he was going to go.

He made plans, with Groot. They took out the real and verified maps, they wrote to the railroad, and the old man was forever doing sums, calendar estimates, calculating time, mileage and provisions, and behaving for all the world as if he would be going, too. Until one day Matthew ended another planning session with "So you will watch over Dunson. And these damn rats we have again."

"Uh-huh," said Groot, with never a note of protest or regret. "If you think he'll notice it. I'm getting cats."

"He'd notice if we weren't here."

"You think so?" Groot was becoming belligerent now.

"I'd be thinking of it, if there was no one here."

"Don't mean *he* would!" Groot was ready to burst now. "Don't mean he'll give me one word, either, while you're gone! Fine fate for an old man has been your friend."

Matthew sighed, and leaned back in his chair. "Do you consider there's a way to talk to him?"

Groot shook his head. "Not a chance. The cats maybe, they might. Not us. He's weak now, and heavy. He'd not make it out of Texas, and he wouldn't thank us if he got to die anywhere else."

"But you'd make it? Are you telling me that?"

"Maybe not. But I'm not afraid to die here or out of Texas. Texas never held no special reverence for me. Seeing I was born in Rotterdam in Holland."

"You don't mean to go back there?"

"No idea where it is, what it is. Matthew, you know it, I would like to keep on moving. That so much to ask?"

"Then maybe I stay here," said Matthew. "Eckersley or Laredo, they could run the drive. They would anyway, if I was there."

"Matthew, no!" Groot dropped his papery hand on the table where they were working. "You got to go, get out of this empty place. Tess and Susie aren't coming back, and your brooding for 'em won't bring 'em. Way you are, it's better they don't come back. You're a young man, still. Get out there and look around. Take me. I might surprise you, and you can talk to me. Never could talk to no Laredo or Eck."

"Nor to Tess?" Matthew added.

"I don't know that. Not that talking's necessarily the only thing."

"Both of us then?"

"I'll tell Dunson," said Groot. "Least, I'll say the words over him."

Matthew watched Groot go up to Dunson's attic room, and he waited outside as Groot pulled up a chair next to Dunson's, looking out to the north. He heard Groot's low voice, droning and drifting, like a fly in the room. It was so close to the sound of the wind in the eaves of the house, he could not always pick one from the other. The figure of Dunson never moved: the stroke, the shock, had left him weathered and unresponsive, but with a secret sentience no one could be sure of. This was the last of Dunson's danger.

Groot came out of the room, grumbling to himself about the futility of it all, thinking already about the big books he would take on the trip, books to read before a man dies, and of the best disposition for the chuck wagon.

Matthew waited until Groot had gone away, and then he went into Dunson's room. He came around the room, sideways so that he might see the light on Dunson's slipped face. It was like a fallen slab of rock, the force dragging the eyes down, the mouth tipped over one way as if weighted. A tear slid down Dunson's sloped gray face, but there was no way of judging whether it meant anything or whether it was just the helpless seepage of water from the eye. Matthew marveled at the fine, silky white of Dunson's full hair: it still grew, fresh and hopeful, on his wrecked head. He put his hand on it, combing it a little, and an interior, mild groan came from the head, a kind of settling sound. Matthew looked at Dunson and one eye shut and opened. The pale blue eye seemed unaware. But the lid closed again, and the sunken mouth shook at its edges as if some giant there was struggling to regain his feeling. The effort went away and Matthew noticed in Dunson's lap the silver-framed photograph of Tess, with Susan on her lap. And the tiny Susan held a broken doll to her airy dress. The doll? It was too small to see if the toy's black hand held anything. Then, as Matthew examined it, the picture slipped and slid onto the floor. A rat was in the corner watching them, its head cocked in an attitude of pity. Matthew picked up the picture, polished the silver and set it on the table beside Dunson.

"I'm sorry for you," said Matthew, "that I let them be taken away, and never understood the joy they were for you."

The hulk of Dunson was surely dying. He did not eat, and he must soon begin to diminish. So active a man dies quickly if he stops, and the carcass needs to be put out in the open so that the weather can clean it up. Matthew had thought of having Dunson put in a cart, and driving him out to the high ground, placing a shot behind his ear and tipping him out on the ground. But it required a severity and a command of gesture that only Dunson had ever had.

He saw Dunson's own gun, oiled in its holster, six feet away on the wall, and he took out the gun. It was loaded, and it shone from Groot's regular attention. Dunson's boots were also freshly polished —they might have been carved from a dark wood. For they never moved, creaked or cracked now. They waited for the man who filled them to sink and vanish.

Matthew needed to leave, but he stopped in the doorway. The rat had disappeared. The adopted son faced the back of Dunson and the blaze of the window beyond him. Dunson's hair was on fire, and the man was unaware.

"If you're hearing," said Matthew, "or if you're not, I thank you for serving as my father. It's a hard thing to have to think of getting by without one." He wanted more, but he could not find decent, soft words, and so he only added, "Dunson, Dunson," so quiet, it was like a shovel in his head, patting down the loose earth on a beloved's grave.

He hoped his own head would fall from his shoulders and roll away into a forgotten corner.

But he was left standing, the survivor, one of the helpless bereft.

Matthew Garth

Groot got strong on the journey, a last strength, more precious than that of youth. The old man did not have much to do except sometimes drive the chuck wagon and pretend that he was in charge of the meals and the provisions. In truth, they had set out overmanned— eight men could have handled this herd, but Matthew Garth had taken eleven, as well as a cook (a bright kid who had come by the ranch days before they left), Groot and himself. But Matthew had no mind this time for harsh labor; there was a part of him that thought wistfully of a holiday on the trail. And when he noticed Groot regaining color, weight and some of his old sauce, why, Matthew supposed that maybe he was improving too. For as Groot ate more, finding appetite with the air and the work, so Matthew dropped ten or so recent, house-bound pounds, worn away by the unusual hours of riding. For days at a time, he did not shave, and once he caught himself in a polished pan on the chuck wagon and saw that old lean outlaw look.

"I thank God for David Braxton," Groot called out one morning. "Whoever he may be." And then the old man rode up close to Matthew and said, "What do you know? I believe I'm seventy-five today. Or maybe it was yesterday."

"We spin this trip out," Matthew grinned. "You'll see eighty."

"Know the secret?" said Groot. "Once I got shot of my teeth— took on a new life."

They had set out early, in March 1879, and they went along easily this time. The trail was clear enough—there had been maybe two million cattle on it since '65, and the ground was pounded down, hooking this way and that to avoid marshland and pick up good water. There were signs along the trail now, comic warnings about Indians, and they saw initials carved in trees. At regular intervals they found blackened circles on the ground and rings of rocks where semi-permanent campsites were made. And there were people along the trail, too, a few lean-to shacks with women and children waiting for their men, or any men, to come back.

It was not hard to foresee a railroad being put down on the beaten track. There had been a slump in the '70s, to be sure, but no one could deny or stop the talk of all the people coming to America, and of so many of them spilling westward, believing prime beef was their reward. It would be a hundred years at least before the glorious encounter of some narrowed European appetite and a Texas T-bone was exhausted. You could see faces grow larger as minds took on confidence, daring and even madness from the bloody fiber of the meat. It was a boom, but Matthew Garth was not always calm about the disturbance or the soaring wealth and power that came to him because of it. He was not naturally a man of power, and he could not free his mind of the way the house—that monument to pioneer wealth—had become the great Dunson's early tomb, hushed and saddened by his fall, so that men felt gloomy going in at the end of the day, not weary but oppressed by it. And if the men felt that, what had Tess felt, confined there every day?

Matthew was left with odd sensations as they made the drive north: it was a source of sentiment, remembering the sites and the incidents of the earlier drive—that nostalgia was the reason for coming again. He had met Tess on that route, saved her, sucked venom out of her shoulder. Had her strike him for that medical embrace.

But he found he wanted the original unknown, the silent, unspoken apprehension of exploration, the liberty of the new; he did not want to see how the cherished points of adventure had turned into drab occasions of common practice. He could recall their crossing of the Red as a Biblical holiday, the dust, the light and the uncharted depths of the water. He could still hear the jubilation in all the boys' whooping as they saw they were going to make it—the dust-covered men plunging into the water, those titans who did not dream of swimming but wallowed there like leathered beasts. And there was, above all, the inspiring triumph, the surety that this large, swollen river had never before been crossed in this way, that it might have flowed on, unknown, unseen, for centuries.

The Red now was announced a hundred miles ahead. There were maps on sale, treacherous no doubt, but full of cocksure lore and anecdotes. There was even a picture, a drawing, of Garth and Dunson in 1865, side by side, not just unrecognizable, but full of an airy jauntiness they had never known. At the river itself, there were flat-bottomed boats, a photographer's tent and a ramshackle bar. It was a known site of the spoiled world, a place where you had to guard your men against distractions. There was a row of girls in bloomers paddling their powdered feet in the Red. There were shit-cabins on top of a slope that ran down to the water. The Red was beginning to become a part of America's plumbing.

And Matthew Garth had to smile fondly on the younger cowboys who seemed as uplifted by the crossing as he had ever been. Was it churlish to rebuke them? Was it dishonest to stay cheerful? They came to him respectfully for stories of the '65 journey. They pestered him, and when he could not recall enough, or be convincing enough about how much finer, rarer, it had been then, why, he heard himself making it up. And he saw the sly winks as they looked at one another, smart Texas boys who heard a line-shooter as quickly as they felt a wind shift quarter.

"Well, sir," said one of the cowboys, to clear the matter up, "this Red is something a man can measure himself against."

And the boys showed one another the photographs they had purchased, all alike, of a cowboy on a horse, the choppy water up to the horse's belly, and the cowboy's face split open with a required smile. A few days later, they saw Indians, docile braves who came up offering them tribal souvenirs, spooking the cattle with the smell of their ponies, snaking off a steer while the cowboys looked at the elk-tooth necklaces or weighed the gimcrack Indian knives in their hands that were likely made now in Chicago and brought in by the case.

It happened, bit by bit, but Matthew would find himself riding on ahead of the herd. He noticed that Laredo, the trail boss, was deferring to him, seeing that this was no usurpation of task or role. There was no offense in it. Instead, it was just that Matthew needed to be away from the rest of the company. There was some fancy in his head, a hopefulness like a boy playing, which liked to feel he was out there alone, with a horse, a gun, a canteen of water and a few scraps of food. Nor did he go only straight ahead, following the prescribed trail. No, he strayed and wandered west and east of it. Sometimes he would come up on a rise and, looking back, see the herd, ten miles behind, following along slowly, like a plow beneath its pall of dirt. He felt some care for it; he could feel the swell of contented ownership. But he was also easier at being so removed from it, observing how slow and steady it was. It was like a man's heart, his system, but Garth now was more the mind, ranging ahead. He took to spending nights out, ahead and alone, so happy he could handle the cold. He could not reliably keep a fire alight, so he shivered with branches and foliage wrapped round him for cover, thrilled by all the inexplicable, swallowing sounds of the forest at night, playing with the snake bracelet that Dunson had torn from Tess's arm when she left.

"Thank you," she had gasped, as if wanting to be punished. Matthew dreamed of her, and dreamed the snake still joined them.

He wondered if, somehow, riding across the nation like this he might encounter her. For he had never gone after her, never gone searching. It was Matthew's opinion that to look for anyone in the huge land was hopeless. Rather, it might be wiser to wait, to let life carry one along or around, until the gradual curve and shuffle of space brought the lost back together again, waiting to see if they could recognize good fortune.

On the morning after one of these nights, Matthew Garth ventured somewhat deeper into a wooded part. So it was he came upon what seemed at first sight only an uncommonly contorted tree. But as he looked more closely, he recognized a man's skeleton, in a sitting or resting position, with a slender, serpentine branch twisted through the ribs and thrusting up through the cavity of his jaw. He could not estimate how old the bones were—Did they date from the war? Was there combat here? But there were no hints of soldiery to the man, only some wisps of clothing, a rusted gun and the husks of his boots. Matthew communed with the long-dead man, the framework abiding, retained by nature, the spirit freed. He was not afraid; this death was tranquil and fluent. He saw nothing hideous in the skull's eyes, with greenery poking through like a lover's grasp.

But he went on, serene and thoughtful, not likely to be surprised again by unexpected meeting. And a day out of Abilene, when he was still on his own, though only a mile or so ahead, and when he was hoping to come up over that last ridge and see the railroad, why, instead, he lost himself. He was in a rolling, wooded area when he ambled his horse into a clearing and heard a young woman's voice call out.

"Why, thank you, sir. Hold yourself right there." It was a woman with brown hair, in a yellow skirt, and she was standing at an easel, apparently painting the sylvan scene into which he had come as an honest traveler, never sensing frame line or color balance. But he stopped his horse and—whatever she thought of him in her picture —he immediately enjoyed the look of her.

Matthew Garth

"I was wondering when a good-looking cowboy was going to come riding out of nowhere," the girl in the yellow skirt told him. There were smears of green and brown paint on her face, and her own elusive scent was wrestling with that of turpentine.

"Were such hopes for your picture alone?" he asked her.

"Oh, I don't believe in being that good," she answered. "Why, painting is not my real pursuit." Nor was she the least perturbed to have him look at her landscape—it was not finished, of course, but what he saw felt pale or faint, not quite equal to her warm brown immediacy or the gentle irony she bestowed on anything she looked at. "I will be a writer," she added, "an author."

The simple act of looking seemed to persuade her into a smile, as if she immediately detected the comic subterfuge in things. Matthew Garth felt he had to toughen up under her gaze, or submit to it. She saw him thinking this; there was even a tremulous hesitation in which they might have turned away or sunk into each other's odor—the paint, her musk, his ingrained dirt from the trail. He could see her inhaling, subtly but deeply, and he wondered if well-to-do ladies did often faint, as he had read. But the moment passed, and they agreed to converse sociably as they went on to Abilene together, overlooking the glimpse of seizure and abandon they had shared. She swung along beside him, but she spoke so quietly that he came down from his horse and walked with her. He put her box of paints on the saddle; it was as heavy as a case of ammunition. He marveled at this mere pastime ready to walk out a mile or so before finding a picturesque spot for her indifferent work.

"Where are you headed in Abilene?" she asked.

"There's a man I know, Frank Melville. We've dealt with him with our cattle over the years," Matthew explained. "He's an honest man."

"The Greenwood Trading Company of Illinois," she answered, with that piercing grin on her face.

"That's correct," said Matthew. "Do you know him?"

"I'm in some way of being his mistress," she said, and she looked away—it was the first time—to let him consider this in peace, or because she would rather not see his reaction. "I never thought to consider his honesty," she said. "I think he's rather past that by now. He's very rich. So we are going to the same place?" Her grin came back with that, seeing prospects in an establishment so much larger than Matthew could imagine.

"Mr. Melville bought our first herd," Matthew told her.

"Yes," she said, "he's spoken of you. He's very proud of you, I think. Indeed, I realize now, riding out of the woods like that, you really are an authentic hero. He'll be delighted that I found you."

"Did you find me?"

"Why not? You were a stray-away from your herd, weren't you, now? I saw you coming along, singing to yourself."

"I was singing?"

"And very contentedly lost, I thought. So I pounced on you."

"Well," he realized, "I did feel that."

They were in Abilene now, an untidy, low-slung, raucous, filthy pit of growth.

"Did you feel me deciding whether to take you there, out there, in the trees?"

He was startled at this candor of hers. "You know, I believe I did."

"Well then," she laughed out loud. "I should have done. I may never get another chance." There was a smile on her face still, to be sure, a readiness to make a comedy of herself. But there was pathos, too, for great chances that were so quick.

Matthew didn't say a word, he was too abashed, too fearful of exposing his own romantic foolishness. How could one withstand the naked neediness of this woman's talk? It horrified him, just as much as he wanted it to go on. Yet he could not understand how he might look so ripe or ready for her wholehearted rapine. Didn't he look hard from the slow drive north? Hadn't he lost that softness of private, tender thought?

Anyone could see Melville's house from the edge of Abilene: that seemed to be the principle of its design. It was four stories high, as big as a hotel, yet empty except for anyone Melville could find to justify his constitutional cheerfulness. He had got louder, or more exaggerated, with age, as Matthew saw it. Not that there was any doubting the genuine warmth of Melville's welcome.

"This is a hero," Melville told the young woman. "I don't mean to bamboozle you. But Matthew Garth is an original Western model." It made Garth feel all the more helpless, or as if his strength was taken away. For as he came into the huge house he thought he would swoon, and he did see the girl's quick hand reach out for his arm, but stop short of it if he could master himself. He recollected the daze from the first time he had reached Abilene in '65. There was something ominous to the spirit in the reappearance of roofs, ceilings and the simple fact of being impeded in a clear reach to the skies. He may have faltered and missed an instant or two as he looked up at the massive decoration in the plaster ceilings, so closed and so solid. He felt like a man looking up at a coffin's inner lid, wondering why it was so engraved if it had only the dead as witnesses.

"There you are," said the girl, full of sweet interest in his state. He was closer to her than he had ever been, while Melville was roaring with that demented, determined frontier mirth, shouting out for drinks and holiday.

"What is your name?" said Matthew.

She did not answer him easily or quickly. "Fleur," she decided. "Isn't that a fancy name?"

"I like Fleur very much," he told her. He liked the small gape of her mouth when she said it.

"It's French for flower."

"What sort of flower?"

"Whatever you wish," she said. There was a tough offhandedness to her now, and Matthew suspected that her name had sometimes been laughed at.

The herd came in, in an hour of noise, turmoil and dust. The cattle were put in pens by the railroad depot. Melville would not let any of the hands go anywhere except to his house. And he arranged a dinner for Matthew, with Groot invited, too, as well as the mayor of Abilene and his wife, and a handful of other businessmen with several young ladies of fully primped and New York catalogue appeal.

"He's got a few of our choice whores in for you," said Fleur. "Abilene, you see, is a mainline town. Good, clean and experienced girls, I'm sure. Just don't say too much to them."

"I don't believe," said Matthew, "that I will be needing any of them."

"Really?" said Fleur. "Well, sir, you *are* bold, I'm glad to see." And she gave him that tempted grin again, before Melville arrived with sherry and a tireless ear for yarns from the trail.

"Well, gentlemen, ladies and gentlemen," said Melville, making a toast. "I give you old friends, the boys from the Red River D ranch, and—I may say—a particular, personal friend, a young man who established my trade, my hat is off to him as he, unaccountably, still seems young, Mr. Matthew Garth."

There were congratulations, and the flashing of crystal and sherry in the soft oil-lamp glow. The ladies came up to Matthew with pretty little dips and curtsies so he could esteem their powder-white bosoms, and the men slapped him on the back and told him he was a fine example and how the livestock of Texas must surely be kept coming.

"And Dunson?" asked Melville.

"He had a stroke, sir," said Matthew. "And he cannot do much. He can do nothing at all."

"But you and he are on good terms now?"

"We do not converse. He cannot. I talk to him sometimes, and I hope he follows what I say. He is well looked after."

"That's good," Melville grunted. "As good as can be."

"Yet I cannot know how things are between us."

"No?" Melville looked at him warily across the meal—beef, with fresh vegetables, sweet potatoes and a batter pudding—as if there was no need to go into the matter further.

"I think the stroke has left him angry, and disappointed."

"He was that sort of man," Melville pointed out, "long before."

"I feel I may have let him down."

"He wouldn't have it any other way, I daresay," said Melville, full of kindness toward Matthew. For he had heard how Garth had had

his wife and child taken away by Cherry Valance, that insolent renegade. Stories worked the trail as readily as disease and new fashions.
But Melville saw no reason to mar this occasion.

"How do you like our vegetables?" Fleur asked.

"My God, yes," cried Melville, in relief. "You can't have had many
on your way here."

"No sir, we didn't," said Matthew, "and I am going very cautiously
with them in case they shock my system."

"Oh, Mr. Garth," Fleur reproached him. "You are too much our
hero to be so cautious. I want you to gorge on them." She teased
him more with her smile. "So that a shine comes back in your eyes.
You boys all look like ghosts, or men kept on a dark closet shelf."

The company laughed a good deal at this, and in the flux and noise
Fleur was able to wink directly at Matthew Garth as she tipped
another spoon of Kansas peas and carrots on his plate.

"Matthew, you should come visit more often," said Melville. "Get
yourself into more business interests than just ranching. You are in
the very best position for speculating with your steady base."

"I wouldn't know what to do."

"None of us *knows*," said Melville. "Knowing isn't the thing. That's
the beauty of it. Do you realize," he began, and he took the silver
cruet set and several spare spoons and forks to make a simple map
on the linen tablecloth. "Here is America," he said. "Now, I put a
line down the middle of the country, top to bottom," and he set a
knife to show it. "See, the knuckle there between the blade and the
handle—that knuckle is Abilene."

The assembly murmured at being so central. Matthew nodded,
and marveled again at the sweetness of the vegetables as he ate.
Fleur leaned over and poured more of the red wine into his glass: it
was the color of brick, but glowing from within, and he was happily
getting himself drunk. Her hand touched his as it passed, and he
knew the skill with which she had managed it.

"Three years ago," said Melville, "in the year of our centenary—
are you with me?"

"I am, sir."

"Three years ago, east of that line there were forty-two million
people—they counted them. Can you imagine the squalor? The
congestion! The sheer, fermenting unhealthiness of it. Not to mention the gloom, the poverty, the near slavery of so many."

"It's hard to believe," Matthew agreed.

"But to the west?" Melville's brown hand was flat on the tablecloth
on the other, free side of the knife. "What would you guess?"

"I've been nowhere," Matthew apologized.

"You live that side of the line," Melville insisted.

"I'll be a fool if I say anything," said Matthew.

"Two million," whispered Melville. "Only two. Do you see my point?"

"So much of it desert, I daresay," Matthew reasoned. "Or simple wilderness."

"My dear Matthew, the wilderness cannot be allowed its simplicity. Forty-two to two is as clear as money, sir."

"It is?"

"You bet on two for the future. Invest in it. Buy it. Beg, borrow or steal to own some of it. There's nothing as sure as the way a great mass of those poor, amazed Easterners are at last going to come here. And they'll likely find themselves hungrier than they ever had the courage to be in Cleveland or New York or Boston. And—more to my point—they will find their heads swelling here with outrageous, inventive notions for building, developing, promoting and acquiring —for the slaves have a lust to own things—that you can build your fortune on."

"Mr. Garth is tired, I think," said Fleur. "I can see him dreaming already. You are such a spellbinder, Frank."

Melville laughed, oddly, as if taken off guard. "Well, maybe I am. I talk too much. But I regard this young man as a kind of son."

"Mr. Melville, I have to tell you," said Matthew, "that I am forty this year. In October."

Melville examined Garth, and concluded, "Then you must make all haste," he said. "America gives you fair warning—it does not wait."

Matthew Garth

Matthew Garth went up to the room to which the unfailingly jovial Melville had assigned him. Indeed, with brandy and cigar in hand, his host walked him down the carpeted corridor on the second floor, opened the door with its flowered porcelain handle (white with carmine roses on it) and fairly bumped him inside with a paternal administration to Matthew's back. The brandy was swinging in Melville's glass from the exertion when Matthew turned to thank him.

"I think you'll have all that you want," said Melville, nearly over-powered by his own pleasure. "I wish there might be all you de-serve."

The coverlet of the bed was turned down. There was a white nightshirt and a heavy, dark brown dressing gown, quilted and em-broidered like a Persian rug, waiting for him on the polished spiral rail at the end of the bed.

There was a painting on the wall of a naked woman lying on her side with her back to the painter. She was beside a frilled stream in a woodland glade, in what appeared to be the middle of a night past waking. Her body was a scoop of milk nestled in the darkness. She was very close to the size of life and protected only by the loftiness of art and the encrusted gilt of the frame. Matthew gazed upon her display and did comprehend the mythic appeal of some call to rescue or ravish women lost in the wilds. But he found the meek array of heedless flesh absurd. There was nothing in the picture as arousing as Fleur's very rapid smile and its snatching intelligence. He won-dered if the obliging Melville had caught one of those quick inti-mations of their mutual curiosity, or Matthew's commotion because of it, and decided to equip his night with a diverting fancy. Matthew had in the past observed the strange clash of courtly delicacy in such pictures and their casual provocation to rape, or worse, in men who professed to be as moved by them as by fine views in nature. But a truly moved man, thought Matthew, is out of control.

He could not prevent the consideration whether, in another room, Fleur remotely resembled this nearly liquid female apparition in the woods, or even whether she had posed for the picture. Was that Melville's unlaughing message? Did painters profess their shortcom-ings and insist on life's examples to study, measure and faithfully reproduce? Or was their method more akin to what he saw as the significance of such paintings—the daring of the imagination when deprived of the ideal itself? Such paintings, Matthew hazarded, were like the visions of men in prison or in a desert hopeless of ever touching women again. Was there not a fairy-like attenuation to the limbs and a glow on the flesh that suggested the artist had begun to forget the particular intricacies of anatomy and was awash with lovelorn impression?

There was a decanter of brandy on the table beside the bed, glasses, and a crystal jug of water with a small weighted cloth on it to keep out the dust. There were cigars, matches and an ashtray as big as a dish. And there was a book in which Matthew could smell new paper.

He examined it: apparently a story, *The Return of the Native* by Thomas Hardy.

He opened it, and there in the hushed room in the silent house, he read aloud in soft nocturnal tones the opening of the book:

A Saturday afternoon in November was approaching the time of twilight, and the vast tract of unenclosed wild known as Egdon Heath embrowned itself moment by moment. Overhead the hollow stretch of whitish cloud shutting out the sky was as a tent which had the whole heath for its floor.

Matthew Garth looked up at his ceiling, crammed with roseate wheels and the frozen foliage of leaves and branches. The solid amber of the brandy stared at him. The cigars waited like sticks of packed explosive. The white of the pliant pillow existed without a will of its own. The woman in the picture was as still. Matthew waited for his pulse to slow. He was not a reader, but those few lines from an unknown book had crept up on him. He knew this Egdon must be in Texas, but he had not heard of it before.

He thought the gentle knocking was his heart, or the beat of feeling in his head. But it came again and he appreciated it was the door. When he stood up, the carpeting was ready to consume him. He could not hear himself move across the room to what he was certain was Fleur, enigmatic, enchanting but challenging at the door. And of a loveliness he could not distinguish from the beguiling atmosphere of twilight and the peaceful, lambent feel of Mr. Hardy's recent words.

"I was considering you might have nodded off very quickly," she said. "Like a tired man with nothing on his mind."

"If that is the measure of it," he answered, "I doubt I will sleep for a week."

"What a pretty speech," she said, surprised by the troubled inward examination so evident in his features. She was wearing a dressing gown of white, with pink and peach flowers on it: she was like the door handle he held, but not as cold or hard.

"Are you available for a conversation?" she asked.

In answer, he drew her in away from the visibility of the corridor. "You are not nervous?" he asked.

She lifted his hand to the pulse in her throat. Her hand was colder than the china door handle, but her throat was as hot as summer. Her eyes leaped as she saw him count the giddy beat of her expec-

tations. "I would not have come if it had not made me afraid," she
assured him. He believed it; he was clear in his own mind that she
was a threat, that somehow she had urges or freedoms in common
with Cherry Valance who had charmed Tess away from him, whis-
tling her out into the night and the bare Texas emptiness. There was
something desperate in it, something beyond reason.

"Frank Melville is my good friend," said Matthew Garth. She
halted in the middle of the room; she had been strolling forwards,
ahead of him, so artlessly leading him.

"What is that meant to say?" she demanded.

Matthew Garth stopped several steps away from her. "Here in his
own house, and you his . . ." He did not know how to repeat her
word.

"His house is just a show," she said. "It is like a theater where,
as a rule, he can get no audience."

"It is his home."

"No, his home is in Pennsylvania. That is where he has his wife
and his domestic arrangements. In Abilene, he is at business. You
heard him say how vibrant it is here at the knife's hinge."

"But he loves you."

"And you, too."

"That is hardly the same."

"He knows you lost your wife. He has a concern for you, and he
saw that you were not dexterous enough to make terms with one of
his professional women."

"He has said these things to you?"

"No." Matthew did see how easy it would have been for her to
smile, and answer "yes" to that. He was ready to believe it and might
have been swayed.

"I likely imagined it," said Fleur. "Well, then, you intend to put
me out?"

Matthew was crushed by this integrity he had assumed. "It is not
. . . not by choice," he said. "Do you not see that there would be
violence to his trust?"

"In this mausoleum of the Greenwood Trading Company," she
finished it off for him.

"You make him sound like a lost soul."

"Not lost. But he has given up being a fixed man. He is all for
progress and change."

"I must be frank with you," said Matthew.

"That is entirely up to you," Fleur told him, striving to be chilly.

"I have never made love with anyone I did not love."

"And that only with one woman?" she guessed. He did not have to respond. His blush showed the wound Tess had left.

"Why did you let her go then, your wife?"

"It was her wish, her need. I was helpless if I would not be her jailer."

"Do you think she will ever return?"

"I did."

"Matthew Garth," she said in a very low, sentimental voice. It made him think of the pity and inarticulate love he had felt in the doorway behind Dunson. "One never knows who will come back. It is a profound urge, that returning. But not often indulged," and she tapped her fingers on the book on his bedside table. Then, "Sir," she said, "I bid you good night." And she dropped a swift curtsy in the middle of the room, and was away in a silent rush that left him cooled and afflicted by the glimpse of tears on her blind face. She was clumsy with the door, rattling the handle, and he heard her distraught scoff at being so upset. Matthew Garth cursed himself in the empty room and thought of dying with so many things never risked.

He sat down on the bed, poured a glass of brandy and sought to steady himself with the firm lines of print in the book. But his mind could not grip them or be still. Though he scanned the words, he could not follow them. But neither could he prevent the accumulation of mood, loneliness and dread. For, at least, he knew, this book—and surely she had picked it for him—spoke of foreboding.

Matthew Garth

He knew there would be no sleeping now in his stately bedroom. The stuffed palace of Abilene was too heavy with the possibilities of doings or waiting hopes in other rooms. He wanted to shout "Fire! Terror!" just to have panic clean the place out.

Matthew was angry with himself that he could not, somehow, dominate the house, stride through it, taking this antique or that person, whatever he wanted, like the model of Western prowess they called for. He might pick up things for which he had no need or taste but which, in the taking, would assert his unhindered will. Wasn't he, after all, the sort of man this great, brimming, vacant and available West was designed for? Hadn't Melville cast him as its hero, its protagonist? And maybe Melville had sent him the best female bounty he had, of the same pedigree as the cigars and the brandy, so that authority should be made manifest? Suppose Melville had whispered, "Show me," in the hush of the house. But Garth had been too timid, too modest, too demure, too helpless, too obscure, recessive and gentlemanly, too much his own observer, just to reach out and take the opportunity. Too much Matthew Garth.

He was likely smiling at the dilemma, there in the richly furnished room, at whatever hour of the dark Kansan night it was. It did not seem difficult for people to recognize the lounging danger, the outlawry and the smoke of violent plunder in such as Cherry Valance. Everyone had respectfully ascribed Tess's departure to that, assuming that the woman had been devoid of purpose and the other man as predatory as a wolf coming down on a helpless creature. Why could no one see such malice, such outright selfhood in him, in Matthew Garth? Why, if they bothered to look at him for more than one polite moment, couldn't they see his anger, the towering urge to fill space with outrage? Didn't they notice the monster Matthew feared so much? A small gaunt man made quietly mad by space, opportunity and the freedom of the first page of a story? Once upon a time. . . . Matthew Garth, trampling the time, dancing on it. Surely Miss Fleur had seen or felt the inner heat of it? Why, then, was he left alone again with his own inertia?

Matthew quit the room in his gracious fury, and thought to stroll about the sleeping house. There was a perfumed air in the corridors, like some scent put down to stifle the malodors of men, their work and death not too far away. He recalled that dead man he had found out on the prairie, and he wondered if a wind was blowing in on Abilene from that Southwest.

There was light in one of the salons downstairs, and Matthew made his way towards it. He could hear a small clicking sound from the bright room, as if someone there was cleaning a gun or testing its mechanism. But it was the sound of the ivory balls of billiards. A single man was at the table, a tall, thin man who had taken off his jacket and was poking the balls here and there across the stealthy verdant baize.

"Not my game," the man announced when he saw Matthew. It was a remark that prevented the possibility of a match. Yet he went on practicing, moving the balls, a white and two reds, around the table, as a trio, contriving small kissing contacts, endeavoring to maintain a close triangle, an intrigue, full of tiny collisions or coincidences, with no ball ever breaking free of the pattern. It seemed to Matthew Garth like some devotional skill in the tall, thin man— no matter if he had other, more preferred games. The other games seemed more sinister in advance because of the tall, thin man's calm skill in ensuring, stroke after stroke, that the three balls kept so obediently close.

"Garrett," said the man, unexpectedly. He made his name sound like, or give imagined access to, a large, upper empty room. Matthew did wonder whether Dunson was dead already: he made a note of the intuition, a reminder to himself to ascertain the likelihood of some psychic or electrical transmission of thought, borne up from Texas on the wind that also carried particles of death and romance.

"I know you," the tall, thin ball player added, his head nodding aside a fraction to the earlier dinner. Garrett had been there, another guest at the table, silent or laconic, being talked to by the vivacious Fleur, bowing his head morosely, unable to say much in return, yet with a held-back readiness for silent humor in the downcast sloping lines of his long face. He was younger than Matthew by maybe ten years, but he seemed so much more familiar with sadness or failure, those two being hard to distinguish in the deliberately adventurous and positive West.

"I heard, as a matter of fact," the tall, thin Garrett went on, "how you were an example to us all." He spoke without grievance or mockery, but the dryness appealed to Garth. "I felt some sympathy for you, sir."

"I appreciate that," said Matthew.

"Then again, I was irked that Miss Fleur seemed so dazzled by you."

"She did?"

"Hardly took her eyes off you. Was besieging me, as a matter of fact, with enquiries about you. None of which assisted my desire to talk to her about myself." The fellow was lugubrious, his amusement every bit as close and conspiratorial as the trio of balls which he was still maneuvering around the table, limping after them as he needed to go round a corner to get the best, prodding angle for his shot, and seeming to chew on the slight, sepulchral sounds the balls made as they met and parted, touched and spread.

"You are in business?" Matthew asked him.

"I am. Yet my business, I believe, is mainly something to do. It's not exactly me, if you take my point."

"What would you be under the best circumstances?"

"Well, Mr. Garth, some gambling, enough cards and some liquor and some ladies. Apart from that, I am a dull fish."

"It seems simple enough," said Matthew.

"Time was," said Garrett, "but today, sir, you are likely to be deafened by the cries for substantial progress and improvement. In both the land and its poor men. I am in danger of seeming frivolous and, shall we say, minor."

"I think that Frank Melville wants me to sing in that chorus."

Garrett nodded. "Indeed. As a matter of fact, would you care to guess how I am here tonight? I mean, why I merit an invitation and the chance of meeting you?"

"Simple bad luck?"

"Well, I never discount that. But Mr. Melville's prompting is that I encountered him on the railroad. I travel there, you see, selling a new line of goods. A line that has excited, and maybe aroused, our Mr. Melville."

"Greeleyism?" asked Matthew.

"I don't know that it might not be so," drawled Garrett. "This going west will not stop at the Pacific, will it? It goes deeper into the mind's small compartments and into the very structure of the gonads. Mr. Garth, sir, I sell a truss—it is the only word for it—uniquely made to cosset the testicles. It should be charged first and put on, still tingling. The imagination helps in this. It is used before encountering the opposite sex, and it promises splendors: twelve dollars and fifty cents."

"I don't think it's for me."

"I hope not. Though it has another claim—I mention it so that you can appreciate the full indignity of my life. Its maker, a gent in Poughkeepsie, has a theory—a large volume comes with the truss, fully theoretical, for another three fifty—in which he explores what you might call testicular phrenology. You know? The notion of bumps in the skull."

"I've heard."

"My boy says that the balls have the very same lumps and peaks."

"So, what of it?"

"Ah, Mr. Garth, you are altogether too quick. The customer is supposed to be so amazed by this harmony he has no need of other reasons. It does work, too. I am, temporarily, out of supplies—save, that is," he grinned up, over and around the cue stick, "for the one I'm wearing."

"It's of use to you?"

"A matter of fact, I am in my eleventh month without female companionship. I was just considering," he looked at Matthew, level, sparkish, but without raillery, "attempting Miss Fleur. Unless you know reason why I shouldn't."

"Why should I?"

"I wondered." Garrett stood up straight; he winced and put a hand to his lower stomach. "It's a bitch of a thing," he complained.

"It tingles? Truly?" asked Matthew.

"Of course not," said Garrett. "Do you believe men of the frontier would permit unexplained electric currents to pass through their gonads?"

"What is promised from the treatment?"

"The language is vague," said Garrett, "but there's no mistaking the glory. We do say the long days in the saddle can constrict the flow of the requisite bodily fluids. The juice frees them up. How do you like that?"

"There are diagrams?"

"No lewdness, sir, if you please."

"I think Miss Fleur," Matthew guessed, "is the sort of woman might laugh to see this truss."

"I should hope so," said Garrett. "I would assuredly remove it in advance, bathe my privates and put the beast away in its leather case. On the train, people mistake it for a clarinet box."

Matthew was in a merry mood by now. "Twelve fifty seems modest."

"There you are. The fellow in Poughkeepsie is a small thinker. I told him that a higher price might be more emotional. However, he did change his name to something more Prussian. He showed willing."

"Is this selling the best you can do with yourself?"

"Oh, it can't last, Mr. Garth. Don't write me off. I hear that cattle rustling is every bit as simple."

"So is the hanging," said Matthew Garth.

"Well, then, I may have to take the hanging. For I'd hate to offend you. As a matter of fact, I have been thinking of New Mexico Territory. Mr. Melville paints a vivid picture of it."

"And Miss Fleur?"

Garrett looked up: "I beg your pardon."

"He describes her in such a way?"

"He is quietly satisfied with her, I'd say. Too much a gentleman to boast. Of course, the truss gives a kind of technical brotherhood. But I believe he's fond of her. While her man does his time."

"Her man?"

"She has a husband. He's a cardsharp; he worked the trains, too. And he's in jail in Kansas City for it. Mr. Melville is, so to say, looking after her in the meantime."

Matthew asked him, "Are you a family man, Mr. Garrett?"

"Guilty, sir. I left a wife and babe in the Sweetwater country."

"No going back?"

"Well, the farm I had there, it was a bust. And I am a poor visitor to my own failures. You might take me for a cynic, Mr. Garth, but I have a virgin's wish, still, to amount to something."

"I lost a child," claimed Matthew Garth. "Susan," he said.

"How old would she be now?"

"Ah," sighed Garth. His eyes narrowed, like a fighter as an opponent came towards him. "Why, nine, I believe."

"You have her in mind often?" asked Garrett gently.

"I do," vowed Garth.

"Then she's not lost—would you say?"

"Does she think of *me*?" begged Garth.

"Nine's old enough, I daresay."

"You don't think of yours, left behind?"

"Matter of fact, Mr. Garth," said Garrett, and the Irish could be heard, way back before the Alabama twang, "we are the two heroes who seem somehow barred from our sleep. No peace for those who move on. No, not even in the German trusses or their magical shiver!"

Bark Blaylock

"Who's your father now?" asked Curly Bill Brocius, his encouraging smile lurking in the shade afforded by his Chinese straw hat.

"I don't know," said the boy, easy in the warm day and his bewilderment and beginning to be conscious perhaps of some larger, more expansive well-being, of having a good time, of happiness itself, a thing so enormous it far exceeded momentary peaks of bliss and contentment.

They were out on the trail, the pair of them, two days out of Tombstone, riding east. The boy knew that, for at dawn Curly Bill had got him up, shown him the ways of lighting fires, dressed him and made him drink bitter coffee with the biscuits that were their breakfast. All of this in the long, bloody shadows of the rising sun, keeping their backs to it as they worked so that they could see, but then riding off towards it, into its blinding secret. Bark could not look up at it, and so he studied the flaming chestnut hair on his horse's shoulders and his small hands clenched on the rein.

"Don't look, boy," Curly Bill had told him. "In a while, now, it'll climb up. Just close your eyes and go back to sleep. I'll lead us on."

He did trust the amiable cowboy, even if he was known as "Curly" while his hair was as flat as fine straw stuck on top of his head. You never knew why men used some names: you remembered people by names, to be sure (that was surely the purpose of names), yet names were deadly mysterious, too, and they could shift. For in those times, men's nicknames or their whole and given names could alter as they went from one line of business or one woman to another. Maybe Bill had been Curly once, before days out in the sun had beaten his hair straight. Or maybe the curliness had nothing to do with hair, but referred to the twisting directions of Bill's mind, his games, his whimsy and his spinning good spirits. For, without one hint of dishonesty or the wish to deceive, Bill Brocius was the most naturally curling and curled fellow Bark had known. The boy liked to look at the man's lean, rigid outline and picture in his mind the delightful floweriness whereby the inner Brocius deserved his name.

"What are you looking at, boy?" Bill asked—as if the kid was transfixed in some grinning, foolish stupor.

"Just seeing," said Bark, his eyes screwed up—for there was always sun around, and a nearly limitless brightness.

It had taken a day and a night for Bark to catch on to Bill's ways. The boy had been a rather grudging audience on their first ride, wondering what he was doing on this journey with a man he did not much know. There were pangs of regret over his mother's state, and a few tears, as he heard the wind moaning, at the thought of all things out of sight. He wondered if he would ever see Tombstone again, or know the anxious closeness of his mother, the mood that made him so unsettled he wanted to stay a little distance from her whenever he was with her. But the boy could not tell whether it was his true sentiment or the powerful, mourning suggestion of the wind. The quandary brought tears to his eyes.

"Hey now, Bark. You water the ground like that and the rattle-snakes'll come out after us. They have such a thirst."

"No, sir," said Bark, sure that this could not be so. For he cried often and none of the many men he had known had ever mentioned the snakes' taste for tears.

"You never heard that?" asked an amazed Bill.

"Did not."

"Only because you're a sad child and no one dared to alarm you."

"You're silly," said Bark. It was his most complete condemnation. The men he had known were so solid and unshakable, and already he could detect the will-o'-the-wisp that made things up in Brocius.

"Silly, am I?" And Brocius laughed so much his hat fell off—or else he had another trick of tossing back his head. Then he made a show of trying to put it back on, but the hat kept falling off, as if the vibration of his laugh was too resistant for it, bucking like an unbroken horse. It seemed to Bark a terrible indignity, to be played with. He wanted his small sorrows respected.

"You're a worm," he told Bill Brocius. "You're a snake."

"Ah," said Brocius, "you're a stern, brave lad, and you've had a hard time of it."

It was left at that. But the evening won Bark over. He was so tired and so ignorant of the camping life that he could only marvel at Bill's dexterity. For Bill found a stream, and a soft piece of ground, and he was away only five minutes before he was back with a rabbit. Bark was not pleased by the rough, tearing sound as its fur came off; nor did he admire the blue and pink glare in the animal's flesh. But, later, in the dark, he hardly remembered such details when the hot, moist meat came to him, piece by piece in Bill's gentle hand, fragrantly herbaceous and so good he felt filled with energy and courage. So it surprised him when he fell fast asleep while he was eating still. And it did not break his sleep when Bill wound him in a blanket and put a pillow of his own clothes beneath his head.

"Thank you, Bill," he heard a boy mumble.

"Oh, you're welcome, sir," said Bill, who was, somehow, playing a soft, unshrill tune on the flute that he kept in the saddlebag on his uncomplaining pinto horse. Bark heard the upward slide of the first two notes, and the crackle of the fire—like defenses falling.

It was heaven after that. In June, maybe, of 1881, making the way Bill Brocius knew to pick out—for ease and scenic splendor—going northeast from Tombstone into New Mexico Territory. Bark felt he was riding on pillows, simmering in the rich, comforting smell of his horse and the flicker of butterflies that escorted them. He did not know or care how far it was, but he was ready for the ride to go on and on, with picnics, campfires and Bill's airy yarning taking away all anxieties, plucking rabbits or slow quail for their dinner out of the provender of the semi-desert.

Bill Brocius taught him stories, their rise and fall, the balance of expectation and delivery. He told him how the horses were experiencing the days, and how a smart man could read the bitter land and realize where water might be. Bill had a pair of binocular glasses and a small book with pictures for identifying birds of the Southwestern prairie and desert. He taught Bark to look, to be patient, to know where creatures would likely be, and to name them accurately. In these details of voluminous nature, Bill Brocius was a quiet but reliable guide to identity and description. "You see," he would whisper in Bark's ear as the boy looked through the glasses, "it has a white bar on the wing. That is the male." And the bird flew up obligingly, so that Bark could see the jagged flash of white.

The bird book was a source of wonder to Bark: he did not even consider if it was correct or useful. It was *the* book of this part of the desert, and since it included every bird, animal or insect, no matter that they were free to roam, and did not include the men one met out there, so Bark concluded that man's place in the book was as maker and reader. He looked into the inscrutable book, sure of the pictures but perplexed by the lines of broken black which Bill said were reading. Bark demanded access to this code, too, and so in the evenings Bill sat him down and began him on the alphabet, a phenomenon that Bark had not yet encountered. And Bill drew the letters in the dust until it was too dark to see. By the time they were in New Mexico Territory Bark Blaylock knew several letters.

"You're a rapid learner," said Bill.

"Yes," Bark agreed, wanting more.

"It must be on account of your being held back. You're like a dammed river—I mean the useful dammed, not the profane. Why, if we were going to New York you'd be writing a book of your travels before we got there."

"I believe I will," said Bark, conscientiously, for he had learned that even Bill's wildest schemes were agreeable.

"Does your father not teach you?" asked Bill, stirring the fire and yelping as he tried to pick up the hot coffee pot. There was the lather of old scorch marks all over Bill's hands, and he assured Bark that there were some places where all the feeling had gone.

"I mean the marshal," added Bill.

Bark felt foolish. He did want to join with Bill in grown-up conversations. But in truth he was never quite sure which one was his father. None of them made anything like the fuss of him that Bill did, so Bark supposed that indifference was a sign of fathers. In which case, the hotel marshal was a likely one, for he never seemed to have a word for the boy but did always stare at him as if, somehow, Bark had got himself in the way. Then again, fathers were not like the birds in Bill's book. They had no differentiating markings. All of them were tall and dressed in dark suits, and all of them had the same horrid mustache that smelled of drink and tobacco and which sometimes held fragments of food or snot.

"Marshal's a very upright man," said Bill. "He smacked me on the nut once with the side of his gun just to stop me drinking." Bill nodded and fingered his head. "Very decent of him, when he could have killed me. Here, Bark, feel my head, won't you? Maybe the bump's still there."

Bark did feel, amid the lank hair. He felt grit and dust, and his fingers squashed one small hard black bug there. But he could feel bumps beneath the hot skin, and Bill explained to him how a man's nature and whole life were supposedly there in the shape of his skull.

"You may not understand it," said Bill, "but you can count on it. Like the photography. I mean, how does that work?—I don't know. But you've seen the pictures at Fly's yourself. Somehow with you there and the box here, it does take you, squeeze you down to the size of my thumb and put you on paper. You can count on it."

And Bill Brocius then would relax and light up a pipe and begin to tell Bark of things not easily understandable as part of the world if a boy had not been outside the West. Bill told him about cities, seas and ships and how, very rapidly, the world was being filled up with things that sensible men just had to count on without ever witnessing. "I met a fellow in KC," said Bill, "that's a city to the north, who said there was no reason why there couldn't be photographs that moved, just like life. He said it was a foreseeable thing. He explained it to me, but I didn't take it in. He showed me a book with pictures on every page of a man dancing. And if you riffled through the pages and kept looking the man seemed to dance. Said it was a similar principle. I said I didn't doubt him, but I questioned if principle had anything to do with it."

Bill Brocius chuckled and put on the Mexican sombrero he liked in the evening.

"Now, Bark," he began. "I have a serious matter to raise with you."

"Yes, Bill," said Bark, sitting up.

"As near as I can tell we are in New Mexico tonight."

"And I had my letters!"

"That's how I knew. They have a way of getting straight in New Mexico. Anyway, in New Mexico, you see, I am not Bill Brocius. No, I am Dave Rudabaugh here."

Bark nodded and said the name over to himself.

"I mention it because we'll be meeting people who know the name. Just take it in your stride."

"Right," said Bark, and he thought awhile. "Should I be Bark still?"

"You should. There's nothing illegal in having other names, but it's a bad habit when you're young."

"You have other names, Bill?"

"Lord, yes. I'm Lee Clayton up north, and Joe Ferguson on Thursdays. I seem to collect names, you know."

"Like Curly," said Bark, as if he had made the crucial discovery.

Bark Blaylock

It was a fine, high-skyed day in June 1881, and Bark Blaylock and Bill Brocius were trudging through the white sands of New Mexico Territory, the spill like water at their feet. They were walking, leading their horses, for it was kinder on the animals in the shifting ground. The sand was as bright as bone, or snow, and it was easier for Bark to look up at the sky, or, better still, the silvered flanks of his horse.

"We're cutting across the edge of the sands, mind," said Bill. "Just to show you what they're like. You go north of here," Bill waved with his left arm away to the north—his right was holding a tattered silk parasol as best he could over Bark's head. It was one more implement that Bill had managed to discover in his saddlebag. "Why, north of here, we could perish."

"I never saw desert like this," said Bark.

"I hear the Arabian is very similar," said Bill in his nonchalant way. If he didn't know a thing, Bill had surely met another man who knew. And he passed the information on in a generous spirit that warmed Bark's curiosity. Days ago, the boy's skepticism had gone to snooze in the sunny adventure. "In Arabia, which is about where the Bible takes place, young Bark. You know that?"

"Sort of," said Bark. "My mother . . ."

"Ah yes, she's full of those Bible stories."

"Does anyone live in this desert, Bill?"

"No, sir. Not even the heathen. From lack of the water."

"Then how do they live in that Bible desert?"

"Well," considered Bill. Then he laughed. "That's it, Bark. There's wells in that desert. God would have provided them, seeing he needed his stories there for the Bible."

"God doesn't know this desert?"

"I think you've stumbled on the truth, young Bark. Although you see a lot of preachers in our country—"

"Yes," said Bark. Tombstone was crowded with the religious gentlemen who were strenuous in attempting to save the miners, especially the lucky ones, and always holding meetings for the raising of churches and chapels.

"Still," said Bill, "I'm of the opinion that God has not personally yet made up his mind about this place."

"No?"

"I feel the air of his doubt here. He may have meant the place as a wilderness. This desert here, for instance, may just have been a place for God to see how hot he could get it. This is what I think of as a God-forsaken place."

"God-forsaken," said Bark, looking over the curled crests of all the dunes. The words thrilled him. They were forbidding, to be sure, but he felt the challenge and the romance. It was as if God had found a way of letting men know what it felt like to be God, to see this vast empty land, to think of taking it and shaping it.

"It got so hot it could melt," said Bark.

"That's all sand was once," said Bill.

"Yeah?"

"When the earth broke off from the sun—did I mention that?—it was all molten, like something cooking, and the sand formed as it cooled."

"I never heard that bit," said Bark, thunderstruck. There seemed no limit to Bill's wisdom. "It was on the sun?"

"I was told this by an old lady in Denver. She was a schoolteacher. Now this happened a while ago."

"Before Tombstone?" asked Bark.

"So long before you couldn't count it."

It was impossible to conceive, yet Bark had no difficulty with it as a notion. He looked up at the sky to see if there were other burning balls coming.

"And some parts," said Bill, "they still resemble the sun. Like the desert here."

"Are there deserts on the sun, Bill?"

"Not that you can walk on, Bark. But the whole sun has to be deserted. You see, there's a magnificent fire going on there. The only thing that's keeping us warm now. Here, lad, we'll stop and I'll put up the parasol. I think we both deserve a mouthful of water."

There was time to play, too. Bark rolled down the dunes, and he loved to feel the soft sand sliding beneath him. Bill Brocius and the horses watched him, until Bark was so weary Bill had to lift him up and put him on his horse. And Bill found a floppy white hat for the boy and told him to keep it on. All of a sudden, Bark felt afraid of the desert and the creeping increase in the heat, and he was dismayed to see how quickly he was tired.

"Are you sad, Bark?"

"I'm afraid."

"With Bill here?"

Bark felt ashamed, but the fear did not go. Bill told him that in two hours they would be out of the sands, and so it proved. But Bark could not forget that onset of ominousness, as if the heat had been ready to engulf him, the air so hot he could not breathe there without his lungs catching fire. He shivered and shuddered.

"You got you a touch of the sun, Bark," said Bill, and Bark was crazy all that night, sweating and chattering, until morning came and he was swathed in a blanket of his own sweat, with Bill Brocius awake, watching his every change. Kissed him for courage. His own, as well as Bark's. This would be recollected as a jewel in the fever dreams.

So Bill carried the boy into a Mescalero village and he made it clear he was not moving until the Apaches cooked Bark their healing cornmeal, made it thin so that the boy's stricken mouth—there was a small palsy with the fever—could take in the gruel. And in the end the Mescaleros were interested, and they grew lively as Bark became better. And Bill traded with them a crumpled bonnet he had for an old baseball so that Bark could play and get strong again.

With the result, a few days later—it may have been early July by now—when they had made it as far as the undulating grasslands between Lincoln, Roswell and Fort Sumner, and they had stopped in a dry wash, where Bill and Bark were throwing the ball from one end of the wash to the other. And Bark looked up as Bill's throw sailed, to see three riders stopped, looking down at them from the ridge above the wash. Three men somber-looking against the rose sky. It was late in the day and the splash of sunset fell across the wash, leaving alleys of shadow.

"It's not my game," said the man in the middle of the three. "But I'd say you had an arm on you."

Bill Brocius had not seen or heard the men come up—this should be taken as a measure of his fondness for the boy. For he was not an unguarded man out in the middle of Lincoln County. He was surprised, and he stood still, speechless, when Bark threw the ball back. So, to cover for him, Bark went scampering after the rolling ball.

"Who would you be, sir?" asked the same man on his horse. The racing Bark felt a surge of joy, knowing how he could do his duty, and he sang out, at the top of his voice, stooping to retrieve the ball, seeing the knobs and grains of gravel in the wash, all alive in the yellow light, "This is Mr. Dave Rudabaugh!"

He heard the horses above snuffle and move, as if something had disturbed them.

"You know the Kid?" demanded one of the other two men.

"Not I!" shouted Bill. "This boy's light-headed. He's had a bad fever. Not recovered. Bill Brocius is my name. He's a crazy kid. Yes, sir!" And Bill ignored the ball that Bark held out to him. Pushed the boy away and made a loose, fretful gesture with his hand as if he ought to cuff his silly, sick head.

"Didn't he say Rudabaugh?" It was the middle man, the tallest, asking.

"Who knows what he said?" said Bill.

"What was it, boy?" asked the rider. "As a matter of fact."

Bark looked up at Bill for guidance with the new name he had carefully acquired, as hard as the alphabet. But Bill would not meet his eye. No, the cowboy seemed to be addressing not just the three strangers but the whole horizon behind them. His denials were meant to fill up and satisfy all of space and light.

"I don't know," said Bark, wretchedly. The tall man got off his horse; his long coat unfolded as he came down; it fell beneath his knees and cast an oval of gloom where he walked.

"None the less," said the tall man, a word coming on each step he took. "I daresay you know the Kid?"

There was nothing from Bill. The cowboy's clenched face was scanning the sky, the other two men, the range of prospects and possibilities. Bark was beginning to cry: not to be known or owned up to; to be deserted and left for strangers. In the days just past he had formed an attachment to Bill; it was hurtful now to have Bill at an inexplicable loss instead of calmly stepping forward to ease Bark's way and claim him.

"Oh yes, sir, he does!" Bark yelled out. He would not permit the doubt or the risk of Bill slipping away from him. "We are very close friends."

He saw Bill's pained face turn on him, and there was such a loving smile in the agony there.

"Well, now," chuckled the man who had dismounted.

"Don't you see, sir, he gets things wrong," Bill was explaining.

The tall man came over to Bark. His coat billowed, and it sent out sighs of tobacco that enveloped Bark. The man examined him in an amused way.

"You get things mistook?" he asked. Bark looked up at the gentle, sad eyes that did not seem eager about their own questions. This was a troubled man. He moved awkwardly, as if he had difficulty or hurt in his body.

"I don't believe so, sir," said Bark.

"Where are you going then?" the man asked.

Bark looked at Bill, for he had never known or cared.

"We're on our way," said Bill, "to see some old acquaintances."

"Where would they be?" asked the tall man.

"Santa Rosa way, I should say," said Bill.

"Aren't you more headed for Fort Sumner?"

"Are we?" asked Bill. "I'm not too familiar with this country."

"You're in Lincoln County, Mr . . . what was it?"

"Brocius. Bill Brocius."

"Aha," said the tall man, and he turned to the two men with him, still alert on their horses. "My fellows here are Poe and McKinney," he said. "Maybe we'll make a camp here with you." The two men slipped off their horses and came down into the wash. The business of camp began immediately. The man named Poe opened his trousers and took a leak. He sang a little song with the pleasure of the relief, and he flicked his long spout in Bark's direction to goose him.

"Then in the morning," said the tall man, "I can steer you straight for Santa Rosa, Mister Brocius."

"That's considerate of you," said Bill, and he guided Bark towards a sort of annex to the others' camp, just a little way away.

"What's your fellows' business, then?" asked Bill.

"Why, sir," said the tall man, "we are after the Kid."

Poe and McKinney laughed and grunted in agreement, and the

tall man let his slow glance float over to Bark. He winked at him
once, and tossed him an old russet apple that he had. "Not you,
son, don't you worry. You've done well."

"He has," said Bill Brocius wearily, but with heartfelt satisfaction
and desolate pride. "He's a champion."

Bark Blaylock

Bill Brocius took pains to see that this camp was as pleasant for Bark
as all the others. Not that he was unfriendly to the tall man, or to
Poe and McKinney. Bill found a special place for the russet apple in
Bark's supper, remarked on its juiciness and made sure that Bark
renewed his thanks to the tall man.

"Bark, you're welcome," said the tall man. "If I'd known I was
going to meet you, I'd have had some candy with me."

Bill did not encourage more conversation, and time and again, if
it seemed likely, he found unexpected errands and jobs for Bark to
do. These were tasks that had not previously arisen on the trail. The
tall man bore with the interruptions in good humor, but he was at
last able to ask Bark where he came from.

"Tombstone, sir."

"That's a long way," said the tall man.

But Bark only shrugged at that, for while it had been a longer way
than he had ever known before, still it was only as far as it was, and
seemed just the palm of a hand compared with the America that
Bill's stories and reports alluded to.

"He's close to Marshal Earp in Tombstone, this boy," said Bill
Brocius, on the sly. "You ever met the marshal?"

"Don't believe I did," said the tall man.

"Oh, you'd know, sir. You'd recollect."

Now McKinney spoke up. There was an ugly grin on his face, and
his mouth was full of beans. "This boy kin to the Earps?"

"He ain't *with* the Earps," Poe chimed in. The three men seemed
sure that they were on to some rare joke.

"You ain't no Earp, are you?" the tall man asked Bill.

"No, sir, I'm not. Though I know 'em."

"Only person I see close to the boy," reasoned the tall man, "is
you. I ain't seen an Earp all day."

"Well," said Bill, "you can't always rely on seeing 'em first."

Poe and McKinney were now laughing their stomachs off, and the tall man kept the same droll, tired smile on his face.

"Expert ambushers, are they?" he asked Bill.

"They're stealthy fellows," Bill admitted.

"Likely to pounce on us?"

"I couldn't say," said Bill. He seemed embarrassed now by the entire Earp concept, and willing to abandon it.

"Bark," asked the tall man. "You know Marshal Earp?"

The game was beyond Bark, and he saw no reason for loyalty to that aloof, dark-coated, absent-minded scold from Tombstone. It seemed out here on the trail anything could be made up or forgotten.

"I say shits to Wyatt Earp," Bark announced—it was a refrain heard often enough in Tombstone, and now Poe and McKinney cheered him raucously and banged their tin mugs against the ground.

"You got a foulmouthed boy here, Mr. Brocius," said the tall man.

"I have that," said Bill despondently. "All the education you can muster, sometimes it's spit in a hot pan."

"He's your boy, I'd say," suggested the tall man.

"Would you?" asked Bill. There was a rising note of true curiosity in his voice. Even of hope.

"Has something of your looks."

"I never heard that before."

"Anyway," said the tall man, yawning, and about ready for a nap—his yawn set Bark off, too. "He's with you. Out here in these remote places." The tall man tipped his hat over his eyes as he lay back. "Funny thing—that other name," he recollected.

"What was that?"

"Rudeboy, was it?"

"Just the lad's delirium."

"Believe there's a Rudeboy known to the Kid."

"I couldn't say, sir, I'm sure."

"Yeah? Well, you two sleep sound. 'Cause one of us, we'll be watching over you."

"Yessir!" came the musical call of McKinney from what was now darkness.

Bark worried, for there had been no time for his reading lesson, and he was anxious to make advances.

Once in the night Bark woke, suddenly, as if some very cold thing had been pressed on his forehead. He could hear the horses breathing. He sat up in the moonlight and on the far side of the declining fire the tall man, sitting in his long coat, raised a hand to acknowledge him.

"Don't worry, lad," he whispered. "Just a dream."

The following day, the five of them rode in a line across grasslands littered with dry cattle dump where some large herd had moved. The grass was eaten down hard and pale so that the horses' hooves sounded like shoes dropped on a thick carpet. Every now and then, Poe and McKinney would yelp and let their horses race.

"They're careless boys," the tall man confided to Bill.

"What's the harm in their fun?" Bill answered.

And the tall man nodded, "Maybe so."

By the early afternoon, they came to a meeting place of two trails, like lines drawn across the seething brown plain, lines that went up to the next ridge without a tremor of deviation.

"You go on left for Santa Rosa," said the tall man.

"Ah," said Bill, not shifting his horse.

"Didn't you say your friends were there?"

"We gotta go with him, Pat," said Poe. It was the only thing that told Bark they hated Bill and were afraid of him.

"I don't see that," said the tall man.

"Let him go?" cried a furious McKinney.

"Look here," said the tall man. "We can watch Bill here go off to Santa Rosa. We can see him two or three miles off going that way."

"But he'll tell on us," said Poe. "Don't you see it, man?"

"The one thing about Bill I have seen is that he don't tell nothing. If he tells in Santa Rosa, why, I like the idea of him going off there."

Bill laughed at them in as brazen a way as he could manage. "And where'll you boys go, then?" he wanted to know.

"Fort Sumner, maybe," said the tall man. "I may just go in there and talk to Pete Maxwell."

"Never heard of him," said Bill.

"Goes to show," said the tall man, "people you want are in Santa Rosa."

And then Poe started to laugh, for he had just recollected something. "That's right," he said to Bill. "You'll like Santa Rosa, pretty as can be."

"It's a wart," said McKinney vengefully.

"Now, Tip," said Poe, "don't you be so harsh."

"Young Bark," said the tall man, gravely holding out his long brown hand. "I hope I shall see more of you. You were a prince on the trail, sir."

And, just as solemnly, Bark shook the gentleman's hand and there was a parting there under gathering gun-colored clouds, so the ground was darkening, the two going west and the three east, and a wind coming up so fast it seemed to blow them apart. And just as often as Bill and Bark looked off at their recent companions, why, it seemed the other three were always keeping a weather eye on the two of them.

"Did I do right, Bill?" asked Bark after a while. He was so keen to have Bill volunteer the opinion. But Bill was lost in thoughts all his own.

"You did grand, Bark. Likely saved my life. We were in there with a most efficient fellow."

"I didn't know the names," Bark tried to explain. He was still not sure of what was proper, and he had been strangely impressed in the company of the four men by codes of strict knowledge and behavior that left a boy feeling insignificant.

"It's hard with the names," Bill confessed. "The great benefit of being on one's own in the world is just that you can have your name be whatever you like at any moment."

"Did you like those men?" the boy asked.

"It's not a matter of liking, you see," said Bill. "They have their thing to do. And, by a misfortune, it's this pal o' mine, Billy Antrim."

Bark did all he could immediately to forget that name. The day was drawing in now, and they could see it raining in places far away, in narrow shafts of light where the late sun still had holes in the clouds. There was a crackling white line above the horizon, and then a while later they heard the booming fall of thunder.

"It's an ugly day," said Bill. "But I warrant it'll be fine tomorrow. Now, Bark, my lad," he said, pulling his horse to a halt. "I think we'd best make our quiet way back to Fort Sumner."

"Not Santa Rosa?" said Bark, patiently. Nothing was as it promised for long.

"Oh, my sweet, we were never going there. I just wonder whether we can get into Fort Sumner somewhere before dark, and so as our companions don't see us. Think we can do that?"

"Very secret, Bill," Bark promised.

Now, Bill was his old Bill again, masterful and cheery. "Do you think we could make it on the trot, Bark, without you falling off? Otherwise, I'm thinking we're going to be soaked to our skins."

Matthew Garth

He made his way back to the bedroom, encouraged by his encounter with Garrett. For there was someone who, without ever having to mention it, had understood him. At the billiard table, the two strangers had nodded in quiet concert at the same intolerable fates. It had been one of those rare moments in which Matthew had felt an understanding possible in the world, a scheme to things that might flourish if it could be left in peace. This was what he and Dunson had always had, wordless harmony; and Matthew knew how much it had perplexed Tess, so close to him, yet having to face the pitiless pact that excluded her and knowing that she could only spoil their perfect silence.

He was no longer certain which room was his. The heavy paneled doors were alike: the model of a sumptuous hotel returned to his mind, except that in a hotel there might have been numbers on the doors, those arbitrary signs of brief home which, for a few days, lodged in the traveler's soul, as secure as a beloved's pet-name.

Such thoughts mingled with the faint wondering as to whether this was his door. And so there was some prelude to the feeling that overtook Matthew at the threshold, that he was not quite solid or valid in himself, but was an actor who kept finding himself in parts of his play, having to make up his mind to stay abreast of the assurance with which others played. For the room was apparently as he had left it—it was his "old" room—but for the insertion of Fleur, in his bed, wearing spectacles, reading the Thomas Hardy book and so bare-shouldered he felt sure she was naked, just as if he knew her disrobed body the way he knew the topography of the land ten miles in any direction from the Red River D.

She refused to be startled, or taken aback—she was, in her way, as impassive and phenomenal as that land in Texas. It was as if they were a seasoned married couple, and Matthew was returning from the bathroom having plied himself with bicarbonate. She had a supreme confidence in taking the moment for granted: he would have fallen in love with just that, no matter the skin, the shoulders' slope or the touching discovery that those young eyes needed help. She did not look up when he entered—he had no immediate part or cue.

He was not central? Then why was the whole damn business oc-
curring, taking place, in his room?

"This is a most remarkable book," she declared.

"Good Lord!" he shouted. "Why should I care what you think
about that?" Why had anger come when he felt so served by her
brave act?

"Oh, don't think you can get away with that," she said, and she
was very agitated, staring at him through her spectacles, the sheet
beginning to slip from her breasts.

"With what?" he asked, his breath taken away. How swiftly, and
savagely, he could be made defensive. How he loathed his predi-
lection for weakness.

"Don't think you can lose your temper about the book, for God's
sake."

"I have no temper," he told her, and he made it sound like the
deficiency of his existence.

"Well, if you can believe that," she began, and then, "I just hope
I don't have to be the one left to look after those in the way of it
when your majestic restrained temper breaks, Matthew Garth. That's
all!" And she sniffed decisively and made a shortsighted grab at the
very slow descent—the fascinating draining—of her bed sheet.

"I don't see," said Matthew Garth, clinging to order, "that that
book"—he made it sound worse than commonplace—"is the right
place to start."

"Don't take it out on the book," she said. "It's a wonderful book.
I have been sitting here, reading it, *moved*." She said the word with
such feeling and effort, she might have been pushing a bulky ward-
robe. "And I am what you would call a regular reader." She was in
tears. "So don't blame the book! How could you? With all that wondrous evening falling on the world?"

"I'm not interested in the book," said Matthew Garth. He stamped
his foot. "I read a few pages of it, and I admired it. There, is that
sufficient?"

"No, it is not," she wailed, absurdly, self-evidently naked, and
therefore approximately seductive, yet burrowed down in the bed
like a sick, querulous child. "I take a very bold step. Don't think I'm
so modern a woman that I don't step naked into a man's bed—a
man, moreover, who has already once, politely, firmly, not to say
woodenheadedly, turned me aside—so don't think I do that without
fear and trembling, not to mention the wondering whether Frank
Melville won't come in for a *tête-à-tête* with the apple of his eye and
shoot me dead or whip me. Oh, yes, whip me, Matthew Garth! And

all I am doing is only because you are such a pigheaded idiot to yourself—far more, oh yes, to yourself than to anyone else—that you haven't got the wit or the ease or the nerve or the decency to just know you love me and just say to the lovely girl, of course, dear heart, come to me. Please!"

He let the waves of speech die away until there was only sobbing from the heap in the bed. He went over to the window and he moved aside the heavy drape. The house looked down on the stockyards, and he could see the pens crammed with the backs of his cattle, stirring slightly like slugs in a tin of bait. They were fair broad backs: they had kept flesh on the drive, grazing as they came. It had been a beautifully handled thing so far. If only everything was just as tidy as cattle-driving. Matthew Garth also saw the image of the hollow-eyed man looking out at the night and the rolling, moonlit humps of his own tranquil beasts.

"Why'd you start on the book then?" he said. He did not know how exhausted he was till he heard his voice, and saw the gaunt man in the glass mouthing feebly.

"I was nervous!" she yelled. "Couldn't you make one allowance for that?"

He turned around. "Melville would whip you?"

She peeped out from the tumble of bedclothes. "Of course, he would," she said. "Only you'd doubt it."

"I won't have that," said Matthew Garth.

"You what?" He could see her pretty face now, brutalized by her misery and confusion.

"I won't let him do that."

"Oh, there's a thing to say!" She cried again, but it was a different sound now, warmer, with relief welling up, the sighing of mercy, not to say passion. "You destroy me."

"I meant it well."

She sat straight up, bursting through her white sheets. She was immediately naked, her breasts borne just as boldly as an outlaw might brandish his guns. And not a sign of caution. "It *is* well!" She was rubbing the old tears from her eyes. "But you wipe a girl away, just saying that out of the blue." Now she came crawling on the bed out of the clothes. He saw the hair between her legs, the air between her slender thighs, the daubs of swarthiness in her armpits. She came up to the end of the bed, towards him. "That's what I dreamed to hear you say, and you say it so sad, Matthew Garth. Oh, come here, my darling!"

He did not stop her taking hold of him: there was an orgy in being

looked after, seized and ordered. She drew him to the bed, he felt
and nearly heard her sweet air squeezed out of her by his force. Then
she was at his clothes, fussing, cursing, talking to the hooks and
loops, as if they were tricky embroidery. "Oh, your things, all your
things." Yet she made too much of the hindrances, for in moments
she had him bare and in her, and at last he stopped her talking with
the terrific urgency and drive with which he repeatedly drove her
down into the soft bed. Impaling her. Until, like a rising hill, something between a groan and a giggle came up out of this Fleur, the
warmest, liveliest, yeastiest pillow on the bed, the one that smelled
of salt, powder, a fart he had shot out of her and the gutty depths
of her own genius gaminess.

"You are a hero," she told him. She was so serious. Did he need
to be told that?

"Tell me about this husband of yours," he said. Fleur was not
dismayed; she drew his wilting force more thoroughly into her, and
grunted with a kind of digestive satisfaction. "You heard about him."
She was gloating a little, pleased to learn that men discussed her.

"He's in jail, I believe?" said Matthew.

"Precisely," she said. "And I don't see how I could leave a man
while he's in jail. Would that be courteous?"

"You're resolved to leave him?"

"Just as soon as he gets out," she said, tracing the outline of
Matthew's lips with a finger.

"What'll he do?"

"Oh, well," she surmised. "I'm likely to end up with a whipping
one way or another in this. You're not going to interfere with this
one."

"Wouldn't seem my business."

"Husbands have a right to do some whipping, do they?"

"If the fellow's about to be abandoned," said Matthew.

"Whipping wouldn't alter that," she pointed out.

"But he might have a need. I mean, I think the woman could
understand it."

"You whip your wife when she left?"

He hadn't, and Matthew knew Fleur was sure he hadn't.

"Wish you had?" she asked, her voice curling round his defenses.

"I believe," said Matthew Garth, "something in me reckoned I
deserved her leaving. A coldness."

"Whipped yourself then?" she mentioned it as a rumor, and it did
stir him.

"Do I feel like that sort of man?"

"I don't know," smiled Fleur. "I'd need more practice with you. Of course," her fancy soared, "I will employ any excuse."

"You are cold-blooded about leaving your man," he told her.

"There's women would have just moved on. Left him to find out."

"So he'd come after you."

She laughed at that. "No, he wouldn't. He's a lazy fool. He wouldn't have the will for any of that."

"You don't know."

"Oh, I do, Matthew Garth, I do." And she sounded so delighted: isn't it always knowledge that gives the headiest pleasure?

"So you plan on leaving him for me."

She looked at him afresh. Something in his limpet-like tone warned her that he meant to be difficult.

"Do you assume I mean to marry you?" he asked.

"I don't assume a thing, sir," she promised him. But she was taking heed of the steeliness he had shown her. She never moved away from him: he could feel all the hot places where their flesh adhered. But her wits were circling around him, studying the whole enterprise of the man. She picked up the silver snake still on his wrist.

"I didn't get this off you," she said. "See how the snake is going after its tail?"

"I wear it to be mindful of my daughter."

"Do you need a sign for that?"

"No," he said, helpless, ready to roar or scream.

"Is it your chain then? Your daughter would not want that."

"That's a closed circle," said Matthew. "I don't take it off."

"It's open," said Fleur. "It comes off." And she slid the silver off his hand. "My," she realized, "it's heavy."

He took it back from her and let it slip back, to knock against his wrist.

"You must have it, then?" she said.

"I must," he told her, but the words were spoken to her breast as he came in again, levering, propelling, mining in this adoring young woman, so fiercely and inventively she cried out in fear and wonder and her small back arched violently as if from pain. In an instant, he thrust his wrist with the bracelet between her back and the bed, and then forced her down. The silver circle pushed into both their skins, and she groaned again in comprehension.

Bark Blaylock

Swift surges of violet and otter gray passed through the lowering skies like a hand smoothing out wrinkles in cloth. Bill and Bark were riding headlong into a thunderstorm, its bruised colors lit up by the sun sinking behind them. They were riding in that hush and hiatus where weathers meet and think of colliding. The light was so pure, the air so noiseless, Bark had the odd inkling that he and Bill were being seen, far off, by some unknown observers through a telescope, galloping without progress or sound on the silver edge of focus.

But when the rains began, all attempt at subterfuge or cunning sidelong approach was abandoned. The roll of thunder spurred the horses, and the immediate, overhead rustle of lightning was not seen, but still it sent a shudder through horses, riders and the very ground. Even in the battering deluge, Bark thought he saw a scrub oak tremble and smolder as the force went through it. In a minute, the light was gone and there was only the sluicing, fish-colored fall of water and the dollops of mud that came up from the horses' hooves. One smacked into Bark's face, thrown up by Bill's horse. The slap hurt him, but the rush of air wiped away the sting. He tasted the earth and he spat as vigorously as he could to clear his mouth. In such hectic forward commotion, the pain was left behind. Bark did not notice that he was going so much faster than he had ever been on a horse. But he felt the danger when Bill made his horse veer off and then fall in a yard behind him and to the side. It was as if he was there to scoop up the flimsy Bark that might lose all grip on the soaked, slippery saddle. Yet they made it, the pair of them, rushing in and out of the rain, as drenched as swimmers and exhausted by the need to cling on through the gallop.

Then, suddenly, in two or three leaping strides of the horses they were out of it: the rain was as dense and defined as a field of corn. And now they were riding on springy ground in dry air, with the sun shining and a mist up to the horses' bellies where the earth steamed. Bark could smell dirt, dung and all the herby aromas of the grass and the sage. He noticed the spout of water from Bill's hat come to a stop. He saw the slick sheen of the horses' flanks as water rolled off them. When he looked back the storm was gone, or so small it had wandered into a dip in the ground. But there was one sure evidence of the rain: the air sparkled; wherever Bark looked there was a brightness that would have served the first-ever morning in the Territory, a cleanliness that had not heard of dust, of age or weariness. The full extent of nature was stretched out in the low, kindly light of the setting sun: the damp was simply that of the creator's fresh paint. Bark sneezed three times, the new evening air was so peppery.

"I think we've gone to heaven, Bark," said Bill. "Who ever saw anything so handsome?"

"I never did," Bark marveled, thankful that Bill was there to see it with him.

"And there is our Fort Sumner," said Bill, with all the contentment that comes from destination.

The ground between them and the four white buildings seemed level and very manageable. But the slant of sunset gentled away the distance, and then Bark saw the sliver of brightness pick out the Pecos River that was still between them and the tiny figures of other children Bark could see playing in the meadows on the far side. From where they were, the river looked like a blade half-buried in the ground.

"Did you ever cross a river?" asked Bill. "Well, this is your day for it. And a perfect day, too. Look at the water, will you, all stirred up by the rain."

Bark's spirits sank when they reached the edge of the river. It was wide and running so fast, with such a will of its own. There was a torn-off branch that went past as quick as a bird flying. The sound of the rushing water was all that Bark could hear.

"I'm afraid, Bill," he had no hesitation in saying it.

"We've got to get across, lad. And I am not in favor of the bridge."

Bark could not guess why the bridge was unsound, and he did not think to dispute Bill's sense of necessity. Bill was unwinding a length of rope. He made a loop of it, and dropped it over Bark, pulling the rope tight under his armpits.

"There, now," he said, cheerfully. "You're held secure, and here, I tie the other end to my belt." Bark watched the adroit hands slip the rope in and out; he saw chunks of knot materialize; and he felt the solid bond between them.

"We got to trust the horses, Bark. They like to swim. But they'll let the current take them. Grab hold of the mane and your pommel and remember I've got you. I've crossed countless rivers like this, and you'll see what a pleasant sensation it is. Just let your horse carry you—pretend you're asleep."

There was no waiting on further discussion. Bill urged the two horses into the water, and in a stride they were lifted away, off the bottom, slipping down the glassiness of the stream. Bark tugged on the rope to make sure it was there and he heard Bill's answering laugh. The horses' heads stretched out on the water, like boats, heading on the slant across the current. Bark felt their legs kicking as he saw the bubbles rushing past at the level of his lap. It was the cold that startled him most, and the tug of strength in the river. He thought it would take the horses hours to get across, and he wondered if they had enough left in them. He laid his own face down so close to the scud of water along the horse's neck and whispered to his animal. He loved his horse and its valor.

"What a horse I have," he marveled, discovering the true wonder as he said it.

When he looked up, he saw Fort Sumner slipping past, and he noticed dusk was setting in. As he looked ahead, he saw the last chinks of light on top of the water being extinguished. He felt the rope drag at his chest, and when he looked up he saw that Bill was half out of his saddle.

"Give us a pull, Bark," he spluttered. "Else I'm gone." And the boy leaned with all his might and love to one side so that his horse felt the instruction. And the horse's surge restored Bill to his saddle.

"Thank you, sir!" Bill called. Bark felt a great wish to sleep, a tiredness that came from overpowering the river and from the happiness of having served well.

"You're a champ, Bark," yelled Bill. "Don't go off now." So Bark gave Bill what he took to be a real adventurer's grin. But he made a mess of it, his teeth bit his lip, and he tasted his blood in the tears of the mashing pain. His mouth felt like a sore but he spat it all out, the blood and spittle sliding down his face until a little wave off the Pecos came up and cleaned him off.

Then the ground staggered, and Bark pitched forward on the horse's neck. Could the river jolt like that? But the water fell from him, and the horse, creaking and slipping, was on its feet. They had made it across the vast Pecos. He felt Bill's horse behind him and then the steady stepping motion of the two animals coming through the shallows and up the earthen bank.

"Great God, Bark," said Bill, "don't ever forget you crossed this river. When you're an old man it may be the best thing you have."

"We did it, didn't we, Bill?"

"Us and the horses and the river. We did it, son." There were lights in the distance, away higher up the river.

"Is that Maxwell's?" Bill wondered of himself, under his gasps.

Bark stayed silent; he knew he was not looked to for an opinion, and he could tell from the tone of Bill's voice that there might be a test still to come more severe than the river.

"I say we walk the horses," said Bill.

It was what Bark wanted. For he could better air out his wet clothes by walking than by sitting in the saddle. Bark saw that Bill gathered up the harness on the horses to make no undue jingling noise. They set out towards the light, moving through cool, feathery grasslands.

In about ten minutes, it was possible to discern the outline of buildings. It was a mild evening and the light wind was still warm. All the rains had gone away and this part of New Mexico seemed becalmed and enchanted again. There were a few lights in the buildings, rooms aglow with stinky oil lamps. But there was only one tapping noise to be heard. As they went on towards it, it became a hammer working on wood, ticking off the time.

Bark saw a split door half open and a white-haired man inside making a coffin. Bill stopped the horses and went up to the door, holding Bark's hand.

"Sam," said Bill.

The old man looked up from his work. "Evening, Dave," he said, without surprise.

"The Kid here?" asked Bill.

"I heard it. I ain't seen him though."

"Garrett?"

"Wouldn't surprise me. Would surprise me if he didn't come."

"Where'd the Kid be?"

"With her, why not? Wouldn't you? I'd be loving her."

"I believe I would."

Bill looked around at the other buildings. "Pretty night," he said.

"Rained earlier," said Sam.

"Mind if I leave this boy with you, Sam?"

"So long as he's not a fool, I don't."

Then Bill spoke quietly to Bark. "I have to find a friend of mine. Won't take me but a while. Get in there by Sam's stove. Dry your clothes."

"Very well, Bill."

The interior smelled of wood, and there was sawdust on the floor. The old man said nothing as Bark came in and carefully closed the half door. As unobtrusively as he could manage, Bark went to stand by the stove. The air there was warm, and he felt safer.

"Out in the rain?" asked the old man.

"Yessir," said Bark. "And we swam across the Pecos River."

The old man stopped tapping in nails, and examined Bark. "You're a liar," he told him.

Bark did not argue. But he took off his shirt and pants and laid them on the stove. He shivered a little in his underwear and moved closer to the stove.

"Evening, Sam," said a new voice from outside. Bark saw the tall thin man they had made camp with the night before.

"There you are, Pat," said Sam, not a jot more taken out of his way. "You worked it out, did you?"

"Took my time. How are you, Bark?" He lobbed the greeting into the workshop. "That's a good boy you've got there, Sam."

"I took him for a liar."

"Oh no. It's the world that's the liar. Bark," said the tall, thin man. "Take a stroll with me?"

"In my underwear?" Bark was amazed.

"It's a balmy night," said the tall man. "And I have a blanket here. Come on with me, won't you?" It did seem like a very firm request, and Bark somehow knew that this tall, thin man had to be watched.

Matthew Garth

If he could hear his snoring, he would wake in shame. But he sleeps too deeply, where vanity does not know him.

Heroes do not find victory in every moment; not if they hope to be men, too. Matthew Garth lacked the scruffy and humbling vitality of mere manhood. He saw the range as his setting. His uncommon longing for magnificence was always likely to outstrip his tenuous career as a real man, used to ordinariness, small illnesses and disappointments. This zeal against failure left him aloof, irritable and a trifle literary in some of his expressions. He frightened people. And the hesitant may make a career out of that.

Which hurt him. In wanting to be admired, he hoped he was a

democrat; he did not wish to go beyond the reach of his good people. With a hunger that suited his lean look, he waited for those few human associations where he could believe he was normal, subject to all of man's fundamental drama and glory. But awkwardness and the daily shabbiness of shared disillusion affected him like reports of the plague. He remained fearsome.

So much for preamble; let snoring bury it. He had not planned it this way. For as after exhaustive, searching and captivating sexual forays with Fleur, in which not only was the body fully used but the mind stretched, as he felt sleep coming up on him as silent as shadow on the ground . . .

He had resolved to doze for twenty, thirty, minutes, waking well before dawn, alert and able to tip and coax a sleepy Fleur back into most of her clothes (there were some the plain function of which baffled him), guide her to her room, then—after proper remonstrances of further affection to her—be back in his room, available for whatever carefree sleep the night afforded, and still ready for the early start on a day that had to load the cattle on the train for Wyoming.

However, there is this scene for us as late as nine o'clock on the following morning: that of Frank Melville and Groot edging into the curtained room, perhaps fearing some fatal attack—though Groot had got himself a concealable pistol, for he had noticed the same tardiness in Miss Fleur and he retained a moderate suspicion of Mr. Melville's eternal equanimity. Anyone who puts so much of himself into the show of hospitality, Groot had decided, has a suppressed devil.

The two tiptoeing men drew back the heavy drape (thus permitting, if there was time, a view of the stockyards and the loading well under way—Matthew Garth's worst fears are met: he is a gentleman rancher). The light revealed the bare, upthrust and flawless bottom of Fleur, the more hilly and prepossessing in that she was lying across Matthew Garth, undisturbed by but vibrating to the boom of his assured snoring.

"Times are changing, I suppose," Melville observed to Groot, stooping to pick up the fallen copy of *The Return of the Native*, and reflecting on the slipperiness of novels and their part in the change.

"This has been an unhappy young man," said Groot, indicating the spread-eagled Matthew. Groot was feeling better because of the reconciled quality in Melville's reaction. He let the Derringer drop to the bottom of his pocket.

Melville sighed, "I trust he's going to feel more secure now," letting his eyes travel across the tangled sprawl of bodies to convey his irony.

That Groot loved Matthew Garth—and had done for years—may be affirmed by the sympathetic understanding in what he said next: "He'll grieve when he wakes and finds us here."

Melville glanced at the old man: "You say we should just melt away? Let time take its course?"

Groot shrugged. It was a delicate point: the loading was getting on very well, and it was hard to estimate the affront to a Garth of having him realize his part in such work was only that of the boss, strolling here and there, offering tobacco and terse, worldly greetings to one and all, presiding but scarcely relevant.

"That goes too far," said Melville, a little grumpy now. He had rights in the situation, and moral superiority was the least easily relinquished. "I'll be decent to him. But I don't see crawling."

"No, sir, Mr. Melville," Groot whispered. "No call for that."

"Anyway," Melville recollected, "there is the matter of the rustled animals. If a man's been robbed, he deserves waking."

"That did it," said Groot, and he put his rough hand on Matthew Garth's throat in a way he knew worked. The dark eyes came open, and wakefulness was only five seconds later. It was as Matthew Garth had estimated the night before: he could pass from deep sleep to readiness quicker than most men.

"Yes," said Matthew Garth immediately, as if a ghost had commanded him to own up to his presence.

Then, "Christ," he added, and those burning eyes closed in mortification. For he had perceived everything, all the ramifications, and was a man who would never sleep well again. When his eyes reopened, he was already in the vigorous act of sitting up, and removing himself from the bed. This had the effect of throwing Fleur—whose waking pace was nowhere near as vengeful—not just from him, but from the haven of the bed itself, so that she slid to the floor in the way of *The Return of the Native*.

Frank Melville swept a coverlet from the root of the bed, and dropped it on her nakedness. (A woman could have done worse than him.) But she was so completely ripped from her Matthew that all her agony was fixed on his going. She registered neither the coverlet nor her need of it, her desire for the elemental ground of Matthew Garth was so great.

"Where are you?" she moaned, and Groot was jarred by the distress in her voice. He had heard that nonplussed agony in Tess, and for the first time he faced the possibility that Matthew Garth had been something other than a victim.

Garth was in his pants, fumbling with a shirt the arms of which were still inside out. In his fury, he tore at the cloth, and then rounded on Frank Melville.

"If you so much as raise a hand against her, I'll kill you."

Melville was sober at this fierceness, and at the lurid idea.

"He wouldn't," Groot pleaded. There was arrogance here such as the old man had not guessed at.

"You won't need to, Matthew," said Melville. He reached out and freed the sleeves in Garth's shirt. "Just take care of her."

"She's married already, I'm told," said Matthew.

"I don't want to hear any more," said Melville. "Groot, you speak to him." And without another word, Frank Melville walked out of the room.

"Well?" Garth demanded.

"Fifty head," said Groot, "gone in the night."

Matthew Garth strode to the window, scarcely noting the stunned, undignified twist of Fleur on the carpet. He looked out at the stockyards and saw the toy cattle making their neat way up ramps and into boxcars.

"Who did it?" he wanted to know.

"That fellow Garrett's gone, too," said Groot. "Remember him?"

"Not in the house?"

"Melville thought as maybe he had taken Miss Fleur away."

"On his own?"

"Some say he's up to it."

"That's how he repays hospitality?"

"What do you want to do?" Groot was thinking he was too old for much more of this nonsense. "You want to go after them yourself? We're meant to be out of here tonight."

"How many head?"

"Forty-something. A small pen off to the side."

"Melville kept no guards?"

"We were having a fine time last night if you recall."

"I would say he was responsible."

Groot waited for the full duplicity.

"His insurance," said Matthew Garth, very calmly.

"So you don't want to go after them?"

"We should file a complaint with the local sheriff."

"We could do that."

"I'll do this in the legal way."

"As you say."

Fleur was by now awake: it may have been this chilly discourse that brought her to her senses.

"You're leaving tonight?" she asked.

"The train leaves," said Garth; it was not his fault.

"I'll come with you."

"Your husband—"

"I'm coming with you."

"That'd be nice," said Groot. And he gave her the best old man's salute of a smile he had.

"You said you could not leave him," said Matthew Garth.

"I'll come back to leave him," Fleur promised, and if that seemed involved or comical, there was a gravity in her that dispelled laughter.

"We have things to talk about," she told him.

"I'll be in the yards," said Groot.

"I'm coming," said Matthew. There was a desperation, in case he was left behind.

"In an hour," said Fleur. "He'll be there in an hour."

"Whatever," said Groot, and he winked and hopped out of the room on his bad leg.

"I'm going now," Matthew Garth told her.

But all that Fleur did by way of comment was to emerge from the coverlet around her—it stayed stiff and erect for an instant, like a tent. She stepped lithely up onto the bed, crossed over it, came down to the floor, opened up his pants and took him in her mouth. There was no sound, yet she shouted with all her might, knowing so much was in the balance.

———

Bark Blaylock

"I was thinking I'd see you again, Bark," said the tall, thin man. He had slowed his stride somewhat so that the boy could keep up. But he was very watchful and not unmindful of how a small male figure might show up in the moonlight, walking in his underwear. They were pausing alongside one building, looking at the stretch of ground that separated them from the largest house.

"You must have come across that river," said the tall man.

"Yes, sir," said Bark, joyous that someone else could recognize the accomplishment.

"Man with you was crazy to try that."

But Bark was not disconcerted, and he nodded with the same determined pride. He did not see the faraway, admiring smile of the tall man, nor the dreaming over such a son.

"Who is he, then?"

"I can't say."

"Looking for his friend?"

"Yes, sir." Bark was sure he liked this leisurely, loping man and the feeling he gave of seeing two out of three things as jokes too grave to laugh at.

"You eaten, Bark?"

"Not in a time, sir."

"Well, I'll tell you. Yonder house is Pete Maxwell's, and I hear that Pete has a piece of meat hanging on the porch. It's all cooked. He leaves it there so anyone can cut themselves a slice."

The tall man reached in his coat pocket, and came out with a knife. He pulled the blade out of the handle, and gave it, hilt first, to Bark.

"Why don't you go over and cut yourself some?"

Bark stared at the knife and at a loaded darkness around the Maxwell house. It seemed a way to go in his underwear, and so dark there.

"Ain't you hungry?"

"Yes, sir."

"It'll be a roast of beef. Nothing like it. Warm still."

How hard it was to have this offer on the very day a boy had forded the Pecos. Bark felt so little courage left in his legs. He did not know if he could step steadily as far as the house. In such dark. But he did imagine the glossy side of well-roasted meat, the scent of it detectable in the night. He could savor its juices.

"I'll be watching you from here," the tall man promised.

"You won't come?"

"No, Bark, I won't come."

"I'll get you a slice," said Bark, to give the tall man a reason for staying.

The man touched Bark's head. "O.K., son. You do that."

This is the night of July 14, 1881, and you can have a distant coyote call if you want it as the boy steps out onto open ground. Or it can be so quiet you hear his toes squeezing the dust, and the flutter of the soles of his feet trying not to hurry, for fear of falling on the open knife. But he is too afraid to take it slow.

Bark's knees knocked into steps up to the veranda of the house. He felt the rough wood beneath his feet. Now he was up against the house; there was a streak of moonlight that ran down the building and bounced off the window. It left enough light under the roof for him to see a large thing in midair, hanging there. He closed his eyes and walked up to it, but before he could smell a thing he heard the buzz of a fly and the drip of grease on the wooden boards.

He put up one hand and bumped against the slimy side of meat; it was like feeling a wound or a battered face, like putting your hand in shit. But when he licked his fingers he was mad on the taste.

The knife was so sharp. A slice of the meat fell down on his hand as he cut, limp, moist and so hot still. He crammed the meat into his mouth and nearly choked on it, there was so much. He heard himself eating, and he heard the dithery sound of breeze in the trees. The fly was angry at having to share. No other creature came near the porch. As he learned to see better, Bark saw a swinging seat next to a door, and cushions on it. Maybe this Pete Maxwell liked to sit out in the late afternoon as the beef cooked.

So he cut a second slice and carried it like a letter with wet ink on it back to the tall man.

"What's that?" said he.

"Your beef."

It astonished Bark, but the tall man chuckled and said, "I forgot," as if he hadn't just been waiting. Yet he took the meat and enjoyed it, chewing slowly as he cleaned the knife and restored it to his pocket.

"Well, that was easy, wasn't it?" he said. And he took Bark's hand and walked with him back to the Maxwell house. It was a mystery why he hadn't come in the first instance: Bark knew he didn't grasp this tall man, even if the man put thoughts of Bill out of his head.

They came together to the veranda, and the tall man stood still as his eyes opened for the dark.

"Sit on the seat, Bark, while I go in."

"Inside?" asked Bark.

"You wait here. Want the knife? Get yourself more meat?"

But Bark's appetite was done. He wanted to curl up on the seat and sleep. He belched, and the thick fumes of the beef filled his mouth.

"There you go," said the tall man. "Like a gentleman."

"I beg your pardon."

"Granted, Bark. You're a good boy. You are. You know, it's nothing I wanted, not this."

"No, sir?"

"Not at all."

The tall man opened the door, and it closed behind him. Bark sat on the seat—it moved and the whole thing croaked and sang. He begged it to be still, and then it was quiet again. His feet could not reach the ground. He heard voices inside the building, too low to make out the words. Then there was silence, and then a hand was on Bark's brow.

"What you doing, boy?"

Bark woke up. There was a man above him, not as tall as the tall man. He saw the light shine on the man's body. He had no shirt on.

"Sleeping?"

"Yes, sir."

"American?"

"Yes, sir."

"I'll be. You had some meat?"

"Thank you, yes."

"Won't find better meat."

The man hesitated, then he ruffled Bark's hair and went to the door. He had no boots on; he left no sound. He went into the building. Bark was going off to sleep again when the voices resumed inside the house. Then there was shooting and the tall, thin man came running backwards out of the house. He snatched Bark up from the seat and held the boy to him. Bark could hear the man's heart thumping.

"I didn't want it," the tall man whispered to the child. And then, after a while, he said, "We'll sit on the chair here." They sat down and the seat lurched and squealed from the weight. Bark's hand brushed against a gun in the tall man's hand.

"God alive," groaned the tall man. "Here, boy, move."

So Bark shifted, and it seemed to him that the tall man opened up his breeches, took something cumbersome out and laid it down on the seat. It was as heavy as harness. But the tall man sighed with mercy when he had done it.

The next thing Bark knew, it was light, and there were several men standing on the veranda watching the tall man, and one of them was Bill.

"So you did it, Pat," said one of these men.

"I did."

"With the boy," said Bill.

Bark wanted to go to Bill, but the tall man had an undeniable hold on his arm.

"Just a while yet," said the tall man.

"That's a mean thing," said Bill. He was weeping and he beat his hand on a wooden post of the veranda.

"From a friend it is," said another voice.

"What do you know of that, Pike?" asked the tall man.

"But I know," said Bill, as if imploring the tall man.

"Reckon you do," the tall man admitted.

A young woman came, and she screamed considerably at what was inside the house. But people took that for granted. Other men came, and the man called Sam arrived with a measuring tape. These people were in and out of the house, but the tall man kept Bark beside him on the swinging seat. The men Poe and McKinney arrived, very happy.

"You did it!" cried Poe.

"Shut up, you fool," said the tall man. And then he called out, "Pike, bring me up a horse, will you?"

The group held, and Bark could feel the fear and hate with which it regarded the tall man. Even Poe looked at him with malice and envy.

"Don't you worry none, Bark," said Bill. "That bastard's going."

"Don't call me that," requested the tall man. "Not in front of the boy."

A saddled horse was walked up to the house. The tall man got on the horse, but he did not put his gun away.

Bill came up to take possession of Bark. He had the boy's shirt and his pants; they were dry and folded, like Sunday. But Bark felt sad with women and other children there observing him dress.

"Well, I'm going on," said the tall man.

"Don't look back," warned the one called Pike.

"I'm not going to start that," the tall man replied very candidly, and he looked down at Bark and said, "I thank you, boy."

"Don't thank him, damn you!" shouted Bill.

The tall man shook his head in weariness and disgust and he turned away his horse, walking into the morning.

Bill picked up a small rock and tossed it in the direction the tall man was taking. It fell short of the horse's plodding hooves, as if Bill was too feeble to throw well.

But Bill stood up and shouted, so the tall man must have heard, "They'll say the children ran after you, throwing stones at you, you traitor." Bill was sobbing, and he sat down on the ground so Bark could put a hand there to calm his heaving shoulders. "That's what they'll say," he told the boy. "Won't they?" And Bark was sure it would happen.

Matthew Garth

If Matthew Garth had a narrow face, still it contained a wide and prominent brow beneath which eyes unwilling to relinquish the great task of looking dispelled any suggestion of meanness. Men and women alike felt that the eyes "blazed." But when Garth himself studied them—he had fallen into the morbid habit of using mirrors —his very scrutiny perhaps doused the fire. So he was more struck by the closeness of his face, and the anger in eyes that were too clamped in place. He saw a prisoner, and he knew that one day the terror would escape.

That day in the Abilene railroad yards, this paradox in his face was so sharp people could scarcely talk to Matthew Garth. It was the way of a company of cowhands to take pride in their master. Moreover, there were men still of that company who had been on the 1865 drive when Matthew had "taken" the herd from a tyrannical Dunson, had succeeded in both execution and wisdom, and then had restored wealth, dignity and family, too, to Dunson without any more trouble than the disabusing of the opportunist Cherry Valance.

Those events of 1865 had brought to Matthew Garth a reputation for authority and generosity not common in the West. And for those who came to the ranch after 1865, there was always something in the stories they heard that was not just admirable, but mysterious —the way in which Matthew Garth had taken the law into his own hands, but only kept it, for safekeeping, and restored it to a rightful owner. In truth, what Matthew Garth had done in 1865 was both rebellious and obedient. For a story to be told endlessly, like that one, even when the facts are settled, there needs to be some doubt or controversy in interpretation. That doubt always survived, and it only deepened when, as time passed, the woman, Tess Millay, who in 1865 had seemed clear and confident about what had happened, gave up Matthew Garth for the plainly dangerous and unwholesome Cherry Valance.

So, on that day in Abilene in 1879, Garth's men were happy for
him. The word was not slow to enthuse them with reports that Garth
was absent from the stockyards at dawn because he was in a boat-
sized bed with a young woman of famous beauty. Moreover, the
suggestion that this woman had until recently "belonged" to Mr.
Melville—and thus may have been an adjunct property of the Greenwood Trading Company—only inspired the men with thoughts that
their generally taciturn and modest Matthew Garth had his own
daring and forthrightness securely in hand. No one wished to admit
the least scorn for the cordial and popular Melville, but the cowboys
rejoiced to know their man was superior and passionate.

As for those cattle stolen in the night, the team was magnanimous.
The number lost dwindled: by late in the day it was down to the
thirties, a trivial total when the cars on the train proved insufficient
and two hundred head had to be sold off to Greenwood just to tidy
the pens. So the night's loss could be seen as very minor; and how
could the rustlers be pursued when the entire enterprise was moving
on, by inexorable rail, for Wyoming?

Garth's refusal to discuss the loss was taken by the men as a further
measure of forgiveness in his robust spirit—he accepted circumstances, just as he had once elected to regard Tom Dunson as a
reformed, enlightened character in 1865, when some observers saw
no alteration in Dunson except that hardening might have gone beyond strength or durability into a wayward, autumnal brittleness.
Even if that was so, wasn't it filial of Garth to bow, again, before the
older man?

But what was in Matthew Garth's mind as he paced his own beaten
paths around the labors of his crew? He was like a lion in his regular
and obsessive walking, so different from the bemused shuffle of the
cattle. But not a lion confident of its prowess, rather one that has
not been told any of the stories that have gathered around the idea
of lions. He was a lion afraid of something: of being late, of challenge,
or simply of being seen. For just as Matthew Garth had felt compelled
to attend the work—and did not want to have to talk to any of the
people who felt close to him—so he had a longing there not to be
seen, or noticed. Not because of the theft in the night of some of his
cattle; not because of the question of whether to go after the thieves
or turn a blind eye. No, the great dilemma in Matthew Garth was
the thought of others' awareness of the softening he had yielded
to in the night, and his dread that it might be seen as common
nakedness.

He was so monotonous in his walking that a pall overcame his own men. Of course, they argued to themselves that it was wrath at the loss of cattle—but such an argument was hard once they had adapted to the loss, and seen how it was no ruin for anyone. They supposed that Garth was thinking of something so remote yet pressing that it was beyond them and the slapstick practicalities of getting cattle into boxcars. So they let Garth's concentration be. But it darkened the day and the depot: it subtracted from their good humor, their excitement at taking a railroad journey—a novelty for most of them—the gossip over this new woman of Garth's, and even the wildfire rumor that Wyatt Earp himself, from Dodge City and Wichita, might be a traveler on their train.

If Fleur had won a new beau it was the venerable but pink and glowing Groot. He was her friend, and the loyal interpreter of the myth that Matthew was too occupied. He fussed with her over her packing. He watched for signs of some doubt or wounding in the young woman. He felt the stupid need to court her and to tell Matthew's story in such a way that she saw room in it for herself.

"Our Matthew Garth never rests, does he?" said Fleur. She and Groot were already established in a sitting room in the passenger part of the train as it waited in the depot. As Groot had reasoned, it had the best soft chairs in Kansas. The two of them were watching from the train window as Garth surveyed the final work with the cattle.

"He's not a big sleeper," said Groot.

Fleur was reminded that she had seen so little yet of her beloved Matthew Garth, even if she treasured her journey into his canyon soul.

"Does he grieve over his wife?" asked Fleur. She had reckoned all day that Groot was the one who knew enough to tell, or who saw the utility in telling her, how the facts might aid her. She had picked up enough to accept her Matthew's gathered reserve.

Groot did recall, like it was a picture in front of his face, shutting out everything else, the look of Tess screaming at Matthew Garth that he was to do something, to beat her or kill Cherry Valance. And then the resolute, burning emptiness of Garth's face as he waited.

Groot could not tell Fleur that; after all, he was a promoter of this new cause. But he was not inclined to lie to her, either, and he did not know how many occasions he might have to tell her, or her to listen.

"Tess was a woman of strong feelings," he began.

"She grew lonely at the ranch?" Fleur explored. She could see how a modern young woman—even one with a man to love and a child to raise—might feel her quality wasting away in some great Texan spread, and just her nerves left behind.

"Must have been that," said Groot, though he wanted to propose that it had been Matthew Garth's solitariness nothing could penetrate, and which, somehow, became more stark and unmerciful in marriage.

"It was Valance, you see," said Groot, remembering that answer. "There had been this fellow on the drive, Cherry Valance. He and Matt took to each other like puppies. They were always together, snapping and sparring. Now, Valance was a no-good—anyone could see that. He'd been with Quantrill, and he didn't hide it. He was a wild, larky fellow. You couldn't trust him, but he was an entertainment."

"Matthew liked him?" Fleur asked.

"Something in him. Sure kept him around." There had been a boisterousness, a showiness, in Cherry Valance that allowed Matthew Garth to stay hidden.

"He maybe studied him," suggested Fleur.

"Cherry was the one met Tess first," said Groot. "Cherry was in the group that got to her wagon train. And he felt she was his, maybe. Then Matt came along. And Cherry was second place. But, don't you see, there must always have been something in Cherry that Tess liked."

"Or was intrigued by?"

Groot was trying to recall the looks on faces, so long ago. Memory was not made for this: such fleeting glances were not part of nineteenth-century intelligence. It disturbed Groot that Tess might have been drawn to Cherry all along, might have been moved by his braggart darkness. For Valance had a presence, and maybe she could see through it so long as it wasn't there, smiling, before her eyes.

"Anyway, Dunson shot Cherry, when he came into Abilene. Just over there," Groot pointed his finger at fourteen years ago. "And Cherry, he was hit bad, and we didn't see him for years. Forgot him. He was the sort of man no one expected to live long."

"He went away?"

"Whatever."

"That always means somewhere, doesn't it?"

"I suppose," Groot agreed.

"Don't you ever wonder that people you knew once, they're somewhere just as real as wherever you are, doing something? They haven't gone away—but they believe you have."

Groot thought of a place called Holland, and of Napoleon Bonaparte, the bogey-man that had sent his people west. "I don't know where Cherry went, but he was a lot older when he came back. And he'd had a hard time of it."

"Did he smile still?"

"Time I saw him he didn't. But maybe she could still make him smile. I didn't consider that."

All that Groot could recall of this part of the story was the over-powering wind around the ranchhouse in Texas. For the time had come when Tess was beginning quietly and carefully to go crazy, and somehow it registered that the wind was bringing something up to the house that spoke to her of change.

Groot never knew how it had been done. But Tess regained her looks, some dash of youth, and she started to go on long and un-accountable walks. She came back red in the face and hungry. Groot had watched her sometimes, on the horizon, walking, bent over against the wind, a dark figure full of purpose. Nothing had been said inside the house. But time and again Matthew had asked for her and sought her and she had not been there. And once, at dusk, Matthew had been sure there was a man outside, waiting under the trees. Tess had said, oh no, he was dreaming. But she hadn't looked. And then she went out walking all that night. And Matthew had gone after her, but never seemed to find her.

"Valance had come back?" asked Fleur.

"Maybe he had just found himself in our vicinity and he said to himself, 'Isn't that the D?' And so he took a look."

"What would Tess have thought?"

Groot was as careful as he could manage. "She may have believed she was being rescued, or tempted."

"She didn't want to go?"

"I don't think so."

"But she could not bear to stay? How romantic," said Fleur, glory-ing in the shape of the contradiction. Then the train lurched and all the cattle, the crew and the two lovers set out for Wyoming Territory. And Fleur was the kind of woman likely to be moved by such a coincidence.

Matthew Garth

"Away, with a shriek, and a roar, and a rattle, plunging down into the earth again . . ."

Miss Fleur Hickey closed her book with a slap that woke Groot from his slumber. But the grinding revolve of all the locomotion immediately carried him back to sleep again. It was harder now for him to stay awake, for since the train had set off he had felt the guiding whirl of so much machinery like whorls of water in a pool carrying him away.

But whereas Groot was ready to give his last energy, like oil, to the wheels, Fleur was driven and inspired by them. What with her book and the ceaseless, arousing circulation of the train, she had to be up on her feet, walking with it. Motion consumed her and took command of her. It did seem to Fleur that an acute constellation of the physical external and the interior ruminative had come upon her. This was her ideal, and she was delighted, for hitherto she had thought that it was to be found—and there far from reliably—only in sexual encounter.

A train was a world unto itself—she had already made that note in the leather-bound journal she kept with whatever book she was reading. For, though they were still more hopeful than decisive, Fleur had intentions on the word and its arrangements.

This train appealed to her as a civilization—as a collection of bodies—not just because of that sense of coupled continuity in a line of cars and carriages, but because she was not sure where it began and ended, or what forms it took. Were the cattle boxes between her car and the engine, or did they make up the long tail of the beast so that the stink of the animals could trail off into the air of Kansas and Colorado? Just because she had come on board early, she had not thought to observe this structure. And so she did not know where she was, or whether there might not need to be one engine at the front pulling, and another at the back pushing this immense Leviathan of traffic.

Further, once night was complete—an hour after their commencement—it was no simple thing to be sure the train was moving through or across territories. With such unmitigated and inscrutable darkness outside, it could have been that the thorough, constitutional agitation was just that of a rooted locomotive as time and journey rattled through it. There were other things in the stream—smoke, from the engine and the tobacco, porters with reports of doings elsewhere on the train, and the indefatigable notion that Wyatt Earp might be somewhere in this surging metal worm.

"And where are you going?" the voice demanded of Fleur.

She realized she had reached a car with tables, with Matthew Garth sitting on the other side where he had been served whiskey. She had the impression he had had plenty already.

"I was walking," she answered.

"Walking on a train?" The idea seemed fanciful to him, as if the larger motion ruled out human exercise.

"I thought I might come upon you."

"How far do you think you are coming? Before you go back. To quit your husband."

"I will go when it is safe," she said.

"When will that be?"

"When I judge I can leave you."

"You are doing a great deal of leaving," said Matthew Garth, pretending to be drunker than was the case.

"I believe I am making progress," she said.

"Ah. You are one of that church."

"I have no church."

"You are confident that progress is being made, that our prospects are improving. That amounts to a national religion. How can you explain the railroad without it?" and he waved his arm to include the whole swaying empire that was carrying them forward. "Across the country in . . . what, ten days? All the advantages of the God-forsaken will be gone. It is America's invented religion to make up for the lack of God. Getting there. Progress."

"You are against it, Mr. Garth?"

"I seem to be carried along, whether or not I like it."

"I have heard you described as a vital innovator yourself."

"Guilty," he announced.

"Are you dedicated to thinking poorly of yourself?"

"It's a natural condition."

"I had hoped you might be excited."

"I am getting old."

"Is that where your locomotive is taking you?"

"Can you save me?" he sneered. She desired some challenge, and had sought to engineer it. In her elation, she did not hear the nihilism in his voice—it could have been the perpetual musical din of the train that covered it.

"Come," she said. She was standing and holding out her hand to him.

"A walk?" he asked.

"Exactly," she said, undeterred by the currents of his aversion or difficulty. "It's your best chance of meeting Mr. Earp."

"Who?"

"Wyatt Earp the lawman. He is said to be on our train. You must be the only one who has not heard."

"He could, perhaps," Matthew Garth was seeing it as he spoke, "go after my rustled stock."

"I think," said Fleur, "in view of his legendary stature, to say nothing of his going west, that that is a mundane consideration."

"Well, you're not going all the way west, are you?" He pounced on her with the point: he could not resist a clinching detail. (He had once locked a trunk of Tess's, seeing it open for the taking, without realizing that she had lost the key years before. He offered to smash the trunk, but she declined and let it stay locked. Never opened again.)

He was getting to his feet, rocking in the staggered series of the train, waiting for her to say more. But there was only her balanced smile in an undying proposition of disagreement and loyalty. He loathed her calm. He thought of striking her, blaming it on unsteadiness from drink and locomotion. But his hand died.

"You think too highly of your fools' Wyatt Earp," was all he said.

At which, Matthew Garth fell off his small feet. The train had slowed, not through any decision of the engineer's, but rather as an arrow is slowed by a wind that deflects it from straightness. There was a long slow curve, with a gradient, too, perhaps where Kansas met Colorado. The long caterpillar of cars had to adjust, each fixed item having to enter the curve. There is allowance in the making of trains, of course, the wheel mountings have some play for the sweep. But, still, it is a height of man's command of physics when the straightforward can go round the bend. All manner of shifts, bumps, swallows and coughing occurs in the machine: this is where grease and oil must do their work. If it all operates without derailment, it is fluent, sweet, and the mind soars with the prospect of travel.

Going forward at night, in 1879, with boxes and cars that are linked yet separate—like siblings—the train might be compared to a narrative in which the elements do not know they are parts of a train, though they may wonder why, occasionally, their own motion seems weighted by another load.

So we may think of a train, or of some kind of purposeful, progressive locomotion that has Patrick Floyd Garrett with between thirty and forty purloined Texas longhorns making his way south and west, and thinking that perhaps New Mexico offers the chance he deserves; that has one of Matthew Garth's cowhands, the youngest, dreaming of adventure and of some turn of events in which he will be hailed as the Lonesome Kid; that has a locked trunk kept by Tess Millay who became Tess Garth and who is now Tess Valance, and who is somewhere in the desert near Yuma, as Cherry Valance wonders whether his luck is not south of the border—Mexico!— where wilderness may be valued and brought to flower, while Susan Garth, the daughter that Tess has taken away with her, plays with the sealed trunk, investing it with all her hopes and all the open-sesame of games she plays, as yet alone; that has Ethan Edwards, somewhere between Comanche country and a new life, summoning up spent energies to find someone else who must be saved; and Bark Blaylock, who is only three or four, at "home" in Lamar, Kansas, with his mother Celia Blaylock who is agonizing as to why Wyatt Earp took it into his head now to make a train journey to Denver— unless his head is turning already to other futures and liaisons that do not allow for her; that has Groot, so asleep he must be dying, and Matthew Garth who is lecturing himself on the great pressure in him to break out of his reticence and isolation, and Miss Fleur who is only twenty-one pages away in her journal from the discovery "I *shall* be a storyteller."

And others, not so evident or apparent, yet they will come to pass over the same country—large as the land seems there is only so much of it.

And suppose against all likelihood that Wyatt Berry Stapp Earp *is* on the train, sauntering its length in the middle of the night, the habitual policeman, humming to himself a wordless song of his own about the best outlaws wearing badges. And in his circumscribed way he is thinking he has had enough of Dodge or Wichita and the clinging Mattie Blaylock and he is conjuring up that restlessness which can be enough to make a dull man famous, with luck and the right storyteller at hand.

And he comes to what, for want of a better word, we might call the observation car where he sees a young woman sitting on the rail, her back to the world hurtling past, her two arms raised to grasp the

metal posts that hold the roof of the car. She is sustained there in
this perilous brink by a man's grasp and clutch and by the evident
fact that the man's rod is in her, there amid the froth of underskirts
and moon-white skin, and that he is pounding into her as if he was
the piston on the train, and she was getting there—the idea of it.

"A man saw us," gasped Fleur.

"Damn him," said Matthew Garth, urging his own ghost out of
his body and into hers and wondering whether he should say, "I
love you."

"I bet it was that Wyatt Earp," Fleur drooled and giggled in his
ear.

And Wyatt Earp does consider going up to them and arresting
them—jurisdiction be hanged! But they are too much for taking in,
too extreme and frenzied. They are like a river, a mesa, like distance
and the sky. So Wyatt Earp adds a drop more frustration to his bitters.
He tells himself the nation is out of control, and that policing will
have to be more drastic. It is likely . . . well, it is possible that on
this night he makes an extra hardness in himself that in two years
will open fire at that O.K. Corral.

Fleur Hickey

This is where a chapter, a Matthew Garth chapter, is redeemed or
rescued by Fleur Hickey. Not that the transition promises anything
as pliant or harmonious as happy marriage; much less the embodi-
ment of one person in another, or the gift of rights and responsibilities
by one to another that goes with the permissions and certificates that
cover care, property and financial arrangements.

No, it would be safer to see the shift from one name to another
as a mark of separation which will widen into difference and difficulty. Of course, such forces of division, even of antagonism, are
not excluded from the civil state of marriage, that interlocking action
and contract of the republic. So they should not astonish or dismay
those who have wed.

Purely from the point of view of narrative, in distinguishing Matthew Garth from Fleur Hickey we are not saying they will be less
than together—thinking of each other, and an obligatory shadowing

factor whenever anyone else thinks of either of them—even if they do not often meet again. There are meetings never forgotten or escaped, for they have introduced a level of knowledge and meaning that no experience outgrows. They are the source of experience. The ardor that looks to new horizons can only use its old, pained eyes. Do they strive so hard to see the new because they are afraid of re-encountering that old ghost? And of having an earlier, wounded conversation picked up again, years and miles later, exactly where it left off? We remember what we did not say; it is not discharged. Late in the nineteenth century, a realization will settle in America that minds are not large enough for anyone to be lost.

Agreement was reached before the train arrived at Denver that Fleur would turn back there. It felt a simple, direct trip as far as Denver, one on which someone could "go back." Beyond there, the line spurred and twisted over and through the mountains as far as Cheyenne—though, in truth, Cheyenne was on the main line first, and Denver's indignation had brought it a spur. Beyond Denver, the eye beheld another kind of West, that of mountains. Such landmarks define human affairs; they serve as stops and barriers. They are the pieces of furniture in a blind man's house: known, felt, taken as fact.

So Fleur would go back to Abilene. She could make notes and read all the way, thrilling to recent memories and assurances of reunion in x months. Matthew Garth had sat down with her and calculated, and he did not see how he could fail to be back in Abilene by July. Time for Fleur to explain the unavoidable transitions of life to the imprisoned Mr. Hickey, time for candor, decency and the material steps of divorce. Matthew Garth gave her enough money to take a room in a good hotel in Abilene—he did not bother to ask whether such a place existed. She said she had no need of his money; she was not without funds. But he insisted, and she happily took that for a profession of love. Not that lovers believe in money; but they are anxious to find proofs that the world can witness.

One hour east of Denver, Matthew Garth said to Fleur, "And Groot, I believe."

She did not need more. The old man had not been eating. He did not complain or show anything like symptoms. But he was losing strength, and it was not credible that he could leave the train and resume the wholehearted physical traveling that would be required for Montana. The train's comfort had allowed him to loosen the grip he had on his own spent body.

"I'll take care of him," Fleur promised.

"He could be with you at the hotel in Abilene," Matthew reasoned, though it was evident he did not believe in Groot completing that journey.

"We'll have to tell him," said Fleur. She was nervous of that.

"He knows." Matthew Garth was sure of it.

"Even so," said Fleur, "I think you must speak to him."

"He knows," Matthew insisted. He was surprised that she did not recognize it.

"But I think, Matthew, he would want you to say so to him. It can't be taken for granted."

"Why not?" said Matthew. He was flummoxed, calm but ready to be angry. Something in this Fleur's mind was determined to open doors he knew should be kept shut, otherwise they would flap in the wind.

"Do you intend I should tell him?" she asked.

"He knows. I keep telling you."

"This will be your parting."

Garth turned physically away from her and her point.

She did not know how to say it more clearly without endangering her trust in him.

He was haranguing her now. "He expects me to say *that*? He wants the awful, obvious . . . softness!" He dragged the word out of himself, like a bullet of poison or a small cancer that could be pinched and removed from good health.

This awkward conversation also served as a warning to her that she should expect no effusive farewell at Denver, or offer such herself. Instead, Matthew Garth kissed her once quickly on the mouth and once on the cheek and then left her, having to hurry for the sake of business.

As for Groot, Matthew said, "Well, I'll see you soon. Be seeing you soon," and Fleur never registered the gesture he offered in the repetition.

The older man sought a handshake. Matthew granted it, but Fleur could see from Groot's eyes that there had been no gentle lingering in the touch, only a manly encouragement, the stamp of form.

Fleur did read on the train back east, but only when Groot was sleeping. And it seemed now that he was making efforts to stay awake, as if the threat had presented itself to him. He was therefore eager to talk, and concerned to pass on a few things to Fleur.

"What was he like as a boy?" she asked Groot. For she thought that subject would please him.

Groot's eyes and recollections filled. "It was just me and Dunson and him. There was no woman to look after him."

"Dunson never took a wife?"

"Never took a woman. Not after he was on the wagon train."

"He had a sweetheart there?" She was guiding him along, feeding him questions more easily than she could the bread and warm milk that was delivered by the porter.

"There was a girl there," Groot agreed. "And Dunson left her. You see, me and Dunson, we turned south, down into Texas. And those wagons were going to California."

"He let her go?"

"He wanted her to come out when he was settled—"

"He would not take her?"

"No, ma'am, he didn't."

"The fool."

"He thought that later. I do think he did. You see, the wagon train was hit by Indians. And she was killed. For sure."

Fleur was more interested than she had expected. She was, certainly, an imaginative young woman, which is to say overimaginative. And she was playing with the fancy that her own mother, in San Francisco, had come across the country at about the same time, from Missouri to California, and had met Indians along the way and told stories about them and still had feathers and trinkets she had traded for. But Fleur was sure her mother had said these savages were helpful and inquisitive, a little randy and suggestive, just like any gang of wild American boys, looking for a drink and a girl.

"There must have been so many wagon trains," said Fleur. "Over the years."

"All of them," said Groot.

"So Dunson was perverse enough to leave this girl, yet never look at another?"

"Put all he had in the ranch, and in Matt."

"I'd say that was more foolish than letting her go in the first place."

"That's Dunson!" the old man smiled.

"But it leaves Matthew Garth innocent of female company."

"That's how Matt liked Cherry, I think," said Groot. "Cherry told him about women."

"Dreadful stories and the wrong women. And all the time there is the figure of Dunson to make him think no man needs a woman!"

Groot laughed at this and nodded. A line of dribble slipped out of his mouth. "You got a tough one," he agreed.

"Dunson loves Matthew?" she asked him, as quietly as someone afraid of waking a child.

"For a fact!" said Groot.

"But he likely doesn't say so?"

"What's the need in saying it?"

"Groot, you are as bad as the rest of them. Don't you see that a woman enables such things to be talked about?"

Groot was grinning at his secret thoughts.

"What is it now?" She was humoring him.

"You don't ask *me* about women."

"So you had an active career, did you?"

"For a fact."

"And now you mean to boast about it?"

"Well," there was a blush in his old cottony face. "You won't mind me thinking about it?"

"No," she told him. "I wouldn't mind that. Were you happy, Groot?"

"Time to time," he allowed.

"You have relatives?"

"I wouldn't know 'em," he said, cheerfully.

"No children?"

"They wouldn't know me."

"There are a few, perhaps, here and there, down in Texas? Or over in Mexico?"

It was a fond, warming question, and a waft of rising air for Groot. He cried a little, quietly. But then he smiled some more to think of boys and girls that maybe he had left, in Presidio or Val Verde, or in those little villages over the river. It did not hurt him not to know the seed or its fruit, but rather, the thought of spilling and of his last remains feeding the ground held him and pleased him—he could see the faces of those young, stars and flowers—and so he turned over to look out at the passing night and stared straight through the ghost of a wreathed moon, the reflection of his own subsiding face, as he imagined, and died.

And Fleur Hickey had never seen a death or a dead person before, and she took heart in the peace left in this old man's abandoned eyes.

Matthew Garth

After leaving Cheyenne, the Red River D trail crew and all their cattle
were alone with Matthew Garth. There was no mistaking this sentiment, or their apprehension. For once the cowboys had become
reacquainted with their horses, and had reassured their animals and
themselves that they were free spirits who could race and turn,
pounding the grassland beneath them, buck and yell—as, in other
words, the energy that days on a train must lock in burst out again,
so the crew appreciated the watchful figure of Matthew Garth on his
horse, some way off, on a gentle rise, not so much observing them,
not taking notice, or showing interest, as waiting for them.

He was, indeed, this Matthew Garth, looking away to the north,
and there was an expectancy in his stance and the lift of his narrowed
eyes that suggested he could see farther than anyone else. The cowboys felt foolish, and they hushed up so quickly there was something
fearful left behind in the air after the noise.

If they sought to explain Garth's detachment, the cowboys put it
down to the departure of Groot. For that old man had talked to
everyone; he had listened to all the men on the trail, and they had
seen him intimate with Garth. So they had a sense of community
and a misapprehension of being "with" Matthew Garth. This vital
cohesion to the team was now gone, and in its absence the cowboys
could not have detected an extra veering into privacy in Garth himself, a soundless, poised encroachment on magnificence. For whereas the young rancher had admitted to himself previously a wistful
ignorance where women were concerned, now he believed he had
exaggerated the mystery. He told himself he had done well, had
excelled, had risen above the uncertainty. A very different opportunity had faced him—the inhabiting of his own doubt and weakness. But he had passed that by.

Laredo, the trail boss, could not fill the gap left by Groot, for he
had grown used to leading the herd on his own. So Garth saw a job
being done with his cattle which he could not assist in, and should
not interfere with. This left him little role except that of unspeaking
god riding along with them as warning or obscure example. It made
the men a little more religious.

There was also a Cheyenne scout waiting for them at the depot. His name was Tall Bull, but the trail crew would call him nothing but "Cheyenne Joe," and he grinned along with the corruption. He was an ingratiating, lost soul, ugly to American eyes yet the wearer of garish American clothes—a filthy yellow coat and a top hat that he had acquired in Cheyenne. He was ambitious and hopeful of promotion in the Greenwood Trading Company if this drive went well. At first, he had assumed he would consult with Matthew Garth on the route, the terrain and the particularities of the rivers in Wyoming Territory. But his chatter dropped away after the first day, and Laredo instructed him quietly not to bother the boss.

The Cheyenne wondered how anyone could ever get on with the white men if they were bitter in their superiority. He drank more in the evenings, and so picked up a reputation on the trail for being insolent and unreliable. One day he buried his crumpled top hat and the garish coat: the cowboys murmured to themselves about savagery renewed, kept their distance, but began to trust his directions so long as they were stated in a terse and graceless manner. Tall Bull wondered if some similar process of warping accounted for Matthew Garth's solitariness.

Wyoming was new to the crew, and it was a marvel to see herds of buffalo parting for them so that they could usher their Texas longhorns north. They shot a buffalo one day and roasted the meat that night, or as much of it as they could manage. They told themselves it was strange and sulfurous next to beef, as well as altogether tougher and less pliant to cookery. But they liked the fur on the beasts, and they cut themselves pelts for their girls in Texas, and they would hang the pelts from the chuck wagon so they might dry in the day. Tall Bull had a modest success in teaching them to eat the buffalo tongue, cooked, then allowed to cool and sliced thin— the tongues seemed piquant and alive, they were so fresh, and it made the men laugh to feel the juice from this smooth meat in their own mouths.

Tall Bull carried a plate of the cold tongue to Matthew Garth with a dollop of the canned condiment the Americans liked. He held the tin plate out to Garth.

"I've eaten," said Matthew Garth.

"Good," promised Tall Bull, pushing the plate forward again.

"Thank you, no," said Garth, and he got up and walked away. It was a fine evening, and he thought he'd stroll.

"Mr. Garth don't eat your shit, Joe," said one of the cowboys.

"The worse for him," laughed Tall Bull.

"You shouldn't say that, Joe," said Laredo. "Maybe he'll whip you if he hears you."

"You are playing with Joe," said the Indian.

"No, sir," said another cowboy. "Our Garth here was raised to the whip. His father, man named Dunson, always kept a whip on the trail."

"I never see it, this whip," said Tall Bull, looking from one set face to another.

"Don't mean it's not there, Joe," said Laredo. "Big magic whip. Mr. Garth carries it in his hand."

"You think Cheyenne mindless," said Tall Bull, though he said it in a muttering, grumbling way to himself.

Matthew Garth had wandered away, carrying his tin cup of coffee, promenading into a thicket of pine trees. It was cool and like twilight under the trees; he saw the flash of small chipmunks hurrying from his advance. The ground rose, and he followed a winding path. After about half a mile, the ground leveled off. He could look back and see the herd and the camp. He went on deeper into a gloomier, more sequestered part of the forest, until he came to a pond as still as its water was dark. There was no movement there but gnats dancing above the surface of the water, moving repeatedly in an inane pattern that spun no silk or gold, but which evidently held or fulfilled them and was as regular as manufacturing or the inner forces of nature.

Matthew Garth, sitting on a rock, leaning back against a pine that disappeared above him in the forest roof, had a hard-on. He took it out in the air and stroked it. He closed his eyes and summoned up the image of a naked Fleur Hickey. He set her on the roof of a moving railroad car, her legs open until it was the train itself moving in and out of her and she was howling like the train's whistle with the fricative satisfaction of it. He had her turn somersaults, with the train battering at her body and her contented smile spreading all over it like a puddle as black as the lake up here in the hills.

Holding tight on himself, Matthew Garth walked forwards to the lake and let the gray drops of glue fall in the black water. They looked like the eggs of frogs, like spots of spit, until they lost form in the dark water. He sighed to feel the release and waited for the throbbing course of his blood to subside. He pictured himself, idly, flailing the nakedness of Fleur with pine branches. He could see the imprint of all the needles on her skin.

"Hey, boss." It was Cheyenne Joe, bobbing with complicity on the other side of the black pond. He had his thing out, too, in his hand, and he was proud of it and of the game they both might play, sparring across the water.

"You want Cheyenne woman, boss?" asked Joe.

"Come here," said Matthew Garth, and he put his thing away as the cheerful Indian walked round the edge of the pool, following the forward thrust of his nut-colored hard-on.

"Put it down," said Matthew Garth.

The Cheyenne winked and made a game of it, straining a constipated face.

"Won't go down," he reported.

Then Matthew Garth hit him in the middle of his face with his right fist. Joe sat down, shocked, in the black pond. His arms went back into water that was suddenly deeper. He shouted in panic and only just recovered his feet on the brief, shallow edge of the pool.

"Can't swim, Joe?" asked Garth.

"No, sir," said Joe. There was blood tumbling from his nose. He put his hand up to it and the broken nose squeaked. He was asking why the boss had struck him, when Garth hit him again in the stomach. Joe could not breathe. But another chopping blow hit him on the side of his head, a blow that slid over from the cheek to the nose. Joe felt that whole nose shift. Then a bolt came up and struck him in the throat, lifting him off his feet and Joe knew it was worse, he was about to die. There was no play or pity in Garth.

Matthew Garth watched the Cheyenne fall over backwards into the deeper water. His head rose, a mashed, broken head, wet with blood and water. Then the choking sound stopped and in a few moments the gnats returned with a new commotion, moving crisscross over the sodden hump of Joe's back as the waters became flat and composed again. Matthew Garth guessed that his right hand was broken.

So he carried his tin cup in his left as he sauntered back to the camp and made ready for the night.

He awoke before light from the pain in his hand. He could not bend the fingers.

Laredo came up to him.

"We haven't got our Joe, Mr. Garth."

"Gone off?" said Matthew.

"Looks like that."

"Damn Indians," said Garth. He became garrulous with Laredo; he felt fond of his stolid trail boss; he reflected with him on the nature of loyalty and the intractability of the Cheyenne, on the true inaccessibility of savagery.

"He left his pony," said Laredo. "Don't understand that."

"You can't understand them," Matthew Garth assured him.

"Your hand, sir?" asked Laredo.

"Wrenched, I daresay, yesterday."

"I got a glove you could have," Laredo offered.

"Why, thank you, Laredo," said Matthew. "I'll trouble you for it, I believe. We'll get ourselves another."

"Sir?"

"A Cheyenne, man. There are villages along the way, for sure. We'll stop and hire ourselves another."

"Joe wasn't worth much."

"Who knows," Matthew threw his trail boss a comradely grin, "we'll maybe get ourselves a squaw. Don't look so solemn, Laredo, it's my hand hurting. Not yours."

So Laredo went away and got the old gauntlet he had in mind. It was agony putting it on, and it did not much guard or help the hand. But it did signal the stress and the fierceness in their Garth which Laredo could not for the life of him explain. But he reminded himself to watch out for Garth in case the difficulty of riding became too great.

"Ye Christ," Garth said to himself, giddy with the pain and the isolation that had no doctoring. "I'll be crippled from it."

———

Matthew Garth

In Matthew Garth's mind, on the way up through Wyoming, his right hand became as extensive as the herd he owned. His greatest effort lay in not referring to it, not yielding to its pain, and not disclosing how hindered he was by it. There was next the policy of not disclosing how it had been broken. The knuckles in the back of the hand were so enlarged he had to slit the gauntlet in order to get it on. Not even Laredo noticed this. None of the men appreciated Garth's plight or the terrible control he employed to muster a passing remark or a nod of recognition. He told himself he was a masterly actor. Yet the extraordinary tension and striving of his whole body for successful pretense made the drive less easy to endure for anyone.

By day, Garth clenched his alarmed horse with thighs that acquired the intensity of forceps. He sat there as the slow progress elapsed, clamping the retained copy of *The Return of the Native* to his saddle with his left hand; the leather-clad right kept the pages from skipping in the wind that tore at all erect things on the prairie. He read, or rather, the words passed through him. Sometimes he read a page over and over without grasping it. There were phrases he knew by heart ("Eustacia Vye was the raw material of divinity," for instance, or "Reddlemen of the old school are now but seldom seen") but could not fathom through. The book was the only thing that kept him from crying out, though something in the inner damage he was doing to himself ensured that he would abominate books thereafter.

At night, like a creature caught in a trap, he wanted to gnaw at his own wrist and leave the tattered hand in the vise of pain. He would dip the stump in hot black pitch and be free of the agony. Whenever they came to a stream or a river, he contrived to let his hand dangle and drag in the cold water. That numbing was as peaceful a release as he had ever known. But the pulse of the breakage came back, beating through the water, heating it, until his crazed expectations believed it would boil and bubble. If ever he could fall asleep, he had dreams of amputation, terrible stories in which he left wicked parts of himself here and there, red and purple with poison. For five days he had had a fever.

Only then did the Cheyenne cross their path. This was not a village, but a band of about a hundred on the move. The cowboys saw the Indians coming up aslant of them from the southwest, and for several hours cowboys and braves made sightseeing forays back and forth full of trepidation, bravado and curiosity. The two groups came together for a night's camp on the banks of the Powder River. The camps were half a mile apart, but there was visiting and small trading, and the Cheyenne were altogether appreciative of and patient with the white man's cautious decision to go everywhere with loaded pistols and rifles.

"They are asking if we would trade some cattle," Laredo reported to Garth. "The chief says his people have been hungry this last winter."

"What do they have as trade?" asked Matthew.

"They don't say," said Laredo. "They just laugh and look at the sky."

So some of the cowboys went to the Cheyenne camp that evening, and there was a Cheyenne ritual, a dance, in which several men, one by one, danced with sticks in their hands. There was a drum set up nearby and at the height of the dance each man used the stick to beat on the drum. Whereupon the Cheyenne tossed the stick in the direction of the cowboys. One of these landed at Matthew Garth's feet.

"What does this signify?" said Garth.

"They're all mightily amused," observed Laredo.

Then one of the Cheyenne approached the two men and, in broken English, conveyed the fact that it was a divorce dance in which the casting out of the stick symbolized the abandoning of a wife. Thus, by chance, several women who, by Cheyenne standards, were esteemed for their looks if not their character, were, so to say, available. Were there, perhaps, some cattle in a similar state?

"A head for a head?" asked Matthew Garth, and this equation seemed to please the Cheyenne.

There were Cheyenne who turned their backs on what occurred that night, and those who watched from a disapproving distance. Only a few men served as the impresarios, leading out a line of young women, squat, demure but hardened to the American eyes that scanned them, searching for hints of sentimentality. The cowboys waited dutifully for Matthew Garth to make his selection though no one doubted which he would take: a girl taller than the rest who did not seem to be only of Cheyenne blood, and who had a more knowing and fearful regard for the Americans. Thus it was an orgy in which the rights of proprietorship were observed.

Before he went to his debauch, Garth had the wisdom to ask Laredo to be sure there were some of the crew not part of the transaction, but awake, watchful and armed.

"They could cut our throats when we're asleep," said Garth— there has never been anything more rigorous or righteous than the paranoia of the early prairies.

The girl of Garth's choice walked ahead of him to a tepee that stank of grease. She lit a stub of candle, and their shadows loomed above them on the walls of the tent. Matthew studied the young Cheyenne woman: her face was filthy, but in her eyes there was still the phantom of some pride and social stature that came from generations of knowing the world was full of people not worthy to look at her.

"Love," said the Cheyenne girl, not with intent or accuracy, but as if it were a name or a call that she believed could win recognition.

"You speak English?" said Matthew Garth.

The girl shrugged—these other words were too much for her. Instead, she made a repeated, violent gesture with her clenched fist that could only refer to the sexual act and its heady brevity. There was no way of telling how old this female was: she might have been anywhere between fourteen and thirty.

"You are Cheyenne?" he asked.

She picked up on this. She nodded, but then she shook her head. She laughed and repeated the two contrary actions.

"What is your name?" asked Matthew Garth. Then he said "Name" and touched her chest. He felt the warmth beneath her buckskin garment.

There was no response, but she had felt the awkwardness when he pointed with his left hand. She saw the glove on his right and stooped to look at it. He did not know if he dare let her touch it. Could she see or smell through the glove? Did she know how crooked the hand was? Her dark eyes came up to him, full of concern.

He could not stop her. She had a knife and she cut open the glove. But she was more delicate in the operation than he expected. She peeled back the flaps of glove and talked to herself in her tongue; he could hear the disbelief. She brought the candle up to his hand. It was so bloated and gnarled, he could have wept. Her own hand was blunt, scarred and old-looking. Her fingernails were as scratched as an animal's hooves or horns. But she did not jar his hand or threaten it.

She came close to him, stood up, lifted her skirt and raised his hand inside the skirt. He had to come up on his knees to follow it. He felt the hand touch the moistness between her legs. She grinned to indicate the contact, and he tried to grin back. Then she squatted a little and came down on his hand. The pain was terrible—she had enclosed him in her—but she would not let him go. She leaned over him and with her free hand held his forehead: again, she talked to herself about his heat.

Then, when he could not bear it any longer, she slipped off him. His hand was wet and it reeked of her rankness. The pain was so great, he could only sit on the packed earth with the hand in front of him. The Cheyenne girl went away, out of the tent. She was gone for half an hour. When she came back, she held a pile of large leaves in one hand and a gourd in the other. She gave Matthew Garth the gourd and indicated that he should drink. It looked like thin milk in the tallow light, but it was cool and tasted of mint.

The leaves covered a warm plaster that smelled sweetly. The Cheyenne girl took the paste and laid it on his hand as a poultice: it felt hot. Then she put the leaves on top of it and lightly bound it together with twine she bit off with her teeth.

She made him lie down on the ground; he felt drowsy already, and wondered about the drink. The girl put out the candle and in the sudden darkness he heard her garments moving before her body draped itself all along the length of his. She undid his breeches and there, in the dark still, she put him inside her and said "Name" beseechingly at the tidy accomplishment.

He did nothing. He lay there like an invalid or a dead man while she moved up and down him, flexing with the strong grip in her hips. He knew that he was coming, or that it was coming up through his corpse, but he was never sure whether he came awake, or in the deep dream of ease that followed. Somewhere he heard the groans and grunts of her contentment.

When he woke, he was dressed and buttoned up. The Cheyenne girl was nowhere to be found, but the glove was back on his hand, stitched up. He could feel the congealed weight of the poultice still there. There was no pain, and Matthew Garth lay for an instant recognizing the undeserved order that had come back to him. He smelled beef cooking outside, and he wondered if he had become a monster yet.

Matthew Garth

The hand was wrong, a disorder was rooted in it, he knew, not to be removed or smoothed out. But the pain had gone. He was not sure whether to think it had trailed away into the air at the ends of his fingers, or gone up, up the arm and into the main part of him. He wondered whether it might break out elsewhere as the caged thing sought other exits. But Matthew Garth felt himself again, troubled only by the silent consistency with which the men overlooked the spider that was his right hand. He called it "spider" because he could no longer close the hand, or bring thumb and forefinger cogently together.

This state of mind coincided as they came closer to Montana with the presence of God on their trail. He was brought there, or hailed, by the youngest of the crew, a Will Powell. It was Will, asleep on the train, dreaming that he might be recognized one day as the Lonesome Kid. This Will was a slender cowboy who did not seem possessed of ordinary strength or endurance; there was a tubercular air about him. Yet his companions in work had learned how a strange tirelessness held him, a stamina that must come from within his quiet good nature. It may have been his appetite for duty, or his meekness—no one could recall—that had appointed Will Powell as guardian overseer of the cattle and the others' peace of mind during that night when Matthew Garth and the manliest of his men had their various ways with the Cheyenne women.

There followed from that night a kind of unassailable, humble rebuke in Will Powell that took out his Bible from his saddlebags and began reading to the other men in the evenings. They could not disregard or dismiss his flat voice or the sturdy rhythms of retribution it recited from the Old Testament. Not that Will Powell ever preached: he did not carry on from his appointed text with any considered moralizing. He only read and then looked up, his youthful eyes shining, his small, blond head nodding, as if to say, "Well, isn't that it . . . ?"

There was a suggestion that these dire strictures met the case of the trail crew in Wyoming, and that Will's tact or grace would not underscore the point or even allude to accusation. But no one spoke out, injured, against the invisible pressure of his suggestions. The men suffered it. They did, among themselves, reckon that Will Powell was most motivated by being left out of the Cheyenne night. But they could not dispel or deny the gentle tide of his commentary. Their uneasiness mounted, and it struck Matthew Garth as the grudging quietness of reproach and suspicion.

The men were unhappy for many evident reasons. They were tired now from the work and the journey, and yet they had to admit that they were not even at their destination, let alone on the way home. And these cowboys were unlike those on the 1865 drive—even if in some cases they were the selfsame men—in that they had developed a true sense of home. In 1865, many of them were used to the trudging marches and the instability of war. But, even before that war, these were roamers and escapers, men moving west out of failure, remorse and anger, men who claimed "home" was a lie made by women and creditors. So they had undertaken that first cattle drive—so much more of a venture into the unknown—with light, rapacious and nomadic hearts.

By 1879, however, they had attached themselves to a swelling ranch. They had become Texans, they had built houses, and they had, most of them, found wives, sweethearts and children. Thus, they had never set out with those ringing cries of adventure and wanton escape that marked the Texas dawn of 1865. They had gone solemnly, with professional regret and a mental calendar of due return.

There was also the somberness of Groot's departure—which most men knew presaged his death—and the inescapable discovery that their Matthew Garth was an uncomfortable man, a leader who could exist only at a distance which reminded them of their own inadequacy. This was not a difficulty any of them could have put into words—until they heard Will Powell's readings of guilt in Biblical men—but it made an atmosphere that undermined the fine, summery weather on the trip. They had an irrational experience of riding beneath dark, sinking skies; and the anxiety overwhelmed meteorology.

As for the opportunity they faced with the Cheyenne, they were torn between their sense of themselves as masters of the open spaces and their longing for home. It was easier to yarn beforehand about the Cheyenne women, and how they would take them, than it was to do the taking or think about it afterwards. No matter that the native women had been placid or obedient, or even intrigued: the men believed they had departed from some white man's self-expectation. They had exploited the Cheyenne, but ruefully, with more sadness than pleasure. They could not have done it if they had not been a group or if Matthew Garth had not seemed driven by the need and the occasion. The inaccessibility of the Cheyenne women had been too grave and large: the men wanted understanding and a motherly forgiveness. And so, with a furious endeavor, they were trying to forget the event or replace it in their fantasies with vengeful slaughter in which the provocative Cheyenne were eliminated.

"These readings," Matthew Garth said to Will Powell.

Powell's face had become serene and lovable in the last few days. There was no doubting that something powerful yet saintly had overtaken him.

"How do you come upon them?"

"I open the Book, Mr. Garth."

"You have not read them before?"

"They provide themselves for me."

"Have they sinned—these men?"

"It is not for me to say so."

"Have I?"

Powell looked at his employer, and then he looked away behind him to the hills and the sky. He said nothing. But he smiled at Garth.

"This country," said Garth, "needs law. I am the friend of that construction. But law is, quite simply, the enactment of reasonable order, the preservation of life and property. Why, it is as useful as a good map and a horse in the wilderness."

"Yet the map takes away the wildness," said Powell.

Garth struggled with the countering line of the argument.

"And God has made it wild," said Will. "That is the beauty of it."

"But if it is wild," reasoned Garth, "then men should act like animals. Killing to eat. Taking the best ground if they can hold it. Acting out a thought."

"I cannot say, sir," said Will Powell.

"Whereas," said Matthew Garth—he was so eager for definitive proof or insight—"man may make himself decent. By contracts, rights of ownership, a code of law, men to enforce it, wire to show where properties begin and end. This can be done, surely?"

Will Powell did not know how to satisfy or appease Matthew Garth. He was not a developed teacher, much less a complex arguer. It may simply have been that in his own reading he fell in love with the cadence and the stories of the Bible. And so he spoke them aloud, and liked to think of them soaking in, like rain on corn fields, or like dump slowly turning into soil. There were passages in the Bible that sounded more clearly than any explanation, and which were more remarkable than the skeptic's best question. These songs matched the spaciousness of where they were.

So he and Matthew Garth sat gazing at one another in packed silence as darkness fell.

Next day, up ahead of them, a boy rode over a ridge on a pale brown pony, without a saddle and only a rope rein. He was a lad of maybe twelve, and the cowboys led him up to Matthew Garth.

"Is this Wyoming still?" asked Garth.

"I wouldn't know," said the boy, "but I suppose it may be Montana Territory."

The boy came from near Sheridan, and his name was Nate Champion. He was with his father, a couple of miles up Clear Creek, panning for gold.

"What are you champion of?" asked Garth, to make his men laugh.

The boy watched their humor and muttered that he didn't know, except it was nothing.

"We're from Texas," said Garth. "Heard of that?"

Nate whistled. "Met a man a few days ago," he said, "foreign gentleman who was going on down to Colorado. He was a picture-maker."

"How was that?"

"He did paintings. He would put the country on canvas with a paintbrush. He had a wagon and pictures in it bigger than windows."

"He do a picture of you?" asked Laredo.

"No sir, he did not," the boy answered modestly.

"What will you be, Nate, when you're grown?" Matthew Garth asked him.

"Oh," the boy's bemused gaze turned to the distance, as if the question urged him out there. "I reckon I'll be a rich man and own it all hereabouts."

The cowboys laughed, and Nate's pony pranced, as if to music. But the boy was so adept, he rode its twists and turns with skill.

"I knew a painter, too," said Matthew Garth. "This was a lady."

"No lady could have done these pictures," said Nate. "No, sir— they're that large. You could know your way by these pictures."

The herd and the crew moved on. They began to turn to the northwest, hoping they were indeed in Montana. Matthew Garth told them it could not be far now, that once the cattle were delivered to the Braxton ranch they could go back at a good riding pace to Cheyenne and the railroad. The men cheered up at this, and they urged the cattle on. But Laredo warned them not to hurry, for there was a pace at which the cattle arrived with meat on them from the bluegrass pastures they traversed. Hurry a herd and they came home string and bones.

Matthew Garth now resumed his habit of riding on ahead, and that riding left the cowboys happier still. Ten miles or so behind him, they tried trick riding and told stories. Without ever addressing a policy directly, the group rehearsed the accounts they would give of meetings with the Cheyenne. They began a campaign to make Will Powell stay in the north in that God was more clearly resident there. Their exposure to the wilderness began to fade; the nakedness was covered over.

And one morning Matthew Garth, riding, came upon a woman in a meadow. A horse and a pony were tethered beneath a willow tree, and the woman was playing with a little girl of no more than ten years. They had a homemade boat they were floating on a small stream that curled through the meadow. Garth stopped his horse to watch the mother and child—there was something in her caring stoop, and in the child's trust, that allowed no other relationship. He thought of the couple he had chosen not to search for. It was true, fate did provide versions of them.

Then the woman saw him and she came walking up the slope

towards him, not boldly but without timidity, putting up her hand to shut out the sun that was full behind Garth. Seeing this, he moved down the slope in a half circle so that the woman was no longer dazzled. Her hand dropped and the sun fell on her face. Matthew Garth knew for the first time, with a momentary loss of center, that maybe he loved all women.

"Thank you," the woman said. "My name is Frances Braxton. You are not, perhaps, Mr. Garth of Texas?"

"Happily," said Matthew, and the woman uttered a discreet "Hurrah" for him and for her good fortune in meeting him. Garth felt a great urge to put his hand on his heart and tell her, "Name, name!"

James Averill, 1950

His wife, Betsy, had on her faraway look, the one that promised some unpredictable change in direction. They were in their seats with a few minutes to spare before the concert. It gave James Averill time to study his wife: there was no risk of her catching him in this; that engaged frown of hers had carried her more than miles away. She was gazing at the wall beyond the orchestra, but she was no more seeing that than hearing the small tuning notes of the players. No, she must have some venture, some idea out of sight that her great, idealistic strenuousness would bring closer; or else it was like a goal out there in the dark that she had identified and which, by hauling on the ropes of desire, she might draw not just herself, him, Boston and 1950, but the world of feeling and awareness, closer to.

His wife, Betsy, this brisk, brilliant, brittle, bristling, British bringer of a woman. Brigandish? Yes. Brimming? No, not quite. This bride that he was thinking how to rid himself of, with such a removed concentration that she might not notice or comprehend any casual request to leave. He feared an explosion would be necessary.

It was a warm afternoon in Boston, in June 1950, and the fervent interests, ample resources and complex desires of the Averills had brought three of them together for a program of American music. James from Charlottesville, Betsy who had been in Boston, and Sally, their fifteen-year-old, who was down for the weekend from her school in Vermont. James Jr. could have been there: there was a spare seat with Sally's morning purchases piled on it. But Jim Jr. had flatly refused to hear the music. He had gone to Fenway, instead, with a buddy and the buddy's uncle, likewise down from Vermont. At nearly ten, he was granted this license, but Sally had had no choice, only the morning shop as a tacit bribe.

For they were honoring two of Betsy's "things"—not just Boston, Symphony and Pops, for which she was "more than Friend," but American music.

"I cannot understand," Betsy said in that Kensington hurricane of clipped elegance she favored when scolding the Averills' America, "why you people will not take care of your own music. You make such a fuss about your freedom, and then let things go hang."

"That *is* freedom, Mother," Sally had drawled at lunch at the Ritz. "Let it look after itself."

"But, darling, it won't. There's such a thing as responsibility. And taste," she added, trying the cold lobster.

"So we tell the people this is good?" asked James. "And we preserve it, like those dismal English cathedrals so exhausted and praying to fall down in the damp?"

Betsy's dry gray eyes surveyed him, and then passed on to the salad. "You're a natural reactionary, James, you don't have to make any effort."

They were at the Ritz because the Beacon Hill apartment was really not large enough, with both the children there, and Betsy putting on a small "do" after the music for some Friends. So James had taken a room at the hotel for the weekend—which the kids showed every sign of occupying on the principle of novel, fresh-purchased freedoms being the cutest.

"I love hotels," said Sally in that sulky, restless way of hers, so stressing the "love" (she made it sound camp and dangerous) that people looked up at nearby tables. "You can do *anything* there."

James smiled politely: he had, until then at least, speculated about getting that gauntly attractive librarian in from the Houghton. Have her bring some of the Averill papers over, and then ambush her with historical hair-splitting and champagne. He fancied she was a sexpot: restricted, tight outwardly, but then, once freed . . . once offered the liberty of a neutral hotel room, with linen that would be laundered by strangers, or replaced. So he had thought, but now his own children had lazily commandeered the room and summoned friends on the phone. They were like him.

"You should read this," said Betsy—it was a sheet of paper, with typing on it. James Averill did, quickly, wonder whether this was *it*, some compromising letter (an Averill paper!) she had come upon or had sent to her anonymously which would convict him.

"It's a poem," Betsy added, "written by the old man himself. His premise for the first piece."

James sighed, with relief and disappointment: he would not have been averse to a beginning of the end, so long as the full, dreadful scene did not have to occur at the Symphony Hall, with Sally as a greedy observer.

He kept the sheet of paper in his hand. The "old man" was something-or-other Ives. As far as James knew (he had good young researchers on his staff), Ives was a joke, an amateur composer without melody or much else. But Betsy had taken him up: she had plans for him, those farsighted prospects which might have been more appropriate if Mr. Ives had not been so close to eighty.

"Can I see?" asked Sally, stealing the paper from her father's hand. Very close-up, under the shadow of her mother's valiant and remote gaze, she shot her father a fat, sexy wink. James did wonder what Sally got up to. But the girl read the paper with a rising curl to her generous lip. Sally was like her mother, James thought, so long as Sally's face was very still. There was a stamp of resemblance, a kinship less in the look than in the way of looking. But when Sally looked, or spoke, or thought, there was something low-down always—it was funny, dry, earthy and conspiratorial, whereas Betsy's face was forever on the point of flight, or soaring—her taut pale skin was like the fine shell of an aircraft, and her eyes were those of the sky and horizons. Not for the first time, James felt pangs of earthbound wonder and daunted desire for his airy, insistent, craze-ridden wife. All those "things" of hers—Ives, Symphony, the refugees, the care of animals—they somehow put him in the role of the ordinary, the businessman, the "Oh, James" who beheld her lofty causes from below.

"This is going to be beyond me, I suppose," he whispered to Betsy.

She turned those soft, hurt eyes on him, as if she felt this private remark had been calculated to catch her just as wingedness took over. "There's nothing beyond us," she hissed. "Nothing."

Then there was applause as the conductor, Richard Burgin, walked onto the stage. The applause subsided, and Mr. Burgin turned to face the musicians. There was the endearing moment as everyone gathered their would-be coughs together, like infants squeezing their bladders before the circus. James settled back for daydreams of the Houghton librarian, and even of Miss Nora Stoddard in Santa Fe. What would she be doing now? It would be noon there. Perhaps she was galloping on the high desert, or examining a remarkable Susan Garth landscape, unseen for fifty years. He would go there . . . that would be his next trip. He deserved it, didn't he? And all the way away in New Mexico, dalliance could go unnoticed. Why, he wouldn't really *have* to notice it himself.

James Averill might have gone off along this glide of reverie if the music had begun in a regular way. Very often, music was all he needed. He could sit in awful movies, held by the romantic strings; he could drive a hundred miles farther at night on a sequence of good songs, sung by Sinatra, Tormé, Jo Stafford, Peggy Lee, Lee Wiley, Lena Horne, or Billie.

Indeed, he relied on the oiled ease of music to get him through this and any other of Betsy's concerts. And he could get through all of Beethoven thinking of girls he had had, or would have had, here and there, the rise and fall of the music sooner or later coinciding with the measure of his romancing, and the music always like progress or journeying, a train carrying him through the landscape.

But this piece by Ives, this "Three Places in New England" or whatever it was called—*had* it started? It was like turning on a radio and getting no program, just the tuneless, rustling accumulation of indistinct noise or presence that signified "on-ness," as opposed to the radio being "off."

But there *was* something. It was far off, as far away as Betsy's gaze; he was communing with it before he perceived it, like waking up in the heat of Africa after going to bed in January Vermont. There was a pattern in the strings—James Averill was not sure it could be called tune—like breath trying to claim a body. Indeed, he felt that the hall was a corpse or a possibility that this air had sought out in a spirit of rescue or reclaiming. There was something as mournful in it as Lear finding Cordelia and hoping his words, his grief, could start her breathing again.

There was now a clear ridge of melody, a fragment, a murmur, old, cracked and so tragic. He felt the pores in his skin expanding as blood filled them. He was being stirred. He thought he recognized the melody—some macabre air of patriotism—but then it stopped; and when it resumed it was altered, further dismayed by the effort of being played.

He realized that he was involved. Sitting forward, he wanted to help or nurse every detail. He was straining to hear. Then came a lurching, walking refrain behind the sad song: the two of them were together, at different paces, like trains lumbering in opposite directions at night so that you see, for a second, a lady in a gray suit, half asleep, framed in the slide of windows, going . . . to Kansas City perhaps . . . and in your own drowsiness, you say, alas, farewell, how lovely, gone forever.

There were several things going on simultaneously: he had never heard or known such activity in music before—alarums in the brass; a plaintive, experimenting piano; ghosts of plucked basses tiptoeing amid the throng; the faded, dead pump of old glories still lost in the air; and always the wistful strings drawing up that broken melody —like hands sifting through dirt for gold. "Good God," he said quietly.

Why had he thought that? He had never panned for gold in his life. But something in the music had unlocked in his mind and body a moment from someone else's experience—it was akin to an unexpected smell: coffee, roasting coffee, in a library, or the smell of a woman's body on a spring day. He knew, without dispute, that his father once, for a day or a season, had panned for gold and been shaped by the process, so that prospecting went into the structure of his desire.

It amazed James Averill to see some people were talking during this extraordinary music, and some leaving.

When it ended, referring to these departures, he said to Betsy, "Ridiculous!" and her anxious face fell, shot down, the iridescent streamlining of a pheasant reduced to a bag of bones and crushed feathers. She turned away from him.

Afterwards, outside the hall, Averill asked his daughter for the sheet of paper. At first she had forgotten where she had put it, or whether she had it still.

"It must be under my seat," she supposed.

"I'll get it." And he was on his way.

"James!" Betsy's voice stopped him. "Presumably, you won't want to bother with my little party. I'll call the hotel later."

"No," said James Averill, "I'm coming."

"Really?" she said, unsettled, but not ready to risk more damage or more hope.

"I'll walk up in a moment," he promised her. He held her hand.

"Very well," she said, briefly lost to the daze of all her arrangements.

He went back into the hall. There were several black people sweeping out. He hurried in case this paper was already tidied away. But it was there, on the ground, folded, like a clue. He picked it up and a black woman nodded to him politely, waiting to bring in a vacuum.

"Thank you," said James Averill.

The woman grinned, and Averill stopped in his tracks again.

"Did you hear the music?" he asked.

"Yeah," said the woman, amazed at the question. "Yeah, I did."

"Wasn't it marvelous?" He wanted to find adherents.

The woman laughed. "Well, I wouldn't know." She was ready to turn on her cleaner.

"But you heard it?"

"Yeah."

"What did you think?"

The woman's face settled; she put her routine aside. She looked around to see if help or distraction was at hand. But it was just the two of them, and there was no getting away from it. She would talk to this wild-eyed, handsome but untidy man. He seemed harmless. She'd tell him.

"I didn't like it," she said. "I really didn't."

He smiled at her. He had to have more.

"It made me scared," the black woman said.

"Like ghosts?" asked Averill.

"More than that," she said. This fellow was simple. Hadn't he heard the whole building shudder and come so close to shouting "No!"? "*I* was afraid," she repeated, and he saw in her aggrieved eyes the threat to order that had passed by, like the subway, threatening to leap out of the ground.

"Yes," he said, "that was it." And he thanked her.

James Averill

As he walked across Boston Common towards Beacon Hill late on that Saturday afternoon in June, he was walking into small children playing on the grass. So he stopped, and found a bench: there was an old woman at one end of it, sprinkling crumbs on the ground for pigeons from a wrinkled paper bag. He asked if he could sit there, and the woman waved a frail hand at the empty space.

He saw the Common crowded with all the slow sports of a weekend. James Averill was touched by the profuse, untidy ways in which American cities could accommodate the easygoing pleasures of so many ordinary people. He felt the confidence and content that any wealthy man would like to enjoy, and he wondered how many other people now on the Common had heard Ives that afternoon, and with his mixture of woe and wonder.

Now he read the page. He recognized the old, upright font of Betsy's typewriter. She had taken the trouble, no matter that the paper might have been swept up with all the Symphony Hall garbage. And so he read the poem:

> Moving—Marching—Faces of Souls!
> Marked with generations of pain,
> Part-freers of a Destiny,
> Slowly, restlessly—swaying us on with you
> Towards other Freedom!
> The man on horseback, carved from
> A native quarry of the world Liberty
> And from what your country was made.
> You images of a Divine Law
> Carved in the shadow of a saddened heart—
> Never light abandoned—
> Of an age and of a nation.
> Above and beyond that compelling mass
> Rises the drum-beat of the common heart
> In the silence of a strange and
> Sounding afterglow
> Moving—Marching—Faces of Souls!

The voice came from close to him. "Are you all right, sir?" It was the old woman, still holding the emptied paper bag—perhaps she kept it for bringing crumbs to the birds.

"Why, yes, thank you," he told her. "I heard some fine music this afternoon."

"Ah," she said, "there's nothing like the music. I'm poorly myself." And she looked at him gravely, her lips pursed, not sure he was fit for her intimate communication.

He felt in his pocket and took out a dollar bill. He folded it and passed it across to her. "Won't you get yourself a cup of tea and a sandwich?"

"Oh, sir," she said, her hand fumbling for the bill. Her hand was cold, he could tell from the brief touch.

"Can I help you?"

"I'll sit here awhile."

"I'll get you the tea," he said, standing up.

"You want the dollar?" she asked, though she did not offer it.

He told her to keep it and he walked as far as the refreshment stand and came back with a paper cup of tea. He wasn't sure, but he put a little milk in with it for her. And he got a small cake with raisins in it. The old woman smiled as she saw him return. She had watched him all the way, but he could tell from her eyes that she had expected him to walk away.

"My lucky day!" she cooed.

"Mine, too," he told her. There were times when James Averill had the urge to go into politics, to do something profoundly testing with his money, his time, his attractiveness and that sense of loss or failed hope that came upon him. Here on Boston Common, with the enigmatic poem still echoing in his mind, he vowed to look further into the possibility.

The old woman was sipping the tea noisily and breaking pieces from the cake to ease her soft gums.

"Where do you live?" he asked her.

"South End," she answered, crumbs dancing on her lips.

"How old are you?"

"I was born in 1876," she told him proudly. "In Clonmel, County Tipperary."

"Laurence Sterne was born there," said James Averill.

"I met him," the old woman told him, devoutly. Averill smiled, stood up and said goodbye to her. She looked up, her eyes narrowed in the late sun.

"You're a good man," she said. "Don't be so troubled."

"I'll try not," he agreed, and he raised his hat to her.

He felt he should stride out now as he went across the Common in the direction of the hill. It was still warm and the damp of sweat grew in the small of his back as his suit coat flapped. There was a softball game to his right, and some dad, naked to the waist, hit a high, slow pop-up that had his children gabbling beneath it, and then making way as the gray bomb fell to the grass. The dad whooped as he rounded first, then slipped, sliding on his ample belly—even jittery, second-attempt fielding got him in the run-down. He looked ready for a beer.

The trees were motionless in the heat on the hillside, and the few people out and about were going very slowly up, leaning into the slope. A pretty woman came down towards him, swinging with her speed, and he felt the billow of her skirt just as he caught her scent. He stopped and turned to watch her go: the backs of her shoulder blades moved like pulses beneath her burnished skin. She had been going too fast, and too enrapt in her own pleasure, to give him the time to smile at her, let alone speak. He felt truly hot now, and winded by the hill; he needed more exercise—he needed a regime.

He heard the party before he was at the house on Mount Vernon. All the doors and windows were open in the hope of catching a breeze. Yet the apartment was crammed with elderly people in suits and ties, sipping sherry and refusing to wilt in the hubbub of talk. As soon as he was there, he wondered why he had come.

"Jeepers, it's hot," Betsy breathed at him as she slid past, handing him a sherry and then moving on with a tray of refills.

He studied the pictures on his own wall, like an admiring stranger: the Lartigue of the figures running beneath an early curlicued flying machine; the small Vuillard and the set of Rowlandsons; the John Gutmann of the woman getting out of a swimming pool. Not bad, he thought.

Woodfull was at his shoulder, a gray bean of a man with that hooked stance and the sour, querulous humor of a semi-professional New Englander. He was on the board of the Symphony, and so frankly smitten with Betsy's high-strung, dithery grace he had nearly forgotten his own skepticism about American music.

"Fine event," he admitted to James.

"Remarkable," said Averill. He had mastered the terseness of Woodfull's discourse.

"Bodes well for our Fourth."

"Ah," said Averill, foundering, but climbing to avoid making a mistake. There was something bigger, he had heard, set for July 4th, a something he had preferred not to look into yet. After all, with any skill he need not be in the East for the holiday. He might be New Mexicoing it with Nora Stoddard.

"Met Ives?" Woodfull asked.

James Averill had not thought that Ives might be at this party, in his apartment. He was afraid to meet the man who had composed that afternoon's music. James Averill never knew how to convince the very talented of his respect and their worth, and of the link, the correspondence. He feared being facetious, stupid or overdone. He had seldom had good meetings with creative people, and so he had come to avoid them on principle. But Ives was so sudden and dramatic a discovery, and waiting for him in his own apartment. He knew his face was sweating.

"Come," Woodfull ordered, and James had to follow him, careful not to jostle sherries, cruising past floral shoulders and the backs of Brahmin necks, catching sight of Sally trapped in a corner by the only young man in sight, one hand thrown up above her head so anyone could study the unshaved hair in her armpit. Her blueberry eyes swiveled, following him, and he made a face at her to show his horror at the heat and the pomp.

Then he was standing beneath a tall man, erect in tweeds, with a corduroy vest and a plaid shirt buttoned at the neck. He was balding but there were frosted bushes of hair on the sides of his head, and the head itself was so craggy and so unmarked by perspiration it should have been rock. His eyes were narrowed, but they twinkled at James Averill.

"Take that coat off," said Charles Ives. "You'll fry."

They were introduced, and Ives dipped his head. He had the toughened sheen of someone who took very little seriously when he went out, who was there for absurd reasons of policy. But he had a sunny disposition that seemed quietly insane, or out of common reach.

"I was very struck by your music," said James Averill. "I loved it."

The old man bowed from the neck, his head tipping slightly to one side, as if to say he didn't normally bother with complimentary small talk but since Averill was evidently above average . . .

"They seemed to have fun," said Ives.

"The audience?"

"Oh, them! I meant the band. It's hard for them, you know."

"But rewarding, I would think."

"Now my secret's out," said Ives, and he barked out a chopped-off laugh. "Man should never lose his secret." Averill realized that Ives was all the time swaying where he stood. But it was not the threat of fainting; rather, it seemed that he was hearing a rhythm and was gaining strength from it.

"You've found each other," said Betsy, coming up behind James.

Ives's eyes now took them in as a couple. The swaying stopped. "Your wife is an angel," he said to James. It sounded less like his grateful opinion than an urgent message, a saving word, being passed to Averill.

"You're wet," Betsy murmured in his ear. She must have felt the damp through the back of his jacket.

"I charged up the hill," he told her.

"Idiot. It's ninety-four. Come with me." Her imperious cool hand took his, and she was already in whim-swept motion.

"There's no need," he protested. He didn't want to interrupt her work.

She had him at the door of the tiny bathroom. "There's every need," she said, and whipped him in, all in the same motion as she opened the door.

"It's hotter in here," he said, but she laughed and slipped his jacket off. It fell on the floor.

Betsy then stepped nimbly into the shower, drawing him in too. The water was dripping, as slow and heavy as the popped-up softball.

"Betsy?" he wondered. He could not believe it.

But his wife had flipped open the belt on his pants, wedged herself into the cool tiled corner of the shower and hooked her outside leg under his arm. He saw her soft silk dress fall back, the cream of her thighs and the incidental erotica of her banded stocking tops.

"You like the music," she said. It was the surprise exciting her.

"I loved it."

She had him out, such fast hands, and moving in towards her. She had no panties on.

"Show me how quick you can be," she urged.

She was so cool, still, at least as refreshing as the tile, just a slip of a thing at forty, flat-chested, lean and so anxious for him. She moaned lightly when he knocked her against the wall, and he noticed that, quick as he came—inspired by her untoward haste— she was racing up behind him. In an instant, she was like a fine handkerchief, collapsed and sweet in his arms. She sagged into the wall. He leaned in, crushing her, and a thrilled noise came up from her body.

"Don't we have fun," she said, and then, "No, no, stay," as a desperate struggle to keep his balance promised to carry him out of her.

He moved to be more solid, and now she was secure, poised on him, bouncing on his pole. She giggled and said, "It's been a lovely day."

And not even dark yet, he thought, seeing the piece of paper with the Ives poem on the floor. This fucking passed all understanding, it mixed their colors fatally. Whatever he did or thought, it washed that history away.

The paper had come out of his jacket as she discarded it. He looked in the mirror over the small hand-basin, and he saw Betsy's eyes beating through the glass, the wall and ranging so much farther than

New England, energized by their soap-smelling sweat, by the slithery collision her loins held on to.

He found later that Betsy had not locked the door of the bathroom —at a party, for aging Friends, with drinks all round. Suppose one of them had come in and found him so breathlessly encumbered with her in the shower? Did she not take the Symphony seriously? Or did she hope for more from it than it could offer? Why was she testing danger so? Suppose Ives had come in? Would he have declined to notice, or turned his silent, shining, rock-like visage to watch, to admire secrets and the old peril trying again?

Susan Garth, 1950

"What have you got?" Susan Garth had asked her, very early on, foreseeing the problem.

"Got?" asked Nora Stoddard. The question had been so penetrating, like a fighter's whispered dare in the first clinch of the last round.

"For wheels," the old woman wanted to know.

"I've got an old Buick," said Nora. She was proud of its stately sway, its wood and leather inside, and its rolling speed along the highways.

"That's no damn good. You want something like one of those Jeeps. I've got one. Put my stuff in the back and go anywhere. God didn't make roads in the places he was proud of, you know."

"My Buick wouldn't get to where you live?" Nora did not want to sound stupid. She realized how little she had ventured out of Santa Fe.

"Might get there," Susan Garth mused—she was cracking the joints in her crooked right hand. It sounded like kindling, just set light to. "I was thinking beyond that."

Susan Garth lived in a house she had built, off the road a way between Window Rock and Fort Defiance, over the Arizona line, in Navajo country. They had let her build there, or perhaps they had never contested her independent action.

She was getting herself in a position to invite Nora Stoddard. Not just to get out of the reach of the recording machine, or even to put the young museum woman in a predicament where she could look at a lot of the pictures and some of the subjects for those pictures. But to be *there*, away from this smart clutter of newspapers, machines and gossiping office staff. Somehow, Susan Garth knew, she had to get this decent, willing but naive girl to see the problem in the pictures, their absurdity. And there wasn't a chance of that, probably, without living longer in some place the busy Miss Stoddard could scarcely contemplate. But you had to try, Susan Garth told herself; and at her age, it surprised her to find there was no useful hurry. You had to work on the long shot that these new young might be awake.

"You could get out there on Sixty-six," said Susan Garth. "Then go north at Gallup. You know that?"

"Of course," said Nora Stoddard. "I've been all the way to Los Angeles on Sixty-six."

"Doesn't mean you know it."

"You're browbeating me, Miss Garth."

"Expect I am. You could go by way of Chaco."

"I could?"

"Chaco Canyon."

"I've always meant to go there," Nora remembered.

Susan Garth smiled at the plaques on Nora's office wall and the Stieglitz picture of the Flatiron Building in the mist.

"Yeah. Well, come on Sixty-six. I'll meet you in Window Rock. Noon on the Saturday."

"Are you inviting me for the weekend?"

"I am," sighed Susan Garth, "but don't bring a cocktail dress. Just a good coat and some bourbon. And leave Baby behind." She pointed at the tape recorder, so loaded and piously objective on the desk.

"I knew you didn't like it," said Nora.

"No electricity," Susan told her.

So, on a Saturday morning, early—for she meant to dawdle and look carefully—Nora Stoddard set out in her Buick. She had two bottles of Jack Daniel's, her copy of *Across the River and into the Trees*, and a strawberry and rhubarb pie she had baked herself. Actually, the second, for the first had not worked out. She had a heavy jacket, a sleeping bag, a blanket—she even tossed in her gun and a box of shells. And a small Coalport creamer that her father had given her. She was going into Indian country, she thought, equipped to trade.

She drove south to Albuquerque, and she stopped for breakfast on the edge of that city rimmed with sunrise: eggs and biscuits in a café she shared with farmers and truckers, the men calmly ignoring her but maybe moderating the ferocity of their diatribes for her sake.

The coffee was the strongest she had ever had, as if the dust from the floor was periodically added to the beans. When she paid at the counter, an old man sitting there turned to examine her without warmth, modesty or offense. Nora felt her skin prickling.

"Gonna be hot today?" she muttered to the man, without looking at him.

"Hotter'n hell."

"Good," she growled.

"Hotter'n your ass."

"I like that fine."

"You'd better."

"If I don't want it to fall off?"

She swept up her change, like a tough hombre, and went out, riding on the admiring, raspy cackle of the old man. Sometimes she felt the West was like a movie, but a movie at rest, just waiting for any visitor to set it in motion with the right, hardboiled lines. She grinned, thinking what if the old man went for her?

It was still early, so she had the low sun behind her as she drove west. This was the most beckoning light. She could see the hair standing up on the corpses of jackrabbits hit in the night by trucks; she could see the variegated pinks and reds in the broken bodies. The shadow of the Buick yawned out in front of her, and she tossed her hair to see her own image ahead, lovely and alive. She put the radio on and the blast of some big band nearly lifted the car off the blacktop. "I've got you," she sang along with the radio's brassy smooch, "under my skin." And she turned and twisted her body like some doll vamping a respectable banker.

"Aren't you just a little horny?" she asked her imaginary Wells Fargo companion, and she invented all the blushing, yielding and eventually ardent afternoon for the empty space beside her and the shadow-box vehicle on the road.

She thought of James Averill, and of how she might write about this weekend to him. After all, it was why she was on the road and excited. No matter the long shot. She knew he was married. She had never met him. Yet she did entertain—at the same time as she laughed at herself—the remote but clear prospect of maybe marrying the scoundrel. It was farfetched, but she was not so much out of her mind that she would not settle for a short, dramatic affair with him, failing her easy accession to hostess for the Averill millions. There was word in the museum community that such liaisons were possible. James Averill, it was said, was always looking, generous and polite. So she was tickled how in their letters so far there had been such a valiant strain of mutual idealism, as if they were searching for honorable reasons to get into each other's pants.

These thoughts made her hurry. It was only a little after nine and she was coming up on Gallup. So she pulled off the road and stopped, but she kept the car radio on for the news. It was all Korea: troop movements, MacArthur, and some talk of another La Motta-Robinson fight, before music came back. So she took out a sheet of paper and started to write:

Dear James,
    It is Saturday morning and I am outside Gallup, N.M., on the way to a weekend with Great Lady Garth. The country is more beautiful than I thought or remembered and—blazing along in my Buick listening to Cole Porter—I thought of you, so I thought I'd write to say so. In a mad mood?

Nora

Then she drove into Gallup, bought an envelope and a stamp and sent the letter off to Boston before she had time to reconsider.

Window Rock at eleven was very little to speak of. It was desolate, wind-ripped and forsaken. The country was extraordinary all around —the huge, crumbled mesas, the pithy green of the meadows, and, quite simply, the looseness of the infinity of it all, the feeling of some empty quarter, a void of geological wonder. But the habitations were small and ill-kept. There were a few Navajo on the streets, bundled up despite the warm morning. Nothing seemed to be going on, apart from the tattered ponies that wandered the roadside looking for grass amid the garbage. There was nothing on the car radio, either. She had gone out of range of Kay Starr and the Dorseys. There was a wind that sometimes rocked her parked car and worried away at loose flaps in some of the resolutely square and minimal housing. It didn't seem to be that dignified being a Navajo. She wondered why Susan Garth had elected to live here.

Two minutes before noon a Jeep drove down the middle of the one street in Window Rock. It came right on up to Nora's Buick and stopped, window to window.

"Follow me. It's three miles."

There was no greeting and no more explanation. But the Jeep swung through a tight circle and Nora fumbled to get her beast in motion before the Jeep vanished. They went north on the road for a mile and then Susan Garth turned off to the left on a dark trail, into rising ground. The Buick bumped and wallowed, but it dealt with the transition.

Nora followed the dust. They were climbing steadily if unappreciably. When she looked back through the rear-view mirror it was a surprise to see the ribbon of road they had left, like a stream.

Now the road turned more sharply. There were slabs of rock passing by and the dirt road became a small canyon. Then they were level again and out in the open and the Jeep was making a half circle ahead of her so that, free from the dust, she could see the house.

There was no reason to suppose it was the greatest house in the world, Nora told herself. There were probably a few better, in Paris, Bel Air or Tahiti. She wanted it for herself and James Averill. As she got out of her groaning Buick, she saw Susan Garth, one ruined hand still clamped on the driving wheel, watching Nora's reaction.

From their approach, the house was low, made of wood and stone. But as you entered it, you went down several steps into a large room filled with light from the western view. You realized then that the house was perched on the top of a steep slope. As Nora came up on the wall of window, she saw a small patch of ground where one could sit outside and then the complete fall and the canyon, with scrub oak and piñon clinging to the violent slopes.

"It's magnificent," said Nora Stoddard.

"No plumbing, either," grinned Susan Garth. "There's a privy," she nodded as Nora's eyes widened. "Know how I got it?"

"You built it?"

"Some of it myself. Some I just told them what to do. Bark Blaylock did most of it, bless him. One of those times he believed he was in love with me."

Susan sat down in the chair and swung her feet up on the antique trunk that served as a table.

Susan Garth

It was the Sunday, and the air was so baked in Monument Valley it was on the point of turning to crisp—as if visibility itself could be transmuted by heat into the fine hard layering of fossil. Nora had asked if she might drive, but Susan Garth rejected all assistance. She remained attached to the wheel like a believer, never relenting or relaxing, coaxing the Jeep over rough ground, using her once broken hand to guide the bucking vehicle. She disdained dark glasses but looked into the searing light with bloodshot eyes so closed she was like a beat-up fighter. Susan surely knew all the ways they were taking; or else, she knew the character of the terrain, as a boat learns the rhythm and geometry of waves, even if it does not know such names.

The weekend had already exhausted Nora Stoddard. It was not the astonishing things she had seen, or the emptiness of this America. Nor was it simply the defiance of Susan Garth, the furious determination to be no one's foolish old woman, never to give pity or appreciation a chance. At eighty, this Susan Garth drove the Jeep in the midday sun; she had split wood the evening before, broiled a whole fish, demonstrated the ways of a dry privy where the wind rose up from the canyon and dried one's gaping bum; and she had dispatched a hawk, caught in the studio, and then shown Nora Stoddard prints, from forgotten negatives, come to life again.

After dark, the fish half in their bellies and half given to cats with wicked ears, crushed or chewed, they had sat outside in coats within a few feet of the canyon's edge, tossing back Jack Daniel's. Miss Garth kept returning to the bottle, with something on her mind— as if the whiskey might be wrong.

"Know what time it is in India?" Susan asked her out of nowhere.

"Must be tomorrow."

"Must be morning there. Never did go there."

"Did you want to?"

"Why wouldn't you want to go anywhere?"

Nora felt challenged in the darkness. This old lady was so bloody-minded; she gave no opening for tenderness or nostalgia.

"What do you think of dying?"—Nora was a fighter.

"You know," said Susan Garth. "The thing about it is, in India they're not worried about me dying."

"One day they may know your work in India."

Susan laughed. "God help 'em. You believe that?"

"I do. Your pictures would move them."

"What do we know? We know Dickens, Mozart, Shakespeare. Except we make Shakespeare up. But before that? We don't know who made the cities at Mesa Verde. One day we won't know the cities. Not if one of these fine New Mexico bombs goes off. Or if it doesn't! Time'll do it, too, just as surely. You think any of us is going to be known a *blink* from now?"

"I daresay not. But names may last. I think we should try."

"Try to be famous? Try to be on the cover of magazines?"

"Do the work that gets you there."

"Only one work will count. Or ever has. Have babies. Get fucked. And I, young woman, who may be famous in Santa Fe because of you, I am a virgin. A miserable virgin. Whereas I could tell you're not in the dark."

"You can!"

"Can smell you," Susan Garth grumbled. "Good smell."

"So I should have children? Keep the whole thing moving?"

"Can't you feel the river running through you?" said Susan Garth, a prospector's grin on her face. The question came with such dire feeling it silenced Nora. She did not understand the image: it seemed either obscure or too sentimental, too obvious. But there was a need for reassurance in Susan's voice that signified much more than the grief of her own childlessness. It was as if she felt Nora carried some larger, total responsibility.

"How do we suppose," reasoned Susan Garth, "that somewhere, when we're dying, there aren't going to be people sitting under the trees somewhere, in love, with the best raspberries they ever tasted, with chocolate, and the light so perfect? How can we imagine they'll notice us dying? The nerve!"

Without much understanding, with Susan lecturing and Nora suffering her own helplessness, they got along. Susan would take no praise for the fish, and she did not discuss Nora's pie. But the two women ate together, simultaneously, sometimes in unison, their jaws clenching on the thyme-lined fish. That fundamental experience could not be evaded, and it was what Susan Garth had intended.

They had gone halfway down the canyon to pick the thyme, clinging to the severe walls, so much less secure than the outcrops of juniper or wiry grass. But they sat there on minimal ledges watching the shadow creep up the canyon walls as the sun set and seeing birds swoop and hover in the depths.

One of those birds was in Susan's studio, an oblong building that flowed from the house. They heard its scraping noise when they went in. The bird was up against the skylight, too frantic or too much bird to find the narrow way out, the way it must have come in. Its sidelong black eye looked at them, rigid in terror, and the hawk tried to flatten itself against the glass, its wings bent like the arms of a kite.

Susan Garth looked up at it. A few small white feathers drifted downwards, picking up the light.

"Can we help it?" asked Nora.

So Susan had sighed in a disgruntled fashion. She had found a stepladder and a broomstick, and she had gone up the ladder to a point where with the broomstick she could push the skylight open wider. The hawk would not help itself, so the little old woman had come down the steps, shaking her head, she had found her gun and shot the bird.

"There," she said, holding up the weight of the hawk and tapping its beak with her revolver. "Now let's look at some pictures." Later, she had gone to the edge of the canyon, held out her arm and let the hawk drop.

"You had to do it," said Nora, full of the idea of woe. So Susan laughed at her, not cruelly or derisively, but with that aged wonder still amused by the trickiness of children.

There were printed photographs on the studio walls—pictures of desert, ravines, the snow-capped Sierras—always the distant prospect of some natural disaster to smooth surface in an alleged globe. There was a rawness to the pictures: Nora was not sure how far it lay in imperfections in the processing, or how far in the rather violent, unsophisticated placing of the camera. For it did not feel as if the ideal or picturesque vantage had been chosen for viewing the scenes. The land was too powerful for composition. There was some peril, or some doubt about surviving, in the point of view—it could have been difficulty or innocence. But it gave the unmistakable impression of a photograph from before the age of photography, unaware of the new medium's clichés and habits.

Susan Garth had a box full of glass plates and another of undeveloped rolls. There were files of negatives never printed. There was at least as much chaos as there was genius, and it was plainly beyond the old woman's clerical control. Yet the neglect hurt Nora only. Susan Garth was ready to pass on with things unseen.

"I used to take pictures, you see. I was too busy. And the processing was always hard. When I started I had to teach myself. And the equipment you had to carry!" She shook her head from the weariness of all that carrying.

"But it made you strong," Nora said.

"Wore me out," Susan contested.

That night, the Saturday, she developed a few negatives from the past. She used a battery-driven lamp, and she worked in the dark as if she knew it through and through.

"I don't know what they'll be," she proposed, as they watched the images swim into view in the trays. They were pictures of a pretty young woman, alone, with a seashore behind her. The camera was near the girl, and she looked so agonized it was remarkable she did not appreciate the camera was close.

"Sharon Pawley," said Susan Garth, flat as your hand. "Nineteen fifteen."

Nora waited for more. Should she know this name? Susan Garth was still inspecting the poised image of the unhappy beauty. Her face was bleak, as if she was looking in on a past beyond rescue or encouragement from her own private window.

"*She* was famous," mocked Susan. "Handsome, isn't she?"

"I think I've heard of her," said Nora.

"Think so? Must be famous!"

"It's very fine," said Nora.

"I don't mean none of that. It may be all that survives from a picture, a film."

"She looks so sad," said Nora.

Susan Garth stopped moving. "What?" She looked at the picture. "No, we had a lovely time that day."

Nora couldn't follow the line of Susan's thought. Instead, she suggested that for the exhibit catalogue Susan should write something about how she had taken the pictures.

"Write it myself?"

"I could help," said Nora. "If you needed it."

Susan Garth reflected on the several problems beyond Nora's grasp. "All in the silver," she said. "I would have to get into that."

Nora looked down in the sink where a gentle splay of cold water was running over the prints, cleaning them. The water was pumped uphill from the level of the road, and it came slowly. The young woman in the photograph lay there in the sink letting the water take off all chemical bitterness. Nora had the first inkling from the talk of silver how photographs were liquid or molten ideas trapped on paper, that alchemy was involved. She knew, without having to ask, that the Sharon Pawley so vivid in the silver was dead, and that the threatened liveliness in the pictures had looked into a dead end. There was an indignity involved, Nora saw now, in perfecting the young corpse, and keeping her fresh, years later.

She fell asleep in the house smelling the resin of wood, the bourbon in her head and the gunpowder in most of what Susan Garth had said.

In her room—that chaste, square space—Susan Garth contemplated a kinship between herself and her guest. They were neither of them, maybe, unified persons. The voice the world heard and the voice with which they talked to themselves were strangers, opponents even, or twins parted at birth, blind to the loss, unaware of the wound that was their eyes. And Susan Garth wondered whether this schism was—in 1950—a debility or a special opportunity, the inner nerve of modernity. Once wounded, does the organism start to turn towards a new kind of life, damaged but more intricate? Did women know this gap between voices better than men? There was a grimace in Nora's face, the one warning in her beauty, and the thing that caught Susan's equally hunted eye.

And on the next day, the Sunday, Susan had ordered Nora out in the Jeep for a drive. The air was dry and clear, but there was something pressured or thundery to it, a danger Nora could not argue away that came from being so far out in the semi-desert. She did feel that weather there must be faster than in "normal" places, more dramatic. She had to consider what might happen if the Jeep faltered. Of course, there was a road, and a road promised linkage. But people died sometimes when they wandered off the road; they walked in insane circles round their empty water cans. There was no other traffic on the road, and Nora could not rid herself of fear as they saw in the distance the ruined red crags and towers of Monument Valley.

There was something so mournful in the eroded surfaces. It spoke to so immense a passage of time that all human agitation had been given up. The Navajo might regard the valley as their sacred ground, but if you were not Navajo then surely the abandoned panorama told you only that you were unsaved, ignored, not known or named. And there was something terrible in the blood color of the rocks. She had heard of red earth and stone, but never seen or felt it so deeply. The hue was as recent as the spindly buttes seemed ancient. The red was now, watching; it was the absolute refusal to let you have a name. The passion in the color was violent, disorderly, tumultuous. It was madness in triumph. The spatial intervals were grand and sure, but the towers, seen close, were as tragic as people who have lived decades in an asylum, for whom there is no saving demise.

Susan Garth did not stop the Jeep. She did not discuss the valley or its atmosphere with Nora. It was as if only motion, a ceaseless current, could endure there or be human. Nora realized she had seen

no photographs of Monument Valley in Susan's work—yet evidently
the old woman had lived nearby for much of her life.

They passed through a small town, Mexican Hat, with a bridge
and a river that split apart the rocks. Then, again, they were out,
climbing, in open country with a view back of the somber red chim-
neys of the valley, forsaken factories. The heat was more intense.
Even the rush of air in the Jeep was too hot for ease. Nora flapped
at the air with her hand—it was so warm she could not be sure there
was life in the air.

Then Susan Garth drove off the road to their left. They were in a
rolling, gravelly area, with the feeling of being upon some insecure
plateau, crusty but like an ocean. They drove for three or four miles
like this, with Nora having to hold on to the hot sides of the Jeep
and Susan easing their way over the stormy ground.

Suddenly, Susan Garth stopped the Jeep. Nora heard the metal
creaking and cracking. She wondered if the radiator was close to
boiling.

"Now then, you," said Susan Garth. "You just get out and walk
forwards in that direction." The old woman nodded towards a slight
rise in the ground. "Take it slowly."

The directions were not brutal or arbitrary, but there was no escaping them. There was something destined in this stop—it could
have been as carefully arranged as that one picture they had brought
to life. Nora knew she would have to go alone, but only because the
solitude was part of Susan's design. It was not fearsome, but a mark
of the privilege or trust. "It's not far," Susan added.

Nora stepped out of the Jeep into the crystal silence. She had
never known such a quality in the air, for while no sound registered,
still there was an encompassing presence, a tone, a system that
was "on" enough for silence to be named. It was like being deaf
in a lung, a bubble rising and falling on the inhalations, or like
being a wave in current. In any town Nora was agnostic; in smart
company she was a witty atheist. Yet here she was certain of that
presence. It did not make her religious—after all, this was 1950—
but she knew instantly and completely the fragility with which all
people hold their convictions. If the world lived in Monument Valley,
she said to herself, we would be a holy tribe. But the valley had to
be empty.

About ten steps before the edge she knew something enormous
was coming. Five steps early she perceived the fact of a chasm in
the ground. But then she was lost.

No, she did not fall, although she no doubt wavered and thought of the descent. The place is still there, you can go yourself and see that words will not manage it. There are tourist postcards, and it is tempting or reasonable to think that they are better than nothing. Yet, consider—they may be worse.

Nora Stoddard stood on the precipice. As she estimated it, more than a thousand feet below her, a river wound its way like a snake in three muscular bends around terraced cliffs. The river was muddy, but she could see places where the sun defined the ripples of motion in it. She could even, very faintly, hear the breath of the water; it must be a torrent down there. But it was the terracing of the cliffs that was most remarkable. She could believe that thousands of Egyptian-like slaves had toiled to make the layering so perfect and exact. But she knew it was only time and the wind, that thing called exposure.

This is a place that beggars description, and so it overawes the ambition of human intelligence. Nora Stoddard wanted to scream, to faint, to die—surely some people would jump into the chasm with a cry—"Geronimo!," whatever—chasing their echo all the way down.

She did not know how long she stood there, and she did not consider Susan Garth's patience. For this was why she had been brought there. It was the reason for the weekend. This old woman did not care whether her photographs were shown, for she had witnessed the irrelevance of photography long ago. No, Susan Garth had absolute designs upon her. Nora had never previously considered that she might be that worthwhile.

But at last she tottered back to the Jeep, where Susan was writing a letter to someone. The old woman did not look up; she could not bear the sight of the impressions.

"It's called Goosenecks," Susan told her.

Susan Garth

"What river is it?" Nora asked Susan Garth.

"The San Juan," said the old woman. "It goes on west into Lake Powell. That's where it meets the Colorado River, and so it takes that name through Grand Canyon. Not that the river knows it, you see."

"Thank you," said Nora when she had sat down in the passenger seat.

Susan Garth regarded her with a sly, fond envy: for isn't the first experience always the grandest? And now virginity was the only thankless advantage she had over the young woman. So Susan leaned over and kissed Nora lightly on the cheek, at the corner of her mouth. Nora felt the feathery sweetness of raspberry, while Susan came away quietly shocked and thrilled at the potent sexual charge in Nora.

"We have to go?" asked Nora.

"Stay as long as you want. You can always come back. Lot of people can't take too much of it."

Nora appreciated that truth. "We should go."

So Susan reversed the Jeep and they bumped and lurched their way back to the road.

"I'm tired," said Susan. "You drive."

They changed places, and Nora learned how toy-like the Jeep was. It made her admire Susan's calm as a driver, for she had had the fitful vehicle feel like a battleship.

"I'll buy you a beer," said Susan. "Continue your education." She made a sign to Nora to take a dirt road off to the right, headed directly into the lee of one of the red mesas. There were tire tracks, and then they passed a corral surprisingly crowded with horses. Next they came upon a parking lot, with several trucks and trailers and some fancy cars. Nora wondered vaguely if this was the camp for the slave crew that had built the layered cliffs.

"There's a kinda hotel here, with a bar," Susan explained. "They're making a movie."

Nora parked the Jeep and they walked into the stuffy bar. There was a mob of people inside that would have seemed impossible out on the road. Susan got a couple of beers and they sat at the bar with them. There were photographs on the walls of scenes from Western pictures.

"Over there," said Nora. "Isn't that—"

"Yeah, that's him. He's O.K. Stupid, but he's O.K."

"It's a big picture?" said Nora.

"I don't know. I suppose."

There was a stir at one of the tables where a disagreeable-looking man in spectacles and a pipe was holding court. He stood up and came over to the bar.

"Thought it was you," he said belligerently to Susan.

"And I was afraid it was you."

"That's friendly." The man had the air of someone who expected to be wronged.

"What's to be friendly for?" The old woman knew just where to prod him.

"Ah, we go back," he told her. "Doesn't that mean anything to you?"

"We don't go back," Susan told him, curtly. "I gave you a job once, that's all. Don't rub it in."

The man shook his head and stole a glance at Nora. He had cunning, hurt, lustful eyes—but the mixture was so furtive as to be funny.

"And don't make up to her," Susan warned him.

"I was not!"

"She's a decent woman. Not one of your actresses."

"Did I talk to her?"

"Could you? I wonder that."

The man was pushed beyond his limit. "You're the most bothersome bitch I ever met!"

"Well, thank you, I'll remember that," said Susan Garth, nodding brusquely in mock time with his furious, deploring gesture.

"And good luck," she told him pitilessly.

He poked his pipe at her. "It sounds like a curse," he said.

"Wish I could," said Susan Garth.

With a handful of drinks, the man went back to his table. His pipe flickered like signal flags as he told his companions what a terror that old woman was.

"Who's that?" whispered Nora.

"Oh, I forget his name. Come on, let's get out before I'm sick."

They drank up and Nora followed Susan to the door. But they were stopped at the threshold . . . by *him*!

"Well, stranger," grinned the tall man, looking down at Susan in his bantering way.

"Well, yourself," she answered. "Doing another one, then?"

"I gotta look after him."

"He's an idiot."

"Come on, now," the tall man remonstrated, and he swayed with what he insisted was a joke.

"What is it this time?" asked Susan.

"I don't know," the tall man told her. "The same. Cavalry—you know."

"Nonsense."

"Don't be like that."

"You don't like it here."

"I never said I did. I come for him."

The old woman shook her head over this inane sketch of companionship. "This is Miss Nora Stoddard," she added grudgingly.

The tall man smiled happily. "Well, I'm glad to know you," he said, and he shook Nora's hand, quite content that the pretty girl could not take her eyes off his face.

"He's losing his hair," said Nora when they were outside, on their way to the Jeep.

"Yeah, but the mind went first."

"Why are you so angry with them?"

"I knew 'em when they were boys," said Susan Garth. "You know what he did, the glum pipe-eater? Last year he put a shot of Goosenecks in a picture. Just to brag he'd been there. And he had baldie throw a whiskey bottle down there!"

"I didn't see that," said Nora.

"Know what else he did? A few years back he did a Wyatt Earp picture. Here! Filmed it here! The cretin. I'll drive. I'm better again."

And she seized the key and drove all the way back with a wrathful speed that never stopped ranting against the follies of the picture business and made the tires howl on tight curves.

Five Letters

Fort Sumner, New Mexico Territory
July 15, 1881

Ethan,

We was too late. You may hear it before this—but Billy was killd by Garrett. In the dark. A lowdown trick not that I blame G. He hadnt a choyce. Or he did not find one. Bark is a fine fellow. Would make any man proud. He was there but unhurt. So well be coming back to Tomb. What else. Hope the lady is more herself and that Earp has taken sick. And died.

You are a hero E looking after things.

We have had a grand ride.

Yours, Bill Brocius

I send this by coach.

. . .

Santa Fe, N.M.
June 18, 1950

Dear James,

I have seen such things—not just the lady in her lair, living on the edge of nothing like some cross between Robinson Crusoe, Prospero and the wise witch of the West; not just more of her pictures, enough to stuff a National Gallery; not just *John Wayne*! holed up in the only bar for miles, making a movie; but places on this earth I cannot describe, as moving as great music. More so.

There is a place I saw where I just felt I wanted children to have them see it. But I do not have any, and I hoped you would be understanding.

Nora

Abilene, Kansas
June 1, 1879

Dear Matthew Garth,

Groot died yesterday: very peacefully, as far as I could tell. He did not complain, and he was talking in that good, gentle way of his until near the end. I know this news will not come as a shock to you, or even a surprise—I think I am grateful that you trusted him to me for his departure. You know, really, that is what you did, passing him over to me. Well, the trust was repaid. He died easily and he had talked about you, and of his love for you. You were fortunate to have this old man, as I was to hear him.

I didn't know what to do but write to you and bury him here in Abilene. Did he have other relatives anywhere—in Holland, perhaps? If you know where they are, and would rather not yourself, I will write them. We buried Groot today. It was simple, but the cemetery has a fair view and the man who did it was very civil. Frank Melville assisted me in making the arrangements, not that there is a lot to do in these cases. I have ordered a headstone in granite with only the name—I found Nadine Groot in his wallet—and Abilene and the date. Any of this can be changed if you are not satisfied.

Frank Melville has been well disposed to me, and very respectful. There has been no recrimination. Indeed, whatever his dismay, he likes us both well enough to swallow it. I would think myself very fortunate if you were not so far removed. I have to be a model of patience to wait for you without going mad. So I read books all day long, which must be very good for me (though there is no library). I am now reading my way through *Dombey and Son* which I had begun on the train with you. (This happens all the time: times of day, colors in the sky and small tremors in my organism all make me think of you.) But as I read this part, I thought that you *should* find your Susan—lack of her, or the ignorance, is too much:

> What is the proud man doing while the days go by? Does he ever think of his daughter, or wonder where she is gone? Does he suppose she has come home, and is leading her old life in the weary house? No one can answer for him. He has never uttered her name since. His household dread him too much to approach a subject on which he is resolutely dumb; and the only person who dares question him, he silences immediately.

Well, Matthew Garth, I dare, at this distance. The heaviness is too great to bear. You should not think you have survived it.

I have also seen my Mr. Hickey in the jail, and found him as amiable as ever and as indifferent to seriousness. He listened to me very gravely and said that of course I must be free. I cannot say that I am cheerful about it: the prison is a dreary place, and I am not confident that he will ever manage well out of it. But a divorce is to be executed, and I will have the services of the lawyer of the Greenwood Trading Company. None better here —and not much competition.

So it is likely when I see you next I need no longer be Fleur Hickey, but can go back to Fleur Blue. My father was a Travis Blue and he was a wagon master on a journey west in, I believe, 1848—much the time you came west. He was from Texas you will be happy to hear, though French before that: he was Bleu once, I suppose, just as I am Fleur. Well, on that journey he met my mother, whose name then was Denver McCreadie. She was a musician and singer in a small group of players that came with the wagon train. She is still a professional on the West Coast. But my father died at the battle of the Wilderness. So, more or less, I came to be here: I won't test your credulity with how I fell for Mr. Hickey.

The only other thing to say is how much I love and miss you and long to be with you once more on the observation car of a hurtling train, risking life, limb and good reputation.

I hope that Wyoming pleased you and that you may be weary of cows so that you will hurry back to your

Fleur

Ft Davis, Texas

April 9, 1879

Mr. Garth,

Regret to inform you, death of Thomas Dunson two days ago on the ranch, your abode. I could not be there but I am informed there was nothing to be done. He had some fits and began walking at the end with a great deal of talking. You are his sole heir.

Yr obdt servant

William Pigg

Ganado, Arizona

June 19, 1950

Dear Bark,

You don't have to get hot and excited, but I thought you might at least respond to my card. You are, you know, in large part to blame for my "career." This silence doesn't mean you're sick, does it? At our age, one does not want to hear of any maladies in our last remaining contemporaries. Better to be as the young hope we are—bundles of amazing energy who will one day drop tidily dead, with no mess or debts.

I have been observing the young: my Nora Stoddard begged her way up here for a weekend. I like her well enough, even if she is not the brightest creature I've ever met. She is generous. She sleeps to all hours, eats like an army and grows woozily poetic with liquor. I also suspect her of a varied and lurid romantic life. Why not? Those of us who hoped to keep things just so and in their place have little to show for it but a clean, well-lit place.

Anyway, she has asked me to write something for this exhibit she threatens. She has come to the estimable conclusion that taking pictures then was not as it is now, and that I should provide some treatise on the primitive system. This may require that I trace the weird instance of my stepfather Mr. Valance's silver. After all, if he had not been a prospector I might never have been a photographer. So I am writing to you now wanting a damn sight more than a postcard. I want to know what you remember of it all. You *were* the writer.

Would you be up to a trip out here? You could get the train to Gallup—I know that—and I would meet you there. I won't say that it might be our last chance because that sentiment is enough to scare *me*. Just assume as usual that I am out of my depth—think of Langtry!

By the way, we stopped off at Goulding's—Nora S. and I— and you can guess who was there. I didn't give an inch and I nearly got the Irishman to start a fight. But in the end he is too cowardly to throw a punch at me. As you know or must recall, I would lay him out as soon as spit in his spectacles. It's a wonder they haven't flattened the whole valley with their doings. How clever it was of the Cavalry to do all of its maneuvers in Monument Valley, thus avoiding contact with the real hostiles!

I shot a hawk the other day. One shot. You would have grinned, you miserable old bastard—I use that word in the time-honored and technical way, you may be sure.

SG

Bark Blaylock

It was the summer of the president, 1881, a time of heat, long-range agony and of disturbed minds which, fearing the tenuousness of law and order, went about wearing guns; it was a time of woe and anger, of menace and inspiration, when men might resort to the easy purchase of firearms for something to hold on to. Before they are fired, guns are comforters that can fill a nervous hand as well as the rosary, a ten-cent cigar or a pair of aces.

For though it was not known yet in Tombstone, when Bark Blaylock set out for New Mexico with Bill Brocius, President James Garfield had been shot at 9:20 in the morning of July 2 at the Baltimore & Potomac Railroad depot, at Sixth and B streets, in Washington, as he prepared to board a train that would carry him to his wife and some relief from the heat in New England. The man who fired upon him was a Charles Julius Guiteau. Yet Bark and Bill had ridden east with other things on their minds. And, arriving as they did at Fort Sumner in the evening, they did not receive the news. By the time they did hear of it, it was nothing but incidental—or, as Bark estimated, coincidental—to the local death of William Antrim, or William Bonney.

Indeed, there was a time when Bark—only five or six in 1881— was not sure but that it might have been President Garfield shot in the dark at the Maxwell house. And though, a day later, before leaving Fort Sumner, he did see in a newspaper (Bill was seeking to educate him—as if that covered all the other ways in which Bill kept the boy in the dark) an engraving, an artist's representation, of Mr. Garfield in the act of falling, still wearing his hat but supporting an expression of great shock on his face, still Bark suspected that the killing in Fort Sumner (which he felt had come first) was somehow a signal, a spur, to the shooting in Washington.

"My God! What is that?" President Garfield had been heard to cry as the shots (two) were fired. The words were in the caption to the engraving and Bill Brocius employed them in his attempt to teach reading to Bark. For his part, Bark could not see the president's cry as the proper response to bullets entering his body. Surely that shock would be beyond words. No, Garfield's speech was more what a man might utter as, unraveling a mystery, he came upon a clue that began to explain things. These were the two shootings Bark had encountered—in the sense of someone firing directly and deliberately on another—and so he could not see how they failed to be associated. Moreover, his ride with Bill seemed to have had as its great purpose their discovery. And so the general excitement, or agitation, in and around Fort Sumner became for Bark Blaylock a kind of elation, as when a child believes he may be beginning to understand adult things.

There was even more controversy and arousal in Tombstone when they returned.

"Now, I don't know, young Bark," Bill had warned on their journey home, "just what we'll find there." So Bark had been ready to take the hint: he had expected nothing less than confusion and suspense.

There was much talk in Tombstone of Earp, Earps and Earpism. It was this town's version of the elusive yet possibly resolving harmony at Fort Sumner between the shootings of Messrs. Antrim and Garfield. Moreover, whereas Antrim was cold dead in the morning,

Garfield lingered—it was befitting the potency of a president, Bark reckoned. Yet in every description he heard the great heat of Washington was very active, sustaining Mr. Garfield while serving as torture for him.

"You see, boy," said the tall, gaunt Ethan he had last seen with his mother, "President Garfield lies stricken in his bed there in the equatorial heat customary in Washington. If only cool breezes could soothe him."

At which point, Bark's mother came rapidly into the room where they were, calling "Earp! Earp!" like a hound.

The tall, gaunt man had stood up to restrain or embrace her and he had said, "Here, here, Mattie," with a great amount of forlorn caring in his voice. So that Bark had felt for him.

And they were residing now, since his return, in a hotel in Tombstone, and it had always been Bark's general, if imprecise, understanding that the Earps were hotel creatures.

Later that very day, Bill Brocius had asked him if he had seen Earp yet, and Bark had said he had not.

"He's fixin' for a fight, I hear," said Bill, full of grievance.

This had not seemed odd to Bark, for surely something like a fight would be necessary to relieve his mother's distress. She was so disarrayed that Bark had to trust she still remembered him, or regarded him as hers. He was therefore the more sweeping in his gestures of affection and ownership to assert that she was his. She observed these signs in puzzlement, withdrawing into herself lest the boy touch her.

"There's more on the gunman," said Bill Brocius, showing Bark the latest edition of the *Epitaph*. The Guiteau in question was a man of thirty-nine, born in Chicago. The newspapers by now had full intelligence of his life of failure, whether in the fields of theology or law. He had passed time in the Oneida community in New York State, and he had been admitted to the bar in Chicago. But without success. He had married and divorced. And in 1881, he had found himself in Washington anxious to make an impression on President Garfield as a writer of jim-dandy speeches. He had also sought foreign service on behalf of his country, and a note survived, written by Mr. Guiteau to the president, that said:

> I expect to marry the daughter of a deceased New York Republican millionaire and I think we can represent the United States Government at the Court of Vienna with dignity and grace.

This offer had not been taken up, and so Mr. Guiteau had purchased a British Bull Dog .44-caliber revolver with a bone handle; and bullets, too. He had been seen practicing with this gun in some of the desolate parts of Washington. Then, on July second, early in the morning, knowing of the president's intentions, he had gone to the depot of the Baltimore & Potomac Railroad and waited in the ladies' waiting room. It had been from that doorway, as Mr. Garfield passed by, that Guiteau had fired two shots.

When apprehended, he had made a muddled statement including this remark: "I have ideas but no reputation." A letter was found in his possession and it had announced:

> To the White House. The President's death was a sad necessity, but it will unite the Republican party and save the Republic. Life is a fleeting dream, and it matters little when one goes. A human life is of small value.

Bark could not but be stirred by these words when Bill Brocius read them to him. It seemed in the nature of such shootings that the man shot had no chance to say anything, whereas the shooter expressed visions of splendid eternity and American momentariness to an attentive crowd. There was, inevitably, the hush that greets the climax of a great performance. Mr. Guiteau had been impelled to give voice to his ideas. Thus the gun: it was a way of commanding attention.

While contemplating these things, sitting on the floor of his hotel room where he was deploying building blocks, Bark saw the polished black boots of another tall man come into the room. Only with this arrival did Bark appreciate that he had been otherwise alone.

"The boy," said this man.

He was dressed in black, and in a black hat, and he had a mustache that was a virulent red color. He wore a gun belted to his side. Bark did not feel intruded on by this man, for the man appeared at ease in the hotel room.

"No Brocius?" he asked Bark.

"I suppose not," said Bark, trying to think when he had last seen Bill. "He told me about the killer," he added, hoping to be of assistance.

The man's hand fell upon his gun, as if a pain had suddenly afflicted him there.

"He took you to the Kid's death?"

"I am the kid, sir."

"You were in Fort Sumner?"

"Oh yes. We crossed the raging Pecos, Bill and me."

"You did?" There was a sneer on the man's face. His heavy mustache jumped with it. "It's shameful," said this Wyatt Earp, "taking a child." He looked down on the infant and, very thoughtfully, he added, "Young Bark."

"Yes, sir?" asked the boy.

"Nothing, nothing."

And the man with the mustache went off to his lunch.

This was Tombstone, now in September 1881—and if the summer was passing, the tension in the city only mounted. One bullet, the papers said, was lodged irretrievably in the president's body. It had entered between his tenth and eleventh ribs on the right side, some three and a half inches from the spine. Surgeons were at hand. Alexander Graham Bell was invited to search for the bullet with electrical devices, but he had no joy. President Garfield was sinking, and in the middle of September it was decided to take him by train to the New Jersey shore, to Elberon, and a cottage there. Was it the journey or the freshening sea breeze that did it, or was the fact of death as immaterial as Charles Guiteau had said? Garfield died on September 19.

In Tombstone, Wyatt Earp did not fail to see the lesson in the summer of 1881. This was a fearsome land where the natural virtue of opportunity, of man's honest ambition and his search for power, wealth and happiness, could be struck down—out of the blue—by demented loners whose only credential was failure. These were reckless and irreligious souls able to stand up out of the darkness and nowhere pointing a gun in accusation and rebuke.

There was a need for lawmen to see those pointing hands before they fired. Thus, in New Mexico, the taciturn Garrett had managed to anticipate that monstrous rogue and wild-dog killer, Billy the Kid. This Wyatt Earp was of a dullness of mind that longs for inspiration and which had known so many outrages to his dignity—the decades of failing to unearth gold or silver, which the lucky few derided as a lack of character or the loss of God's favor; having to witness on a moving train the bestial coupling of man and woman with such disregard for others that one or both of them might have fallen from the train, causing a delay in the schedule; and having to endure the surreptitious remarks of the Clantons that his wife was a whore and the Barclay he had been ready to regard as a son was nothing but the bastard of her infamous trade.

O wronged Earp, betrayed hero!

This Wyatt Earp held on to his guns and knew that the moment was coming. The spirit of retribution, the imperative of gunplay, was in the air. He could smell it just as surely as surgeons detected the odor of death in the fetid Washington bedroom as the heat passed so slowly outside.

He practiced and he began to tell others that the name was spelled E-A-R-P.

Matthew Garth

"I regret, Mr. Garth," said Frances Braxton, "that you should have come this far to find sad news awaiting."

There was something demurely prepared in this handsome woman. It might have given warning of her intuition how—after the letters reporting the deaths of Nadine Groot and Thomas Dunson— there was worse to come, in the sense of immediate vexation.

Matthew Garth was touched by Mrs. Braxton's solicitude. Ever since meeting her, out there in open country, and as she had conducted him to the Braxton house, with explanations that her husband was away, to the north, exploring *et cetera*, he had been affected by the quiet firmness of the lady which had not hidden, but rather had seemed to guide him inwards to a waiting warmth and tenderness, a readiness to address his pain and trouble. How he yearned for some attentive softness into which he could deliver himself.

"On the trail," he whispered to her, in the very large hallway of the Braxton house, his eyes still fixed on the two letters that had been there waiting for him, "I had to kill a man." He wanted to say more, but he was so dependent on implication, that liars' music.

Frances Braxton was more moved than she had been in nine years by this nearly instant and barely audible confession from a stranger. She cried quietly on discovering that certain depths of sentiment and compassion still existed in her; she had thought that in the windswept ranges of Montana they had dried up. She knew—and this was her vital conclusion, erroneous as it may have been—that there would be no second chance of such a burdened, insightful and sympathetic man finding her in that wilderness. So alone and so removed, a person becomes mightily attuned to signs: there is no stopping that religious moisture rising.

"I am sure it had to be done," she said, laying one hand on his arm.

"Oh, it did," he assured her, and he saw the tears in the corners of her eyes, shining in that hallway in the afternoon like dusky pearls. This woman was in exactly the best light for his mood and need. He felt boulders being slipped away from his conscience; he felt ease and gratitude with this beautiful light-trap of a woman. He could see in the sere illumination that came through the leaded glass door that she was angelic.

"Your hand," she asked—she saw everything. "What has happened to it?"

He felt her cool touch, tracing the heated sprawl of his hand.

"I broke it on the way," he said, "and it healed as best it could." It did look like a tangled root system, embarrassed by being pulled out of the earth.

Frances Braxton, before her marriage—as Frances Reid of Virginia —had had nursing training. She had been, aged eighteen, a nurse to the Confederate wounded at Chancellorsville. (In years to come, she and Matthew Garth may discover the likelihood—no more than that—that they were in Richmond, together but unaware, for a month in 1863. But that comes far too late to interfere now in Frances Braxton's great need for a fateful, destined meeting. It is her salvation, after all; there is time yet for her to learn the cruel vagaries of chance, and see whether she can still smile at the comedy.) So, now, in 1879, she felt his disfigured hand and wondered if a rebreaking could restore order. She could not doubt the suffering in such an operation, or fail to see the new healed strength in the crooked hand. And this was a time when people were more prepared than they are now for both suffering and irregularity.

"My God! What is that?" said Matthew Garth, taking two steps back.

For as his concentration slipped away from the letters, and moved to Frances Braxton, standing in the enchanted soft halation of 4 p.m. in the hallway, he appreciated a massive force of nature reared up behind her like the wall of a canyon or the face of a sheer mountain.

It was nature, yet it was a picture, a painting some eight feet wide and perhaps twelve feet high, a painting which, in its ornate ormolu frame (or fencing), required the full height of a wall that went up beside the staircase to the upper floor of the house.

It was a painting of a mountain in which the snow-capped peak took on a peculiar, beacon-like intensity by virtue of the extra light that struck it from a window in the floor above. The mountain, with all its attendant foliage, including a lone deer and the expanse of country that was the foreground of the picture before the mountain thrust up, seemed to have entered the house. This illusion was so complete, Matthew Garth believed he could feel the cold of the snow or that the deer, alerted, looking up over its shoulder, had scented him.

The more Garth examined it, the more there was to see. He went halfway up the staircase, and it was like climbing the mountain. But this vantage allowed him to study the many fine conifers, the narrow steel-backed lake and the yellowed meadow beyond it, as well as the awesome incline of the mountain, the mists it took on as it rose, and the clouds in the sky.

"This is astonishing," said Matthew Garth, for he could see that the great canvas was not just a representation of the scenery, but a picture hallowed by what a man feels about the limitless spirit in landscape.

"It is Long's Peak," said Frances Braxton from below. "That is in the Tetons, in Wyoming, I believe, though I have not seen it."

Matthew Garth shook his head, not just to show that he had not seen it either, but because *this* mountain, the one in the house, seemed undiscoverable in Wyoming, or anywhere else.

"We were lately visited by a gentleman," she continued, "a Mr. Bierstadt, a painter. He makes tours of our Western panoramas, seeking subjects. He has a very large wagon. Mr. Bierstadt worked on this painting while he was here. I should tell you that Mr. Braxton took it into his head to purchase the painting."

"Why, yes," said Matthew Garth, full of understanding.

"For a large sum of money."

"Your husband is an enthusiast?"

"He is an impulsive man," said Frances Braxton with hardly a pause. "Mr. Bierstadt is in quite a line of business," she added. She went to a chest in the hallway, opened a shallow drawer and took out a photograph.

"That is Mr. Bierstadt," she said, handing the picture to Matthew. "He has many copies of it, and leaves it where he goes as a keepsake."

The small photograph was as startling to Matthew Garth as the large painting. For it was a picture of two men, utterly alike, in the same dark frock coat, with the same heavy mustache, sitting together at a round table, the one man pouring the other a drink. The two men in the picture did not look at each other; the one was intent on pouring the drink, while the other gazed away. They were unaware of anything untoward.

"Do you see?" asked Frances Braxton.

"How similar they are," said Matthew Garth. "They are twins?"

"No," she said, and she laughed, just behind him, so that he felt the wavering, musical spill of her laugh. "It is one man. Mr. Bierstadt meets Mr. Bierstadt."

"That cannot be," said Matthew. He was hoping for some law in optics or physics, not just a rule of conduct, that would not permit it. This was not the first photograph Matthew Garth had seen, of course. But every other he had encountered before had been some imprint of identity, a vouchsafe of appearance. He did not understand photography very much better than, say, the Cheyenne. He had been told the process. But he did not follow it, and he cloaked the enterprise in some allowance of the imagination (his limits and its magic) such as he employed for the workings of the steam locomotive, the origins of children and the explosion in a gun that did not blow up the weapon or the hand holding it.

But he had never seen a photograph in which the properties for transmitting the authentic look of things had been made into a fraud or an impossibility. He looked back at Mr. Bierstadt's painting and then at the cunning *carte de visite*. He could not reconcile the two or believe that the same mind was involved. As to the precise way in which two Bierstadts were side by side in one picture, he felt only horror and the itch to destroy as a response.

"This is very wrong," he told Frances Braxton.

"I am afraid so," she admitted, though she could see that his quick fear had not let him work out the fatal connection, the cause of offense that awaited him. In fact, the foolish photograph amused her, in a ghastly way. But Frances Braxton had given up the ghost some while ago, away up there in Montana with her relentlessly enquiring husband.

At that moment, there was an unusual stirring on the porch of the house, a bustle and the shouts of joy of Frances's daughter, Jane, the child who had watched Matthew Garth on their ride in with such respectful wariness.

"That will be my husband," said Frances Braxton.

Whereupon, she threw open the front door of the house to reveal two figures on horseback approaching and the small figure of Jane scampering towards them. One of the men on horseback, the one wearing a smart city hat, had raised both arms to greet her, or to show the child where he was. And then he leaned down from the saddle and lifted the girl up into his arms. It was a gesture of such affection that Matthew Garth was moved at a distance of a hundred yards. While Frances Braxton groaned and beat her fist on the door-post.

"Are you ill?" Matthew Garth asked her.

"To lose one's child," she said, looking dread in the face. How could this woman read his life?

With his daughter perched in front of him, David Braxton came riding up to his front door.

"Who is this?" he called out.

"Mr. Matthew Garth," his wife told him.

"No cattle?" Braxton's eyes widened as if at the prospect of miraculous dispensation.

"They are behind me," said Garth, "coming up from the south. We have lost a few, but you will find them in excellent condition."

"Well," said Braxton, as he swung himself and then his daughter off the horse. He was a small, lean man, unremarkable except for darting eyes that had never found satisfaction anywhere, and which, as a result, could seem devious and unstable. It was David Braxton's grudge against the world that it had not always recognized his search for genius in these rapid eye movements.

"You must come in, Mr. Garth," he said. "My wife is wild for company—aren't you?" His quick eyes moved across her face with the snap of a whip.

He led them into his library and he was pouring glasses of whiskey.

"I have been up in the vicinity of Canada," he said, "roaming and rambling to my heart's content." But David Braxton's gaze and twitching attention gave so little hint of peace.

"The cattle will be here tomorrow," said Matthew Garth.

"Ah," sighed Braxton, and he veered away on an impulse, scanning the books on the shelves.

"Jane, my dear," he asked, "hand me down *Tristram Shandy*, won't you?"

And as the child went up the hickory library ladder, Matthew Garth heard renewed sounds of despair from Frances Braxton.

Susan Garth: On Silver

Being a draft towards an essay on the early career of Susan Garth, as photographer, at the request of Miss Nora Stoddard—on her own head be it—with asides and remarks by Miss Garth and Bark Blaylock, who asks to be known as "a friend of long standing":

I saw some sort of a ghost, that was my start. I don't know how else to put it. Here is what happened, or the best recollection that I can now muster, maybe seventy years later.

We were at that time moving around the western edge of Nevada, seeing that my stepfather, Sheridan Valance
—Where did that come from?
—It was his given name, and now at last he has an occasion for its use as he was in the prospecting business. Not that it was too business-like; indeed, it is a way of life based on the "shot in the dark," listening to rumors, judging whether to trust them or were they blinds intended to send you off directly *away* from the real stuff? A prospector listens to everything, wants to believe, but becomes hardened in suspicion. It is not good for the children who may be around, but that's another story.

Sheridan Valance—who was widely known as "Cherry"—was a prospector especially torn by the calls of curiosity and anxiety. He was convinced that great secret lodes still existed in unmapped spots too quickly dismissed by others. And so he was a connoisseur of ghost towns, which accounted for our being—he, my mother and I—on a tour of the abandoned silver mines of Nevada. What happened there one day in 1875 or '76—it *was* '76, for my mother was heavy with Liberty; a great weight, in truth—must have occurred in Mina, Lida, Marietta or one of those places where there were just a few shacks cracking in the sun. They are mournful sites, for nothing dies as fast as absurd hope. A grave is a somber enough place, but a ghost town can make you reflect on the feebleness of all endeavor.
—What has this got to do with it?
—My Nora will like it; she's got a high-falutin' streak
—Whereas you are plain as a cup of cold coffee?

—Whose life is this? I can give it a touch of color

On that day, as was frequently the case, I was on my own, exploring, and I came upon an entrance to a mine. It was a tunnel driven into a hillside and there was a door shutting it off. This door had the look of being firmly sealed—I think there was a rusted lock. But the door was not secure, and not really heavy. Even I was able to open it.

This, as best I recall, is what transpired: there was a poorly built stone wall facing the door, a support for the tunnel, and it had fallen in some places, leaving holes. One hole exposed a piece of silver: this was not ore but some artifact of silver left by a miner to salt his mine. As I opened the door, with a strong sun behind me, I saw the form of my shape in the doorway become outlined on that piece of silver

—No one'll follow that

—My shadow left a shape on the silver

—The light worked on it?

This was more than a child understood, at that time; yet if I had, it could not have been magic. I believe there were some chemicals in this mine, left over from work, and that in time they had made this piece of silver sensitive. And so, in its primitive way, it took an image. As far as I have read, this is not unlike the first images recorded in France around 1840 by Daguerre and Niepce. It was a matter of getting silver that was "alive" or "active" and then suddenly showing it some light. To this day, that's all it is.

—What's this "it"?

—Photography, you fool

—Say so. You're leaving "it"s around like garbage. They don't have no antecedents

—like a lot of us, Bark, aren't they?

I told my mother, and Sheridan could not help but hear. She, I hope, recognized that I had had some sort of unexpected, informing experience.

—Unless she was boozing

—That was later

He started to work that mine with a vengeance. But the one imprinted piece of silver was all he found there: and he used it to make the handle of a whip. My mother was probably as mystified by the occurrence as I was, but she did what she could to explain the phenomenon to me. She said she believed she had some other old photographs in the trunk, but we hadn't been in there for years on account of there being no key

—My father could have been in there for all I know, dead as
Houdini

—Could still be there!

So she sent off for books, and they did come—maybe it was from
my father, in Texas. At first, this thing photography did not impress
me: for it was a direct impression of life, whereas I felt I had discovered a ghostliness about myself that was already in that mine
there before I got there, a premonition, a shape waiting to be occupied. Which is more stimulating to a child

—You've never believed in ghosts. Why are you pretending
you do?

—This is not ghosts. This is simply wondering if what you do isn't
foreseen.

—That's God, that's worse

—No, it's not God, either, Bark. It's just being open to see how
there is some story there if you can only make the parts fit. And
don't forget my father is somewhat of a ghost.

—He'd be a hundred and ten!

The result of this was a gradual education in photography—or one
as good as my poor life could provide. I should say that I was never
properly taught, and not then able to have fine equipment. For good
or ill, my work has had the flaws of self-education, and the stub-
bornness; I believe if people are ever taken with it, it is because of
the difficulty they feel in it.

It would have been when my stepfather had moved us on to what
was then the boom town of Bodie, in California. This had streets
and a crowd of people, and they were hauling the metal out so quickly
they left holes people would fall into. Bodie was all very well, but
you could drown in the snow—this happened to kids I knew—and
I still believe I can tell someone who lived a spell in Bodie, for they
are leaning over from the wind and do not bother to listen to anyone.

It was there that my mother and I made a camera for me. We got
a good box and an old bellows from the blacksmith so that you could
fold it up. My first pictures were collodion plates, and not many,
since they were hard to come by. But the whores in Bodie liked their
pictures taken, and I got a few damaged plates from the man who
did it.

—I bet he did "it"

But harder still was the way of working, for one had to develop
those plates while they were still wet. I made many a hash of it, and
Cherry said he could not understand a kid persevering in so many

disasters. Moreover, the trouble in my right hand would be no help either in the delicate operations.

—And whose fault was that?

—Yours for having a hard head

In Bodie I was a spectacle of general entertainment as I would trek around the town trying to carry all the equipment as well as a developing tent and chemicals that were likely stale or the wrong ones: I got pictures that looked like modern art!

—They'll know that's a joke?

There are stains on my hands I cannot get rid of from that time, and some acid burns. Very likely it was the folly that appealed to me, though I can still recall the satisfaction in getting one good print at last. I have a few of those still: the hills around Bodie; the desert flats in Nevada; and a few people, including one of my friend Bark's mother in Death Valley the year before she killed herself. It was after she had done it that I looked at the picture and realized maybe I was supposed to see what was going to happen.

—Everyone knew it was going to happen

—No one did anything

—What could we do?

—I could have shown her the pictures. For she can't have known how she looked

—Would have scared her to death, on the spot

Now, I know today how far the lovers of photography treasure the romance of the wet collodion days. I have seen the wonderful, adventurous pictures of William Jackson up in the Tetons with his boxes and his tent; and the mules that had to carry all that stuff over mountain passes; and the man with the camera perched on some pinhead peak in Yosemite, with a black cloth over his head, unaware of the drop and the bear, looking like Buster Keaton. Let me tell you, cameramen were lost, dragged down by the weight of their load. And if you have never had to pick or blow dust off drying collodion before it dries, you do not know purgatory.

So, it is all very well to attribute just the popularity of photography to Mr. George Eastman—"You press the button, We do the rest." For myself, I think he rescued the young and decidedly imperiled art from its terrible handicaps. Don't tell me we didn't have more time to think about pictures when we could pay less attention to the hazard, the burden and the dust. You do not today see any purists maintaining their allegiance to wet collodion and a wagon-load of materials. There may be beauty or the resonance of history in some of those pioneering views, but you should remember we had no choice.

—You never had to take the pictures

—No, we didn't

—You haven't said why you did

—It's not a thing I'm comfortable with

—Comfort! Good God!

I think I was fourteen when I got my first roll of film: it was a paper roll with a gelatin emulsion, and there was no need for it being wet. A few years later, my father, Matthew Garth of Texas, gave me the first proper camera I had

—Why do you tell that lie now?

—Same reason you tell any lie whenever

and it took the Eastman rolls. Or rather, as I now recollect, it was my father's second wife, Frances

—I should hope so

who was active in this. It was she who was the first person I knew—though I did not meet her for some time—who had some appreciation of photography. She sent to Rochester for the camera; she mailed me books and pictures by hoity-toity Stieglitz and Curtis so that I had something to aim at.

Still, I am drawn to reveal what might not be noted, and which I do not understand even now. I took pictures, I daresay, because of the wild places I saw and because the means for taking them were at hand. But I was never an enthusiast. From the very first moment, on pushing back the door of that mine, there seemed to me something in the light so quick and vanishing as to forbid the taking. This disquiet has never left me. I am not sure that when my form appeared in the silver it was not a warning as well as an invitation. It is always so hard to read the full consequence of a new prospect. Just so, in our West, there is no beauty without wildness, and the greatest beauty may depend on being never seen.

—That's done it

—I hope so

—She can't like that

—I don't mean her to

October 26, 1881

Camillas S. Fly had been out very early on that day, taking his cart in the direction of Huachuca in order to obtain scenic studies of the sunrise (for delivery to his man in Poughkeepsie).

He had run short on sunrises in the desert, which were also one of the most favored subjects for miners in Tombstone who wished to send some information or impression of the locality to their dear ones in all the Eastern strongholds of family and civil optimism. Better by far to overlook the squalid streets of Tombstone and the jostle of unwholesome people on its sidewalks. Those Easterners wanted something new and idealistic. Send graven images of the Biblical desolation of the spot; these were so much more reassuring to those left at home to wait and wonder.

Thus the miner in folklore was a solitary enquirer, a pilgrim with a spade, with just a mule and fickle fortune as his associates—not a rodent scratching at the ground, poised to tear at those others whose bloody claws glittered with the precious metals.

Camillas Fly believed that the Lord had put these metals underground so that decent people should not have to observe the evils of mining, and so that the burials might be a little easier. Miners were a nasty, filthy, crawling race with an unhindered sense of envy that should be locked up at night and given food only so that they might be diverted from eating one another. He knew it was the duty of those in mining towns who were not miners to stay above the vicious beasts, to set them an example, and, ruthlessly, to keep them in order. Camillas Fly's own contribution to this campaign was to provide them with artistic visions of Arizona and becoming portraits when the oafs could be shaved, dressed and propped up long enough for the exposure.

Never a complacent man, Camillas Fly was disgruntled this day because there had been clouds at dawn that competed with the grandeur of the sunrise. He would have to go out another morning, and the mornings now were colder than he liked. So he returned to Tombstone, to his appointments, conscious of his own problems, that high state of middle-class concern on the frontier.

Miss Josephine Marcus was doing everything in her vigorous initiative to rise to that level of American manners, and so she had arranged to have her photograph taken. To that end, she had spent two months endeavoring to lose weight and polish her complexion; and, by dint of self-effacing economies, she had enough money to purchase a dress at the Fashion Saloon just opened on Allen Street.

This photograph had several purposes: to send to her parents and her sisters, as evidence that she was well and doing well, not just alive but ascending—there should be an air of aspiration and fine prospects to the picture, something, Josephine imagined, of the subject, herself, adopting a very positive, not to say pert, attitude.

Then she would see that Wyatt had a copy of the picture, in a suitably sentimental frame, so that anyone in and out of his hotel quarters could recognize a staked claim. For this Josephine Marcus had just detached Wyatt Earp from his wife: and takers know how quickly taking can be managed, and what infectious thoughts it breeds. Therefore, it was important that the picture have an appeal—an allure, perhaps, a seductiveness—that might fascinate Wyatt Earp when Miss Marcus in the flesh was having her dowdy days.

But more potent than either of these purposes was Josie's *own* need of a photograph. How did a person know whether she was making a mark in the world if she was, so to say, entirely shut up in herself? The photograph, that extraordinary mark of progressiveness, permitted an extra intelligence, the point of view outside oneself, a way of re-forming one's appearance and directing one's impact on the world. Josie Marcus was not a good actress—not on the stage; but she had an acuity of mind that noticed how well performing served in life. And she perceived it in photographs. So she was sitting for her character.

As for Ethan Edwards, he carried his desire to rescue others like a rock. It made him strong, but it fatigued him, too. The strain told in his stooped shoulders and lined face. This force of effort was everywhere, and Ethan was not sure it stopped short of madness. He had felt the terror when he came back with Deborah, the dread of ending the search. So when he had handed over the girl, he knew he could not go into the house. He had looked in, from the threshold, then turned away and gone back into the fire of the desert, confident the door would close behind him. How many other children must there be, out there, for the finding?

This West of America was full of stories of the very young taken in raids, by the Comanche or the Cheyenne, and brought up in the tribe and the tepee. Then there were the young who in the commotion westwards had become separated from family, boys and girls who had watched parents starve, children who had come later on the train only to find no one to meet them. Did parents fade away? Did they give up their young as they struck out for themselves, for the luckiest strike? Was the way West an opportunity for escape, for freeing oneself of all limitation?

Wherever you looked, there were foundlings, orphans, the lost. There was no way this land of opportunity and challenge could ever furnish enough searchers to go after them. But Ethan Edwards had only ever felt ease, or a use for his power, in seeking the lost young. For he was as moved by the picture in his mind's eye of a waiting child, as he was by the ragged red rock columns in southern Utah. He was a hard man—he had always been told that. And he had spent so long in remote places, on his own, that he knew he was not comfortable to others. He had heard people call him mad, and he was not offended; he was curious about the possibility, for he had never much admired the things or ideas others thought normal. But he could make tears just by thinking of a child out in the desert, steadily walking to keep from terror or dismay.

He wanted to save Bark Blaylock. Not because of any character he saw in the boy. He did not know how to look into a child, and he saw nothing in Bark but the numbness that seeks to endure shock and alteration. No, Ethan wanted to save Bark, because Bark was there. There was no reason to search again. There in Tombstone, in 1880 and 1881, he had come upon the plight and opportunity of this boy who might be Wyatt Earp's son but who was being discarded by Earp as the lawman exchanged his fading wife for a smart, dark-eyed showgirl. Not that there were not other notional fathers in contention, a large enough circle for Ethan to gain entrance. So he would have the boy's picture from Mr. Fly, to show young Bark he was a personage, a being who counted, a champion as Bill Brocius had called him. They had an afternoon appointment at Fly's Gallery, and Ethan gave the boy a bath.

And Camillas Fly was striving to persuade Miss Josephine Marcus she looked her best with her long, dark hair down.

"I see it," he said, closing his eyes to suggest the fineness of the conception, "as like a shawl."

"Ah," said Josie. She had her heart on it piled up, but this was daring, and didn't Wyatt himself like it when she swept the length of her hair across his body? Didn't it tickle the marshal?

"This wouldn't seem abandoned?" she asked Fly.

"No need for that. The composition can be ethereal. You would be like a muse."

Josie didn't get it yet; she didn't really understand the approach until, days later, she saw the picture. But this Fly intrigued her, and she did admire photographs that went beyond mere accuracy. (It could also get her parts, perhaps, if she ever went back on the stage in something more than bloody *Pinafore*.)

Moreover, Fly was now arranging her, and it was a not unpleasant sensation. He sat her on a stool beneath the skylight; she could see how well her red dress looked. Then, gently and artfully, he took out her pins. In a moment she felt the silent collapse of her long hair.

"My word!" sighed Fly. There was no doubt about it.

"I must brush," she decided. As she did this, Fly set up his camera and perfected the composition. He talked to her to keep her sweet.

"I hear, Miss Marcus, that you will be marrying our marshal?"

"Fifty-fif," she said.

"It will be an adventurous life, but a model."

"Well," she told him, in time with the brush-strokes, "I like the traveling sort of man better than the kind that sits back in one town and writes rows of numbers all day. I prefer a little excitement."

"And excitement is so worthy a cause," Fly agreed, noting to himself the complete inability of the dense Earp to add up even a short column of figures.

"Yes," said Josie piously. "Wyatt is a peacemaker. Which is what we need."

She tossed the hairbrush on the floor, eager to be complimented.

"What do you think?" she asked Fly.

"I believe you should raise your head."

"Uh-huh," she said, looking up.

"Now, lower your eyes. Regard the camera as your slave. Be an empress. Now, still—thank you."

Josie's languid aplomb met the brass lens cap, the cap came off and Fly counted under his breath to fifteen before returning the cap. Josie Marcus had not wavered or aged; for fifteen seconds, she had held back time, and she just knew she looked grand.

"You must give Mr. Earp my compliments," said Fly.

"I will," she promised. "We're having a celebration dinner to-night."

"And the object of celebration?"

"Don't know," Josie remembered. "He hasn't told me yet."

Josie was winding up her hair, preparing to go out on the streets again, when the door to the gallery opened, and there stood a man and the boy at the top of the steps that came up from the corral.

"Aha," said Josie, "aren't you the little boy?"

"Yes, ma'am," said Bark.

"I heard about you," she told him.

"He doesn't know," said Ethan.

"Mr. Earp knows," Josie assured him.

"Mr. Earp," regretted Ethan, in his slow, wondering way. Bark took his hand with a mind to consoling him.

"Well, I said 'Hallo,' didn't I?" said Josie to Bark, tipping up his chin so he would look at her.

"Yes," she added, "you've got Earp eyes. But then, Mister," she turned on Ethan, "so have you."

She went away in a pretty flourish of skirts. Bark did think she was very lovely, and he had not minded having her look into his eyes, for it gave him the chance to examine hers.

"You want your boy pictured?" Fly asked.

"That's it," Ethan said, with surprise. "My boy."

"We'll do him as a fine young Earpist."

"No," said Ethan. "Sitting in that chair." He pointed to a high-backed chair with a red velvet seat.

"Unsuitable," said Fly. "Too big by far for a boy."

"In that," said Ethan.

"He'll look like a dwarf."

But Fly put Bark in the chair anyway. The boy's legs were far from the ground.

"Put your hands up on the arms, Bark," said the tall man. Bark did as he was told.

"See what I mean?" murmured Fly.

"I like it very well," said Ethan.

Bark observed the argument. He looked up at the windows and the roof. He liked the white light that filled the gallery, though he was a little afraid of the box that stood on three wooden legs. From time to time, Mr. Fly would go behind the box and study it.

"You waste my skill, you realize," said Fly.

"How so?"

"My experience, my eye, may I say my vision?"

"You can do it?"

"Do it?"

"Take it?"

"Any fool can expose film. The knowing when and where is the refinement."

"He's only a boy."

"Very well, Mr. Earp."

"What did you say?"

"I said, 'Very well.' "

"You take me for an Earp?"

"You're with the boy."

"Very well."

And Camillas Fly fussed all the more with his set task, just to show the subtleties. It was in taking that extra time that he did not get as far as doing the picture. For there came the sound of gunfire from the corral.

"Don't go out," said Ethan. "You'll get yourself shot."

He stood at the door, looking out through the small side window.

"What is it?" demanded Fly, crouching as low as he could, looking up past Bark, high now in his chair.

"Earp," said Ethan. "I believe he has done for some of those boys. There are bodies in the corral."

Matthew Garth

"Sir, would you be wanting *Tristram*?"

He was startled by the question, and the austere, straight gaze of the child asking him. What was her name? Jane. She was the only other person up. It made everything feel stranger. For Matthew Garth had come down at his usual time to find the downstairs silent and empty. The dawn came in misty and he had watched the shreds of it moving across the fields. He wondered if he would see his own cattle, lumbering, oblivious and bulky, dark meat coming out of the skim of morning.

The child was fully dressed. She must manage it herself. These were odd ranchers who were not working yet. The little girl was waiting for a reply.

"What did you say?" His first words on any day now seemed torn from his head, like a bandage sticky with blood or pus.

"*Tristram?*"

"I don't know what that is."

So the child went to the library ladder and up to the eighteenth century. She presented the book to Garth.

"I'll make our breakfast," she said. There was a solemn look on her face, unsmiling, yet claiming him for company. He reckoned her for being independent but lonesome.

The girl stepped out to the kitchen. He could hear her feet on the stone floor, and the muffled clang of metal. Matthew Garth considered the book she had selected for him. When he opened it at the title page, he saw a picture of a man in a wig with a large nose, a pointed face and eyes like a hunting animal. It could have been Braxton, he thought.

He entered the book and found matter that was both familiar and disconcerting to a habitual rider:

> A man and his HOBBY-HORSE, tho' I cannot say that they act and re-act exactly after the same manner in which the soul and body do upon each other: Yet doubtless there is a communication between them of some kind, and my opinion rather is, that there is something in it more of the manner of electrified bodies,—and that by means of the heated parts of the rider, which come immediately into contact with the back of the HOBBY-HORSE.—By long journies and much friction, it so happens that the body of the rider is at length fill'd as full of HOBBY-HORSICAL matter as it can hold;—so that if you are able to give but a clear description of the nature of the one, you may form a pretty exact notion of the genius and character of the other.

Garth could not grasp this, but he had an uncommon inner tingling—as if electrified—that his system *knew* it. He turned the pages further and the binding of the book fell open where some prior reader had slipped in a photograph. It might have been to mark a place, but when Garth assessed the picture he knew that *it* was the heart of the matter and that this *Tristram* was only a hiding place for it. It was a picture of a young woman in just her drawers, turned towards the viewer so that her breasts were evident. There was a look on the woman's face that seemed to say, "I know you're there."

Matthew Garth was reminded of that evening in Wyoming when Cheyenne Joe had drowned. Hadn't he felt then the occasion for some stimulus to his self-manipulation? Hadn't he, in his innocence of such things, tried to conjure up an image, like this, now before him, complete and obedient, obliged to keep to his clock?

"Will you take eggs and biscuit in the kitchen, sir?" He slapped the book shut, but he knew from the girl's prim gaze that she had some premonitory intelligence of what it was about.

"Well," he said, standing, "you are likely to be an ideal wife one day."

Jane Braxton tolerated this awkward flattery. But he could only suppose from the small, tenacious courage in her face that she had no high estimate of being a wife.

The child's parents did make their appearance, an hour after she and Garth had disposed of the studious breakfast. Braxton laughed a good deal at being forestalled, whereas his wife said she had every reason to trust Jane's capacity to look after a household. But as soon as she was able, Frances Braxton took Matthew Garth aside for urgent talking.

"Mr. Garth," she said with the asperity of one determined that the point shall no longer be obscure, "other arrangements could be made." She was shaking.

"I beg your pardon, Mrs. Braxton."

Now she was vexed: "If prior agreements are not met."

"Yes?" He felt an unaccountable temper arising in this confusion.

"I believe I might be regarded as compensation," she hissed.

"Damnation!" he roared. There was nothing worse than feeling the coils of the unintelligible dragging you down. But she was miserable at his anger.

"I am so wretched," she cried.

"My good sir," called the melodious voice of Braxton from another room. "I see your stock coming, like a flood lapping over the hill."

Frances Braxton kept watch on the two men as the day went by, and the cattle filled the view from the windows of the house. By noon, Braxton and Garth were sitting side by side on the top rail of a paddock, watching the cattle come. She could see Braxton's wiry body heaving with twisty laughter, boyishly exhilarated at the spectacle of his new herd. Then, with scarcely any other movement, Matthew Garth's arm swung at Braxton, toppling him from the rail. It must have been a mighty blow for those cowboys nearby—Garth's and Braxton's alike—were fixed upon it and on the prospect of hostilities. Matthew Garth got down from the rail, spoke vehemently to the prostrate Braxton and then strode into the house.

"You did not tell me this," he said, with bitter outrage. "Not again." He had been afraid of Cherry Valance; he could admit that to himself. But Braxton had none of that menace. He was a fool who deserved punishment.

"There must not be violence," said Frances Braxton. "Your men and ours do not know why. We disgrace ourselves if we fight."

Garth was astonished by this remark—was there, after all, some higher cause that could condone cowardly reluctance?

Braxton came into the house, rubbing a swelled face, but laughing to himself still.

"You are a humorless cowpoke," he said. "I was afraid of that all along."

"Oh yes?" asked Garth, too agitated to be still. "Well, I have read your *Tristram*, let me tell you that!"

"Yet you are full of spleen," said Braxton. "It is a very simple problem: I do not have your money. You can wait until I am rich again—it will not be long these days. Or, I daresay, you can lead your poor cattle all the way back to Texas!"

"Be quiet!" Frances Braxton ordered him.

"Are you saying so?" asked Braxton.

"No money," said Garth. "How is that?"

David Braxton's arm came away from cuddling his battered face and pointed upwards to the mighty Bierstadt painting of the mountain. "I paid for that," he shouted proudly, as if hoping the words would carry to anyone high up on the mountain.

"How much?"

"Twenty thousand dollars. A bargain," said Braxton with glee.

"He cannot take the cattle all the way back," explained Frances. "I will go with him."

"What's that?" asked Braxton, for the first time interested.

But he had no answer, for Matthew Garth had added to the complex transaction: "I will take the painting."

Mrs. Braxton groaned involuntarily. "No," she said, imploring, catching hold of Garth's arm. "Me."

"Good Lord," said Braxton, very quietly now, an irresponsible man, but not unaware of nice moments. He looked from his wife to the painting, and back again.

"You may come, too, as you wish," conceded Garth.

"You had better take me," said Frances Braxton, white with panic. "You will look the fool otherwise. Accepting a picture for a herd!"

Matthew Garth could follow this calculation: in his head he heard such talk, conspiring against him. He looked at the woman and the painting. "It has value," he supposed, nodding up the stairs.

"Even so," she gasped. "Say it was me."

He smiled at her and shrugged: she knew the life it meant.

So there was no gunplay up there in Montana in 1879, and the Texas herd could relax in their new pasture. The painting was taken down and, at Braxton's learned instruction, carefully garbed in water-proofed canvas before being loaded on the chuck wagon.

"Measure it against warping," said Braxton, quite riveted by the craft.

Will Powell remained in the north, to father outlaw preachers. A silent Frances Braxton packed one bag, spoke briefly with her daughter about some necessary visit, and walked out of the house. The cowboys were stunned to realize they were turning round so fast. But she insisted on a start. The woman walked about, as violent as an Indian in a dance.

There are hours of madness in sane lives, hours when insurrection takes over and calls itself freedom and courage. Frances Braxton could not pass another night in the house, straining for the sobs of her child. So they rode off, with her hearing screams that would carry to Texas as faithful as migrating birds.

James Averill, 1950

It was a dominating necessity with James Averill that he be always busy, overextended and driving himself to take on new things. This may have been, in part, the resolve in a very wealthy man to keep ahead of the guilt that can come from privilege. He had a daydream of dying en route, in the saddle or in a cockpit of action—so that people might say, admiringly, he never stopped or took it easy on himself: James Averill was always looking for a better America. (And a new girl, he added, quietly.) Not that he intended dying.

There was another advantage in a ridiculous schedule. No one had any hope of checking on him. He was famously late, and just as notorious for his indignation if people assumed he had forgotten a meeting. By no means, he insisted: just because he was late didn't mean he was less determined, or that, in the enforced extra time, he hadn't seen a new, unexpected approach. He loved surprising people—and so they gave up relying on him. In this way, his chronic busyness became mythical. And so, in the flux of meetings, arrangements and hurried restaurant phone calls, he could more easily squeeze in attachments and rendezvous that pleased him not just because women pleased him, but because they were secret, not in the "book" his secretary kept, but his alone, comically contrived and so unbelievable it was easier for him later to guess they hadn't happened.

He conceived of this maneuver, and he loathed the cynicism as much as he could not live without it. So he labored to maintain a true openness to all things: he read everything; he kept up so his heart might burst; and he talked to strangers. With his two children above all, he showed a youthful appetite for ideas, events, phenomena and prospects which he believed was the most educational influence he could have on them. His son was still very moved by it, though Sally was shrewd enough to see how tiring and how manipulative it was. Which is not to say she was unmoved. But she was older, and aware that a parent who needs the child's admiration has enough of the lost soul for the wise child to keep a distance.

Let us observe twenty-four hours in James Averill's life, from June 1950, to take an example of his frenzy.

On this day, in the family house in Vermont, he is up early enough to spar in the backyard with his son, watched by just a tethered goat and the modest, verdant mountains. It is a robust session in which Jim Jr. is encouraged to hit hard, if only to test the new red Everlast gloves his father has purchased. They work up a very good sweat which they sluice off in the pond a half mile from the house. James's schedule is such that getting to and from this pool has to be done at a run.

He makes their breakfast (scrambled eggs and bacon with muffins) and then drops Jim Jr. off at his school on his drive to Boston. This he manages in time for an 11:30 meeting of the Averill Trust, followed by a lunch with three bankers and a newspaper editor at which far-reaching plans are discussed, and everyone agrees that if anyone can do it, James Averill can.

From the lunch, he goes to the Houghton Library to meet the gaunt, young, female librarian who knows about his father's papers. With her, he establishes to his own satisfaction that his father must have had a warm affair in Wyoming around 1890 with a whore named Ella Watson.

"You're not disappointed, are you?" the librarian has asked.

"Good Lord, no!"

"I expect James Averill reckoned he was entitled."

This leads to a kind of goading small talk for which he really does not have the time, but which is her entitlement, he allows, before he takes off her spectacles and puts them down on a cold metal

radiator, hikes up her skirts and takes her there, in the stacks, noticing once as he breathes deeply that the papers of James Garfield
are within a foot of his pounding temple. It amazes and gratifies him
that the librarian is left all atremble, and so he gives her another
twenty minutes and buys her tea.

That sacrifices the early flight to La Guardia he has hoped for, for
he vows he owes himself one restful hour. So he takes the later flight,
and Sally is impatient and unruly at the hotel, waiting for him.

"Dad, you really should keep your dames on time," she tells him.

He merely grins at her, letting her think she is a smart-pants,
guessing that if he argues she will know there is something to it. So
he buys her a Chinese supper and then rushes to Birdland where
he tells her how to listen to Charlie Parker. He is so enraptured with
the hectic music himself he never notices young blacks giving Sally
the eye.

Later, from the hotel, he calls the librarian and tells her he has
been thinking of her. He waits long enough to know he will be
waking her, and she is duly impressed. Then, for two hours, he
reads Willa Cather's *The Professor's House* (which his wife has recommended) before retiring for the night.

In the morning, he takes Sally to the station and puts her on the
Boston train. Then he sends his son a cable:

"SAW JAKE LA MOTTA LAST NIGHT. THINK HE'S SLOWING. LOVE DAD"

He makes it up and loves the game.

In the cab to La Guardia, he finishes the *Herald Tribune* and from
the airport he telephones his wife, gets her secretary and leaves "Just
love." Then he gets on the flight to Albuquerque, estimating that
there is time to finish the Cather book as well as consider how to
handle Nora Stoddard.

PART TWO

That Summer, High and Blue

1881–82

In 1881 and '82, there were fifty thousand miles of railroad west of the Mississippi River. One hundred million pounds of barbed wire were being sold annually to section America. The first electric power plant was opened, in New York City, and there were sixty thousand working telephones in the United States. John L. Sullivan won the bare-knuckle Heavyweight Championship of the World. Charles Darwin, Garibaldi, Emerson, Longfellow and Dostoyevsky died; Stravinsky, Henry John Kaiser, Franklin Roosevelt, Samuel Goldwyn and champ-to-be Jess Willard were born. Jesse James and Tsar Alexander II were shot and killed, the first by Bob Ford, the second by a group calling itself the People's Will. *Iolanthe, Ghosts* and *The Portrait of a Lady* appeared. The word "horny" was coming to mean "sexually aroused" as well as just "angry." I was eleven, eating it up.

In Tombstone, in Arizona Territory, in the aftermath of the October 26th shooting outside Fly's Photographic Gallery, Sheriff John Behan (who had until recently been the beau of Josephine Marcus) arrested Wyatt Earp and John Holliday for the murders of Billy Clanton and Tom and Frank McLaury. Virgil Earp was relieved as city marshal.

The trial was held amid bitterness and dispute; the factions in Tombstone had such an earnest willingness to give the best testimony that no evidence can be deemed reliable. But Justice Wells Spicer did order the release of Messrs. Earp and Holliday, and though he censured Virgil Earp for enlisting armed help to go up against the Clan-

tons and the McLaurys, he admitted, "I can attach no criminality
to his unwise act. In fact, as the result plainly proves, he needed
the assistance and support of staunch and true friends, upon
whose courage, coolness and fidelity he could depend in case of an
emergency."

The verdict was published on December 1, despite the testimony
of Sheriff Behan that the Earps and Holliday had fired first on men
who did not want to fight after Wyatt Earp had challenged them,
"You s——s of b——s, you have been looking for a fight, and now
you can have it."

But on December 28, 1881, after dark, Virgil Earp was fired at on
the streets and badly wounded; and on March 20, 1882, while playing
billiards, Morgan Earp was shot and killed. Thereafter, Wyatt Earp
and John Holliday made a campaign against the Clanton-McLaury
faction, killing several others, including—it was said—Curly Bill Brocius. Yet no body or trace of Brocius was ever found in Arizona, or
anywhere. It was during this campaign that Wyatt Earp saw fit to
quit Tombstone. With Josie Marcus, he headed for Colorado and a
fresh start.

But during that winter of 1881–82, apprehensive that anyone
looked on with less than kindness by the Earps was in danger, even
warned by a fugitive but amiable Bill Brocius, or simply persuaded
that Tombstone was no place to raise a young boy or care for a
disturbed woman, Ethan Edwards took himself, Mattie and Bark
Blaylock out of the town and headed gradually west, coming by
halting stages into the southern spike of Nevada where, variously,
there was said to be silver, space, the epitome of liberty, and nothing.

On the Red River D Ranch in southwestern Texas, Matthew Garth
and Frances Braxton were married by a judge making a tour from
San Angelo. At that ceremony, Mrs. Braxton had only to aver that
she was an unmarried woman. Nothing had been done to sever or
dissolve her ties of marriage with David Braxton, except the putting
of a thousand miles between them. But in those times the reach, the
paper and the digestive tracts of the law lagged behind the proclivity
for emotionally truthful but factually false assertions. And so Garth
and Frances were married in a silence that had set in between them
and which observed little more than formal announcements.

Matthew Garth reproached her in his mind for the problems she
had caused between him and Fleur Hickey. On the journey back
from Montana, he had said nothing about Miss Hickey to Mrs. Braxton. He had not even entertained her with some reassuring story of
a woman he had known once in Kansas, the sort of diversion in

which Frances might have felt the graver significance and appreciated
that it should only be mentioned lightly or anecdotally. Matthew
Garth said nothing because he was in the process of denying Fleur
Hickey to himself. He thought that lies might wither and desert him
if he refused to speak. His fierce will was his only companion.

Their train did pass through Abilene, and this steely Matthew
Garth was not above the sentimentality that foresaw Fleur there at
the depot, a lone, hopeful figure, waiting on every train. So he said
they would travel on to Kansas City before going south. This surprised no one: the cowboys had been sober witnesses to Garth's
recent life; and Frances Braxton had no idea that Abilene was a more
suitable or time-honored place for their alighting. But during the halt
in Abilene, Garth was not to be seen. He took that opportunity to
explore the closed freight cars to be sure his Bierstadt was traveling
well. He marveled at it in the dim light available; hiding with it, he
treasured it.

Fleur Hickey did not frequent the depot: she trusted that Matthew
Garth would telegraph to her. She was, anyway, too busy. For her
days were divided between helping to establish a library in Abilene
and in writing her first book—a novel about a young man, so un-
hinged by failure and solitude that he makes an attempt on the life
of the American president. He was a rover and promoter who had
gone West but found no satisfaction, and who then turned back
towards the organizing East in a spirit of recrimination. It would be
called *A Gun to the Hand*, and it would launch her career.

She did notice that Matthew Garth was late; she came to the open-
minded conclusion that something had happened to interrupt their
plans—in other words, she did not blame Matthew Garth, or let her
distress mount against him. Not even the garbled and then gradually
straightened story that came through the Greenwood Trading Company (for commerce is a railway of narratives) convinced her she had
been wronged. Fleur Hickey was not a person who lapsed easily into
that anxiety. She was a great idealist, but she retained a large respect
for chance and things she could not know or understand.

She waited longer for a letter: for there was also the matter of
Groot's burial, and she knew she was indulging her lover in not
regretting the lack of some acknowledgment or thanks from him for
that.

In the spring of 1881, she decided she had waited long enough,
spurred by the news that a New York publisher had accepted *A Gun
to the Hand*. (Oh yes, you must recognize that she had in no way
capitalized on the shooting of James Garfield. She had anticipated

it, having written her book in 1879 and rewritten it twice in 1880. It was the shadow of prescience—no matter how ominous—that gave her special impetus and encouragement. For in July 1881, she would feel that she had heard America's secret breathing.)

She went south herself, moving by way of Fort Worth, Austin and San Antonio, coming to Uvalde first and then to Del Rio, a pretty town on the bank of the Rio Grande. From there she sent a gently enquiring letter to Garth, mentioning nothing of affection or desperation, but allowing that she was in the locality.

Letters in those days could not fail to be noticed. When the delivery of mails is irregular, arrivals are events. Frances saw the letter come and marked that Matthew Garth said nothing about it: this was hardly less laconic than keeping one's peace if a tornado struck the house. She did not question him about it: she had learned it was more diminishing to have to confront his refusal to discuss personal matters. As so often before, her eyes rested on the doorway to the parlor where, years before, Tess Garth had recorded the growth of her daughter Susan—of me. There was an unsteady column of short black horizontals and a date written on them. The column stopped at thirty-eight inches in the spring of 1874. Frances had been in Texas long enough to dream this was the same measuring scale she had made in Montana for her Jane, a scheme that had stopped at some fifty inches in 1876 when Jane felt too mature for its continuation. But the parent never grows that far up. In Texas, Frances Braxton Garth had traded grief for hope in me, whom she had never yet met. And so I benefited, and another woman in Montana—one I never saw—what of her?

In truth, Frances had better hopes of what she and I might be for each other than she had for rekindled paternal feeling on Matthew's part. If ever he looked at the lines of growth on the doorpost, it was as if he was noticing scratches in the paint and planning a fresh application.

So when, two weeks after the letter arrived, Matthew Garth declared he would go to San Antonio to sell the Bierstadt, Frances asked him to get a camera while he was there which could be sent to his daughter as a gift.

"You will sell off the painting?" she asked.

"I have decided, Mrs. Garth," said he, examining her face in a rather belligerent, testing manner. "I am a businessman, after all. Once you have made up your mind to be rich, one's policy is very clear." And he thrust his hand forward, cutting the air in the ranchhouse, as if he were a pathfinder in the Rockies, or Kit Carson in Bierstadt's panorama.

"You might be richer if you kept it."

"I hear Mr. Bierstadt's stock is already falling. If only the canvases shrank with it."

"I believed you liked it."

"I did," he said, and then, more sorrowfully, "I did." He could not forget how he had been used.

Matthew Garth went to San Antonio in the fall of 1881, his wagon lifted along by the huge sail that was the painting. There was a westward wind that nagged across Texas, and he would raise the Bierstadt to collect its force. The few people he met marveled at the apparition of mountain snows surging across the dry sweeps of Uvalde and Medina.

He was free of the picture in San Antonio, but only for ten thousand dollars: Mr. Bierstadt *was* past his prime. There was a German down from Fredericksburg who pronounced himself thrilled by the painting, and he added to the ten thousand dollars a new hand-carved wooden bed in the form of a sleigh which he had brought to sell in the city. Moreover, the German was able to advise Garth on the best camera to buy, for he was himself an amateur photographer.

Thereafter, Matthew Garth went directly and as quickly as the heavy bed allowed to Del Rio. He had it in mind to present the bed to Fleur Hickey, it being so evidently a site for lovemaking that that activity might not have to be requested in words or burdened with larger examination.

Fleur was most moved to see him, and delighted by the workmanship in the German bed and the bold sweep of line that gave it the effect of prow and stern. She did perceive the way the bed was meant to smother doubts. But, in writing, she had come to love words and her confidence with them, and she was no longer content with passionate silence.

Which does not mean, there in her small house in Del Rio—made smaller by the ship of a bed—that she refused lovemaking. But she entered into it as from a few feet away, engaged but observant. Otherwise, she might not have detected the change in Matthew Garth.

"What is that?" She held his penis delicately. Between her thumb and forefinger there was a sore, about the size of the new nickel. It was red and it was moist from suppuration.

"What?" he asked. He would not take his eyes off her. He had refused to notice the damage to himself, or its inflammation. "You mean my hand?" he said, and he raised the bunched knuckles so they were in front of her face.

"This," she said, and she pressured it a little so that he had to wince. "What is that?"

"I hurt my hand in Wyoming," he said absent-mindedly.

"What did you do there?" Fleur was afraid of an answer.

"Went north," he said, smiling.

"You should see a practitioner," she said, and she pointed to his penis.

For the first time, with care—indeed, with reverence—Matthew Garth studied the chancre on his penis. He knew it had grown.

"Poor thing," he murmured.

They made love: she shut her eyes—duty had begun and she could feel how close she was to punishment.

"You will be here," he told her, "in sweet Del Rio. So I may always visit."

He went back to the ranch, and Frances sent away the camera, to Bodie in California. But I had already left there, so the camera had to pursue me as we went south towards Death Valley where I would meet Bark Blaylock. This was in the early summer of 1882, and it was so hot in the valley I was sure we had got there in error.

———————

1950, Plumbing

Nora Stoddard has been as proud of her silent ingenuity as she is horrified and fascinated by the block. There is a part of her revolted now whenever she remembers that her toilet is . . . stuffed up? Impossible? Yet another side to her, the wayward veering, has let the congestion wait, or grow. That macabre patience sometimes lifts up the lid and contemplates the stricken, coiled mass—just as the upset lady pours disinfectant and perfume on the mess. (These two unyielding sisters watch together as the turgid stew foams and colors.)

She takes adroit leaks, and she is a strategist of her own modest dumps. There are the bathrooms in the museum, airy adobe cubicles where she has always repaired with *The New York Times* or *The Ring*. She has visited her mother's bone-white bathroom, in Shinbone, and she has sat on the lip of eternity in Susan Garth's outhouse. There

are the challenging, dank places at the backs of bars. By standing on
a chair, and then putting one foot on the draining board, she can
squat over her own kitchen sink and let the beer out. And she has
always liked to pull over on the highway at night, mooning the lights
of passing traffic. This is New Mexico, the West, and people go when
they have to. It is more principle than biological mechanics.

So, for a week, she has managed to live without her own plumbing.
This has led her to reflect on how the old-timers made their arrangements. The movies are eager to have you think wagon-training had
been hard, but they show no latrine carts bringing up the rear. Those
boisterous cavalrymen were always sneaking booze, but never taking
a leak. Nora wonders what the scheme was when a wagon train
stopped at night. Were there designated bushy areas, and pissing
orders to avoid congestion? Was it men one side of the trail, and
women the other? Or was this performance so natural then that some
communal naked witness was taken for granted, and thus ignored?
Were there waterworks in the frontier town, or was the West an open
sewer? She has heard how, in the desert to the south, where they
have exploded the bright new bombs, they have wired that section
off because the ground there now is so filthy, so poisoned. She smiles
to think of old-time Westerners in the desert, close to death from
thirst, finding a bucket of water and using it to wash away their
morning shit. Where does it all go? Is there ever a chance that that
river running through Goosenecks will be just a piping system, flush-
ing out the West's excrement?

Anyway, she says to herself, grinning in a sulky way, it isn't her
fault, that sweet stink in the bathroom. It is this Jubal's fault. She's
called him. He's said he'll come. But nothing. Susan Garth may have
recommended him, but he is probably another piece of that New
Mexican white trash, swaggering hombres who hang out at saloons
and are likely on the run for shooting up road signs. But on the
phone he has sounded a funny guy, and Nora Stoddard has never
learned in her European exposure and her Eastern education how
to ignore the laughter of a handsome thug.

"So, where are you?" she asks, when she has had a beer and got
him on the phone.

"I came by."

"You did not."

"Weekend."

"I didn't know you worked weekends."

He chuckles. "Yeah. Ladies like to use the bathroom then, too,
you know."

"Why didn't you leave a note?"

"Note?" His voice is dreamy and speculative, touched by the suggestion but not persuaded writing ever helps.

"I still have my problem," says Nora.

"I'm coming." Stop nagging.

"Now?" She is unsettled by this suddenness.

"Sure. You want?"

Do plumbers work at night? Is the rate then exorbitant? Does she have to get dressed again, stop relaxing? On the other hand, this whimsical fellow maybe has to be taken on the spur of his moment.

"O.K., then," she says cautiously, and she hears him put the phone down. Of course, if he has come by at the weekend, he must know where she lives. But she isn't sure she has ever given him the address. Wasn't he going to call before he set out?

It is after nine before he arrives: leaving quickly, he must have then delayed—as if something else has come up, or just to make her wait.

"Jubal?" she asks at the top of the stairs.

"Here he comes," he laughs. He is narrow in the hips and wide at the shoulders, with long dark hair, like a Navajo but not one. He comes up the stairs lithely, drilling through the space, so all she hears is the clank of his bucket and the tools inside it.

He has a battered Stetson and he keeps it on in the apartment. Without asking, he noses around under the guise of having to find the bathroom. Nora stands and watches him: she has put on jeans and a tee-shirt for him.

"Hey," he says, smirking as he comes to the one closed door. "The powder room?"

He makes a play of opening the door with servile care, in case the Queen is in there cutting her toenails. Then he stops and looks back at her over his shoulder, hit in the face, askance and startled.

"How long you left it?"

"I went away—I told you."

"This is high," he says. He puts his bucket down and dares her to come into the bathroom with him, to join in the smell.

"It's all me," she tells him from the living room.

He takes out a pack of cigarettes and lights up, to combat the smell. As an afterthought, he offers her one. It surprises her, but she takes it, and he keeps the match going in his cupped hand for her. The cigarette is stronger than she likes, but she blows the smoke as far into the bathroom as she can.

"You just left it?" he asks her. He is guessing the maneuvers needed to get rid of her own personal waste. His eyes trace the furtiveness. "Not healthy."

"Educated people," she says, "never can take care of themselves." She resents his interrogation, but she believes her answer.

He looks at her as if she is insolent. "You educated?" is what he says.

"I went to school."

"That don't keep your john clear."

"It's a fact," says Nora. "Can you do it?"

"Bet I can," says Jubal. "You don't want to watch."

"I don't?"

"I got to get it out." He makes feeling gestures with one hand to suggest the kind of work.

Nora is inclined to watch, just to see if this toughie pukes, or is lying to her. And maybe she ought to know how to look after herself better. But then her phone rings, and as she turns to it he tosses an old sheet on the bathroom floor and picks up a wrench.

It is James Averill on the phone.

"Oh, yes, how are you?" she says. Jubal has left the bathroom door open. "It must be late where you are."

"Eleven-thirty," he says. "Railroad time."

"What's that?"

"Before we had time zones," he says. "It was called railroad time, originally, because all over America there were different times, and the companies wanted to make it clear what time the trains left."

"I never knew that." It seems an odd thing to be talking about. She hears Jubal grunt, and there are heavy swimming sounds from the bathroom.

"I'm coming out to see you," he announces.

"By train?"

"No," he laughs at the idea of such slowness. "I'm flying. Tomorrow."

"I'm so pleased."

"I thought I should warn you. In case you weren't there."

"I'm glad you did."

"I'm at a hotel in Santa Fe. I'll call you."

"Oh yes!" She is shouting, she realizes. "How exciting."

That is that: thank God she is getting the bathroom done! She puts the phone down and notices the receiver is damp from her perspiration. James Averill! For how long? He hasn't said. Yet, she has the impression she is to be on call. She'll have time tomorrow to get the pictures together. She wonders which hotel? Or what time his plane arrives? At Albuquerque, so maybe he is hiring a car? Should she meet him? She has been too happy to be sensible. Will she fuck him? Of course she will, she knows; but that is not the question. The question is much more the timing, the attitude to it, the long-term implications, the relationship, the funding, even . . . the prospects.

Jubal is standing in the doorway holding his bucket. It pulls his arm down.

"Done," he says.

"Oh," she says, standing up, and having to glimpse the contents of the bucket. "You were fast."

"If it's not fast," he grins, "it means you gotta take it apart."

"Yeah?"

"I have to get this to my truck," he nods down at the bucket. "I'll be back, tidy up."

"Want a beer?" she has the wit to ask.

"I'd like that," he says on his way out.

She gets the beer for him, but he won't touch it until he has completed the job.

"There," he says. "Take a look."

She scans the bathroom: it seems cleaner than it has ever been. The john sparkles, and the water in the pan is worthy of a certified oasis.

"What was it?" she asks.

"Shit and stuff," he says, into her face.

"What I thought. Anything I should do?"

"For what?"

"In the future. As a precaution." It is inane, trying to impress this guy with how diligent she will be. She feels like a housewife auditioning for an advertisement.

He looks at her and at her tee-shirt. "There's this great bar I know," he says. "In Glorieta. You wanta go out?"

"Tonight?"

He mimes perplexity; why ask if not now?

He hasn't said what she owes him. Is this the bill?

"It's late," she apologizes. She has James Averill to think about.

"Yeah?" He seems younger and abashed.

"What do I owe you?"

"You don't owe nothing."

"I must."

"No. You're a friend of Miss Garth."

"That's not right."

"You're not her friend?" He is grinning again. It is his game.

"I hope I am."

"There you are. You come out with me some night. Some other night."

Nora laughs at this. It is easy enough to put it off, and even if it comes to it, he is so hard and knotted she could keep awake, and better still—she sees now—he is a boy, in awe of her, not hard to keep in line.

"What's your name?" she asks. "Your full name?"

"Jubal Valance," he says, putting a stress on the last syllable.

1882–95

Death Valley in those days was not kind to the legend of American fatherhood. Old-fashioned paternity was like the water there, treasured in its absence. But I have come to appreciate what a woeful task fathering is, and how much discretion and sympathy is required in children if men are to keep trying at it.

There were two families sweating there in the heat, and several tortured fatherings on show. I had the merest recollection of my authentic father, Matthew Garth. For I had been only three when Cherry Valance lifted my mother out of Texas, and we had no portrait for me of a daddy. Had there been one, no doubt, the oaf Valance would have used it for target practice. And, as time passed, he might have hit it.

My mother, Mrs. Tess Valance, as she had become, was not unwilling to talk about my father. She did not bother to make him a scoundrel or a monster in my eyes. It was easier to regard him as a nullity, since Valance did such a complete and observable job as beast. My mother was forgetting Matthew Garth: that looseness of memory is obligatory if you have exchanged an overly inward Texas rancher doggedly approaching wealth for a self-deceiving, hopeless Nevada prospector whose eyesight is going. (The eyes are traditionally favored for the lighting on glints of gold or silver in the slurry that is the prospector's daily fare.) Cherry Valance needed spectacles, but he clung to his own code of robust health more, so he knocked into things and imagined plots laid against him.

But I knew of Matthew Garth from the letters sent me by Frances, his second wife. These came with gifts of prodigious expense and utility, gifts that educated me and changed my life, packages from a stranger I could never repay, unless the lady eventually liked my pictures.

Frances Garth gave me extensive news of my father, most of which, I decided later, was invented, as much for her benefit as for mine. This epistolary father was a man she longed to know. His busyness accounted for why my father was not writing himself. He would, Frances promised, very soon, next month, at Christmas, when he returned from San Antonio or his current trip to Mexico.

He had expanding concerns: not just cattle, but railroad stocks, barbed wire, property and so on. He never did write—or not until the very end. And I decided it was because of his hand. This intelligence came as one of those confirming echoes from a nether world I chose usually not to hear. But in one letter—in '86 or '87, I think —Frances mentioned his "crippled" hand. This was not long after I had broken my hand on Bark Blaylock's head: and I assumed it was the same hand, the right, in both cases. Of course, I was not prevented from writing, despite some imperfect healing. This was a kinship with my remote father, a chance resemblance, yet I felt it more than all those characteristic affinities like the calculation of minds and the uses of hope.

I do not say I felt deprived. Not at all. For I had determined, very early on, to eliminate that sickly tendency. I have had no weakness for pity, and I may be alone because of it.

Valance, too, was a father, but his nastier inclinations were not hard to divert. He was disposed to be a stepfather with a heavy tread. Yet I learned early how explanation, or any lucid utterance, baffled and dispatched him. If you had a capacity for whole sentences, you saw little of the man. In my opinion, it was this that made my mother more absent-minded and vacantly cheerful as the years went by.

There had been a time, I know, when she was a lively and snappy woman. "I was a heller once," she told me, with such a melancholy fall of her head. She had left a wagon train to go after Matthew Garth; and then succumbed to the fleeting allure of Cherry Valance, some moonlight in which his grin shone. But in keeping company with this new husband, she had had to make herself subdued, long-suffering and hardy. She had had to live with her rash decision. How good for all of us that she could do this without becoming morose. Instead, a rather foolish, indifferent gaiety becalmed her.

My stepfather was also able to console himself with real fatherhood and a son who never threatened his faith in action rather than words.

This clunk of a boy was born in the town of Bodie in 1876, and he was named Liberty to honor the year and its celebration, but also because, like other wastrels, Cherry Valance reckoned he had rights on everything, so that "Liberty!" was his watchword.

As to Tess, more of the turbulence was taken out of her in having Liberty. Not that he seemed her child, or she his mother. I never felt a call for jealousy. But he was like rapids that ran through her river, and then later when you looked back the river was placid again, flatter and reduced. Liberty exhausted her, and made the river less than it might have been.

Then there was Bark's kin, the Blaylocks, until his mother killed herself. This woman, named Celia or Mattie, looked to me a goner from the time I set eyes on her. She was largely left alone, as an invalid, and she could not abide heat or sun, which made the valley an ordeal for her. I never saw signs that she knew where she was or what she was doing. She had a way of wandering off—and that's what took her finally. She would start up conversations that had no bearing on anything anyone else had said, and she had tenacious fits when she would smash anything to pieces. I lost a camera like that, one of the first of the Kodaks.

As I said, she would go off, and we found her dead from a fall in the area now called Zabriskie Point. I have little doubt but that this was by her own volition. In her last months, Mrs. Blaylock was of a misery not to be witnessed. It may have been the unhappiness of her existence, or it could have been a small change in the composition of her brain. We are vain enough to weigh and ponder the former, but our organism is fragile and it takes many knocks.

Her man in Death Valley, Mattie Blaylock's, I mean, was Ethan Edwards, a majestic fellow, somewhere between prophet and scarecrow. I don't think they were married, and he made no direct claim to be Bark's father (one of the few!). Yet he raised the boy, did surely care for him, and fostered his hopeless romantic principle of affection. This Ethan was the man in our Death Valley. Though older, and not always well, he could have handled Cherry Valance had it come to a struggle. That it did not tells you my stepfather was of the same opinion. So Ethan protected us (from everything except nature, heat and himself), and even I sometimes thought of him as "Uncle Ethan," an address that annoyed him and could bring on one of his scowling rages.

He buried Mrs. Blaylock. He repaired our houses. He worked in the borax mine. He took charge of the schooling we had, what with the books and magazines sent by my stepmother, Frances. He was the law in our end of the valley. He was a fine man for children growing up, for he acted the part and knew how to bestride an empty, God-forsaken landscape, how to stand in the wind until the brim of his hat curled, how to command a doorway and walk in his ruminating way across open ground. I was forever trying to photograph him; he caught and schooled my eye. But he was quicker than my shutter. There was some rare, enigmatic spark in his living motion never there in stills. Not that he helped. He hated to be photographed, and was the first person who told me those stories about Indians saying cameras stole men's souls. Whereas, of course, the horrible news of the camera is that we have no soul anyway, just our spiffy skins!

Ethan took time with us. He played with us: we had a baseball in Death Valley—no bat, but bits of timber we broke in pieces playing. He was not an understanding or easy man—he told me one evening how that had been burned out of him in the war and on some decade-long rigmarole of a search he went on for his niece. That evening in the valley, I did not know how far to believe him: it was a confused story. But he was not one who practiced lies. Not like Valance, who did nothing else. That does not mean Ethan only told the truth. But he wanted to pass this story on, and he must have thought I was fit for it. I wasn't then. Maybe I am not entirely now. But I must count Ethan as one more sad aspect of the fathering urge, for he had rescued this niece of his from the Comanche out of longing for a child. And maybe he should not have done . . . not in the long run of consequences.

The identity of Bark's real father was one of our best games. That might have ruined Bark, and I'm sure I was more cruel to him than anyone, because I was closer. But I think it only encouraged his surety that there were big things far away, riddles to be solved, and a pattern that involved him. Ethan talked about Wyatt Earp. He pretended to be Earp in ambush and shoot-out games. He had a black coat he wore to be Earp, and a horse-hair mustache that fell off if he started to sweat. I don't know that anyone ever told Bark, one hundred percent, Earp was your father. There were other names—you had to suppose that Mattie Blaylock had known men. And "Uncle" Ethan never ruled himself out, or never made himself less than the male Bark could trust, or listen to. All of which is prelude to the loss of trust that's bound to come. So Ethan likely wasn't Bark's father, but it was with him Bark saw through fathers. And that's a service.

Now, I have known people squirm on my behalf hearing I grew

up in Death Valley. Don't take that name to heart. A man died there in 1849 when a party of travelers got lost. But only one died! And if places were named after death—instead of Concord, Lincoln or Springfield—why, everyone would come from Graves. And probably fewer people have died in Death Valley than wherever you're reading this.

No, those were grand days. You can get used to the heat, and learn to abide by it. There is water enough. After that, there is just a dry air and an absence of germs fit for a sanitarium. Who knows, maybe silence helps you live longer? There's plenty in Death Valley, so you can hear your toenails growing sometimes. It's gorgeous, too, in that infinite, stark way, a photographer's dream—yet days so clear you put the instruments down and behold the light.

The society we had! The burros, the snakes, the Gila monster! Mrs. Blaylock did not last, I know, but a madwoman is an inspiration to kids. Tess was a good dancer who could hum while she moved so you never noticed the absence of an orchestra. Every day there was some farfetched joke to tell about Valance, and the challenge of seeing just how many prospectors' rumors he would sniff after. His Liberty was a punching bag we all made use of: I never heard of kids really close without them having that sort of stooge or idiot. And Ethan was our boss. Surely he had come to the valley by intention: his travels would have discovered it years before. He knew the extreme place it was, and he probably thought himself lucky to have us there to play with Bark and box his ears, even if I did rear that boy on wolfish blow-jobs where he feared being eaten whole.

You might have reckoned Bark and I would end up in love. Maybe we did, every day, with time to fall out again before supper. Bark can't have liked having his ears crunched, and he had that over- powering need to think on things out of sight or reach. He would grow weary of a girl at hand, especially one older, smarter, who spat his jism in the dirt. And one who had too much hardness to gentle him truly, too much to let him imagine a me he could not see. I was not lovable, I daresay, or made for it. Maybe I was more deprived than I saw, or maybe I was more like my father than a stranger had any right to be. But in the silence, Bark and I loved each other. If we'd never met, we'd have been the happiest of couples.

1950, Happiness?

Flying over Kansas (Abilene may be below), James Averill comes on this in *The Professor's House*, the book he has determined to finish before landing:

> Happiness is something one can't explain. You must take my word for it. Troubles enough came afterward, but there was that summer, high and blue, a life in itself.

His robust egotism believes any book he reads is secretly directed at him; finding how is his suspense. And he prowls within a book until the entrance appears. Well, there he is, definitely high and blue at however many thousand feet in the droning Dakota, looking forward to what may be an adventure, novelty, new things that will revive him in the way the daily paper does if he has it at dawn.

But Averill gets the point about happiness and how it often keeps to the past, like a golden deer you glimpse in your rear-view mirror, when mechanics and mortality will not let you go back for it. You must have passed so close the deer was immobile with apprehension. But you did not see it—we are so full of ourselves in the present tense, thinks Averill.

He has known such summers; or he has come to appreciate them as he looks back: 1906, riding in the West, no matter that his father was silent and preoccupied; 1910, at Newport, the first year he could crew on the boat; 1922, his junior year at Harvard; 1936, going with Betsy to Berlin for the Hitler Olympics, loving her amid warning signs; and 1944, striking through France under Patton.

Good years, great years—or good enough. There was never a complete relief from flaw, regret or boredom. In 1906 his father had been too melancholy, and in 1910 too absent, to see Jim's development; at Harvard, on the drive to Chicago, there had been the mishap and the girl who was scarred; in Berlin there were the indications one had to overlook to stay and have a good time; and in France, he had lost all his best friends, leaving no one to share the exhilaration.

"So, tell me, Nora Stoddard," he says to her within two minutes of meeting her, "what do you want for yourself? Are you happy? And, whatever the answers, why?"

They are in the bar of his hotel in Santa Fe, where he has invited her on his first evening, for dinner. He looks at her: she is tall enough, and he admires the long legs and the hair that drops down on her shoulders. He isn't sure what to make of that untidy air she has. Is it a mark of the voluptuary, or a kind of loutishness that may be stubborn or difficult? In having affairs, James Averill has detected a repressed, pained beauty that is most fertile. It is a sign of women who feel wronged or excluded; they are avid material. But this Nora has a rangy assurance. She seems satisfied, and surely knows he is assessing her. He wonders if he is happy, or if it is only alertness being there, judging the likelihood or reward of a conquest. He does feel something in Nora Stoddard whereby he will get what there is to be had only by going all the way. The prospect makes him feel old.

"Want now? Today?" she asks. "Or want some day?" She sees a man who does not seem his age, which must be close on fifty. This is appealing, but it leaves some worry—his as much as the viewer's—that he is never going to look properly seasoned or matured. He has the youthfulness of too many interests; it seems too smooth for failure. Maybe money makes him smoother.

"Some day," he answers. "Today's wants I can deal with."

"Just like that?"

"A good meal, conversation, company."

"Suppose I want to go Mexican dancing," she says, not sure what that would be, but seeing Jubal Valance.

His hand comes up, the wrist cocked, as if holding castanets.

"You're unbeatable, I see." This supremacy of his irks her.

"I'm interested in whatever you want."

"No kidding," she sneers. Something in her wants to shock him. She examines his confident face—so open, such a mask.

"A major museum," she begins. "Money—money for me. Places in New York, Paris. A Mercedes-Benz. Zabaglione. Montgomery Clift—"

"This isn't Christmas!"

"—Burt Lancaster . . ."

His eyes widen in a mock-defeated smile, egging her on.

". . . James Mason, above all James Mason, Claude Rains, Richard Widmark," she sighs, as if she might be spent, "and John Ireland."

"What would you do in your major museum?"

"Whatever others don't do."

"Apart from Susan Garth."

"Her house, too, and the canyon it stands on. That country! I would like a museum that was a whole stretch of life, with real rocks, an abandoned pickup truck, garbage by the roadside, next to the wildflowers and a deer. Do you see?"

"Isn't that what life is for?" he asks her.

She shrugs. "So, I'm not a suitable person."

"You think museums are . . . graveyards?"

"Safe. And tidy. All custodians and tasteful skylighting. But if a museum showed us *life*," her hands are out, savage, palms up, "we might realize we need to look."

It is more than he has expected, and more than he can contain in one good line.

"Might be easier," he murmurs, "to get those movie stars for you."

She laughs violently at this, for she has been led farther than she meant to go, and she is sure she has been reckless in lining up that parade of studs. She is grateful for being eased away from her own exhibition.

"What about you?" she asks. "What do you want?" She grins, and then does as he has done. "James Averill."

"I could say I have all I want."

"Why don't you say that?"

"No, really." He tries to keep a straight face.

She grabs a handful of nuts from the bowl on the table and counts them out. "I thought all you had is a lot of money, the Averill tradition, a beautiful English wife, two adorable children. And the freedom to fly off to Albuquerque if you choose. No wonder you look so hunted."

"Do I? Is that it?" He is taken aback by her directness, but intrigued by what she sees.

She has only said it at first, without looking. The thing that leaves him young still is that alertness in looking, or hunting. James Averill does seem, even at his age, to be caught up in a desperate contest, incapable of rest. His gaze is traveling, as progressive as a bullet roving across open ground. "It's an unsettling look," she says.

"I'd like to run for office," he tells her.

She thinks of another jovial fraud, her father, the senator.

"As you pointed out, I have a lot. I have been well treated by fate. But I have . . . energy still. I'd like to be of use."

"You think it was fate?"

"What else?"

"You picked the right parents. The good school. The bank, the lawyers, the club, the wife . . . Natural selection."

"The only one of those I picked was the wife," he decides to say, "and that hasn't entirely worked."

"So you keep picking?"

"I beg your pardon."

"You have affairs."

He doesn't respond, but he carries their glasses back to the bar and gets the same again. She thinks the pause is comic but stylish, until she notices how much she needs it.

"That shows?" he asks her: it sounds like a problematic backhand.

"I was rude."

"Not at all," he tells her. "I had been thinking whether I would, or should, ask you into bed."

"Or could."

"Exactly."

"What did you decide?"

"I thought I had a chance."

She smiles.

"But now . . . you've changed the rules."

"I have?" She cannot follow this.

"You've been honest," he compliments her.

"Well," she sighs, "maybe I don't even get my dinner now."

As if to assure her, he stands up and holds out a hand, showing the way to the hotel dining room. They go in, in single file, and a Mexican waitress seats them in leather chairs. The menus are the size of peace treaties. But they need something to read for five minutes.

"How long are you here?" she asks, when she has decided.

"I was leaving it open. I might ask my son to come out."

"To see the West?"

"He's a terrific kid," says James Averill. "Terrific." And he hears the terror in his voice, as if, for the first time, he is a stranger observing himself, concerned for the peril he may be freeing.

"I'm not easy," says Nora Stoddard.

"The worse for me if that's what I seem to want."

And so there in Santa Fe they eat, without noticing, a fine dinner, for all the world like two independent travelers sitting alone at opposite ends of the dining room, sharing nothing but hope.

1895–96

Do not take us for bumpkins there in Death Valley, not when the world was spinning with its new age. We got about, Susan and I. She was always hearing of places to try her camera on, and I had not forsaken the valor of a lad who had once crossed the flooding Pecos. So we had explored along the eastern edge of California, from Bodie to Calico, observing the three Ms—Mormons, missions and miners—and not much else, except for eagles like scratches in the air. And we had been on a boat down the Colorado all the way to Yuma, as well as tracking in the Panamints and going as far as what would be Los Angeles, which was beginning to be something in the 1880s, with people coming in on the train from Kansas and Ohio saying this was it. Fools. I had seen the sea.

Scotty was always telling me we were unversed—not that we heeded him. Rather, if Walter Scott said something, it was most likely he was hearing how it sounded or selling some project. If that man ever found the truth, he put it in his pocket and shut up so as not to start a rush. But he was a pal of ours in the valley, and he had gone off with the Wild West Show of Buffalo Bill, which was his exact breed of nonsense. Well, he never let us forget, and sent us postcards from Chicago and Baltimore. There was one from London in which he said he'd seen Queen Victoria.

"Don't tell her he did," is what Susan said.

But give him his due, he'd been across the sea: he had an ashtray off the ship. And he was telling us, whenever he got back to the valley, how there was no place like home, but no knowing it until you'd been away. With one thing and another, therefore, we made up our minds to try Texas. It was in 1895 that we settled the plan, and Susan wrote her father to say at last she was going to visit.

Ethan didn't see the need or the reason, yet I believe some old wandering energy of his approved the urge. He talked about Texas and New Mexico, trying to recall old trails. But we reckoned to go by train, especially when Mrs. Frances Garth, Susan's stepmother, sent us two tickets.

"She says it's providential," said Susan. "Says my father was just about to set out to see me. But since he is sickly and we are going there, he'll stay put."

"Don't tell him," I offered, and Susan said she wouldn't.

So here is what we did in the late fall of '95. We went down to Los Angeles to get on the Southern Pacific. You may ask why I went along, and was there anything between us? I went because I wanted to—wouldn't have gone otherwise—and not from any consideration that Susan Garth couldn't have done it on her own. She could have gone to Peru and back, Peru, South America. It was our habit to do things together: we had been all those years in the valley without anyone else, except Liberty Valance, and he would have made a snake and a rat into friends. We were a pair, in our locked, argumentative way. People sometimes picked us as a married couple, just because we had a knowledge of one another. But that knowing can doom matters of the heart. And though as kids she had done dirty things to me, that was only her whim and loneliness. She wanted everything to be her way. We relied on each other, that was our system.

Neither of us had ever lived so snug as on that train, and we had a top ticket from Mrs. Garth, with good meals, sleeping arrangements—to lie in bed on a train, letting the miles slide by like water!—and a drawing room with armchairs. Not to mention the lively society on board, the musical evenings and opportunities for level games of skill and chance. And until I'd had to squeeze past a perfumed lady in a moving corridor, I didn't see how exciting the twentieth century was going to be.

We had a two-day journey, and it was a treat to follow it on the map—out through the big cactus fields to Yuma. Then on into Arizona, all of one day rattling over the desert until we came to Tucson. I was proud there to be able to describe to Susan the proximity of Tombstone. There were other people on the train (commercial men and promoters) pleased to hear about it. So I did a little Scottying, yarning it up, yet not giving anything away. For instance, I did not and I do not like to talk about Wyatt Earp at all, because people give you a wary eye. They have heard too much Earp, and only stories they've never heard before will satisfy them. Which means *new* stories—made up that morning. So they can feel they've heard the hot, new legend!

Then we were in the southwest corner of New Mexico, and I was fondly looking for country I had crossed with Bill Brocius fourteen years before. But the shocking thing was the progress wherever you looked. This once was desolate territory, and now you couldn't go twenty miles without seeing some building and a general air of purpose which—I will be candid—I could as soon do without. Not that I don't wish every man to have his chance. But every man a winner is against nature. A sporting nation needs a lot of losers, and hopes they will be civil.

You could smell Mexico at El Paso. There was a man on the train who had been stationed there a few years back during the last hunt for Geronimo. Susan said she had lately seen a picture of the old chief in his new "home"—in Florida!—leaning against a tree, somewhat sad, but defiant still, and with that mouth like a straight line. We pondered on the steady loss of the wild things of the West— which is proper, though I take the pity as a sign of softness in us, too. Geronimo was likely puzzled we didn't kill him, instead of having him stand for his picture. Susan says she has not done people much because it is too upsetting for them, or us, to look back and see what has gone. Yet I think that decision is also part of her cranky meanness.

It was at Alpine, in Texas, that we came off the train and hired us two good horses for the ride on down to the Red River D. As it was getting on for Christmas, we anticipated some festivity in the Garth household, even if Mr. Matthew Garth might continue indisposed. Susan had one of her best pictures, a far-off view of the Sierras, framed for them as a gift—it was from the two of us.

The size of the ranch was a wonder: we were nearly a day riding from the first wire to the house itself, and there were cattle all over the land, like red sage.

"I surely understand the gifts I have been getting now," said Susan Garth, as we rode along.

"Why wouldn't you be heir to all this?" I asked. I had no accurate idea of wealth then, but any fool could feel the swell of this outfit.

"I don't believe my father has taken any account of me," she said.

I would have scorned that line, yet Matthew Garth was not at home. Frances, his wife, came down the steps of the house towards us, holding her skirt out of the dust and with the other hand up at her eyes shutting out the sun. I never will forget that sight or feeling. Not that she was our kin directly, but it was a powerful emotion meeting her at last. And her so pretty.

"Don't cry, you fool," Susan hissed at me. But I could not stop, and Mrs. Garth and I very soon were in each other's arms soaking ourselves, which is a wonder. Susan stood there, grinning fiercely at us in her suspicious way, and discovering her horse had a problem with a shoe she just had to attend to.

"Your father had to go on one of his trips," Frances Garth told Susan. "I am so very sorry."

So we had our Christmas there without him, and it was a good time. Mrs. Frances Garth was a gracious and kind woman. She told us about her very own daughter who lived in Montana and was married to a rancher named Logan, and how she hoped to see them soon because she was a grandmother. (People lived then with kin in their minds largely.) She had pictures of them: you do see the service of a camera, keeping people mindful. But Susan told me later she believed such pictures only reminded us of absence—she has always had this perverse streak to her.

The talk turned a good deal to photography, and Mrs. Garth showed us newspapers that told about the progress towards moving pictures. I did not see how this was possible, let alone desirable. The two of them had to explain it to me, with drawings and bad-tempered impatience from Susan, that enough still pictures gave an *impression* of movement. Susan had already been reading about this innovation, and she let on how it was elementary—which turned out a joke on her!

In the course of this Christmas, Mrs. Garth said how she believed her husband might be intending to be in Langtry, Texas, early in the New Year as there was a boxing match promised to be held there. She showed on the map how Langtry was only a hundred miles farther east of Alpine, and there was a railroad. So we might like to try it. Now, she was not easy about this. At the time, I considered it her uncertainty as to whether he would be there. But there was anxiety, too, over what we would see. Moreover, Mrs. Garth told us more fully that her husband was no longer strong, though very determined.

"He does not believe enough in doctors," she said. "But keeps it to himself. I would be glad if you would encourage him to see someone."

"Why will he listen to me?" Susan asked.

And Frances Garth said a strange thing: "Oh, my dear, don't you see how very afraid of you he is?"

Susan laughed. She wanted not to understand it. "Why's that?" she asked, as if the man were crazy.

"He believes he failed you."

"He has nothing much to do with me."

"That is failure."

I liked Mrs. Frances Garth very much, and I wished that her step-daughter could have had more benefit of her company and wisdom. But Susan just wrinkled up the skin above her nose—not a pretty gesture—and sniffed at it all.

Anyway, it was in this manner we came to Langtry. I could write you a whole book on what happened there, but you would not believe it. Let me just say that once we were on board that train again, there was no doubt about something happening there. The talk was so excited and exciting it made the fight itself seem momentous—whereas, it was a minute and a half, and lost to record!

Langtry was a spot on the map, a railroad junction that grew most likely out of the crew camp, on the north bank of the Rio Grande. As the place was small, so its potentate was large—in his own head. This was the Judge Roy Bean of notoriety, a bearded, dumpy sack of a fellow, stupid when sober and slower drunk. He had assigned to himself what he called jurisdiction west of the Pecos! This amounted to much ponderous reciting from law books and the hope of luring developers into the area to make it known and rich.

The name Langtry was from the foreman of the crew laying rails. But Bean knew that was too plain. He was a dunce with a flair for promotion, and so he said he had named it Langtry after Lillie Langtry, the actress, for whom he had a wounded fondness of the sort that is blessed by neither party ever setting eyes on the other!

Bean had a saloon which also served as a mock courthouse. He actually asked me to write "a few suitable speeches and sentences with an ominous ring" for him. It was all theatrics, but cowboys would come in from miles around to hear him, thereby giving the saloon some business. I have heard it said he kept a bear, but I never saw the creature. I suspect some strangers saw Bean a way off and just concluded from the smell it was a bear.

In his promoting of Langtry, he had contracted to put on a boxing match, between Bob Fitzsimmons, "Freckled Bob" or "Ruby Red" from England, and Peter Maher, who had been "presented" with the Heavyweight Championship by Corbett when he retired.

On the face of things, Langtry was no place for a big contest. But somehow, Bean had angered the state of Texas, the Texas Rangers and even the government of Mexico so that they all regarded the fight as illegal. I do not know the details, but I am sure this controversy was a cooked-up matter. For there is nothing as desirable or as American as that which has been forbidden.

Bean had a solution: there was a small island in the stream of the

Rio Grande, opposite Langtry, and he was claiming that this island was "nowhere," or what he called "at liberty." The fight would be held there.

We were in Langtry by the end of January, and the fight itself was in a state of simultaneous announcement and postponement, with the telegraph worked to death. Bean was as interested in us as he was in any visitors, and it was plain that he recognized the name of Garth.

Fitzsimmons arrived at Langtry early: he had no doubt taken one of Bean's dates seriously. And he was irked at the delay, so he put out a call for sparring partners. I took it into my head to give it a shot with him, for he was not a big man, only one hundred seventy pounds, and I had boxed all my life, well enough to keep the snarling Liberty subservient.

Let me tell you, I did not fancy Peter Maher's chances. I was quicker than Bob, thank God, and I made him work, which he liked. But he had perfected body punching in a way that was a frequent devastation to my system. He had mottled fists—the freckles and a fine gingery hair were all over him—that managed to find my solar plexus and leave me stricken and unbreathing. But he was a gentleman, and we would take some beers afterwards and talk about fighting, for which I was a happy student. Bob had killed a man in the ring, or had one die on him, and he had knocked out Jem Hall in New Orleans for forty thousand dollars!

"Which they deceived me on," he added, smiling. He was a friendly, casual man, not at all puffed up. I venture to believe he could have fought all day—he was a natural pugilist, with fists like snakes.

And then Peter Maher appeared, in a large party that included a moving-picture camera, some drunks and revelers and sundry showmen, and Mr. Matthew Garth, with a lady and a lawyer.

This Garth, at last, was not taller or more robust than his daughter. He was, I believe, in his fifties, yet he had such gray hair and so ravaged and exhausted a face, with a greenish hue beneath the tan, that he could have passed as twenty years older. He was the sort of man one flinched from touching, as if a rot had gone all the way through him and pieces of him might break off. Yet, if it was illness, it left him trembly and alert.

He saw his daughter from far off, having been advised by Bean as to who she was. I was watching, and I know I saw in him the urge to vanish. But he mastered it and then strode up to her, staggering the last few steps, spent in strength. There was a kind of

impromptu fairground springing up, and he gazed at the clowns and
tumblers as if they fulfilled his vision of madness.

"Well then," he addressed her with a terrible bravado, "at last you
choose to visit me. Only now! Your wretched father!" He was shaking, like a tragedian. "Don't think you will get anything from me
because of it. I am not so rich I can be fed upon by anyone. Talk to
my lawyer, Johnny Garner, he's here. He will settle. I'll give you a
sum, and that'll be final. No more calls on me."

He drew breath. A shine of sweat as gray as quicksilver lay on his
brow. His eyes darted here and there; he could not make them still.
Then he groaned, as if calculating death. "Well," he asked, "when
are you coming again to see me?"

1950, Taking

He has not decided yet if his high spirits are from the air of New
Mexico in June, his encounter with *The Professor's House*—in which,
it seems to James Averill, a dry, settled academic has his cramped
family existence illuminated by a story from the West—or the fra-
grant, dimpled particularity of this Nora Stoddard, lying beneath
him, and rendering up the gasp of fertile earth and flowering if he
so much as moves.

"Can't you rest?" she asks him, for she feels so close to drowsiness.

"Never better," he lies, like a Dracula who itches from the creep
of morning light coming round the earth, but keeps on smiling, to
show off his pink teeth.

They are on the floor of her office above the museum. It is a
Saturday, and they can hear the muffled sounds of visitors looking
at the pictures. The offices are closed, but Nora has her key and has
come in so easily, it is obvious others could do the same. Is that why
he has elected to take her there? Is it the danger; if so, is the danger
more his or hers?

He is examining what he is doing in a way that is not James Averill's
custom with affairs. Years before, more than half his life ago, indeed,
he had worked it out: that there were many women, lovely enough
to be taken, willing, more or less available (that was an argument in
their heads), just so long as the apparatus of consequence was not
invoked. That was how he regarded such matters. A dozen times a

day he felt horny when he met or saw some woman—and every other day or so (he doesn't keep count), the irresistible quickness acts on it.

But he is a busy man who has become the more beset by appointments, details and obligations as he grows older. So he does not have a boy's taste or time for wooing. Once he had hunted, patient and ardent, like a lone tracker, the Blackfoot in the winter Dakotas, going after the one timid deer seen in a month. That was wonderful and enthralling, as well as pathetic. Now, he feels . . . well, he feels more like that man, the engineer, Mulholland wasn't it? who had somehow drawn off another world's water for Los Angeles and said to the city, in so many words, "There it is. Take it." Noah Cross has told him that tale, and they have smiled over it together, rueful but admiring, men of the decisive brigade.

Yet James Averill is no barbarian or robber. Not even Dracula was a rapist: despite their early alarm, his pale maidens always sought the fatal kiss. They gave up the ghost with a will. He despises any touch of brutality, force or bruising; though a connoisseur of speed, he does not think any woman has ever felt hurried by him. Or hurt. Or not for more than a few days, and that is using "hurt" only in its fitful, emotional sense.

There are some pangs: he doesn't intend to excuse himself. But the world builds confidence, history and character in handling those hurts. He is very struck, James Averill is, by Hemingway's proposition that we are all of us hurt, damaged and broken, but that it is where the breaks heal that we are strongest. He has offered this theory to his own doctor, and the man has agreed, there is something in it in the nature of bones.

So James Averill asks women, or kisses them, or touches them. He is very deft: he can read refusal, distaste, disdain, or a truly virginal dread that should not be spoiled. And he can back off with a very expert air of apology or surprise, as if he has been inadvertently bumped in the darkness. He has the best manners he knows, and he does those little dances well. Moreover, most women know who he is; they understand the wealth, the background, the attitudes of heritage. They know they have been at no risk.

Others accede. They smile or fold themselves into his embrace. They like it. They slip down to the nearest decent horizontal surface without dispute; they fall like petals from the rose. And James Averill enjoys that spill of petals on his desk just as much as he does the tight, loaded bud. He is a man for all moods, a collector.

But in twenty-five years, he has detected a pattern, a regularity, that only an idiot would overlook. And he refuses to be such a complacent passenger to time or experience; one has to profit from it to justify one's existence.

As he looks down on the closed eyes of Nora Stoddard, and on the hills of her, all blindly witnessing him, he tries to judge the profit, or the nourishment. He knows one thing—that with any woman it is not the act itself, the carnal collision, he calls it, but the knowledge, of having faced, met, had and known one more mind or soul. The quest is for understanding. And Nora Stoddard is a rarity for him: she is a whole book, instead of a newspaper sensation half-read over someone's shoulder rocking on the subway.

Women have become for James Averill too like their photographs. He has not lost his appetite or his enthusiasm. He wants as many, and even at his age is as able. But he has realized they are alike, so many of them, and in his mind's eye he cannot always recall one rather than the team of them. And although he has nothing against older women, has no doubt but that they know more, have earned irony and humor, and in many cases have bodies free from modesty or compromise—still, he notices that the women he *sees* are all of one age or moment. It is as if his eyes screen out anything but seventeen to thirty-two.

On the face of it, that is ridiculous. How can it *work*? Yet, year by year, he finds it to be so. Not that James Averill meekly neglects other women: he does go farther afield. But only as an act of will, the determined policy that says I will get an elk today, and which involved looking for them, as if they were one particular grain of sand in the desert, or one unique turn in the canyons of Utah. And they can be found, sooner or later: the searcher gets his reward. But suppose he relaxes, suppose he is simply out to enjoy the day, letting life pass before him like sky. Then, surely, it will be one from the narrow age-range that catches his eye. He has decided there is something in those women, something that waits and wants to be seen, some decision whereby they have pressed their beauty, their presence, all to the surface just for the moment of observance.

There may even be a greater severity in the last few years: is the focus shrinking, to seventeen-to-twenty-seven, that unequivocal firmness, the unused hope and defiance, the beautiful vulnerability now evident for the first time in his daughter, Sally? It is an offered secret, a full center waiting to be known—and it preys on him more, and makes him sometimes inclined to pick buds apart, to do away with their hard, intimidating freshness.

But the shift frightens him: for it means he is moving, traveling towards . . . the end, growing not older, but closer to the certain limit, the prospect which somehow all the urgent daily news deters him from seeing. That is knowledge, too; and the quickness tries to fight it, to make it go away.

So he has developed an intellectual bent to his womanizing, or the superiority of someone flying over the canyons in a plane, seeing the passage of all the views and secret places, getting the big picture. He sees that female flesh is a commodity like the cracked ground in Utah, Arizona, New Mexico and Colorado. The beauty is constant: in one it is the mark of youth, in the other of great age. But he has gained the lofty perspective of geology, and it helps him see that in both—the young skin and the ancient ground—there must be some greater mystery, something more worth the knowing than the having or the taking, in an instant, as in a photograph, permits. He is resolute about it, but he is afraid. And he knows that he cannot just take Nora Stoddard and move on, without seeing himself as a demon, or worthless. She challenges him. She is not necessarily the best or the finest he will ever meet: you cannot hold out for the ideal; he cannot wait forever. Sooner or later, he has to recognize an affair means enough for divorce and remarriage. He is bold enough for the battle.

Otherwise, he is only the corridor, the time and the thrill you beauties slip through. He is an old lech, a voyeur, a mere womanizer. One can stop and count one's mercies, of course: any intellectual can see that. But James Averill has been over that before. He is of the opinion that a man lessens himself if, seeing desire's flower and opportunity, he backs off. You have to take it; not to do so is cowardice, denial and a yielding to mortality. Not to live fully is to start to die. America and this West were founded on that.

Now, James Averill knows the objections, the pleas that this can be no more than a justification for piracy, for robber barons, for raping the land, decimating the Indians . . . and so on. He agrees. The challenge requires gentlemen, men of education always ready to question themselves, open to experience and doubt. But the pioneering impulse, the magnificent spirit of exercised liberty, must never be relinquished. Take it, he says to himself, seize this day!

"Here he comes again," laughs Nora Stoddard. "You are something." She is droll and satiric, but she is impressed, too. "We could find somewhere more convenient," she adds.

"This is not going to be convenient," says James Averill, in triumph.

"It's not?"

"It's going to be bloody awkward, and difficult, and painful."

"I didn't think I was that hard a lay."

"I beg your pardon?" Querulous. He is all at once lost.

"You make it sound like digging in under fire."

"Just this, Nora Stoddard. That I mean to marry you, whatever the obstacles, whatever the world says."

"Will the world be bothered?"

"Oh, I think it will, a significant part of it."

"Boston?"

"Not just Boston. The James Averill you see has been approached by Washington."

"Really? Poor James Averill," she strokes his bobbing head. "You should talk to my mother about that."

"Ah yes, Senator Stoddard." Her stock goes up.

"Ambassador Stoddard." Even where she is, prone, squashed by him, Nora conveys the tic and tremor of a curtsy.

"Your mother," Averill realizes. "Is she here?"

"She said she'd be interested to see you."

"I must," he decides immediately, and with a palpable erection of duty that Nora has to rise to.

"To discuss the difficulties?" she asks demurely.

"Well . . ."

"To signal your intentions."

He presses into her. "It's not a joke," he warns.

"Don't frighten her. Just talk about New Mexico and the flowers. She's had a hard time."

"We will see her?"

She nods, but then she has to ask: "Can we go back to my place and fuck in peace?"

James Averill is as touched by the word as by the prospect. He goes with a will, sure of how fortunate a man he is.

1896

That Matthew Garth looked arsenical gray in Langtry
My father was attached to death, dragging its slimy shadow
You regarded him with horror and disbelief
I thought, so this, this is what I come from, this decay.
No one noticed, though, it was all Bob Fitz versus Maher.

He was torn in two, wanting to embrace me but deny me.
He was a man who likely had a constant fever.
Such opposing forces made him shudder so.
But there was no doubting the power or his will.
In the pictures I took he blurs; he could not be still.

There was a woman with him, Miss Hickey, the famous author.
Did you ever see such a woeful, betrayed countenance?
She kept notes of every happening in a leather-bound book.
Writing to ignore the ooze of this dreadful, aching man . . .
Storing up material—I could see how she worked
. . . and the greater dread of his far-reached infection.
I talked to her of writing: she said she had a novel
No need to name her mistress, I asked her what he had
Going very strong—she'd call it *Is This It?*
She took me in a corner and whispered "syphilis."

Then Bean approached you squarely, holding out the box
Why do people think a camera is ready to explode?
He said, "It comes alone, girl, without no operator."
Could I then take charge of the filming of the fight?
I said I would assist you, "Think of this good luck!"
I knew it from the outset: I was a cold, dead duck.
It would be a piece of history, the earliest movie fight
You were so busy chattering, you never saw my fright.
I asked, "Are there instructions, pictures how to do it?"
I told you, Bark Blaylock, you're such a racing idiot.

"Will you be quiet?"
  "Won't you talk to me?"
  We looked at each other across the sealed apparatus—the camera, the black bag, and the cans of film we could not open, or look at, without destroying. We had been there two hours, the likely loading path of the film spiraling with our argument. And all the while there was that fatuous song on Bean's calliope, endlessly rhythmic, drumming up the trade.
  "Think of something else," Bark advised.
  "What'll that do?"
  "Come at it unawares, take it from the side."
  "It's not a cat, you fool, it's a problem we can't solve."

"Sometimes," he reasoned, "if your mind's all clenched up, and you relax it, why, the answer becomes apparent."

"So what do we talk about? I don't know why I brought you."

"You need me."

"Like a headache."

"I'm someone to talk to."

"But do I have to listen to you?"

We looked at each other, held together by antipathy. We were like a model, plus and minus, in a book on electricity: opposites attract, just and only so long as they can beat at each other's brains—it's all Maher vs. Fitzsimmons.

"We could talk about Miss Hickey," Bark suggested.

"What about her?"

"Don't you think, her and your father?"

"Think what?"

"They came together."

"She's a modern woman, and a writer, too."

"But I think she's *with* him."

"Well, I'm *with* you, more's the pity."

"You know what I mean, Sue. I know you do."

"You think she's screwing my pa?"

"Him her, more like. But screwing."

"Spirochetes," said Susan Garth.

"What's that?"

"That's what's whirring around. That's the action. That's what I said."

We sighed in unison and different difficulties. The Texas afternoon wound remorselessly onward toward fight time.

"Well," said Bark, "it surely starts here, goes through there, and comes out here."

"Are you pissing?" giggled Susan Garth.

"You don't seem so pleased to see your father."

"I'm not, I'll tell you that. I could have done without it."

"You'd have wondered. Don't tell me you wouldn't."

"You're the one says wondering's fine."

"It is," said Bark. "But so's knowing."

"What *do* I know?"

"How he is?"

"Just because you see someone, you know that?"

"You pick up a lot."

"And there's a lot I'd rather not pick up, thank you."

"The question is," said Bark, "what the film looks like."

"Of course that's the question!"

"Well, you're the camera person."

"I don't know what it looks like."

"You ain't read about it?"

"I've read, but I haven't seen."

"Seems to me," said Bark, "even if we get it upside down all we do is have them boxing on their heads."

"It does that anyway."

"It does?"

"The image is inverted. In cameras."

"We're going to have to try it," Bark appreciated.

"No. You are."

"Why me?"

"Because it's a matter of putting the camera and the can in the loading bag. And doing it. Right?"

"Yeah?"

"My hand's no good for that." She held up her old chestnut, the right hand, and added, "Your rock of a head."

"Not my fault!"

He considered the problem.

"You could put one hand in the bag," he said, "and I could put one."

"What's the sense in that? We aren't courting."

"I don't know what to do!"

"So study the camera first. Work out the path."

"Talk to me while I do it?"

"I'll hold your little thing, Bark, if you like. While you're tied up in there I could really give you a pull."

"You do, I'll kill you!"

"You don't think it'll help you come at the problem from the side, so to speak?"

Throughout the afternoon of February 21, 1896, people in Langtry, Texas, advanced on the fight, or what had become known in the days beforehand as "the big fight." Judge Bean had assembled a small fleet of punts and skiffs whereby, for a considerable fee, the sporting folk could be ferried across to the island in the middle of the Rio Grande.

Authorities in both Texas and Mexico were making many arguments over the propriety of this, but Bean was above them all and said as how in America no one could obstruct the freedom of people to embark on small boating voyages. It was observed how, very late in the day, some of the authorities themselves traded in scruples for tickets to what was called "Bean-land" or "Bean's Yard," if only to obtain clearer evidence if the matter came to trial.

Even so, there were not a hundred people on the island at the appointed hour. "Not too many," Bark Blaylock said, and Bean turned on him with all the vitriol of a showman pushed to his limit. "Damn you, boy, that's what the camera's for. Millions *will* see it!"

There was the Judge, Bark and Susan Garth with the loaded camera, an instrument they carried so carefully it might have contained a cup of coffee for which they were under orders not to spill a drop. There was Matthew Garth, Miss Fleur Hickey, Garth's lawyer from Uvalde, Mr. John N. Garner, a referee, George Siler, and, not forgotten, Peter Maher and Bob Fitzsimmons, the two of them cracking jokes together.

The ring itself was white wood with canvas stretched over it, and four posts with a slack line of rope making a square. About fifteen yards back from the ring there was an encircling stockade of white bed sheets—no one in Langtry could estimate how Bean had come by so much fresh laundry. On one side of the ring was a platform and a walk-in box. There were squares cut out of its front, and it was through these that a camera and a camera person were to see the fight. That same side of the ring was otherwise unoccupied, with spectators gathered on the other three sides.

"Good luck, Bob," said Bark in passing.

"Put your money on me, my son," said Fitzsimmons.

"Bet on the Englishman, I hear," Bark told Matthew Garth.

"They're trying to have my cash," Garth warned Garner. "Put it all on Maher. He's our boy."

"Are you comfortable?" Bean asked Susan Garth, shutting them in the box.

"I just turn the handle," Susan told herself. "That must be it."

"Is your view right?" Bean demanded to know. "I'll change anything you want."

"Will there be blood?" asked Fleur Hickey, not quite sure whether she was afraid, or ought to be.

"Don't you worry, Miss," called Bob Fitz. "I'll rattle his noggin, but I won't disturb the red stuff. Just spell my name right."

"Ladies and gentlemen!" roared Judge Roy Bean, and as his clarion cry raised stillness and a volley of echoes from the cliffs on the Rio Grande, he fell into a fit of coughing from so exercising his throat.

"If we get it wrong at first," reasoned Susan Garth, "we'll get the next roll right."

"We didn't tell Bob that."

And so the big fight began and Susan started diligently to turn the handle on the side of the camera.

The pale figure of Fitzsimmons darted between Maher and his slow shadow.

"Can you hear it?" asked Susan.

Bark put his ear to the side of the camera.

Bob Fitz feinted with his right.

"I hear the handle."

Peter Maher edged away from the proffered punch.

"It must be going through."

In the late afternoon light, there was a flash like a jumping trout as Bob's speckled left arm struck at the base of Maher's rib cage.

Maher grunted. The crowd moaned.

And Bob's freckled right went in on Maher's jaw with a crack, like a sapling snapping.

"A minute and thirty-five seconds," regretted John N. Garner.

"You can stop turning," Bark told her. "Bob just did him."

"I don't know if it started," wondered Susan. She looked up and saw the mean, blunt eyes of Roy Bean swiveling to glare at his last hope of treasure.

And in the camera, moved, stirred and circulated, but not used or fired, does the glue of silver know there has been failure, or is it gloating quietly, having survived again?

1950, Turning

There are two things going on, two lines of force and intention thrusting into the warm air of the New Mexico evening.

James Averill is visiting the Shinbone house of Hallie Stoddard with Mrs. Stoddard's daughter, Nora. He is a family man from Boston, Mass., out West to look into the possibilities of the Susan Garth photographs. He is at a loose end, knowing no one else, so it is reasonable and hospitable for Hallie to have him over. Averill wishes to impress the mother with his civility, his good sense and his model existence; for he believes that he may shortly wish to present himself to her as a son-in-law and a sound prospect. He knows there is an incongruity, a fissure running between his legs wherever he stands. But he reckons a gentleman and a survivor is nimble and adroit enough not to fall into the chasm. It is a game, he tells himself; and he always does well at games.

There is another shape to the night, a very busy, surreptitious spin of sexual complicity. James and Nora have spent the afternoon like spaghetti—soft, warm, inextricably entwined, in a sauce called love that makes them shine. They have boldly come to dinner after a final, exhausted fuck, without bathing, with sweat and sex crystalline on their quivery thighs. They wonder how they smell in the cooked night air. As they walk to Nora's car, a dog comes up to them with amused interest, its cold nose jabbing at their slippery crotches. And they cannot stop touching now in the Shinbone house, where Hallie trots in and out of the kitchen to the lamb and her salad: they quickly assess the angles of the open, New Mexican design, the timing of a kiss, and plant hands in each other's treasured, fetid places, their faces dark with triumph.

Two things? Hallie Stoddard has two more: she must play the somewhat silly, unobservant mother to permit their reckless play; and she must conceal the inner rifling of things she knows about these two self-confident deceivers, things that might arrest their dance. Should she tell? She may not have to decide.

"Mrs. Stoddard," says James Averill, "I believe my father knew the senator a little."

"Very likely," says Hallie Stoddard. "Ranse was widely acquainted. Far more so than I, of course." It had been Hallie Stoddard's way to leave business and professional matters exclusively to her late husband, Senator Ransom Stoddard. After all, Ranse had been so much more at ease if those affairs of the large world were left, privately, to him. He did not like having to explain himself at the end of the day. And Hallie was weary to death of the pomp and pickled clarity of the explaining.

Hallie has on her best absent-minded air: but with all the pressures gathered there, she can feel a turn taking her, a twist of insight, and a quiet, inadvertent way of maybe forestalling one more of the world's earnest disasters.

"But I do believe I knew your wife's poor mother in London," says Hallie. "She was very gracious to me—I fear I was not the greatest adornment to the Court of St. James's."

"You knew Daisy Lycett?" says James Averill, beset now with

intense interest. For he had never met Betsy's mother and had only heard the most general accounts of how remarkable, amusing and unpredictable she had been, and what a great loss.

"I don't know about know," murmurs Hallie Stoddard. "One feels in such cases, afterwards, that one can't really have known the person."

"How do you mean?" asks James Averill. He is going very cautiously now, for he feels some elusive iron in this apparently unthreatening old woman. He has seen her eyes watching him, and they do not suit the genteelly cramped face. He is being led, he knows it, and if it is beguiling, it is also rather sinister.

"She was so gay," says Hallie Stoddard, "so very active, always looking for new tasks. She moved mountains for War Relief, you know, after 1918."

"I had heard that," says James. This sounds so like Betsy and her high-strung need to take flight on good, sociable works.

"Oh, yes," says Hallie. "She and her friend Clarissa . . . what was it? So many parties. A house full of flowers and people. At the center of things. Ascot, Henley, the cricket—I did like that myself, so very peaceful."

"You watched cricket, Mother?" asks Nora.

"Yes. At Lord's. Have you been there?" Hallie asks Averill.

"No, never," he regrets. "It's winter usually when I'm in London."

"I remember the pavilion, with red brick, dark glass and white-painted wrought iron. Very pretty. I sat at Lord's. Often."

"With Mr. Averill's mother-in-law?" asks Nora.

"What? Oh no!" Hallie remembers. "No, she would have been too busy. Dallowell, that was the friend's name, I think. No, Daisy would have been out and about. Then, one day, poison."

"I did not know that," says Averill suddenly, but she has drawn him close to guessing it. Her bitter eyes bespeak no easy way out. James sees a small vial, tipped into the lovely mouth.

"They never said," she continues. "They don't seem to have to in England, do they?"

"I heard just that she was ill," says James.

"I'm sure she was," Hallie reassures him.

"You mean of disturbed mind?"

"I suppose so," says Hallie, very thoughtfully, as if this has only just occurred to her. Whereas, in fact, she always felt sure that Daisy Lycett had done it clear-eyed.

"This was widely known?" asks James Averill.

"I wouldn't know." She leans forward. "I haven't upset you?"

"Not at all. One always wants to know."

"Oh, do you think so?" asks Hallie, full of an old lady's fastidious interest.

"We have to know, Mother," says Nora, hushed but brave enough to beat a way into this secret society.

"Really?" Hallie sounds full of doubt, yet too polite to argue.

"You can't bury things," her daughter tells her.

"Well," says Hallie Stoddard slowly. "I'm not against burying. It would have helped your father."

"Mother, you're wicked," says Nora. "I knew you were in a mood to tell one of your stories. Out with it."

"With what?" Hallie's eyes open in poised alarm.

"Whatever you mean to tell."

"I don't know what you mean."

Nora smiles at James Averill. "Mother is Norwegian, you know, a land of tales told at the fireside on winter nights."

"You're sure you're fit to hear?" Hallie asks her, as dry as ice.

"If she's not, I am," declares James Averill.

"Oh, Mr. Averill," laughs Hallie quietly, "I wouldn't have you bored."

"Why have I come to the West if not to hear the old stories?" he demands to know.

"Well, it's not for me to say what brings you here," she says politely. "Who ever understands such things?"

"Mother, you must tell. I will never speak to you again if you don't," says Nora Stoddard.

"Oh, too much temptation," says her mother, with an eerie wistful chuckle at the foot of her voice. Averill tries to recollect what he has ever heard of Norwegian witches.

"Well, you know the great fame of Ransom Stoddard? Himself?"

"Senator and ambassador," says James Averill.

"Here in New Mexico," Nora explains, "it's the shooting. He once shot a desperado, Liberty, whatever he was."

"Is that what you call him?" asks Hallie. "Poor fool is all. At any event, yes, years ago, before Ranse was famous, when he was just a lawyer—"

"I did hear about this," Averill believes.

"I expect you did. He shot this so-called outlaw—a rowdy, a drunk, a man who would not buckle under. Out on the streets. Just like the films. But he didn't."

"The man wasn't shot?" says Nora.

"Oh, the man was. Dead all right. But it wasn't Ranse who did it. No, there was a friend of ours, Tom Doniphon—he lived in this house. But I've altered it. Enlarged it." She waves her small white hands at the house surrounding them. They realize it is listening, too. "Tom did it. He could shoot. Your father's prowess with firearms was limited to starting races and firing salutes."

"That's wonderful!" cries Nora. "The whole thing was a fraud?"

"I don't know about that." Her mother has flinched from the word. "It was a kindness on Tom Doniphon's part, and it surely helped New Mexico become what it is."

"And Ransom Stoddard?" asks Averill.

"Him it ruined," says Hallie.

"Ruined!" the girl cries out. Averill now hears in Nora's voice the same grim foresight he had felt a little while ago.

"Didn't you ever notice he was ruined?" Hallie inquires. It is the tiny woman who is the killer.

"He was a politician," says Nora. "I knew that."

"He was a public figure," Hallie answers, without mercy.

"What does that mean, Mother?"

"There was no private man. That was hollowed out of him."

"You mean," asks Averill, "the lie destroyed him? Do lies do that?" It seems too neat.

"I didn't say 'destroyed.' Just ruined."

"He was a great success," Nora points out.

"Really?"

"He was not a bad father."

"Well, let me tell you," says her mother. "Don't ever marry a man who has taught you to read."

"Mother," sighs Nora.

"Yes?"

"He only meant well by that."

The old woman, born in Norway, and taught to read good American by a law-book husband who took her on to Washington and London, makes an elaborate show of coming to her senses.

"Mr. Averill, forgive me. You don't need to hear our troubles."

"Mrs. Stoddard, I've been very seriously educated."

"Oh," she says, "what a nice thing to say."

"The senator," asks Averill, "could not believe in himself?"

"I daresay that was it," she tries to recollect. "The thing is, everyone was sure he was a fine fellow, and told him so. But he was not convinced. He'd have been better, I think, if he'd never been told."

"Doniphon told him?"

"He did. He had a need, too. He drank. He had a life, too, you see, and the secret may have hurt him. Aren't they like that?"

"Sometimes," says James Averill.

"Or it may have been better, I suppose, for Ranse, if Liberty Valance had shot *him*! That's the safest fame." She laughs, as if it is comical and foolish.

"Valance?" Nora asks. The sound comes out like breath. There are different ways of saying the name.

"Liberty Valance," says Hallie Stoddard. "The poor fool who was killed."

"Are there family still? Valances?" says Nora.

Her mother looks up at the raftered ceiling, as if all this thinking is too hard. "I suppose there may be," she allows. "It's a small world."

"And so crowded," says Averill.

1896

In the aftermath of Langtry, amid victory and unexposed fiasco, Bob Fitz had caught up with that very swift lad, Bark, to ask him: "What about Frisco, then?"

"Yes, sir?"

"Got a fight there, December. They've tipped that Wyatt Earp for referee. You're my lucky sparring bantam, Bark. Don't desert me now."

Opportunity! But Bark Blaylock was not quite brave or confident enough to go along without the bonds of obligation—in short, to be needed. He saw in an instant how every pioneer, immigrant or escaper had gone out into the bleak expanse of sea or wilderness from some intense, muddled conviction that he was doing it for the persons left behind, out of the intricate leverage of debt and duty. Never just to yell in the fresh silence.

There, in Langtry, Bark left home, without great consternation or fuss. The one securing rope may rot or dissolve and the craft slips away from moorings without pain or pronouncement. Bark realized it had happened only a day later on the train, and it was Miss Fleur Hickey who told him.

"I am not going back," she announced, looking up from her book, a recent Hardy with a title that made Bark smile at Susan—*Tess of the d'Urbervilles*—and gave them both an oblique pride when Fleur told them it concerned a heroic and much put-upon young woman, a natural and social victim who yet refused the overcast of gloom or affliction—so far.

"Naturally," observed Fleur Hickey, always willing to discuss literature, "this Tess is a person without place in that rocky class system of England. She tries to climb but falls. Defiant, however, not diminished. Whereas, in this America, she could soar—she would become a confidence woman, and her own best fool."

"Please—" Bark began.

"Don't you see?" said the enthusiastic author. "The trickster here first persuades himself. Herself. No need to be charlatan or rogue, but someone entirely self-promoted, radiant with belief!"

"I like that," said Bark, for there was a lyrical absurdity to it that encouraged him.

"I shall write it," said Fleur Hickey, and she made a note in her journal to that effect. "A young woman, a foundling, who claims to be the lost child of wealth, and takes the nation by storm."

"You said you were not going back," Susan Garth reminded her. They were sitting together on the train, with Susan cast in her inevitable role of doubter, energized by the rue of Langtry's lesson, that great schemes may never see the light.

"You two have persuaded me," said Fleur. "I have taken too much. One does not have to do it. There are no chains. We wish there were—we sit quietly, too much, as if there were chains."

Thus it was in listening to the inspirational Fleur Hickey—her enthusiasm flaring up with every extra mile's removal from the tarnishing touch of Matthew Garth—that Bark Blaylock observed the second seasonal change in his life, and the greater, in that it separated him from the famously perilous place, Death Valley, where he felt secure. She extolled the adventurous life and the bracing encounters with new places. What were railroads for, she asked, but to convey liberty and novelty? San Francisco was described as a mine of innovation, business, eventfulness and personality: Miss Hickey made it seem like a stage, brightly lit, where only those with something to say and momentous actions awaiting them were ever seen. Yet, of course, the show was all spontaneous: to go there, seemingly unprepared and humble, was to become a character in the *real* world of America.

"Once you are there," Fleur Hickey promised (and she could write dialogue as quickly as her pen moved), "you will find something to say, some new line."

"And you may confront the majestic Earp," said Susan Garth, who had rather withdrawn into the upholstered seat of the railroad car, but whose sardonic smile shone forth still.

"Exactly," said Fleur Hickey who, on the train, had picked up about as much of Bark's family banyan tree as he had of the plot of *Tess of the d'Urbervilles*. "Settle the matter!"

There spoke one who faced the steady duty, by page 400 or so, to clarify the plot, so that readers would be content to have the characters' lives go on after the last page, without their constant company and concern. The plot mistress does acquire a certain decisive innocence, no matter that her own life is as suspended as Fleur Hickey's had been, living in Del Rio, waiting on Matthew Garth's pleasure, and trying not to notice the evident lack of pleasure or the advance of his deleterious symptoms.

At a moment when Bark was otherwise engaged, and in her declared spirit of clearing things up, Miss Hickey asked her lover's daughter:

"So your money's on syphilis?"

"He has the pox, ma'am," said Susan Garth.

"Really?" said Fleur Hickey, as if the fossil in their hands was now confirmed as one remote civilization rather than another. "Well," she reflected, "I have been with him—I can't say I haven't—so it may be my lot, too."

At the same time, with fleeting knowledge of this disease and the laws of infection, Fleur Hickey did not know what to expect. Her lover, however spectral, did hold so much within him. After that first night in Abilene, she reasoned, what had he *given* her? Wasn't the absurd German bed a mask for his helpless lack of generosity? Was any partner infected, or could the organism shrug off the threat just as it "forgot" so many things? Was Mrs. Frances Garth at risk? Did he couple with her? In her bitter jealousy, Fleur Hickey had hoped not; now, she saw, her spite might have a merciful edge.

Then again, Fleur Hickey was in a state of such unexamined health and robust ignorance, she could not be sure she did not already have this pox. Perhaps it was like being saved, a condition confirmed at the end of the day?

"The medical men in San Francisco," suggested Susan Garth. "They will likely be expert."

"Bound to be," said Fleur, seeing how far the mere brush of sexual

congress could slip from romance to tragedy to farce. It was a lesson
to her that she had grown irrevocably older, and she saw as the train
traversed the desert how she was alone now, dependent on some
mixture of professional care and public amusement.

"You have met the new Mrs. Garth?" she asked Susan.

"I have."

"Does she know?" Miss Hickey could be a benefactor now.

"Post notices in the newspapers?" suggested Susan Garth.

"Ah," sighed Fleur, chastened at the thought of print's power.
"And he was something once, our Matthew Garth. But never easy
with himself."

This Matthew Garth's daughter gazed out at the stark cacti, so
barbarous and solitary, and she could see how a human might envy
their freedom from talk and reflection.

They did not go directly to San Francisco; there was no need, for
the fight was months away. They came off the train at Tucson, and
took a rambling tour north, to Canyon de Chelly. This was the first
occasion Susan Garth saw the place she would make familiar to
people on other continents, whether she meant to or not. The three
of them explored the two rims of the canyon and rode the length of
its floor, the horses splashing in the streams. Susan Garth took two
hundred photographs in the course of ten days, forever seeking to
lose her companions so that she could record the emptiness of the
place.

She did feel her camerawork was bound up in her difficulty with
people. Though the persimmon-colored wonder of the canyon
moved her, and compelled her into the constant seeing and taking
of compositions, still she knew she wanted no one to see the pictures,
or remark on them to her. She would have hoped for the canyon to
be a lost world, the beauty of which was commensurate with its
inaccessibility. She desired some ultimate destiny which she could
invoke to stop the foolish chatter of people. "Ah," she would say,
with grand finality, "you should have seen the Canyon de Chelly."
So young then, and so much in love with rock's grain and texture,
she wanted it gone, or destroyed, just engraved on plates for her to
develop.

They went on up to Salt Lake City and came in to San Francisco
in September from the northeast, finding the place still and hot and
mistaking the condition for regular summer.

"I am informed, sir, that you yourself are known to Ruby Rob,"
said the handsome man with eyes that screwed into one.

"I beg your pardon," said Bark.

"John McCabe," said the man, thrusting out a hand. "John Q. McCabe."

McCabe was a sporting gentleman whose diverse gambling instincts and connections were wary of only one regrettable aspect of pugilism: that it had but two fighters, and therefore a limited span of odds.

"Was the Rube well when you saw him? I hear he flattened Maher. It's the latest intelligence I'm after."

And so Bark got into that business, characteristic of modern American cities, of report, rumor, information—the line. It did seem to him remarkable that whereas in rural locations people saw things, met others and talked with them directly, in cities where there were "too many" people, they read and heard about things, mulled them over in prospect, and duly craved the news as if they might perish without it. Within a matter of months in San Francisco, Bark Blaylock went from a state of happy ignorance about most things to the anxiety that fears it hasn't got the hot late word from Paris, the Congress or Nob Hill, to say nothing of the inside stuff on fighters' conditioning. Bark marveled how he thrived on the insecurity of it all. He became a newspaperman, advancing in one fall from selling them on Market Street to writing for the *Examiner*.

The change in Bark's attitude was apparently matched by a rearrangement in Bob Fitzsimmons' when he reached the Bay in November.

"Any time, Bob," said Bark, as excited to be talking on the telephone as by the possibility of having his wind divorced from his body again in some lively sparring.

"Well . . . maybe, lad," said Bob Fitz sadly. "I've a lot on."

Bark took this to mean that Bob was in negotiation already for a title fight with Corbett. But word was crawling around the newsroom that maybe a fix was in. Fitzsimmons' opponent in San Francisco was Tom Sharkey, a big beginner, and the odds were all on Bob's side.

"It begins to smell," said McCabe, one night in a bar on Polk. "You get a nose for such things, Bark. I heard a story this Sharkey had been a lumberjack?"

"I know the man who wrote it," said Bark. "It was a lumberjack or a miner. They tossed a coin."

McCabe eyed him very shrewdly: "Lumberjack is better, I fancy. Even so, there's humbuggery here. What's a man to think? Aha," he added, nodding across the bar. "Our Arizona Terror!"

"What's that?" asked Bark.

"Mr. Wyatt Earp, the referee."

Bark saw a parched-face grump of a man, still tall but stooped, and plainly fixed on the obstinate, joyless task of being an Arizona Terror to groundlings. Bark knew nothing was going to be settled. But, all the same, with an open mind and being a newsman himself, he battled his way across the bar for a small chat with the man who might have been his father.

"Mr. Earp," he said.

"Glad to know you," said Earp, drunk and automatic, pushing out a paw.

"Bark Blaylock, sir. Would you recall?"

The stupor in Earp's head cleared enough for Bark to see cruel steel balls at the backs of the eyes.

"Blaylock?"

"Yes, sir."

"Knew a woman once, similar name."

"My mother, sir?"

Earp waved an arm, as if it might be so, but what help was that, and he was too tired to make an argument.

"Have a drink," he said wearily. "Bark, was it?"

"Yes, sir," said Bark, longing to get away.

Earp nodded slowly. Some point was down there in the mush, and he was feeling for it.

"Seen Bat?" Earp asked him.

"Who, sir?"

"Masterson. In town for the fisticuffs."

"Oh, Bat Masterson," said Bark.

"Ah, now you know!" declared Earp. "What became of your mother?"

"Died, sir."

"Best thing," said Earp. "Very good." And then he added, "No offense?"

"None taken, sir."

"One thing," Earp said, grasping Bark's shoulder and drawing him close enough for whispering in the din. "For a pal. Bet on the Shark."

"Did he have an opinion?" asked John McCabe. "I'll keep it to myself."

"It's a sure fix," said Bark.

"It is?"

"On my father's life."

"Bark, we're partners, now on."

The fight was held December 2, 1896, at the Mechanics Pavilion, in a city alive not with argument as to who would win, but whether the fight was for real: the question of authenticity was overtaking the fact of contest. Wyatt Earp raised a stir by stepping into the ring to adjudicate wearing holsters and six-guns. He was relieved of these and several buzzes went through the crowd:

—that he was always on the lookout for old Tombstone enemies

—that he wore a money belt fat enough to need protecting

—that the city was a den of thieves

—that the fix was in and he anticipated some wrath in the crowd

—that he was an absent-minded old fart

The fight was a leisurely, humdrum affair for seven rounds, with Bob Fitz less electric than he had been in the sunset at Langtry, and Sharkey stumbling to avoid any substantial contact, but the pair of them upright and virile as if mindful of having their picture taken. Then, in the eighth round, a grim-faced Bob Fitz threw a slow punch which Sharkey, by much twisting and jumping, managed to have strike him near the groin, or as near as anyone would want to go. There was dispute about how wounded Sharkey was. But Earp was determined on the rules: it was a foul, and Bob Fitzsimmons must be disqualified, the loser. The heap of Sharkey had its arm held up by the dismal Earp.

"Never!" cried a fleeced Fleur Hickey. "That man is no father of yours!"

John Q. McCabe came up to Bark in the uproar of that huge, slow-witted, self-pitying beast, the public, when it realizes it has been had.

"Bark, boy, we're rich. It's the north for us. I hear from a man there's a new gold fever in the Yukon. Don't tell a soul!" he shouted.

1950, Beyond Shinbone

Mrs. Hallie Stoddard lied about the house, a white lie such as people can ignore in the blaze of the desert.

The old Doniphon site was consumed in Shinbone's first great muscular stretching after the war, in '46 or '47, when the town lunged out at the desert with pipes, wiring, blacktop, tennis courts and blue pools. The carefully recomposed, charred structure of Doniphon's house was taken out in twenty minutes, and the debris carted away. Hallie Stoddard ordered the largest beam—one with scorch marks on the underside, like hardened blood—preserved. It was employed in her new house, five times the size of Doniphon's shack and a half mile beyond where Shinbone meets the current edge of the desert. Mrs. Stoddard has the finite physical resources to move once more yet, if stupid Shinbone cannot stop growing. She has a site in mind (not that she mentions this—keep the price down) and she has made the calculations on what it will cost to have the water and the sewage trench taken out that far. She has no wish now not to be connected. If he'd been hooked up, Doniphon's house would never have burned.

Albeit less than honest, her house befits the widow of a senator and an ambassador, the dowager to one of New Mexico's crusty characters. But she knows people would expect that one smoke-blackened beam, and it is no trouble to build in the old style. The old style is fashionable again, and no one finds fault with the up-to-date plumbing it conceals. Plumbing is easily excused because it is discreet: a turn of the hand and your sin is washed away, she says, every time. Why, even a Liberty Valance might have been malleable if he had had a pacifying shower in his home and an efficient flush closet. It does make the roses red. Hallie is sure they are brighter from the waste.

Hallie Stoddard is complacent about her lie: she regards it as a "version" of the very open, indecisive truth, a tasteful modernizing, just as the house she lives in is a reworking of Tom Doniphon's way of life. And if Tom had been smarter, more viable, why, she'd have married him. There is no harm in the change, is there? She has a pretty tale about the new building being gathered around the one true timber left—yet isn't that one the interloper, the fake?

It is not hospitable in the West to have to tell visitors everything is changed, that the old stories have been reexamined. It is kinder to bend to what the tourists expect. Hallie Stoddard never notices she is telling lies: rather, she believes that she is some kind of guardian to tradition and ideals. So long as her faith is strong, the facts are at her service, surely? Her people made the West. She will never, ever, turn on its ideals, despite the damage they have done to her life. Damage, sooner or later, is what holds you together, like the primordial slime. She is caught; she knows it: her poise and advantage will crack if the grand old tradition is exploded.

She has noticed lately the feeling that her thoughts and memories are cards that someone else is shuffling. They are all there, perhaps, but the ordering changes, and she has no more way than a gambler of knowing which card will be turned over. It makes her mind very active, but it leaves her feeling helpless and afraid.

Her remarkable garden is watered by her confusion: bloody begonias, eye-piercing lobelia, dahlias that are daubs in the air, and red-hot pokers you wouldn't want to touch. She is beginning to feel menaced by her garden, and wonders if the blooms are lit up by Los Alamos. This garden is famous not just in New Mexico, but in American horticultural circles; she is remembered and corresponded with in England where she was a faithful at the Chelsea Show and a solemn, insidious advocate of cacti in English living rooms.

She would have liked to implant those fanged green succulents in English nostrils or roll them across rose-petal cheeks, all the while engaged in that sing-song, tea-time small talk, with observations like sugar cubes and cress-and-Shippam's sandwiches. All the damp disdain of London—it was a species of poison, and Hallie Stoddard was an authority on the unnamed, unofficial poisons that people dropped in the tea. Her cards, the memories, are brittle and sour from it.

She does the garden herself, in a daylong peregrination—Nora calls it her "prowl"—forever walking about the property, pinching, picking, watering, dusting, talking to the cactus rose, tirading at the unresponsive dignity of the portrait of Senator Ransom Stoddard over the fireplace, never coming to rest, tiny and thin, never exhausting her fear or anger, taking her nourishment on the trot, finding the need to do more and more at once, in case she dies.

She does not sleep. She sits out at night on the veranda, wrapped in a shawl; she makes a Thermos of tea to have by her side, so she does not have to go inside the house. Even then, she cannot settle or sit in one place; a fearful, flickering activity comes over her, like a screw so old its rims have worn flat so the screw can only wind and turn in its hole, without grip or purchase. Yet it needs no oiling; the wrath keeps it free and spinning. Alone so much of the time, she is becoming the perpetual motion of her recrimination.

There is the abandonment, Ransom dying in 1944 of the cancer that was scarcely identified before he had gone off with it. She had counted on years of tending him, talking to him, rebuking his haggard face and trapped spirit, piling on repudiation, torture and contempt. But he got away. Did he have some fast way out, a plug of cyanide in his tooth, like the Nazis? It was so inappropriate that Ransom Stoddard had not had to suffer—for her eyes alone. Oh no, she would have permitted no nurse to soften her own scathing attention to the invalid. He would have had just Hallie, all to himself, without any chance of making speeches.

But at the funeral, Mr. Ambassador Kennedy had been grateful for "the mercifully quick deliverance of that so much alive and vigorous Ransom Stoddard." Still in his Boston overcoat, the man's spectacles had flashed in the sunlight as he scanned the congregation: "But this was always a man of the West, a man made by decision, bold action, such as most of us dreamed of as boys and men." He had mentioned the shooting. Which was hardly delicate at a funeral, even in New Mexico in 1944.

Until the other night, Hallie Stoddard has never mentioned how Tom Doniphon and two others had shot down Liberty Valance, or how the idiotic Ransom Stoddard had elected not to notice the other gunfire, but had opined that his one, wounded effort had taken out the vaunted . . . what would you call Valance? Outlaw? Perhaps. Vagrant? Certainly. Wild, drunken, woebegone, stupid, put-upon, exploited, scapegoat . . . ? More, more, there was always room for more on the broad shoulders of Liberty Valance. Liberty indeed. Free for all. Anyone with anything to hide could blame it on that silvered buffoon. Until they shot him down, at last, the launch for one of the West's loudest campaigns, and the moment when guilt had nowhere else to go.

But she had never known a major event of the West's history that had not been rigged in some fashion. As if Liberty was any danger, except to himself. And the glum-faced Ranse working himself over the years into believing he might have shot Valance—one lucky shot, the gambler's throw—instead of the rehearsal and the virtual writing out of the squalid drama, with Doniphon doing the brave, dumb thing and Dutton Peabody turning it into a scoop for the paper.

It had made her wonder about the earlier event, the start of the Stoddard legend, in 1908, down in Las Cruces, when Ranse had helped defend J. W. Brazel, the man who shot Pat Garrett. There had been an argument, it seemed, between Garrett and Brazel as they were both riding along about the size of a herd of goats Garrett was aiming to buy. And Garrett was in his buggy with Brazel on horseback.

Garrett then was close to sixty, a man much aged, they said, by the effects of having shot the Kid, and being so often asked and challenged about it, a man hardened and made suspicious, a case of prairie paranoia, she had heard someone say. But just by virtue of his age, he had had to take a leak as they rode. He had allegedly adverted to this: "As a matter of fact," he was said to have told Brazel, "I'm going to step down and take a piss."

So he had done: and J. W. shot him in the back. Not a pretty or promising case, with Garrett a reputation. But Ransom Stoddard had had the wit to notice how Garrett had a shotgun in his hand as he stepped down and was laboriously slow unbuttoning, seeing that his left hand was doing all the work. "Therefore," Stoddard's wide-eyed, heartfelt plea had been, "therefore, I ask you to see the very reasonable, the entirely honorable trepidation in Mr. Brazel. He was in dispute with a famous marksman—the man who picked off the Kid in the dark—a man who was supposedly in the act of urination, yet taking so long at it he might have been extricating himself from a suit of armor. And with a deadly weapon in his firing hand!"

J. W. Brazel had got off—self-defense. A brilliant bit of lawyering; and maybe it had all happened just so. Yet you didn't know if Garrett hadn't been shot just to show the guile of the defense and the career of the defenders.

She cannot get over how far Stoddard went on those few accomplishments—it was the New Mexico statehouse that did it, of course, but it was the legend of his Western prowess that won him office first, and then preferment, so that poor Ranse even swallowed the suggestion he was within reach of the vice presidency! To think of that being talked about! And all the while, Ransom Stoddard was a big act of a man, comfortable only when addressing a public meeting, yet compelled to talk in that oratorical way to his own wife and daughter. He was a cunning simpleton, Ransom Stoddard, a man so devious but so naive he could not see how thoroughly he was being used. He was a man who, on a clear day, could talk to you only by screwing up his eyes, as if he stood in waves of cigar smoke and intrigue. Some men walked through life with their heads in clouds of fatuous optimism; his was wrapped in specious iniquity. His only hope was that he was on to every piece of mischief and plotting going on. Whereas he needed to read anything and everything in the papers, and read it three times, before he grasped it.

Hallie Stoddard has her religious group, on Wednesdays, at the house. The several cars drift slowly out of Shinbone, old ladies motoring in a spirit of reverence, for tea, Bible reading, and not so much prayer as contemplation. This is the one time Hallie Stoddard sits still, for she is the center of the circle, the conduit or the medium that may carry the silent urging out there, to where it could have an effect. She has been to Washington and London, and the fame that accrued to her affords the prospect of a nearness to God.

As befits people living there in New Mexico in 1950, they read passages from the Bible that deal in wilderness and destruction. They are much concerned with the atomic testing in the West, and they are perplexed but intrigued by the idea of more intense deserts within the old deserts—the firing grounds where now no one can go, and where, previously, no one would have thought to go.

The ladies of Shinbone have several uncertainties or areas of vagueness in their devotions. Is it the Christian Him they are addressing? They do read His Bible, and there is a good deal of hypothetical discussion of forgiveness, etc. Yet Hallie Stoddard's polite advice is somehow more demonic and fateful in its overlook. Further, the ladies are unsure how to regard the Bomb: it threatens so much, not least their vivid gardens and the ruddy soil of New Mexico.

They do comprehend the notion of instant, widespread death. Not that they are afraid of it. Quite obviously, that force applies to America's enemies—Communists from Mr. Stalin to Susan Garth, wanting to defend native rights! So it may be valuable to be so close to the foundry of astonishing fire and light. And in Hallie Stoddard's gentle but firm description of a wrath on earth they can already see in the immemorial dry gulches of their West the imprint of a death more extensive and searching than funerals can handle. At their advanced ages, it may offer a way of beating a mortician's sleep. The ladies believe Hallie Stoddard is the most impressive person they have ever met. They think of going to see her on Wednesdays more than they think of meeting God. Like her famous past, He will not be there— but she will tilt her head to one side and reminisce, the cards leaping back and forth until she closes her eyes to stop the upheaval.

It is Hallie alone who has her pitch tuned higher and outward, like a great gun firing at the idea of divinity, and making sure she has fresh-cut roses everywhere in the house. They have colors in New Mexico richer than anywhere else, savage colors that would shock Chelsea. But the roses do not last as they do in England. In New Mexico, the blooms can wither while you watch them, and the passing hurts more than the burning colors.

1897

Was it a quickening beginning, or were the last years of the century downhill, hurrying to arrive? I, Bark Blaylock, was twenty-one or twenty-two, and I never guessed I couldn't slow that hurry once it got going.

"The thing I don't . . ." I tried to say.

"Understand?" said John McCabe. "Grasp? Get? Latch on to?"

"Is if you knew the fix was in, why you bet on Fitz. Is that a dumb question?"

McCabe's bearded face wreathed itself in chuckles and worldly tolerance. He shook his shaggy head agreeably as if, yes sir, he *could* see my quaint point of view.

"There's fix and double-fix, kid. I break that to you here and now."

"Yes?"

"One of the slyest fixes," he estimated, "is to put out word on another fix." He was being wonderfully patient with me. "A fake fix."

I could see that, I supposed; but I could also observe the dear, desperate grin of John McCabe, surrounded by his own doubts. How could a man bet on a fight once he had imagined the dread fake fix?

"You told me we'd won," I pointed out.

"Ah," he said, seizing on a nicety. "I think I said merely that we were rich. Or did I say 'flush'? I might have."

"Yet we weren't."

He sighed. "No." Then he perked up. "Not yet."

"You lost it all. You put it on—"

"Fitz was the class. In doubt, go for pedigree."

"—which I was certain to find out!" I waved my arm to refer to the small cabin, the enclosing snow-laden forest and our location, lost, somewhere north, on the way to the Yukon, unable most days to get the door of the cabin open because of the weight of snow against it.

"Aha," he pounced, "I did find our hut. Look on the bright side, Bark, we could be outside with nuts like cherrystones by now. But for old McCabe's luck you'd be a goner. Give me that!"

"Or sitting in the warm in San Francisco, eating buttered toast."

His gloved hand went up to ward off that tempting blow. "Don't say that! We should mention no edibles, butter least of all. We have a head start on the rush, think of it that way."

The hollow truth of it was that we did have a start, an advantage once, but by now a freeze. How John McCabe had learned so early of what would become the Klondike sensation I do not know. I have never been able to rid my mind—acquainted as it was with McCabery—of the notion that it was a lucky guess. You see, this McCabe was a remarkable vessel of intelligence, ignorance, desire and hunch; and it took a while for a newcomer to see how the mix worked. (As for McCabe himself, I am sure he never understood it. He would have turned to old stone if he had.) It is possible that McCabe studied the maps, thought of the most remote places as being likely repositories of rich ore, rubbed his thumb and forefinger together and muttered—he was an inspired, heated talker to himself—"Klondike!" Had he got there and found it bare, there wouldn't have been a soul to observe his embarrassment. "Fine country!" he could have rhapsodized, breaking the ice out of his beard and convincing himself he had always meant to be a solitary naturalist. And as things turned out, so the highly imaginative John McCabe became a hero in his story. Those people intent on "fresh starts" are like authors who want to begin their book again with themselves as unequivocal admirables.

He was, therefore, constitutionally unable to appreciate, or—I would go so far—even *see* our predicament. We had put all my money in the boat trip on the *Portland*, and had a spectacular experience of the rugged shoreline on the way up from San Francisco. Now, in a year's time, the natural starting-off point for the Klondike would be Skagway, where the *Portland* was innocently headed! But as we sailed McCabe grew uneasy that he was being watched and followed by those who knew he had secret information, but didn't have the map of it. He was forever taking me behind funnels or up to the wind-honed bowsprit to talk about our plans.

I never noticed one item to support his fears, but he had a way of turning my matter-of-fact objections into further proof. For, as he had it, I was the callow youth and he the sad veteran of a troubled, dishonest world. That is no easy attitude to contest, not if you're dealing with a brilliant, all-talking dreamer like McCabe. So, to be on the safe side, we got off the *Portland* at Prince Rupert, a couple of hundred miles south of Skagway! To throw the spies off our scent! "Anyway," said McCabe, as we surveyed the blank town, "that Prince Rupert, I hear, was a fine fellow."

Day after lonely day, plodding north out of Rupert on disconsolate horses, we would pause on every rise while McCabe scanned the way we had come with a telescope he had purchased for the task. Not a soul came after us, God save them!

The emptiness of those places is a wonder; nothing moves but the slow, spiraling descent of snow, silent and obscuring. Yet we went especially slowly, beating into the blizzard, to be sure we were alone. And then slower, for the horses knew we were hopeless cases. And the noble, ingenious, blundering McCabe would not be put off his huge gratification at our solitude (you must not think your early Americans were skilled at what they did—their fortitude, their determination, their cultivation of luck were all the offspring of ineptness). Until he woke me one morning with "Bark, I suspect our horses croaked." He was not medically sure of this judgment, so I suggested we carve what meat we could off the hardened carcasses and see if that woke them up.

Then again, within a day we came upon this abject cabin—surely forsaken by earlier fools who preferred death to its confinement—and he elected it as the latest evidence of fate's itch to smile upon us.

There was a hearth and a chimney to the cabin, so we were always hoping to get out into the forest and find wood. But the fire, as and when we could keep it alight, was a threat to claim the cabin. There was a very mean average—of subdued warmth and barely survivable smoke—except that the smoke drove us to open the door, thereby raising the level of necessary heat. We kept warmer, I believe, from the exertion of making and maintaining a fire than ever we did from a cozy, merry hearth.

The snow was our water, our monotonous view and our isolation. We had beans, flour, coffee, salted bacon and several boxes of chocolates which were a delicacy to McCabe, no matter that they gave him dire toothaches. We became knowledgeable with the cuisine of smoky, frozen horse, and we were often nauseated from it—our cabin was circled by our waste, dark piles of the heavy stuff (such a solid mockery compared with our diet) and small rusty pits whereby we restored our water to the snow.

I had brought *Tess of the d'Urbervilles* with me, and read it all through twice, lastingly affected. McCabe tried it, but I awoke one day to find him making playing cards from its pages. He had blackened one side of the "cards" for uniformity, and on the other he wrote the value of the cards. In an attempt to occupy our empty lives, and to guard against the cards being too readily identified, he enlarged the pack. We had the same four suits, but our court was augmented with the wizard, the treasurer and the mistress and our suits did not stop at ten—they went to fifteen. Thus we had a flimsy pack of eighty-four cards, and an opportunity for McCabe to amplify the rules of every card game.

My greatest entertainment, however, was listening to McCabe and his theories. I believe I had been brought along on the trip principally as his listener, as a kid who would marvel at his ideas and serve as the Emperor McCabe's one loyal subject. I cannot recollect all of them, but here is a sampling of his speculative wisdom, uttered from a huddling coat, from beneath the frozen curl of his black derby as we tried to sleep and stop ourselves from wondering when spring would show:

—that women were the supreme, scientific proof of man's imaginative power: delicious in prospect, but crabs when met (this was an additional McCabean opinion on the good fortune of our circumstances)

—that it was the people left short in storybooks one wondered about the most

—that electricity was thought channeled into a wire, and that one day thinking would catch up with it

—that America, sooner or later, would have so many diverse peoples that language would have to be abandoned, and some electrified photography would be required to command popular attention (I have never said there was not a bizarre, ruminating insight in McCabe—but the intelligence that cannot live in its own time is uncomfortable)

—that money in the pockets ruined a suit and cramped the spending instinct; one day we would be able to commit on credit to our heart's content

—that the heavens' infinite extent could be explained only by some vast spiral shape so that, out there, in accord with symmetry, there was another world, identical to this, except that the right-handed were left-handed and vice versa—and one was the real world, and the other was the story in the mirror. But which was which?

—that, as time went by, coincidence would become established as a staple form of existence—for, surely, with more time there would be more coincidence?

—that John Q. McCabe, for one, was heartily glad to be living in the modern world, and that the one duty he felt bound to honor was staying up to date

—and "Gold, Bark lad, gold!," which, I suppose, was less an idea than a kind of climate. At least, it had to pass for our sunshine, until:

"Evenin', gents. Jerkin' off in your beds, are you?" and a great gust of cold came in from Canada or America, wherever we were, as two women appeared in our doorway, rosy-cheeked from the labor of walking in the snow and the sources of a considerable steam arising from sweaty clothes. This very real physical evidence made them more charmingly like the ghosts our reveries had summoned. Yet they also seemed costumed for an ordinary winter promenade in the snow, which promised horses in the offing, and thus a passable trail, something our sojourn had not noticed.

Spring came into our cabin on the sweet, abrasive air of Constance Miller and her junior, her skivvy, Ida Coyle.

"Mrs. Miller," she explained. "From London. That's not 'ere, you know. London, England. 'Eard of it?"

We assured her we had. We told them of our great ordeal, but they took us for madmen—and, of course, I didn't need the several winks from McCabe to shut up about gold. We were on the defensive, straightaway, and our awe only mounted as we perceived them to be very appealing ladies, and Mrs. Miller in particular possessed of a somewhat abrupt, no-nonsense beauty, a trifle forbidding in aspect, to be sure, as if she had learned not to waste time on people's hopes or tender fancies.

"So, boys," she summed it up, "up 'ere all on your tod? No dirty stuff, I trust," and she glared at each of us in turn, like a schoolmarm who's lost her piece of chalk.

"Not us, lady," said McCabe in that orotund and jovial way of his.

"Suppose I sat on your face, then, eh?"

"Madam," said McCabe, "my repasts here have been pitifully simple, but I believe I would recall the taste."

"Sauce!" said Mrs. Miller, with a cunning giggle, and she turned on me. I was alarmed, I may tell you. For she stood there, arms akimbo, meaning business. She had commandeered our cabin.

"You there. 'Ad it, 'ave you? My word, Ida, I don't believe 'e 'as. What's this, then?" she demanded, swooping down on our miserable, makeshift playing cards. She examined them. "Damn it all! Our Tom's book? Defacing lit'ture, that it? You buggers!"

Ida came up and examined me, like a nurse looking for a rash. "No, he's not had it, Connie. Got that lovely look in his eyes."

"All the same," deplored Mrs. Miller, holding out the wreckage of *Tess* in her hands, "this is diabolical."

"Mrs. Miller," said McCabe, "man's inventiveness works in remarkable ways."

"But this is Tom's book, i'n't'?" she demanded. She was very reproachful and moved to give McCabe a smack.

"Mr. Hardy?" I interposed.

"What I said."

"It's a very fine book," I assured her in a tone of piety which, while I felt it, still shocked me, for I saw subterfuge growing in me. It was the closeness and the promise of woman that did it.

"Who did this then?" She proffered the tattered, sooty pages.

"He did," I told her meekly.

"Bloody 'ell," she growled.

I felt the prospect of getting discovered, transported, improved—there was nothing else to it—and I would have sent McCabe to the dungeons of Manchuria if it could advance my eager cock one inch. If Mrs. Miller was a lending-library whore, so be it. Why should I deny my honest allegiance to Thomas Hardy when I might be within reach of losing my virginity? Gold be damned, I had weightier stuff to be rid of.

"What would 'e say?" she muttered.

"Ma'am?" I inquired, drawing a little nearer to her, as if to read the precious book once again. She looked up, quizzical and piercing; she knew my drift and, just between the two of us, she stuck her tongue out at me. It was the hue of strawberry flesh. And with her free hand she gave my creaking prick a friendly nip. "Oooh!" she said at what she'd found. "Didn't know cucumbers grew so in the winter, I didn't." And she laughed like glass breaking.

"Friend o' mine," she said. "Tom. In Tooting. Matter of fact, I've done for 'im now and then." But, catching my absolute wonderment, she added, "Housework! Polishin' his brass, I mean. None o' your filth, lad. Cor, you are a devil!" But the rebuke was proud now, and just a little giddy with her own anticipation.

"You," she said to McCabe. "Take Ida for a walk. Go down to the 'orses, bring up our things. Don't 'urry, Ida. Know what I mean? And don't lose him."

Ida's cackle surely left McCabe the only one of us with a chance of being in the dark. But that was his natural abode. And he would prove a hero of that lonely dark, a fool still, but a character such as he saw far off in space.

O reader, are you there? Do you know or care that fifty-three years ago, in an otherwise abandoned cabin in the snow, I came to lose what, until then, I had not fully realized I had? It is all so long ago. Can the story matter any more than any one dot of snow that has landed there since? Was I ever really headed anywhere more cheerful, or less mortal, than John McCabe? Did seeing his error keep me correct? At least he had his moment, taking out three scoundrels with him, three wolves, in more northern snow, ignored by the very sexually proficient Mrs. Miller. She ignored all men—it was her habit, her rule. No true knowledge of Mr. Hardy had overcome her coldness; she pitied one spoiled volume, but she had not read it. And though she proved amazing warm and moist in the frigid cabin, really she was very practical frost. A most knowing frost, knowing enough to free me, to make me ready for unhealing sorrows. Thomas Hardy had not helped or touched her.

There was no vulnerability in her. Just as she had dispatched McCabe for that moment—and I urged him away, too—I would sooner preserve this odd speech from McCabe himself. It came long before the ladies appeared. I heard him talking to himself one day, in our solitude, when I came up on him quietly in the snow.

He was insisting to himself, over and over again. "I didn't give in. It didn't beat me." But his tears were falling in the snow, leaving clean bullet holes, icy at the edges.

1950, In the Garden

This garden scene could be a still picture, there is such accumulated lack of breeze or motion: the poised wisteria, like frills on a Meissen figurine; the limp sag of the badminton net; the tray that once was tea, with a timeless fragment of cake; the afternoon incline of the Peace rose heads, open but exhausted; the mauve hovering of a thunderstorm; his mother, an elegant stick creature in a floral dress folded in the belly of a striped deck chair. Nothing moves except a single blue butterfly and Jim Jr.'s thoughts.

He is thinking of people and peoples far away: the Red Sox and the Indians at Fenway; the refugees, thousands, tens of thousands, surging this way or that in Korea; the refugees in Europe, still in camps, with less drive, or hope; his father in New Mexico; the indistinct yet certain impression that, over the wall, through the trees, across the small, tidy river, there are Vermonters making their way in and out of unique but unheard-of lives; and the dots on the ground in the film his mother took him to in Rutland, *The Third Man*, the dots that Harry Lime offered to his friend at twenty thousand pounds a dot, "Free of income tax, old man." Not that the dots had to be killed or squashed —no violence was called for. Out of sight, out of mind.

And now the fixity of the heavy, overcast afternoon oppresses him. He treasures his mother's languid collapse: he has walked past her chair, barefoot, silent, observing the rapid pulse in her wrist, inhaling the fragrance of her sleep. She has a high-strung fineness that thrills but daunts him: she is his mother, but she is English and he needs to be an American boy. He decides to disturb her.

"What would Dad be doing now?"

"What indeed?" she asks him back, so swiftly, she can never have been asleep, just lying there with her eyes shut, trying to sleep or waiting out the duration of an ordained "rest"—like a prescribed silence in music. Jim Jr. sees a total respect in his mother for that sort of order—the idea of a text or score that has to be followed.

"He is there?"

"He's somewhere, I should think."

"Do you think of him when he's away?"

Her eyes open; there is a pain in them he cannot yet recognize but it is like the dusty color of the wisteria. He decides that people are lovelier with their eyes open.

"More, sometimes," she tells him.

"Than what?"

"More than if he's here."

Jim Jr. has a mother and a father who often talk of people and peoples outside the orbit of their children—the "they" who are expecting this or that, making arrangements for Mr. and Mrs. Averill, hoping for their interest and support. Jim Jr. does not feel neglected or unloved: quite the contrary. But he has noticed that his parents are often away on different undertakings, and that they can be at home so engaged on papers that pertain to "they" that Jim Jr. and Sally merely exist in their circle and warmth, loved, secure, *here*, yet not thought of. And he can see that what other people, the "theys," value in James and Betsy Averill is their capacity for such thought or attentiveness. They have always impressed on their children the ordinary human need to look at the wants of strangers: with his mother, it is refugees, or those who need rescue; with his father, business and politics. For the Averills are determined their offspring shall see that wealth and position carry responsibilities to the shadowy external world, less fortunate and less endowed. Otherwise, there is something unadjusted, something perilous, in the state of things.

"Do you think of England?" he asks her.

"I do."

"And Grandfather Lycett?"

"Sometimes."

"Do you think of his wife, the granny I never knew?"

Betsy Averill sits up in the deck chair.

"Is it going to rain?" she asks.

"Super," says Jim Jr.

"Mmm. It'll be cool."

"Do you?" he persists.

"She's always there," says Betsy.

"Even if she's dead?"

"She is dead. And always there."

"In the film," he says, "when they're up on the wheel."

"Mmm."

"And Lime talks about all the dots."

"Yes."

"Free of income tax, old man—the way he says that."

"That Mr. Welles is a shocker."

"But they are dots you don't know. Aren't they?"

"They're people, though. Viennese."

"Like Granny Lycett. I mean, if you weren't in the Lycett family. Or our family."

"It's only a film, Jim."

"It was good, though, wasn't it? You said you thought it was."

"But you shouldn't get upset about it."

"I'm not upset." He laughs in surprise.

"Lime is a wicked man. It's a terrible thing he says."

"I liked him."

"Well, that's the actor. That Orson Welles. He's a charmer."

"You said he was a shocker."

"He enjoys being a naughty boy."

"How many people can one care about? I mean properly."

"As many as there are, I suppose."

"Really? I couldn't."

"Why not?"

"Well, in Korea. Suppose at this moment there are ten thousand peasants—are they peasants?"

"More or less."

"All right. Walking down a road. They've had to leave their homes.

And planes come and bomb them. Now. At four o'clock in our afternoon."

"Yes?"

"What can we do?"

"There are ways. We do help. You know, I work for the refugees."

"But we're having a nice time. Having tea in the garden."

"We can think of them," she says.

"I was thinking of Dad."

"So was I."

"When you think of Granny Lycett, is it different from thinking of Dad?"

"No, I don't suppose it is, really."

"Or Harry Lime?"

"How do you mean?"

"Well," he breathes deeply, "there are dead people, alive people and people in stories."

"Yes."

"And they're in our heads together. As well as the people we don't know. The dots. The peasants."

"We know they're different, though."

"But, suppose," he strains to extend the context, "say when my grandchildren are old—a hundred years from now?"

"About."

"Well, then no one I should think would know who Granny Lycett was. I mean, I've only *heard* of her."

"People *will* be forgotten. But they may still be watching Harry Lime."

"Perhaps."

"I did try to know Granny," Betsy tells him, but she notices the oddity of having to use a word, a reference, that in no way fits or was ever used to label the erratic, beautiful Mummy who ceased so suddenly to be. Jim Jr. does not know how to respond, except by going to his mother, on his knees on the grass. She is shaking inside her soft silk dress, and there is an awkward, unpleasant smell arising beneath the perfume. Is it the smell of tears or upset tummy? She puts her hands on her son's strong shoulders, and feels his warmth, his presence and his comfort. There is no mistaking the loyalty, the distraught love in his eyes, the willingness to be her if he could. But she knows his grip is fleeting, that he could easily be, in just ten years, recalcitrant, bored, longing to be a stranger, tugged at by oblivion.

"We have to try," she says.

"I know." He would do anything to reassure her. "Mummy," he sighs and sinks into her lap. He feels the peace of her hands stroking the back of his head, but she feels only that she is smoothing a head from another civilization, a head she cannot possess.

There is a sound from inside the house, it is the tensing of the phone before it starts to ring, not a bell, not a sound even, but like the wind-up to a throw, or the deep breath before a speech.

"I'll get it," she says. And the phone begins to ring, that wobbly call, as if the rural phone lines were sagging from the weight of birds.

"Hallo yourself," she says into the phone. Jim Jr. can see and hear her through the open French windows. A wind stirs at the end of the garden: the storm is coming. He feels two heavy drops of rain on his arm, like fruits bursting.

"I see," his mother says. "Yes, it would be lovely."

She is looking at him across the lawn.

"Why don't I ask him?" she says.

She puts down the phone and comes out, unsteady, swaying, stumbling, laughing at her clumsiness.

"It's your father," she calls. "He says would you like to go out to New Mexico. To see it all."

"Now?" asks Jim.

"Tomorrow. The day after."

"Could I?"

"He's asking. Go talk to him. I think it will rain."

Jim Jr. runs into the house and to the phone while Betsy picks up the tea tray, kicks the deck chair flat and picks it up, too, to put it in a safe, dry place. The leisurely storm begins to pour over their part of Vermont, and there is a tranquil roll of thunder in the mountains. Then, from nowhere, a prickle of lightning breaks apart the air of their garden. They do not see a flash, but they see the place where the air and the day have been torn. The sound begins, of rain heavy on large leaves.

"Oh, do watch," says Betsy. "It's going to be a lovely one!"

April 1906

The Palace Hotel, San Francisco
April 17, 1906

My dear daughter, to Miss Susan Garth,

Once I saw a dead man—and it was me! Why didn't I know that then?

It is a point of fine judgment, here and now, whether I will be alive when you read this. I will be up and out of here by five; I have ascertained there is a passable light at that hour, enough to see to shoot. And this letter cannot reach you on Russian Hill until . . . when? Perhaps eight or nine in the morning? You may read it and wonder! My first letter to you is no ordinary piece.

I want to tell you what is in my mind. I have a disease—I will not name it. It has been my faithful companion these many years, keeping pace with me until I falter under it, eroding, depleting, deteriorating, making me feel like a ghost composed of decayed vegetable, warm glue and wrapping paper. Haven't you noticed? People regard me in this superior hotel as a specter; only my money and their abjectness toward it permit me to stay here. I walk the corridors to frighten them!

Well, I struggled with this companion, and I have lasted longer than the doctors supposed I could. For I fought it. I denied it. I refused to acknowledge it, or let it gain except by desperate, hard-fought battles for every part of me. Even then, I gave it no name! But in the last two years, here with San Francisco's best doctors, it is as if the disease took heart; like a dog hearing the voice of its master. It has rallied and spurted; it has burst out of me in triumph. I am wrecked with it—and so I have made it my friend.

Last Thursday, the doctor I most value (because he did admit he despised me while being engrossed with *my* version of the disease), he told me it is only months before inescapable death resides in me. He thinks I am not maddened by it already! He does not know how competently the mad can act, or how insane performance is.

This is what I shall do. I have bought a gun—would you believe that when I came out of Texas four years ago, I threw out my gun? But it is very easy to purchase another, and I have a sound Smith & Wesson .44 with a mother-of-pearl handle, which will do me nicely—it is like one of the older guns. That Cherry Valance had one like it! The man who sold it to me, south of the Slot, averred that it was very popular with these "dude cowboys," our city sports, those who take pocket artillery up to Tahoe to fish!

I will shortly escort Frances—the forlorn, patient Frances, hoping to be accepted (never!), wondering if she is infected (a proper quandary for one of nature's waiters)—to the opera, to see Caruso and Mme. Fremstad in *Carmen* (I am told I should be excited—but I believe it is *they*, the plump singers, who should be more aroused to think that I and my mission are in their audience—they will read of me, for I will leave the opera ticket in my pocket as a clue!).

It is my present mood to be indecisive as to where my eye will fall tomorrow. I see no reason not to kill the first stranger I encounter—it is the outright principle of the thing, for I have never yet killed anyone, and I will not let death beat me so simply. So it may be a cable-car driver trudging to the depot, head down, or a printer on the *Call* going home. How many can there be on the streets at five a.m.?

But I will have a destination: if I am not halted by God (I am interested to see how early he rises), the police or retaliatory bullets, I will go to Mrs. Constance Blaylock's premises down on Pacific and put that guttersnipe out of her husband's misery. She is a whore, a whoremonger, a vicious fool and the ruin of that gullible Blaylock who has not the sense to perceive he loves you. So this will be my gift to you, my Susan, the Susan I never had, along with the ten thousand dollars a year I have seen to it with Garner is settled on you. For life! But don't be reassured by *life*.

God knows why the glum Bark came back from the Klondike with that raddled wife, or how he has endured her. Tell him to quit prizefight management: he has no head for it. His best prospect, Johnny Chance, has Indian in him—and I never saw one of them fight. I do not know if being rid of his shrew will wake him up, or inspire *you*—I cannot begin to comprehend you in all this, why you do not take the sunny simpleton if you want him. You could, you are a Garth, and taking is in your blood. Don't dispute it, or hope to stifle it.

Then what? I do wonder what then? I have been a ghost for so long now, I might easily persist. Suppose I live inside your camera, daughter, so that when you peer in the eyepiece to compose your fine views—why, there I am, my ravaged aspect, a hair on the lens? So that you remember me.

If you ever did. It has been too late, I know, these few years in San Francisco. We were strangers when we met in Langtry, with only my failings to discuss. And I silence such things—it is my illness. But you must know that, long before debility, you were a steady thought inside me, eating at me. A loss means more to most men than anything they ever have. We are not skilled at happiness.

I was afraid of Cherry Valance. I believed he had a more natural, expressive capacity for violence than I. So I watched him take you and your mother, and the cowardice would never desert me. Men in the West are famous for their fortitude. How so? When most went there as much out of escape as venturing? There has been so much to be afraid of. It is a history not of boldness—that is the stories. In life we have inched forward in our craven way, afraid of the sun, afraid of being noticed, afraid of all the liberty. And to think that Valance gave you an ugly brat half-brother named Liberty. It is as ironic and grotesque as how, when he found silver at last, it was as a scavenger ratting around in photographic processing plants for the metal in the swill thrown away. *That* silver is like sleep in the corner of my Susan's eye.

I should have written to you sooner.

Tomorrow, before you wake.

> Your always loving father,
> Matthew Garth (written with his broken hand!!)

We were on the slopes of Russian Hill, watching the fire spread through our city below. Can you see how this was the first great urban catastrophe of modern times? Another first for the West! In which case, it gave new evidence of the impossibility of simple tragedy. For we were sightseers, picnickers and photographers on the hill, just as much as we were the homeless or bereaved. Injured people limped up the hill for a better view, so they could say, later, they had seen it. It was our city, all at slipped and drunken angles, burning end to end; in a day, the swaggering metropolis of the West of America had been made smoking rubble, a five-cent symbol for false hopes. The fallen columns, the autumn of bricks, were small wreckage compared with the confidence, the designs on the future and our sense of order. People were laughing on Russian Hill at the frenzy of the spectacle and the calm in being spectators: we were not certifiable, we were not ill or disturbed; but we were onlookers at the show.

Susan had her letter; it was claimed, later, in the first exuberance of recovery, that not one letter was lost in the confusion. So be it: in the years since, I have found, "earthquake letters" keep materializing. But Matthew Garth—more solid, more operatic than most missives—he was never found. The shock came at 5:13 in the morning; famous clocks are still stopped at that angle. There was time for Garth to have walked out, and fired on someone in the casual spirit of a window-shopper. No one reported bodies shot in the gathering of casualties. No one found a piece of Matthew Garth, his ticket for *Carmen* or his mother-of-pearl revolver.

My wife snatched his letter from my hands, and scurried through it, looking for gossip.

"Bloody 'ell!" she said. "The nerve!" And then, "This is grounds for divorce, I'll warrant." She was a bitch, but I saw sorrow and dashed hopes in her patched-up face.

I have some fondness for the notion of an indignant Mrs. Miller Blaylock searching in the burning city for a lawyer. It all worked out, in time: I went away, and a year later the news caught up with me that she had gone back to England in umbrage and legal separation. No doubt she described the knavery of American men, and grew into an old lady on tales of how the earthquake had rescued her from a wretched union. Perhaps she tried to sell the story to her Mr. Hardy.

That day on Russian Hill, in a pleasant breeze that would not let the fire rest, her tirade came and went. I was victim, I suppose, of the woman who happened to be the first prospector of my sexual energy. Not that I believed I was unlucky: no, I was that glum fellow Matthew Garth saw, smart enough to see John McCabe was dancing on a fine wire, but not brave or truly wise enough to know I stood beside him. I recall my Mrs. Miller with relish still: she gave me such attention.

When you are young, you assume you are the center of activity, that time and the world are being carried forwards by your progress. You do not realize you are a speck of dust in the current, neither precious nor necessary, and seen only to the extent that you are a constituent of the thing others call dust, the crowd. But then one day can come, when you are thirty or thirty-one, when you see that you are just an odd fellow, failed, awkward, regarded somewhat askance by others, getting ready to be an old man, an incidental, a character perhaps, but no longer fit to be anyone's hero, let alone your own.

"Who was that?" said Susan, peering into the throng on the hill.

"Where?" I wondered.

"I thought . . . I thought I saw my father."

We searched, we did, though neither of us hoped to find him. Nothing. Except the odd superstition that we would go on "seeing" him.

A handsome man came up Russian Hill to survey the city. There was a whisper it was John Barrymore, the actor. He had a pretty thing on his arm, Eurasian, and they stood together, spectacular and alert.

"Look at that!" said Barrymore. "I wouldn't have missed it for worlds."

And I heard an old Chinaman saying, "By-and-by, we will build it up again." I was looking at Barrymore and his girl, and I thought, yes, why not? so long as the builders are as fine and mindless as those two, so long as they can see the city as just their stage, and not a place that was making an attempt on the land and history. But if the cities are here only for our drama . . . then surely they can be folded up and remade. We can do that? And never understand the great travail in the ground that every now and then must throw its rider and roar at all the human vanity. They will build again. And again. But with each change they are less builders and more show-men.

"I'm going to be moving on soon." I was sure of it.

"I was thinking of leaving," said Susan. "But how can you go now? How can anyone?"

We did not talk about the letter, or what her father had said about us. I cannot say why. There was no possibility that we would part, or not see each other again. We would stay in touch. But there was a raggedness to our edges; we did not fit tidily. It was not her father's last show of rage and feeling that chastened us. Rather, we were both of us fulfilled by this new, shattered San Francisco. We had never fallen for its vaunted progress. There was always in the West too much urge to start again. So we were confirmed, standing there, seeing the damage and foreseeing the industrious, the wondrous, the futile reconstruction. I know we both needed desert: it might not be met immediately, and we did not speak of it. She would stay, like a losing gambler. I would go, a vagrant freed. The lonely people who require deserts cannot claim company there, not even that of loners.

Mr. Arnold Genthe was on the hill, very active with his camera. He told Susan she should be working, it was a once-in-a-lifetime opportunity. Susan said nothing but watched him hurrying along to fresh, striking vantages. We remained up there all day until the fires were all the light there was. Then we went down the hill and carried on. Survivors, or cynics? She was always stronger than I, harder and better. I would soften once again—fatally, or nearly so—and she was there to watch and wait for me to get through it.

And Matthew Garth? He may have had the best view of it, at five o'clock in the morning, awake to see the wave coming down the street, with buildings rising on it like small boats. Surely there was glory there, such as we like to think would attend a great hero of the West? Seeing a city made into surf and wind! I cannot say I knew him—or that a day goes by without my wondering how he thought, and how he took his route from hero to outcast.

One other kept his day. On every April 18—until 1932, when she died in a railroad accident in Ohio—Miss Fleur Hickey walked the city in the way one might make a promenade through an unmarked cemetery, seeing every reborn tower as a secret headstone. She had given up her Garth in so many ways. But, as she always said, he had been hers once to give up.

1950, Prospecting

Nora Stoddard is twenty-nine in 1950, driving out of Santa Fe to run into Jubal Valance. Unmarried, at what is, for 1950, an advanced age, she is going to see him (or look at him) without invitation or announcement. She is taking a chance, and she knows it is not just impulsive but wayward. He is the sort of man who might have a Mexican woman in his place, half-clothed, sweating, uncomplaining, sprawled across a torn sofa as he drills her and the radio whines with song from the kitchen where it presides over broken enchiladas and refried beans. If she goes in very quietly, she may drag a taster's finger through the cold food; and see how he does it.

Nora Stoddard, Smith College class of '42, is not glamorous; she is not in a movie, after all. She is only living in New Mexico, but she *is* a central figure in the story: and if you do not need to see her, still you will have allotted her some clarity or presence, something that grips James Averill and interests Susan Garth. This may not be a case for "beautiful" or "pretty"; but she should be becoming, let us say, someone *you* would hope to meet. People in fiction are as opposed to being plain, dull or "not there" as actors are to playing anyone less intelligent than themselves. Fictions cannot be about people who go unnoticed.

But if Nora Stoddard is alive today—this "now," 1990, has to be acknowledged, though it is not the writer's "now"—she will be sixty-nine. She may have retired, emeritus or emerita, from the museum in Santa Fe; or she may have made it farther afield—to director, say, of the Hood Art Gallery at Dartmouth College; or even the author of an unexpectedly popular biography of Susan Garth, noble old eccentric, adventuress, radical, visionary, link to the pioneering tradition; the book might be called *The Light of the West*. One can believe that . . . with Jane Fonda, say, optioning the movie rights?

But she might be Nora Stoddard only, a spinster without relatives, shaken by a fall, her memory going, her pension measured in small change—an old woman not very widely considered or recognized. And she must be thinking of that on her short evening drive in 1950; or if she is not directly dwelling in the problem, then it has become a part of her, a wind that prevails against the slippery rock so that it becomes hard, glossy, free from handholds, and leaves her marginally less accessible or graspable—a difficult woman.

She drives in the new age of relativity: which is to say she can chat at smart dinners about what Einstein said and meant; and she travels all the time in a set of contexts, concentric, enough to resemble a large, unwieldy, wind-tossed umbrella that wants to bump into everyone. She knows the axis of professors and state functionaries in New Mexico, respectable, sometimes engaging men—sound prospects, and probably fuller with character than her far-focused romanticism is prepared to admit. Then there is the sudden recent vector that is James Averill, all bold, intersecting diagonal: warm, touching, intimate, enchanting.

But is he just a bullet crossing her path, slowing to enjoy the aroma and the heat of New Mexico, then off again? Or does he really intend to seek his rescue, his great change, in her? And could she, should she, survive that fearful drama just because he is so monopolized by the allure of his own transformation? It might not be the easiest or most settled existence: with stepchildren, an unspoken notoriety, cold shoulders from the old Averill associates, and an overpowering need to explain, or justify, the mystery—why her? Why this unknown from New Mexico, this near girl, who cannot be described in Eastern cities without some hint of opportunism creeping in? Yet isn't the precipitousness of choice what she wants? Isn't that the saving danger? Isn't a ten-to-one shot at James Averill just the promise that lets her dismiss historians from UNM?

There are other lines of possibility for her—ridiculous, perhaps, but lines the mind takes every day: there is the legend of a stranger, Cary Grant, stopping off for directions and being halted in his tracks, "Oh, I say . . . ," or a John Ireland glancing at her from the pickup that sidles alongside at the rush-hour stoplight, mouthing something indecent and juicy at her through the double windows. And *there* is Jubal Valance.

He is not embroiled in any raunchy trailer. He is in the yard behind his small, squat, square house, grooming a wild-eyed chestnut mare. Nora can see that where he lives he can simply ride his horse out into the open country, that unmarked, unfenced scrub ground outside Santa Fe. He could just ride away.

There is no junk or trash around the house: it is poor or severe, but no eyesore, not an open evidence of uneducated, untamed instinct waiting to spoil or infect—Nora has picked up this squeamish hostility to outlaws from her father, the lawyer, the state-maker, the senator, and so on, the man whose fame and authority were based on a decisive, brave purging of barbarism—this Jubal's grandfather? —the ancestor of this kid who talks soothingly to the jittery mare as he works up her shine.

"I been lookin' for you," he calls out, grinning happily over his shoulder, which is very little lighter than the color of his horse.

"Yeah? I've been around," she taunts. "I've been here," and she shifts her bottom comically in the car to indicate her here: it is not a flirtatious or erotic gesture, just a way of saying "here" is always where the first person singular's eyes sit. It is a cocksure, democratic boast. It shows no disrespect for the complex, surrounding "there," only the courage and the ignorance to take it on.

"Isn't she a beauty?" says Jubal, so that it is not clear whether he is speaking to Nora or the mare.

She is still sitting in her car, watching the evening subside, and gazing at the horse. She looks beyond Jubal, and sees some wire-covered boxes on legs.

"What you got there?" she asks him. She knows there is a directness in her speech she would not let Averill hear.

"Want to look?"

He tethers his horse and nods to her to get out of her car and follow him. It is a wily performance, backing away toward the home-made cages, coaxing her, without words or touch. She slides out and follows.

There are rattlesnakes in the cages under some cottonwood trees, rattlers and one coral snake. The red and yellow rings on the coral are lurid, like new paint: Nora knows this is the deadliest of the snakes.

"They're from here?" she wonders. She believes it is too high, and cold, in Santa Fe.

"I bought 'em off a fellow in Yuma," he says. Famous for its unbearable heat and its prison.

"Why do you keep them?"

"You don't like them?"

"Not a lot," says Nora Stoddard. She is nervous now, the box cages look so flimsy, and the snakes like pure muscle.

Jubal puts his hand on the cages and rocks them. They seem sturdy enough. But the coral's black snout looks up at skin, with only the weave of chicken wire in the way.

"Don't!" she says, pulling him away.

He laughs at her; she sees his crooked teeth. "So," he asks, "what you come around for?"

"I didn't come around. I noticed you."

"You wanna see a movie?" His grin knows it all.

"Not particularly."

"I saw this picture. I was going to see it again."

"What's that?"

The grin. Breaking her in to his rhythm and mindless rule. "I don't know."

"You don't know what it's called?" The archivist, the exhibit-maker, the cataloguer in her is irked.

"About a gun, a rifle. You see." His hands come up, as if holding a gun. "It's a crack shot and there's a contest for it. One guy wins it—but the guy that loses steals it. Then the rifle goes from hand to hand—there's a gambler, Indian chief, some soldier, yeah, and Waco Johnny—"

"It's a Western?"

"Right. You wanna come in for a beer?"

"In there?" She tilts her head at his house. It looks so hot and airless in there.

"You could bring it out," she says, as if not much interested or thirsty.

So Jubal goes to the back door and into the kitchen. She can see it is very plain, bare rather than clean, squared away. He takes two bottles of beer from a sink of water and flips off the caps. Then he comes out, leaving the door open. But he has a fancy whip in his hand, too, a mass of black thongs with a heavy silver handle. The leather is dry and cracked, but the silver has been kept polished.

"Take a look," he says, giving her a beer and holding the whip in one hand, like a dead creature. The thongs look as if they might crumble or fall off.

"The handle's pretty," she says, tracing the engraved form of a racing horse.

"Mexican silver," he says. "My grandfather's. All I got of his." It is a very heavy whip, hardly functional: it is more like a whip of office, a show of what might be cruel power. Nora is trying to judge whether the grandfather would be Liberty Valance, and whether this snake charmer knows.

"What are you going to do with it?" she asks.

"It's mine."

"What did your grandfather do?"

Jubal's eyes stray into reverie. "He was his own man. One of those old-timers. Pretty famous, I hear. Valances go way back, you know."

"Did you know my father shot him?"

He is pleased she has said it, it tells him something. And he admires her, in a grudging way. "Yeah," he says, "I heard. But I didn't believe it."

"People say."

"Don't reckon he could have. Old Liberty was better than that."

"Well, I don't believe it either." She takes a long swig at the beer and comes up breathless.

Jubal is relieved. He is only a boy, she sees, and the line of his shoulders is so haughty, with dried trails of sweat still on them.

"Know what I'm gonna do?" he asks, suddenly. "I'm going to Korea. Be a soldier. Know what else?"

"What?" She doesn't want to hear that bullets have beaten in his graven chest.

"I'm going to be president."

"Of the U-nited States?" she drawls and grins at him.

"What else?"

"Well, boy," she says, and is sounding Texan now and using the beer bottle to cool her face. "You'll have to try me first." And she laughs out loud, like an idiotic kid, at what she has said.

"Don't talk like that," he says.

"Why not, Jubal Valance?" She wonders if she can anger him. Would he slap her?

"It's not right," he says. "I like you too much, anyway."

"Too much?"

"Yeah," he admits it.

"You mean you can't take me inside your little hut and give me what I deserve? Jubal Valance? I'm talking to you."

He doesn't know how to answer. He turns away and drinks his beer. Nora's heart is beating so much she can't think or hear anything.

"Are you crying?" he asks her. "You shouldn't cry." His dark brown hand is on her shoulders. "I don't want to see that." It is a plea.

"Don't go to Korea," she asks him.

"What else am I gonna do?" he wants to know.

"You been to school?"

"Eighth grade."

"You read all right?"

"Pretty well."

"Go to college."

"Yeah?" he laughs. "I'd be an old man before I got out of there."

"I could help you."

He is not sure if he wants that: it is teaching that clouds education for Jubal—he could be lawful if just left alone.

"Tell you books to read," she adds.

"Miss Garth does that."

"You know her well?"

Jubal shrugs. "She's pretty strange."

"What do you mean you like me?"

A blush roars up beneath his tan. He seems naked without his shirt. She puts a hand on his nipple. It is taut and she feels vibrations beneath it.

"What people mean."

"What's that?"

He is at a loss. "I don't know."

"Say it."

"Liking you. Thinking of you all the time."

"What else? Go on."

"Wanting you, what do you think?"

"So?" she leans into him and kisses the nipple. "Jubal Valance?"

Out there, in the evening, with traffic going by, he picks her up and carries her into his house. He is very tender and courteous at first, and she watches him as if he is a boy in a movie. But then she reaches out and holds him, and he has no control. It *is* love he has for her, and a youthful, extravagant delicacy such as he may have read about in books, or worked up in daydreams. She can see herself, eyes shut tight in willed pleasure, as the Mexican woman, but he is so ardent and thrilled. He tells her his name is really Jubilation, and there is no denying it fits him and the soaring that now lightens his face. She gives him money and he goes out to buy Mexican food. They eat it together in rapt silence at the square kitchen table. And she goes away again, before eleven, with the tired, excited feeling of a very complete workout.

"Let him be president," she confides to her car as she drives home with calculated risk.

1910

Jack Chance was as invariable at one hundred sixty pounds as coffee in the morning. He may have been born that weight, I told his mother—a most slender-hipped lady—but that was just to make her smile. You could sit Jack down for a month, feed him steak and fried potatoes, apple pie à la mode, and give him all the Steam he wanted, and he might have made it to one hundred sixty-one pounds when you were finished, just as fast but better natured than ever. That happiness of his was the single defect in his fighting makeup—except for those his management added. He liked people too much.

He was the son of a sheriff in a small Texas town, on the Brazos River down by the Gulf. The sheriff I never saw; he was an elderly man, it was said, and didn't like to travel. But Jack Chance's mother was a character—Miss Feathers O'Meara had been her maiden name, and she was the child of an Irish Confederate renegade who had come West after the war and taken a Comanche woman for his wife—hence the daughter's name "Feathers." She was an arresting-looking woman, with light brown hair and witchy black eyes, and she followed her son's career as a conscientious gambler. And I daresay because she had an itch for Jack Chance's manager.

"Look at him move," said his mother, the first time I saw him spar. "He's got my legs—you could make your fortune out of him."

And my pal, Tex Rickard, who was in the boxing business, reckoned, "Build him up, make him a heavy."

But it couldn't be done. Jack Chance had speed in his physical constitution—not a trace in his thinking—and he resisted bulk the way a vampire hates garlic. He could punch with both hands. He could take a strong shot himself. And he had a left jab to tell the time by. But he was an inevitable middleweight who couldn't find it in himself to work up a necessary, unhindered hatred toward another man, not even for three minutes.

I explained this problem to Jack, with analogies and examples.

"You've got to believe," I told him, "that there's just one loaf on the table, two of you looking at it, and it's fight or starve."

He nodded and said, "Why not cut the loaf in half?"

"All right," I said, "put it another way: there is a rattlesnake in your shorts, and if you don't put this other guy away, the snake bites you."

"How did it get in my shorts?" He couldn't picture it.

"I don't care," I cried. "I put it there!"

Then the kid had the gall to lay his knockout hand on my shoulder, pat it like Father and tell me, "Mr. Blaylock, that is comical. You are one of the best men I've ever met. You wouldn't *do* that, sir. Can't you see? Anyway, it's kind of ridiculous. I'm likely to start laughing now every time I put my shorts on."

"Go without 'em," I encouraged him, and his eyebrows leaped in alarm.

"Still, I catch your drift," he said: thinking made him slow and solemn. "I have to make my mind ruthless."

The truth was, once Jack started thinking he used to get hit a lot —then a kind of pained, intellectual disquiet spread through his face with the bruising.

"I don't see it," I told Tex Rickard. "He's nearly. But nearly isn't the bacon."

"Don't despair," said Tex. "Think on the bright side: he's a nice-looking dope; quarter Comanche. Great name—I tell you, Bark, people like to bet on him. Call him Comanche Jack Chance."

I groaned. "He won't have none of that. Won't have the Nations exploited. Irish Jack Chance?" I tried it out.

Tex nodded in that patient, keep-your-nose-clean way of his when talking to failures. "The thing I don't like is the mother."

"Mrs. Chance?" I may have exclaimed. "She's on him harder than anyone."

"Don't get me wrong. She's a sweet, decent woman. But does a killer in the ring have his mother around?"

"He'd mope if she wasn't here," I said.

"Well, now," mumbled Tex and started adding up some figures. "It's a shame," he said, "because, other things apart, I'd say you had a prospect."

It was 1907, up in Montana, that the Jack Chance prospect came to life. We had taken him up there on a building tour: there were plenty of fights to be had around the mining towns. In Butte, our boy put Montana Jack Sullivan away in a ten-rounder, yet everyone knew he should have knocked him out. A month later, in Helena, he got involved in the worst, read-a-book twenty-round draw with Kid Lee I ever saw. People were walking out from the tenth round on, and Jack was boxing the Kid's legs off, thinking he was putting on a marvelous show, never knowing he was making everyone miserable. The referee "turned" an ankle because he had a girl he wanted to see, and there was a twenty-minute extra delay while they found another. "That rest," said Jack, "that's what saved him. I was about to decapitate him—but he got a second wind."

So I put it directly to Mrs. Chance over supper that night—Jack had gone for a run, because he still had nervous energy! He was a strange kid, it didn't surprise me that he took to the church later.

"Spit it out," said Feathers. "I don't like it when you're anxious."

"Mrs. Chance," I began, "did you ever consider that your presence here might be . . . restraining him?"

"What in hell are you wanting to say?"

"Well," I proposed, "a regular rough fighter—I'd be checking up on him he didn't have more than two girls at a time. If you understand me."

"Very well," she said, and there was a dark grin on her face, more of a smirk, really.

"Maybe, in the nicest way, you have stilled his heart? I'm not offending you?"

"I'm glad to have the topic raised," she said, leaning forward and pushing aside her plate of chops. I doubt she was forty, and even if she came up out of nowhere Texas she knew how to dress and look after herself. She put her finger to her nose, as if an idea, or a sneeze, was coming, and then she came out with it.

"Suppose," she said, "he thought you were playing around with me."

"That wasn't what I meant."

"Wasn't it? I thought it was." She was wistful: "It'd give him a bit of devil."

"Make him angry?"

"I'll bet on it."

"How'd we do it?"

She leaned back and sighed deeply, calling to the waiter for fresh coffee. "Well, Barky," she smiled, "we'd have to, you and I, run a little show for him."

"Ah," I caught on. "Put the idea in his head?"

It seemed to me, in fact, that the matter was somewhat beyond this good woman's guile. I was therefore plotting a strategy myself, and so did not notice things making headway. Not until we were in Sacramento a month later when Jack knocked Pat O'Keefe out in the second round. Mrs. Chance shuddered at the blow—it was one of those punches palpable and shocking at the ringside, with dislodged sweat hurled everywhere as O'Keefe tumbled. She clutched at my arm as if this ruffian, her son, might attack her! As they counted out O'Keefe I saw Jack, confined and restless in a neutral corner, scowling at me and still punching his gloves together as if the fight hadn't started.

"I hear he woke up," said Tex on the phone. "Is it true you're bouncing the mother?"

"Not a word of it," I shouted—the damn telephone has always made me shout, for I can't get it out of my head that lung power doesn't assist the very progressive principle.

"Keep it up," said Tex—I could hear him drawing on a cigar— "and your boy could get Ketchel."

"Stanley Ketchel!" said an amazed Chance when I told him.

"The championship," sighed his mother, and then, "Bark, you're a wonder to even get it talked about. Don't write your father, Jack, but I think I'm getting fond of our Bark here." And she leaned over and kissed me on the cheek with a lot of heavy breathing.

"Mr. Blaylock!" Jack remonstrated, when we were alone. He was as red as a cherry and embarrassed.

"Uh-huh," I said; I was catching on.

"You wouldn't? With my mother?"

"This is not a thing gentlemen talk about," I pronounced. "Grow up, Jack. This is nineteen hundred and eight!"

"Ketchel will kill him," said Susan Garth—she had come along to photograph Jack for a razor-blade promotion. "You know it. Ketchel's the real thing. When he combs his hair he breaks the comb." Trust her to pour water on your dreams. "You should never let Jack in with Ketchel. Jack's never done anyone any harm."

"Oh, you like him then?" I asked—I was stung.

"Not as much as you like the mother," said she.

"That," I said slyly, "is a fix. To make Jack wild."

"Is that a fact? Or are you talking to yourself?"

The rest of 1908, Jack walloped Jim Flynn in Great Falls; he had Philadelphia Jack O'Brien's people throw in the towel; and, in Portland, the crowd were yelling for it to be stopped before Billy Papke bled to death.

"You're cooking," Rickard told me. "You're gonna have an animal there." And all the while Jack couldn't talk to me because his mother was draped all over me, and going into simpery little daydreams if ever I said two sentences in a row. She was a lovely lady, and I was with her more and more.

"You know," I started, the night before the Tony Caponi fight—Jack was early to bed.

"I do," she said, "I'm getting thoroughly persuaded myself. It's strange, you know, until people started their talk I don't know as I ever really noticed you." She had this way of implying it was a real thing, not our game.

"Would it be going too far?" I asked her: she was the expert in these things.

"The worst could happen," she reasoned, "is Jack putting you in the hospital." She laughed. "If he does, I'll visit you."

So a small thing started, of a purely physical and publicity nature. Ask Caponi—he was in the hospital, K.O.'d in the third, and didn't wake for nine minutes.

By then Ketchel was the recognized middleweight champion, beating fellows Jack had dismissed a lot quicker. Not that I didn't have concern over Ketchel: he was, along with Harry Greb, the most awesome fighter I ever saw. Take the Johnson fight. We went to that in Colma, in October 1909, to protest and give interviews on Ketchel hiding from Jack Chance and going in with Johnson.

But you had to give Ketchel his due. Johnson was maybe thirty pounds the heavier, and a head taller. He was a cocky bastard, and a lazy, show-off sort of fighter, but he could hit, and he had a mean streak such that only a life of abuse can give you. But he needed twelve rounds to beat Ketchel, and Ketchel caught him every round, and astonished him. Ketchel was the sort of man you needed to kill a couple of times before you felt safe.

"This'll have weakened Ketchel," said Tex.

"I don't know," I told him. "May make him meaner."

"Next year?" said Tex. "Ketchel vs. Chance? I think I like it."

Well, from then on we were aiming at it. Tex had the promotion, and his summer was given over to Johnson vs. Jeffries, and all the bother he had with that, being chased out of San Francisco—boxing had a bad name there ever since the Earp refereeing—and having to locate at Reno instead. He had two weeks to put up the seats, but still he took over two hundred and fifty thousand dollars, and he told me himself that he was fifty thousand in pocket. He was a wizard.

He told me in Reno—it was a July fourth fight, but Jeffries was too shot to be a nice American winner, "What Chance needs is something ugly."

"Ugly?" I said.

"He's a bit too perfect. People still think Ketchel will maul him."

"Break his nose?" suggested Mrs. Chance.

"I could maybe get drunk," said Jack himself, "and insult some nuns."

We were experimenting with such notions when I got a letter up from Texas:

Dear "Uncle" Bark,

I know you're not my uncle really. But I heard about you from my real Uncle Ethan. I am yours, truly, SHARON PAWLEY, the child of Deborah, who was Ethan's niece and married Martin Pawley.

Well, people say I'm pretty—I don't know. There's no way of knowing here in Texas. So my mother said I should go to the big city and maybe write to you. You are such a hero in our family. Uncle Ethan swore by you as a fine man and American. Could I come? I wouldn't be any trouble to you, and I'd go home if you said.

Yours,
Sharon Pawley

I didn't recall very much about that side of the "family," but Susan worked it out on paper, and I wired the girl to come if she liked. You never know when the greatest and the worst things of your life

are coming up to meet you. It's a wonder we have the nerve to leave
our beds and go out. I speak as a man who, very quietly, had maybe
spent a couple of hours every day of his life calculating the likely
ways to meet his one and true love. Oh, and looked at the faces of
every woman I ever saw, and wondered is that it? Which, you see,
is why I can say with absolute veracity that my burning for Mrs.
Chance—lively as it was; she was a real woman—was neither here
nor there. I was a man capable of a certain amount of formal fucking,
but it didn't mean a thing without loving.

"Here she is," said Jack, grinning all over his Indian face. He had
gone to the depot to meet Miss Pawley.

"Well, hallo," she said—I was making expense checks at the time,
and I got lost in the zeros. This was October 15, 1910, and she was
maybe nineteen or twenty, with black-brown curly hair and a smile
that dropped a trapdoor in your stomach. And she just looked at me
the once, checking who I was. There was this picture-book prize-
fighter at her elbow, ready to have her dance on his chest. And all
she saw was a thirty-four- or thirty-five-year-old fading guy who
needed spectacles to work, but who had surely been dreaming and
waiting. She held out her long, white hand and it was moist and
warm with her perspiration. "Hi, Bark," she said; there wasn't any
uncling.

Then Susan came in with a newspaper, full of excitement. But she
saw Sharon Pawley and I believe she knew on the spot—no one
knew my weaknesses better.

"Well," she said, catching her breath. "That Ketchel has gone and
got himself killed. In Conway, Missouri. A man named Dipley did
it. Our Stanley was seeing Mrs. Dipley on the side. It does happen,
doesn't it?"

"Shit!" said Mrs. Chance—for Ketchel was the prize and the purse.

"Lord," said Sharon Pawley. "Have I brought bad news?"

And I told her, "Don't you worry, kid. Things are looking up."

1950, Traveling

For James Averill III, Jim Jr., it is an adventure, this going to the
West. The sudden invitation from his father involves some time out
of camp—"But *this* will be educational, Good Lord," his father has

claimed on the phone (afraid of the thing being spoiled)—and a drive down to Boston with his mother (she has much to do there for her July fourth Ives affair—so very much she knows it cannot all get done, but it will be a party). Then in the Boston afternoon, while his mother is occupied, someone from his father's office takes Jim to an available double bill; it is *Colorado Territory* and *I Shot Jesse James*. Then his mother will collect him and cab him out to Logan in time for the flight to Albuquerque. And whereas Jim Jr. has flown several times before (seven—he has the score), he has never flown alone.

"Oh, there'll be a pilot, darling," says the understanding Betsy, winking at him past the edge of the *Herald*.

In 1950, nine going on ten, Jim is very much concerned with adventure, with courage and fear, the things that seem so important and so crushing sometimes in being an Averill. He is proud that his father was in the war; he knows there were medals for bravery and conduct, the occasions for which are never talked about. His father's modesty, which he reveres, only makes the performance more compelling. And Jim Jr. knows that whenever his father goes tight-mouthed about something from his own past, it is because there is that something there in a quality he wants for his son, but which he *will* not speak of, because it is most valuable to Jim Jr. if he comes to it on his own. For himself.

Even in all his activities, Jim's father is cooking up things for them to do, many of which have the atmosphere of challenge for the son:

—they will *see* the next Robinson vs. La Motta fight

—they will do a riding holiday together, just the two of them, in the White Mountains, and why not try a little rock-climbing while they are there?

—of course, Jim must meet MacArthur

—to improve at chess, at tennis and at bridge, you need to keep playing people who are better than you are

—and Come to the West—Come Now

Some promises slip: James Averill curses himself then for laziness and for letting down the boy; he does not see that there is sometimes relief when a menacing excursion is canceled. There is an altogether upward rush of feeling, effort, hope and initiative that the father urges on the son. It can leave Jim Jr. short of air, too nervous to try breathing. For Averills place themselves on a mountain—too steep and dramatic for all but the most venturesome of climbers. There is no forceful directing of young talent: Jim Jr. has had it explained to him many times that he could be a lawyer, a doctor, a military man, a writer, a painter, a businessman, a senator, *whatever* . . . but the point is to be high up the mountain, in a tricky spot from which the only relief is to go higher. This is not merely competitive: Jim Jr. has been taught to be a good loser (the language, the smile, the etiquette, the private rationale), and he admires and honors those who overcome him. The Averills are sportsmen, idealists and gentlemen. Jim Jr. knows that while Amundsen captured the South Pole, it was Scott who moved people, who revealed the pitiless unwinnability of the far place. And the mountain is where America sees its future, its examples; it is the peak of public service and performance. The idea of it exhausts Jim Jr., and it has taught him fear.

Try as he might, Jim Jr. cannot eclipse fear. He does often battle it down, yet it is there again next day, like a stray dog, cheerful, loyal and stupidly fond, laying claim to him. He was afraid in England of the bombs, and, worse still, of the bomb sites, the places that must be haunted; he is afraid of the dentist, of speaking in class, of the physical threat in sports, the loss of self in chess, of being alone in strange places, of his mother's sadness and his father's disappointment. He is ashamed of the fear that will not desert him or grow bored with him.

It is a young woman who takes him to the movies, a tall, smart girl who seems stoically amused by a boy's company and by the Westerns they are to see. But it is an afternoon off from duties Jim Jr. cannot guess. He does not think to question his safety with the young woman, or her reliability: his father's employees understand the overhang of the mountain, even if they are not all of them on it.

There is time for them to stroll down to the theater.

"I bet you're excited," says the girl: her name is Gloria.

"Do you know," Jim asks her, "will it be dark when I get there?"

"Albuquerque?" Gloria frowns and looks up at the Boylston sky. "I think it might still be light. You'll sort of chase the sun as you go."

Jim loves the deep red-carpeted shadow of the theater after the glare of the streets. Gloria gets the tickets and buys herself some Almond Joys: Jim Jr. declines all food at the movies—he disapproves of the intrusive smells of butter, popcorn and sugar—he wants to inhale the dry fire of the West from the screen.

He knows nothing about either film in advance, and he has learned that is always best. The strangeness is the greatest attraction: the new world that opens up is such a bounty to the imagination. These two films stir him especially: they are not bursting with confidence; they have uneasy central figures, an outlaw who cannot run far enough into the desert, and a fearful-faced desperado who is not sure whether he is coward or hero. In black-and-white, the two films are more comfortable at establishing the West as somewhere in the past. Jim understands the genre's taste for color, but believes it is helplessly modern and cheery. He prefers the aged feel and the beauty in harshness, and he always wants the weight of loneliness in Western landscapes that color somehow paints away.

Once or twice he looks at Gloria. She leans back with her knees up against the seat in front. She wears glasses to watch the film, and it makes her look more ordinary and more likable. He enjoys the way the light from the screen washes across her face, and leaves a kind of blank, dreamy attentiveness. He knows that feeling: she is there, away, *in* the picture, moving with its flow. He likes her.

"Hey!" she sighs, when the show is over. "Not bad. You like it?"

"Oh yes, I did. Thank you," says Jim Jr., so desirous to please her.

"Yeah. We had a good time," says Gloria, and she seems sleepy and content. (Jim would not mind marrying her.)

His mother is late and afraid of getting later. There are difficulties with the concert, evident clashes of will and reality in the air; her face is set in that pleading grimace that is always looking so far ahead. He is sure that if she could not see so far she would be more peaceful. She scribbles out a note in the cab, as they hurry through the tunnel. Jim Jr. is to give it to his father.

"And give him my love, won't you, sweetheart?" she asks, declining to add that to the note, and straightening Jim's hair with her cool, quick hand. "You'll have a wonderful time."

"Will I be back for the fourth?" he wonders.

She shrugs: "Ask your father. My life is going to be absurd between now and then."

On the plane, Jim Jr. has a program, and he will not be deterred from it, not even by the sweet, uxorious attention of Judy, his designated flight attendant. He takes the Cokes and the sandwiches dutifully, not really responding. He is nervous of the flight and knows that some mental task is his best occupation.

He has brought with him an ideal preparation, his *Boys' Book of the Wild West*, one of his favorite books. Of course, he knows it already by heart, but he has learned the value of preparation from his father and he intends to go through it once again.

The book has an unusual scheme: a bunch of 1948's boys, enthusiasts for the West, are visited by a ghost who invites them back to the West of the past. And so the gang travels through clouds of time to be *there* overlooking the Little Bighorn as Custer's regiment charges into trap and massacre; at the O.K. Corral; in Fort Sumner, New

Mexico, when Billy the Kid is killed; in Northfield, Minnesota, when the James gang carries out its last bank raid; in Indian camps, at cavalry posts, on a stagecoach, on a cattle drive, close enough to Belle Starr to touch, and so on. With many illustrations, more romantic drawings than photographs. There is a mixture of fantasy and research in the book that appeals to Jim. But what moves him most is the frequent ruling of the ghost. "We can watch, but we can't intervene." The gang cannot warn Custer, cannot save the carefree Kid (who does always, somehow, seem deserving of salvation) or tell Wild Bill Hickok that he should not sit with his back to the door.

For himself, Jim is prepared to let the past have its way. What intrigues him is the chance to be there, so close to the danger, yet safe. He hears the fusillade at the O.K. Corral but not even the most perverse ricochet could pick him off. All the way out there in the Dakotas, witnessing Custer's folly, he is also in First Class, cushioned and thoroughly Judyed, flying over Tennessee or Kansas. This is, after all, the privilege of the movies—the wondrous opportunity to be *there* yet undamaged by it, to be moved by the story yet not wounded, to live but not to die.

If there is a coward in Jim Jr.—and he considers that possibility very seriously—then he prefers the safety of the movies. But he has noticed a contradiction that runs through the form—the people in these films are so very seldom afraid for themselves. It is as if they were viewers, like him. Yet they wear old-fashioned costume, they carry six-guns, mustaches and long skirts across the range, and Jim expects more of them. He loves the medium and the genre, but he has begun to be suspicious that no cavalryman is ever yellow (despite the hinting stripes in their uniform), that men blaze away at one another and never ask for cover, that ladies in the desert wear lipstick and eye shadow, and that the simple life of the West is mysteriously sustained by modern conveniences and the lack of true danger.

So, moved by these films, and by their prospect of courage, honor and comradeship, Jim Jr. is disturbed by their serenity. He knows himself, at nine going on ten; he does not shirk what he sees and feels. He is ordinary, he is everyone, and he is afraid of everything. He sees fear as a respectful way of life, and he is most afraid of the terrible, blithe courage that people always show in Westerns.

"I'm going to do that belt for you," says Judy.

"Are we there?"

"Pretty close."

"It *is* still light."

"Surely is. You can see the mountains."

He looks out at the streaks of silver and violet in the astonishing mountains. The air is so clear—perhaps courage does come in the air.

"You've been a champion," Judy tells him.

"Oh, yes," he laughs, for it is expected in an Averill.

1915

She was a rarity then. People called her "the new girl"—as if they'd been expecting her, like the end of the world or unstoppable tanks. You see more girls like Sharon Pawley these days. They are the dreamboats from Arkansas or Texas or Oklahoma who win Miss America, six feet in their high heels, wavering to keep their decks in balance, jaunty, reckless and edible, about as house-trained as Ma Barker and threatening to split their bathing suits with raucous laughter at the foolishness of winning and having a tin-and-tinsel crown jammed into their hair.

They are wild beauties, as true as ice cream, and likely to last as long. So long as someone doesn't come after them and kill them. There's a ripeness to their looks that must pass or take up violence for salvation. They are as fast as the sun in time-lapse photography, a radiance hurrying toward the sea to cool itself. For the moment, though, they are electric vanilla, and some idiot ends up getting them down on film. I always thought that Sharon Pawley was about to catch fire. She was like the foliage on the hills in California in September. Ready to go, the gold that waits to ignite.

I loved her, and I photographed her, and those two furtive adorations went unnoticed in the splashy brightness with which old Bark Blaylock was in love with her, too. He took me for his friend and helper, and so I was: for I don't think I would have dared love her, without being sure of the enormous, blinding thing they had for each other. But the hardest part was when Bark's heart was broken—and it was open season on discussing the fracture—I still had to pretend to be just an honest friend, a hushed onlooker, someone with objective advice. Bark and I, I daresay, were never closer, yet never more at odds. But it may be easier for people to be together if there is some large misunderstanding, or something that goes unsaid.

I must tell you first who Sharon was, for there is no doubt in my mind but that her legend—which Bark knew, or felt, more strongly than Sharon herself (she was all present tense; that's why she photographed so well)—helped him fall for her, or even into her. He loved the history of that girl.

When Ethan Edwards had come back from the war, belatedly, for something more had gone wrong for him than just the end of the war, he had gone to his brother Aaron's home where Aaron lived with his wife, two daughters, Lucy and Deborah, and a son, Ben. It was a time of Comanche raids—1868, I believe—and the savages came down on Aaron's house and killed all of them except for Deborah, or Debbie, whom they carried off into captivity. She was then six or seven, and I don't know why she was not killed, unless it was to serve as a torment to a man like Ethan Edwards.

This was the origin of what Ethan called the "journey," the "search" or sometimes just "the time." He went out after his niece, roaming across the West like a marauder, growing older with the seasons, and Martin Pawley went with him, I hear, for no other reason than that people reckoned Ethan must kill Deborah if he found her. It is hard in such a search to find what you have looked for and not be dismayed, or disappointed by it. Moreover, this "time" got to be ten years, and Deborah was by then sixteen or so, and quite evidently the squaw of a chief named Scar.

Well, they found Deborah and killed Scar—and at that moment Ethan (a man who had always felt bound by solitude to act worse and fiercer than he was) did no such thing as slaughter her. He just picked her up and carried her home, aloft, as high as his heart. But as he told us, long afterwards, in Death Valley, he could not go back into the house or into any idea of family with her. He had become, as it were, as much a drifter, as much a lizard or an eagle scavenging off the land, as the Comanche he had tracked. He went away from the house, just let the door close behind him, and came to Tombstone where his harsh but soft heart was moved by Celia Blaylock.

Deborah came back from the Comanches pregnant: this was hardly a surprise, and I am not even sure it was her first child. She may have left one with the Indians, a young Scar with blue eyes. Well, this child . . . I do not know whether it was born or stillborn, buried or left in some remote place to die. Deborah then was in the care of old friends of the Edwards family, and I cannot estimate how hard they would have tried to keep that child alive, or how far their strict faith would have accommodated fate or forgetfulness. Ask yourself what you would have done on the edge of the desert in 1878, with a Deborah half crazy from not knowing who her proper people were. Don't underestimate the derangement, or overlook its power on Sharon.

A few years later, Deborah took up with Martin Pawley, Ethan's companion and guardian on the search. Martin had been betrothed all those itinerant years to a Laurie Jorgensen, from another of the pioneer families. They were married, too, but it did not stick. Martin, maybe, was as much affected as Ethan by their "time," just as foot-loose and devoted. And how could he get the figure of Deborah out of his head, after he had looked for her so long and hard? Especially when, as I hear, she had taken on the loveliest features of her first people and of the Comanche. So they were married, and Sharon was their child, born in 1889—tall, dark, and a little Cherokee on Martin's side for sure, to say nothing of the influence of her mother's Indian memories.

This was the girl who came among us in 1910 and who, at first, became the sweetheart of Jack Chance. This was so natural, it was obvious; it had to be worked through. They were the two handsome young brutes, after all. But Jack suffered grievously from it. For Bark never looked at Mrs. Chance again, thereby depriving our fighting hero of his one hope of violence—the pain of seeing his mother taken by his manager. Mrs. Chance herself was indignant at all of this: dumped on the one hand, with her best shot at fortune dwindling on the other. Jack Chance had a sad time of it: Billy Papke beat him in a close title fight; Frank Klaus knocked him out of the ring in Pittsburgh; and then the up-and-coming Harry Greb ruined his face forever. Jack took it very well, and he went back to Texas famous, moderately well-to-do, to a life of fronting bars and doing good work in the church.

By then, he had relinquished Sharon to Bark—losing her was not involved. The girl was too headstrong for that, too single-mindedly desirous. She took all the responsibility and always talked to Jack in the same joking, cheerful way. He had never had her properly, never had her enough to lose. And all the while Bark had watched Jack and Sharon together, and that watching had been the strongest force in her life. I never saw Bark so alert, so full of ideas, perky wit and odd charm. For this, you see, was the kind of idiot who had always supposed that some day someone would come along, half as beau-tiful and winning as Sharon Pawley. Oh yes, half would have matched his great hopes. And what had he got? A woman who would be famous for her fatal allure and her scared laugh.

It was in the summer of 1914 that Bark took it into his head to make a moving picture with Sharon as its object of worship—a religious picture! By then, long films were being made and thought of: Mr. Griffith had done his highly devotional *Judith of Bethulia*, and there was talk that summer of *The Clansman*, or what would be *The Birth of a Nation*.

Bark, too, was contemplating a four-reel picture, as long as an hour—though by the time we filmed, in 1915, he was ready for eight reels. He had talked to Fleur Hickey about an old favorite of theirs, *Tess of the d'Urbervilles*, and about the chance of transposing it to the rolling hills of Marin and Sonoma, with scenes on that rocky Pacific shore, in the redwood forests—a rural film, full of the wondrous Sharon Pawley, windblown, her hair like an unraveling rug, barefoot in the grass, running from and towards passion. Fleur was enthused; she wrote what she called a "photoplay," so shamefully vulgar she liked to read it aloud. Her literary standing went to hell. Movie was unhinging everyone.

That was the inspiration, though Bark was too conservative to want to pay Mr. Thomas Hardy anything for the rights—so Fleur's free, rampant adaptation did not acknowledge the novel and was to be called instead *A Girl of the Hills*. It was something to see Bark Blaylock as the idea took him over: for it was not enough to have and love Sharon; he wanted the world charged by the force and glory of the love, and he wanted everyone—I maintain everyone in the world: for movies *are* religious—to witness this wild girl of his. Whereas, maybe, he should have taken her off to the far end of Death Valley—except that there was a quality to her, a thrill that went through the air around her, that might have populated even that barren place.

"We don't know how to do it," I said—for it was somehow assumed I would be part of this film. Bark and I were not good at doing things without our own company.

"We'll find out, Sue," he said, and I did wish he could have loved me. It must be something—even for one summer—to be on the receiving end of such hope and zeal. I felt his energy could make me fly—for as long as I looked at him.

"Talk to these cameramen," he said. "This Billy Bitzer."

"You want me to photograph it?" I asked him. Who else was there? What else was I good for? Yet nothing had been said.

"Of course I do! Make her fit for heaven."

"But with some flavor of a short trip to hell?" I suggested—whereupon he shot me that old pinched, disapproving look of his that meant to tell me I was a heartless cynic.

Anyway, I went down to Los Angeles, and nosed around in the new profession of "lensing." They were all men, of course, and the most novel experience I had was in discovering that these men felt there was something indecent in a woman looking through the view-finder of a movie, something sacrilegious, as if the thing seen was their virgin daughter. The seeing itself was mysteriously male and sexual; it was a cult, a secret rite. But Bitzer very kindly gave me the time of day on film stocks, lenses and filters, and he recommended one or two likely assistants—at least someone who could load the camera without another Langtry disaster.

The one I wanted had another job, so I had to pick a mean-eyed, wash-faced kid named Jack Ford. He was very sniffy when he realized that a woman was going to be the photographer, but he surveyed some of my stills and muttered that he'd seen worse.

"Seems you know a bit about light," he conceded.

"Good of you to say so."

He looked at me wearily, dreading another bad-tempered female.

"You think the film won't come out if a woman does it?" I asked him.

"I never heard of it working," he said. "Who's the star?"

I told him and, of course, he'd not heard of her. So I showed him some stills of Sharon I'd taken out at Point Reyes. I was proud of the pictures and of the way I'd taught her not to shine those eyes of hers straight into the lens. Instead, I'd told her to look and let the camera come up like a shy boy thinking of kissing her. Ford examined the pictures, and his lips puckered.

"She looks Irish," he said.

"She looks better than that," I told him off.

It was like popping him in the nose. He looked up, startled and flustered, and then he gathered himself and gave me that snarly grin of his.

"Well, you haven't sold her short, I'll say that."

"Thank you." I put them back in their envelope.

"No, I could jump in bed with her now."

"She's taken," I told him.

"Oh, I can see that," said he in a dreamy voice.

Did it show? I had taken so few photographs of people, I was myself surprised at the luster in Sharon Pawley's face, and the en-graved, curled whorls of her hair in the wind. We had had a great day out on the cliffs and on the shore, with a picnic basket. She loved to have her picture taken: she learned so fast it was like an adult learning to read, seizing on a wonder that might still alter her

life. I did not know from anything she did or said whether she knew
what I felt. You see, she could easily say she was revealing or giving
herself just for the camera, not for me. But she looked at her pictures,
too, and I saw her interest—it was not unlike Jack Ford's appreciation, as if only then realizing the heat or need there might be in the
person watching. They do say of movies that the camera loves some
people. Maybe. But don't forget the person guiding or feeling
through the camera. Isn't it their nakedness that shows?

So Ford and I went back to San Francisco, after I had done my
other errand in Los Angeles, collecting the last investment from a
man recommended by Tex Rickard—and leaving a selection of stills
at his house so he knew what he'd be getting—a gentleman named
Noah Cross. From his great white house in the hills I guessed he
could pay the money and never notice where it went.

1950, Birdland

Sally Averill is sitting in a corner at Birdland, listening to Wardell
Gray solo while Parker counts the house, her chair rocked over on
its two back legs, her head gently beating time on the wall. How is
she there, alone, underage, in the dark throng of the city, a fifteen-
year-old getting away with eighteen in the shadows, still learning
this new music?

She is there because, with her father, she looked at the exotic, racy
place he had brought her to for excitement, for education, for experience, and thought to herself these things only commence when
one is alone. And she saw the delicious cult of secrecy and surrep-
titiousness at the club, willing to slip past rules; she saw the sidelong,
appraising eyes watching her, begging her to be alone; and she knew
how far a little money would go, getting in—and out. Moreover,
against all expectation, despite her father's earnest instruction, she
liked the music. Bop. She loved that music. After one night, she
wanted more.

And so, at a weekend, Sally Averill has told her school she is
visiting home, and she has instead put on her high heels and her
tight black dress—a "pencil," it is called—collected the allowances
she saves, and she has come to New York. It is her wisdom on the
streets of that city never to be at a loss, a stranger or a beginner,

never abashed, daunted by or interested in what is passing. So she bears the tough, abstracted manner she imagines in a cool young hooker who is studying to be a lawyer—she has this character sketched out in her head so she can answer in the whore's terse dialogue. It works—it does? Someone asked her the way on the street, and she got out of it by seeming too bored to know.

She has a hotel room: she has enough money for that, and enough domesticity in her upbringing not to risk everything. It is a tiny room at the Wentworth, a closet of a room, but it is a place to wait, to lie in the old, cracked bath and scheme. It is a place for calculating or summoning just how much peril and excitement it will take to fill her up.

At Birdland, she slips in. There is a chuckle in the dark from the dwarf at the door: she has not fooled anyone on her age. But that aloof, closed authority she masters—it is oddly English; her willfully ignorant mother has it, a way of not noticing servants?—persuades the man she would not be there, so vulnerable, unless she was there for someone, part of an arrangement it is not wise for him to interfere with. Her character has a destiny—far less pretty or promising than she knows—that sweeps aside formal objections. She has the confidence of a possessed actress, and it may be up to her to see if she can handle the tragedy written for her role, a role she has never read through to the end. Who can? Bop.

She picks a table where a young black couple is sitting, a corner table in its own gloomy aura. They are holding hands, bop-bop, and they look like a haven: he wears glasses and a tweed jacket and she has a large bead necklace that strikes Sally as a charm-like model of decorum. She asks if she can sit at their table and they shuffle over guiltily to make room for her. The young black woman holds on to her man more tightly. Sally smokes aggressively, blowing out as if the air of the club is a conspiracy against her, and she orders a whiskey that comes without dispute. The couple at the table fall silent. Do they know her for a gangster's abrupt babe, bop, an insolent, black-eyed portent of trouble?

She asks the tweed who's playing: she longs to know, she wants to be able, in her bouncing head, to praise these languid jitter-freaks, the musicians; she wants to follow them. But the young man takes the question as sure sign that she is, indeed, not a jazz fan, not a music lover, but a scarlet woman who is there just for the kind of liaison, thrills, that give jazz a bad name. The black man in the tweed jacket looks as if he might be a Ph.D. student, doing a dissertation on African rhythm in the American city. Bass kick.

He tells her that it is Charlie Parker, Wardell Gray, Milt Jackson, Max Roach, Tommy Potter and Thelonious Monk. He is hurt but not surprised that she is so unimpressed by this 1950 galaxy—he knows he is a spectator at history, and this blasé white girl behaves like a bitch at the fights waiting for real blood.

The alto soars, reverses, hopscotching bar to bar. Sally nods curtly at the young black information service, stubs out her cigarette and tongues a possible speck of tobacco from off her lips.

She does not know the tunes the musicians play, or even whether they are "tunes." For it seems to be their object just to get into the music and stay there. She has worked out the pattern of a theme stated first, sometimes with abject, violent speed, a wriggle, to get it over with, and then the run of limitless solos, some of which last five or ten minutes, crescendoing, and each of which is marked by applause as another soloist takes over. She cannot stop moving to the music, keep up, keep on, the beat, bop. She notices that her body keeps the base time, the beat of the drums, the flutter of bass, while her fingers and her hands are playing out the notes of the saxophones and the vibraphone. She assumes that this music is not written, that the themes are known, like old jokes, and that everything after that is improvised—like running, jumping, leaping. But she is learning to see all the small bondings in the group, the ways in which as they spiral off in their own directions they touch and dance. She has never seen six people so close, so carried on by the same momentum. Yet they do not seem, these grave men in drape suits, to talk or recognize one another: it is the music that links them; its surge is the idea of all their spiraling.

The black couple leave her: she is too intimidating for them.

The man at the piano wears a short-brimmed hat, and every other note he hits—she hears every one, sparse, splintered—sounds odd or wrong, until seconds later, three other false notes make a new, sidelong line that is inevitable. The bass player is taller than his instrument, his eyes are closed and nothing moves except fingers that are like small flutes—but Sally has already learned to listen in to just the bass, inward beating: it is the pulse, but its notes are the structure of what the others are playing. The drums are too forceful for her in the small club, but she sees already how this drummer has several different rhythms going at once: she has a vision of him taming spiders, tarantulas that live in the drums, teaching them to scrape and hiss for his cymbals.

The vibraphone player has hammers with bright blue silk heads, and he watches over them, his cobras, studious and elegant in horn-

rimmed glasses until there seems to be a life in the bars of his instrument that sends the hammers flying up and away to other keys.
Is the picture running backwards? So that the instrument seems to
be playing the man and he is now its rapturous slave, his eyes wild
and wide at the fury he finds beneath him, his slick face catching all
the drips of sweat that rise up from its exertions.

The man with the smaller saxophone is stout: he rests the curve
of his horn on his belly and then leans back away from it to stay still
and balanced. But the equilibrium strikes oddly with the unexpect-
edness of his playing. He is the most advanced of them all, and
apparently the undemonstrative leader. His improvisations are more
dexterous, more melodic and serene, at the same time more perilous
and more controlled. James Averill has told Sally that this man—she
knows he is Parker—is a genius, albeit a genius whose music emerges
from a chaos of living confusion, drink, drugs and a systematic failure
to link up with time, place and the world's measured occasions. This
is strange when his momentary instincts of rhythm and harmony
are so acute and piercing. Sally can already see a rationale in the
man's music that the large, external time-scale is a sham and that
the inner connectedness of notes is more crucial—as if what men
and women did might be minor, or automatic, compared with the
tiny leaps of electricity or magic in their heads. Sally does not know
how to articulate what she is trying to think, but the music is leading
her on. She wants to sing with the band: it is the first great ambition
of her life, the first one worthy of the Averills. It makes her cry.

"What's hurting, child?" People notice tears: they wash away
reserve.

It is the black man in tweed. He is back again. Alone. He takes
off his glasses, folds them, inserts them in his top pocket. She sees
the moves, the stages of the act, as if they are eternal and hallowed.
Is she drunk?

"You like the music?" he asks. He has not realized this possibility
before. Tight white people are so strange.

"Yeah, I like it." She sounds, she thinks, like thirteen, and she
hopes the darkness hides her blush.

"Wait for War-dell," the man tells her, and nods up towards the
players.

The fat man and the vibraphone player have retreated to the bar,
and the man with the larger saxophone is left alone. He is very thin;
he does not look strong enough to support his keyed, bespouted
instrument. He starts to play with just the rhythm group. He leans
over to his left and his pants billow as if with air. But it is his rhythm

and it comes upwards until his long jacket is swaying, too, and the sax is going like a pendulum. He plays something that seems simple and droll, but the sound from his horn is so wise, so sad and so complete—it seems to Sally like an ancient natural phenomenon. The phrasing of the number passes into her so that she knows it on one hearing, and she knows this is more than all the idleness of school and the torture of trying to understand her parents, or make them attend to her.

The black man is holding her hand and she gives him a smile as more whiskeys come down on the table in front of them.

"Now you're doing fine," croons the young man.

The number ends, the crowd applauds and the saxophone player whispers into a microphone, "Thank you so much. That was called 'Twisted.' "

"War-dell, War-dell!" the black man with her chants under his breath. And then, to her, "He's my man."

"Mine, too," says Sally, knowing for sure she's on her fateful way, but knowing it's hers and feeling the corkscrew squirrel of the music in her just like a sexual thrust she has read about and guesses is coming closer.

"You with someone?" the black man asks her.

"I'm with the music," she decides.

And he laughs and says, "I'm with you!"

"Whatever," she tells him.

1915

Night after night, in a heat wave in Marin, our clothes and hair smelling of the eucalyptus, the story of our movie bucked, twisted, doubled back, began again. But nothing came between the mortal freshness of Sharon Pawley and the cold resolution of my lens.

I gave up on the story; Sharon simply plunged into her character—the process was convulsive, ecstatic, like being drunk. There were so many nights in the country inns we lodged at when Bark arose, fire-eyed with new story slants, from the bed we assumed he shared with Sharon. At any small hour of the morning, you could find him sitting in the lamplight rewriting the script—or just adding page after page of his wild longhand to it. Sharon never stirred, never woke; she dreamed on, refurbishing the glory of her looks.

I was playing cards one night with Ford and a couple of the crew when Bark came tottering downstairs. He had no shoes on and his suspenders were hanging down from his waist. But he had a notion.

"She could come out of the sea, soaked," he said, "and we could have the camera lead her up the gentle incline of a cliff with the sea behind her." He stared at us. "Couldn't we?"

"We might," I said. "Where would that fit in?"

"Well," said Bark, "after she's gone away."

"She swims back?" asked Ford, the more impatient because he held three kings.

"She might have come by boat," Bark was working it out, "and there's a shipwreck."

"How do you do a shipwreck?" asked one of the other fellows.

"Her clothes clinging to her?" I asked.

And Bark's eyes widened because someone else could see it. "Yes!" he yelped. "Exactly so!"

"Would she do that?" asked Ford. "Can she swim?"

"She'll do it," Bark assured us, so shyly and so proud I wanted to stroke his uncombed hair.

So we did it, and it was grand. She couldn't swim, but she went out into the water that was colder than any of us guessed, and she shuddered and laughed at the craziness of it, and then without being told she went under and came up soaked and glossy like a long-haired fish. And she strode out of the water while I backed off in front of her, holding the camera. Oh, the shot was shaky, but everyone said considering the ground it was a small problem, when really I was only shivering because she was so wet and glorious, like a wound walking into your heart. No one knew or cared how it would fit in the story, but she came out of the water laughing, a beautiful Fury from mythology.

"It's gonna make the shipwreck tougher," Ford murmured in my ear. "That laugh of hers."

"It's a pirate ship," I suggested. "Or a ghost ship. She's happy to have escaped."

And so our picture grew, and became more expensive. It was such a summer, 1915, with ourselves excursioning in and out of the coves and woods of northern California, living on bread and cheese and cherries, making our story anew each day like a picnic lunch, and catching up when we could with the news of Ypres and poison gas, the *Lusitania*, and Willard "beating" Johnson in Havana, and of the extraordinary burning success all through the land of *Birth of a Nation*. We knew and understood the deaths on the Western Front, we were not callous, but we could not stop being happy or occupied. The lack of straight story did not matter so long as Sharon Pawley was coming over some hill as bright and patient as the moon. From day to day, she was victim and temptress in the story—it did not all fit: There was a greater continuity and energy in the appetite she and film emulsion had for one another. I have never known boredom or doubt so suspended. It was Sharon's greedy summer.

The laughter did die. Not that she became despondent because of the war, or tired of running across dappled meadows. No, what made our star reflective was just the sight of herself on the screen. Our base was a large shed in Calistoga, and when we came back there once or twice a week we'd run the footage. I suppose we would have been professional to examine it for "errors," but in those un-hindered days of moviemaking we looked at the film for fun and feeding on—none more so than I, for I was learning and needed the pleasure of work done—and just to see what else we could do with this project. We talked to our story as it unwound on the screen.

No scrutiny was as anxious or as intelligent as Sharon's. She was not always on the screen—Bark did permit other characters. But there was the feeling that she was, if not the screen, then at least the light, the wavering but silvered clarity that let the enterprise exist. And she must have seen herself as she had never done before. I do not mean she was afflicted with coyness or embarrassment as many good-looking people are when their image is broadcast. Rather, her natural, uninhibited grace acquired self-awareness and could not stop some cunning need for control creeping in with it. She saw herself and the effect she had; she saw beauty at work, not just the unique impact of Miss Sharon Pawley. The adoration of Bark Blaylock may have fallen into place as just one example of what there was, out there, available, and such as she merited. I think she began to think of herself in the third person, and that is what took away the laughter. A touch of myth came over her: she might be eternal—would this picture ever die or age? All her riotous irony slipped away, vanished; she had found a kind of worship, full of dread or worry.

More than any authorial or scripting policy, this gravity of hers led our film towards its proper Thomas Hardy–like tragedy. Her Tess brooded more; she moved fitfully or indecisively; there was doubt in the twist of her body and the droop of her heavy head. There was a close-up in which she looked at the horizon as if it were a wire prepared to encircle and strangle her. She emanated the fine, tremulous passion of a deer in hunting season; her hair became as noble as antlers that had had a dream of ending as a severed trophy on some wall.

"Oh, Sue," she whispered to me one day as I ministered to her —the cameraman must measure the beat of light off a star's skin, he or she must go very close, where confidences can be given up as well as intimate pictures. "Why am I so uneasy?" she asked me.

There was nothing anywhere to be seen that explained her apprehension, and I did not know how to answer. So I made wordless, reassuring sounds, mothering noises, and stroked her face: I was so artful at finding excuses to touch her.

"Oh, Sue," she warned me, and she smiled.

"What's that, Sharon?"

"Sweet Sue," was all she said.

Then four days later, as I adjusted a reflective sheet of white cotton beneath her sunken face, she said—or the sound welled up out of her, I did not see her lips move: "You take care of Bark."

"I'm his friend," I said. "Always will be."

"He wouldn't forget."

"Forget what?" I murmured.

"If I went. He's the sort holds on to what's gone, what he never had."

I laughed. "No, that's me." And she looked at me as if I were the joker, the pretty card but never used in the game.

We had a film, if we could find a little more money. The shipwreck had cost more than we anticipated, and then there were the Gypsies (confidants to our Fury), and the wild horses and the falcon—oh, yes, the falcon was very difficult, and left scars on my bad hand. Bark was always awake, trying to raise more money. He let it make up for the way Sharon had asked to sleep alone: she needed that, she had said, to fortify the solitude of her character and to be more lovely. Bark's furious planning had been keeping her awake. Only sleep could nourish her now. She was a kind of demon.

One day as we finished filming, we saw a rogue car parked near our camp. It was a burning-bright yellow Maxwell tourer and a tall man of middle age was sitting in it.

"I came to see what I had here," he called out to Bark. The voice was very clear across the sunset distance.

It was Mr. Noah Cross, and he left no doubt but that there was more money if we needed it, and if the story could be wound up to his satisfaction. He watched the footage, silent and missing nothing, like a lion watching a film about meat, terrifyingly restrained.

So we went on filming as fall came: the leaves turned and Bark worked out our absolute conclusion as Tess would fall from a cliff.

"You would ask Miss Pawley to do that?" asked Noah Cross, never looking at the actress in question.

"Of course not," said a bewildered Bark. He was exhausted and he planned just to toss a costumed, stuffed sack, any dummy, down the cliff.

"Yet the real thing would be more powerful," said Cross, and still he did not dare to glance at Sharon—perhaps he was so thrilled by her he could not. There was a pressure in what he was urging, more than money's request.

"I should," whispered Sharon.

"Ah," sighed Cross, as if he was remembering she was there. "Do you think you could?" He asked this in such a way they were standing there alone: his intentness shut us out. She could not speak, she was breathless, but she nodded at him, and there was a directness to it, a naked gesture that sufficed, so that I knew he'd had her already, and infected her with knowledge.

Cross took charge. He made a soft landing on a ledge a little drop down the cliff so that we could shoot upwards at Sharon falling towards us.

"I'll be there to catch you," he told her.

Bark watched the shot being worked out. He saw plot suddenly coming together in his rapture of a film. He could not bear to see Tess stop or cease. And the camera caught Sharon's falling face as if she was seeing an open razor—it was only a second, but it was a face about to die.

"There," said Noah Cross when it was done. And he laughed out loud so that his laughter echoed back from the cliff face and we all wanted to get away from it.

Sharon drove off with him that evening, still wearing her Tess costume. They left us to cut and finish the film. And then a month later, Noah Cross came up to Calistoga alone, without any mention of where Sharon was or whether she was. He watched the film and he sat back when it was over to light a cigar.

"It's heartbreakingly beautiful," he confessed. "Miss Garth, my compliments on your eye."

"Sue has done splendidly," Bark agreed.

"But it's nonsense," said Cross. "You must see that."

"Not nonsense, sir." Bark could only deny it.

"Oh, but it is. There's no story anyone could follow, or credit. There's just the young woman—and she is, well, she's a genius of an odd, unknowing sort."

"Yes," said Bark, close to some empty peace.

"With a great career."

Bark nodded. Could his head's tired flicker make Cross vanish?

"Which this would ruin."

"This will start it!"

"It will not," said Cross.

"She will do nothing better!" I never heard Bark so certain.

"I own the picture," Cross then explained. "The majority of it. I have a personal service contract for Miss Pawley. I cannot allow this work to jeopardize her chances. Mr. Blaylock, I am indebted to you—you are, shall we say, the pathfinder. But I am the builder of cities, sir. I will pay you five thousand dollars so as never to see you again. Cash."

"What does Sharon say to this?" I asked him.

He turned to me. "Why, Miss Garth," he said, slowly and courteously, "she puts her trust in me and asks to be remembered to you. You, too," he smiled, "showed her the way, showed her, if I may say so, the light. Five thousand dollars."

"And the film?" asked Bark.

"Forgotten."

1950, Mesa Verde

James Averill has driven his son out of Santa Fe, by way of Los Alamos, Cuba and Farmington. They can see the ragged prow of Shiprock to the west, beckoning them on, sometimes more like a webbed hand, sometimes a ruined or forsaken cathedral. James is elated at being out there with his son, exploring, and it makes him drive fast even though he wants the trip to last forever.

"Who is this Jubal?" asks Jim Jr. in a solemn but exasperated way that must have made Jubal himself sneer. There are differences of attitude and history in the loft of a voice that eclipse race or class. Yesterday, Jubal Valance had taken Jim Jr. riding on a small bay horse that bulged with muscle and willingness. They had gone miles,

and the boy had come home happy, caked with dust and too tired
for supper.

"Who is he?" asks James Averill. "Well, he's a local. I expect his
grandfather was a cowboy. He's a Westerner—the real thing."

"Perhaps," says Jim Jr., very thoughtfully. "Do you know what
he said?"

"I thought you liked him?"

"I do. But he said he was going to be president. I ask you!" The
boy cannot forget Jubal's darkening silence when Jim had reported
how he had met Mr. Truman, a couple of times. They had been
resting on their ride, and Jubal had simply wheeled his horse around,
a mountainous chestnut that would keep nipping at Jim's horse, and
set off up the trail at an unapproachable canter. He hadn't spoken
to the boy for an hour, and Jim had known no way of regaining his
new friend.

"He might make a president," says James Averill.

"Oh, Dad!" The son has already worked out a despairing tolerance
for his father's bouts of righteous sentimentality. "How could he?"

"I don't know," Averill admits. "But he *is* the heart of the country.
If he got himself an education, studied law, ran for local office. He
could become a figure of some . . . some appeal." Averill loves political hypothesizing: he *can* see it working.

Averill is thinking that if Jubal were played by, say, Gary Cooper,
in a Capra film, he might be able to redeem the political validity of
homespun virtue and inarticulate candor. So long as he wasn't also,
or incidentally, a lying, brutal, scurrilous opportunist, in which case
he might just settle for being a New Mexico bully boss.

"He's impressive," Averill points out. "As a rider—you can see
that. Imagine him in a good suit, his hair cut; imagine what your
mother could do, whipping him into shape."

Jim Jr. chuckles; they are having fun.

"Teach him to talk," says Averill, on a roll now. "What then?"

The boy is impressed. Jubal does have a strong face, frightening
if he isn't grinning. He isn't anyone you forget. And the name is
potent.

"Well," says the boy, leaning back in the seat, "Miss Stoddard
fancies him."

"Do you think so?" His father sounds surprised.

"She was very kind to him. When we got the horses."

"She was being polite," Averill reasons.

"She smiled at him when she thought I couldn't see."

"How sharp you are!"

"Mummy says Averills are always watching ladies." He smiles, sure this means more than he likes.

"She said that?" His father pretends to be horrified. "We'll have to talk to her."

"Are you here for Miss Stoddard, Dad?"

"I just thought it high time you were exposed to some of this country. Too many satisfied Americans have never seen it—have never heard of where we're going."

"Mesa Verde," says the boy. He has mastered the name. "But why are you seeing Miss Stoddard?"

"There's this photographer she's uncovered—a very old lady. And Miss Stoddard wants the Foundation to help put on a show for her."

"Do you like her?"

"I like her pictures—some of them—very much."

"I meant Miss Stoddard."

"Ah." He pauses to look at the wrinkled surface of Shiprock as they turn north. "Yes, I think she's terrific. Don't you?" He sees that his hands are trembling on the wheel, but the car hurtles on, undeflected.

"I like it when she swears," says the boy.

"Really? I haven't heard that. So you think she'll make a fine First Lady?"

At which Jim Jr. dissolves in mirth, as if being tickled, as musical as a girl. It makes Averill feel a girl's hands are moving all over and through him, searching for his soul, like soap slipped away in water. They do have a good time whenever James can manage and protect a reasonable vacation. He likes to say that all of life is a holiday; what a gift to lose.

"Now," he announces to his son. "I'm not going to say anything about this place. Not until we're there, anyway. I want you to see it for yourself. But you should know it's somewhere Indians lived once, from about A.D. 500 to 1300."

"Gosh," says the boy. "I didn't think there was anyone here then. That's William the Conqueror." He has learned, through his mother, to measure the brevity and recentness of America's history against the interminable gallery of English rogues and heroes. "Mummy would like this," he says.

"Who knows?" says his father gaily, yet pierced. "One day."

They drive through Cortez, and then east for a few miles to the turnoff to the right. The winding road climbs through piñon-covered

hills until they are on a plateau. Sometimes they catch glimpses of
the flat of Arizona and New Mexico, away to the south, like gray
glass.

There is a guide waiting for them, a tall lean young man in Bermuda
shorts and long white socks. Averill has called ahead to get the best
assistance. This is something he regards as everyone's due; yet his
son sometimes flinches from the advantage and the extra weight of
response it calls for. He would have preferred to wander about alone
with his father. Not that the day is spoiled, or less than captivating.

They see the canyons and the cliffs; but the guide appreciates that
a boy is the object of the exercise. Like a wise master at the Prado,
he chooses just five or six Goyas and Velázquezes for the novice,
confident they will make him a devotee for life.

He leads them down the paths to the houses, the towers and then
the Cliff Palace, a stone city set in an enclave, an arc scooped out of
the cliff face. The buildings are in different states of repair, and here
and there some new government cement has been added tactfully
to the face-powder–colored mortar daub the Indians used centuries
before. There are houses of small rooms, with windows like jars
upside down and a stopper at the bottom. Jim Jr. feels peace in the
grave beauty of the construction and the balanced air of the ruins.
There is so little room in the enclave, yet the Indians—the Anasazi,
the guide calls them—had made busy, crowded miniature cities in
which there was the decent, spatial poise of a street of tenements.

"These fellows, the Anasazi," the guide says. "As you can see,
they were fine builders. Here in this city there could have been two
or three hundred people. They harvested food on top of the
plateau—corn, beans, squash—and they would have hunted for deer
or wild fowl in the canyons."

Jim and his father follow the guide down into a kiva. There is a
hole in the floor and a wooden ladder that descends to a small,
circular chamber maybe ten feet in diameter. Its roof is a very artful,
tidy cross-layering of timbers which, their guide assures them, is
original. There is a firepit in the center of the ground and a clever
system of draft ducts to keep the air fresh. Around the walls there
is a series of stone seats like choir pews. The three of them sit down.

"We don't know exactly what the kiva was for," the guide tells
them, "but we believe they were holy or ceremonial places, where
the elders came to pray for rain and to discuss tribal governance."

"I love it," whispers Jim. There is an air in the kiva still of austere
magic, of some sublime judiciousness carefully arrived at. The boy
aspires to such close councils of wisdom and tolerance and he revels

in the firm support of the stone seats. The delicate interweaving of the roof is a marvel: the bare, dry beams and the rock-hard mud between them. It feels waterproof, fault-free, a physical model of order possible to any man on earth. His father looks at the pale, smoothed branches and thinks of Nora Stoddard's polished limbs, and of how he can contrive to be alone with her.

They go back into the light and the guide begins to speak of the destiny of the Anasazi.

"Some time around 1300," he proposes, "they just left this place."

"Why?" asks the boy. He would have stayed there forever.

"It's not known. There may have been drought years and crop failures."

"Did they have enemies?" Jim asks.

"We believe they were peaceful."

"You know," says James Averill, "perhaps they just took it into their heads to move on."

"How do you mean, sir?" asks the guide.

"They may have had no problems. They may have been happy, or content." He is feeling the terrible, hopeful force of boredom that thirsts for change. "Perhaps the spirit came to them, to the leaders down in that kiva, that they must change or die. So they changed." He looks down the canyon. "And maybe died." Why does he find that winning?

"We think they are the ancestors of tribes to the south: the Pueblo, the Navajo, the Hopi and the Zuni."

"Imagine them," says James, enthralled by the structures, "leaving such a city and going out into the desert."

"Well, sir," says the guide, politely. "That could be. Yet I think the years of drought were in their minds."

"I'm sure, I'm sure," says James. He is a poet, humbled by a social scientist. "Whatever the answer, they were brave!"

"And very worried," murmurs Jim Jr., trying to feel his way back through the abandoned silence to those helpless fellow Americans who would be dead very soon, long before the last fall of their elegant, rational stone houses.

1921

I was forty-five or forty-six, and weary of the uncertainty, even if I was not far from too old to care or notice. But as Susan would always tell me, I was premature in regarding myself as an old man. Of course, she knew it was losing Sharon had taken the shine off me, and she was patient and kept close by me in those first months without her, until she had had too much of it and grumbled at me for seeing only my own misery.

"That's what misery is!" I shouted at her. That woman made me so angry, I never could decide how she stayed around so much and I didn't choke her.

"Misery is a common condition, Bark Blaylock. That is, until you realize how common, and then people have the grace to see they're no worse than unfortunate."

"It's knowing she's down there," I cried. "With that Cross."

"Prefer her dead?"

"I might." Dead or never known, I thought.

And she looked at me with lowered, absent-minded gaze. I know she was trying not to show her hurt, for she must have hoped or thought I would surely marry her for want of an alternative. But there I was, nonetheless—with her! She had never talked to Sharon; never even quite looked at her, despite the business of photography. That blind jealousy. It's a wonder what people can manage not to see.

Mr. Noah Cross suppressed our picture without second thoughts. I did hear that he had burned it. And Sharon must have reckoned he was right, for she made these foolish comedies, laughing till you thought her head would split. And they were hits. Everywhere. She never got another chance to develop herself as a tragic actress, some-one worthy of Hardy. I don't know what happened with her and Cross, but in 1920, Sharon Pawley, the "Oh, you kid!" loved by millions, threw herself off the Bradbury Building in downtown Los Angeles. There was talk of her being a drug baby—I don't know, she did have unreliable health and irrational fixations—and there was no mention of Cross. He had taken her and left her, I suppose.

That, apparently, was his way. I read about him, I followed him, and I was startled at the scale of his wealth and piracy. Our picture was not much more than a tip for him, and I hope Sharon was satisfied with her four or five years instead of going off homesteading, as I had fully intended and asked her, to the Pecos country, near Fort Sumner, which I recalled fondly.

So, I moped around the West a couple of years, looking up a few old acquaintances and changed places. I got as far as Fort Sumner and found that the river was considerably less than I remembered, a none-too-deep affair. Maybe the storm that day in '81 had made it flood; perhaps it was luck that I nearly drowned. There were little lean-to souvenir stores in Fort Sumner selling Kid gimcrackery that made you sick, and old-timers ready to swear they'd known him. But I didn't let on—no sir.

But I was forcibly struck in those years after the Great War by the way clear-cut fraud was becoming a national business. My old friend Walter Scott had made a small fortune just by talk of having struck gold. Never bothering with the stuff itself! He was so honest about it, I couldn't dislike him for it. But there were people in the West now writing rotten, fabricated stories, and they were making moving pictures about the "great old days" for which they had the nerve to seek historical advisers. Then there were the Noah Crosses, able to manipulate the world while saying they had acted, or striven, in the saintly cause of progress, patriotism and American enterprise. I heard that Cross had ruined other women, just broken them when he was bored. But how could anyone ever prove the facts against him of the passion or the dread that made Sharon hurl herself down? He cooked facts and served them up as publicity.

"Yet he made her famous," said Susan, needling me.

"What's that do?"

"Maybe it's all she wanted."

"You know? Better than I?"

"I cared for her," she said, and she lurched out of the room, weeping. She was always like that if she couldn't have her way and feel she'd won the argument.

As I said—and I daresay I am wandering, I am not a straight story man—I was wandering over the West, less pleased with what I saw. Until I came to Mesa Verde, the Indian ruins in the southwest corner of Colorado. One day in 1920, I rode up into it, never knowing it was there, never hearing of it, but simply in the stubborn mood of a rough-riding, lone camper, beating his way into what seemed an impenetrable canyon, to find the peace there, the hallowed enclosure and the fine, abandoned dwellings of some ancient people.

This was the first time in five years—the first time, I will say it (this *is* 1950), since I had lain beside the warm, drowsy Sharon—the first time I had felt whole. I stayed there several days—with only a guide there—and I took stock of things.

I might be what Cross called a failure, not to mention a bastard— in the exact sense—a manager of beaten fighters and aborted films, a person much left. But I was still alive. And I had seen the shooting of the Kid *and* the gunfight at Tombstone, neither of which I would ever mention to anyone in the certainty that if I did I would be called a liar. For a society of liars breeds that rebuke. No, Bark Blaylock would be what he had to be, a true bastard, and not a man who'd look for someone to kill when he knew his own death was close.

I wrote to Fleur Hickey about Mesa Verde—she was an old lady then, but busy and not as old as I am now. She said she had a friend, the author Miss Willa Cather, who was interested in the place, and maybe I should go to see her. Well, I had read a couple of Miss Cather's books—*O Pioneers!* and *My Ántonia*—and I liked them. So I thought why not? I wrote to her in New York City and she very politely and encouragingly wrote back, saying I was to call on her when next I was in the city! New York! Who's afraid of that?

"You ought to do it," said Susan. "Go there."

"You haven't."

"What's that to do with it?"

"New York?" I knew she was scared of it.

"It won't bite you."

"I despise it."

"You've never seen it. You have altogether too many set ideas about the things you can't or won't see."

"Come with me?"

"I will not!" As if I'd proposed a wicked weekend!

"Why not?"

"If I do, you'll blame me. Whatever happens. Go and meet a New Woman."

I went. On the train—four days of it. Ridiculous but straightforward. And I turned up at Bank Street in Greenwich Village, where Miss Cather lived. She was giving a party if you can believe it. She was a large, old-fashioned woman with a very direct, friendly face; she wore a white shirt with a loose black tie.

"Come in!" she urged, and straightaway she showed me off to her city pals. I got passed around until I met a sagging, wiped-out fellow who had had too many cocktails and was leaning on a stick to stay on his feet.

"Blaylock? Did you say Blaylock?"

"I did, sir."

"Knew a woman of that name."

"When was that?"

"Oh, '75 or '76—'75 *and* '76, I think. In Dodge City. Bet you never heard of that?"

"Indeed I did, sir. It was a famously lawless town in the old West, where—"

"Wyatt Earp!" he groaned. "Don't say it. Every John Doe's heard of that old sham. Begging your pardon."

"Do you know, sir," I said, "I am what is often called a bastard. In the technical sense, you understand? Well, Mr. Earp, not that he has shown the least interest, is one of the contenders for the role of my father."

"He was absent-minded."

"Of course, it means little to me."

"And less to him!"

"Precisely."

"How old are you?"

"Well, sir, I am to the best of my knowledge, forty-five or forty-six."

"Blaylock?"

"Bark Blaylock."

"What sort of name is that?"

"The one my mother preferred."

"Ah, is that it?"

"I've upset you?"

"No, lad. I've deserved it all."

As soon as you pour out your heart to anyone, he or she takes over—it's *them* that's so moved!

"It was 1875 you were born," he said. "October. I don't recall the day itself."

"Not '76?"

"No, for I can see you even now, in your mother's arms, in Dodge, on July fourth, 1876—the centenary, you know—at a grand shooting contest for a one-in-one-thousand Winchester. Mr. Earp himself officiated and took bets. He was your mother's man."

"I am much relieved," I said. Though in truth, I resisted it—I said to myself Not Enough!

He grinned in a giving-up-the-ghost way: "Relieved?"

"May I ask your name?"

"Bat Masterson."

"Of course!"

He mocked me. "Of course! I was a . . . colleague to your father. His gun. His rival, too. And now I am a newspaper man in this rathole. See what a dire thing time is?"

"You remember me?"

"I recall an infant. I know it was a boy."

"I am older than I feared," I told him.

"D'you ever see Earp?"

"Not since 1896."

"Buy you a drink. Let's get out of this bluestocking parlor."

We went, but on the way Miss Cather told me I was to be sure to come back at a more convenient time. I thanked her. We made a rendezvous.

Masterson was outside on the pavement, swaying as he tried golf shots with his stick. He did not look well. But I saw in the lamplight that he was weeping like a man who has just lost a puppy.

He stuck out a hand. "Masterson," he said. "William B. Masterson."

"Yes?" I said. I wondered if he'd forgotten me.

He put a hand on my shoulder. "You're as likely mine as his," he said. "I wouldn't worry." I could see both his hoping that it be so and the dark, guilty fear that it might be. I did understand then, and I shook his hand. But I knew I should ease his spirits somehow.

"It could have been Bill Brocius, too," I explained.

"Bill?" he said. And then, "My word, you've got credentials. Bill was a creation."

"He was," I said, seeing that old, full Pecos.

"And Earp shot and killed him. He told me so himself."

1950, The Waldorf

Betsy Averill can come and go, pick up the phone, have her calls taken, and never consider the possibility of anything different. It is one advantage, she knows, of being in America, perhaps the last place on earth where her swift, thoughtless correctness of speech and her offhand authority may carry. In England now, in the Labour England she intellectually approves of but would as soon observe from a distance, her voice still makes ordinary people cower—they

are subdued by the privilege of being in her presence. They are likely
to obey, without listening or pausing. The voice is like a heraldic flag
waved over their credulous heads; it shuts out the light. Once or
twice, someone bowed and answered her, "Yes, my lady," led into
believing she was an aristocrat.

"Oh, for heaven's sake," Betsy had said, "don't be such a ninny!"
But she has known her voice could say anything, and get respect.

In America, she may have her way, or much of it, eventually. But
she has to bargain, banter, flirt and negotiate. And she can speak
without having to feel shame about her voice. Oh, it impresses people, it establishes many entrées, but Betsy does not feel her fortunes
are sacrificed to it. She moves along in America, loving the extreme
weather and the feeling that every day she can start again.

She is in the lobby of the Waldorf to meet Noah Cross. She has
encountered him a couple of times at parties, and she knows the
published state of his wealth, probably better than he does, for Betsy
is a very American fund-raiser, even when working for her wayward
causes, who follows the financial press and studies company reports.

Cross comes out of the elevator: he is eighty (she has verified this
first in a library), and he is very thin, but he has not fallen half an
inch from his young man's height, and he has a full, unguarded
stride as he comes silently across the carpet to her.

"My dear Mrs. Averill, I kept you waiting."

"Not at all."

"It's very interesting. I was upstairs seeing David Selznick. Do you
know him?"

"No, I don't. I know his first wife, Irene. I had a little money in
Streetcar."

"Ah yes, the Irene, the empress. You tread carefully?"

"I do, rather."

"David is going broke." Cross made it sound like an appealing
surprise—like a monkey in the elevator. "He wanted to chat about
it. After *Gone With the Wind*—all gone. I suppose that's what you'd
expect. Owes a fortune."

"Good Lord!" Betsy knew she made it sound like measles for an
adult.

"Very cheerful, however. I do like him. No doubt he'll come back."

"He lives here?"

"On and off. Best chance of coming back, I suppose. Mustn't make
people miserable. He didn't ask for any help."

"Well, I will," she laughs as she warns him.

"I should be disappointed if you didn't. Shall we eat?"

They move into the dining room and Cross takes her, without the assistance of the hotel, to the very best table. There is a bottle of Sancerre in a bucket of ice waiting for them, and with a pince-nez Cross quickly confirms the year. He retains the antique device to examine Betsy Averill's features—this takes only a little longer than the wine, but she feels the sweep of sensual appreciation for pedigree, stock and year. It is quite stirring from so old a man.

"How is your father?" Cross asks, unfolding his napkin.

"He's pretty gaga, frankly. He just sits in the house at Shaftesbury, gazing out at the country."

"Mr. Hardy's Wessex. Shaftesbury, I think, was Shaston to him."

"That's right! Not that Daddy takes it in really. I go over a couple of times a year, but I don't think he knows it's me."

"So hard to tell," says Noah Cross. "Isn't it a fallacy that young, alert people know who we are? They see the surfaces and make up the rest. I have left instructions, if I have a stroke, or anything as debilitating—they will shoot me."

"How will they get away with that?"

"Oh, my dear," he smiles, as if the getting away with things is his trick. "And James?"

"He's in New Mexico at the moment with Jim."

"How fine. My very favorite state."

"You see James?"

"Well," Noah Cross considers the question and its possible consequences. "We do meet. We keep meeting, as it were, over the years, crisscrossing. There is a pattern. But we cannot stop. We never have the time to get to know one another. I regret that. I think highly of your James. I can even imagine a world in which he might have particular prospects."

Betsy reflects over the chilled soup whether James is likely to risk their existence together, their system and economy, let alone their love.

"He is happy?" Cross asks.

She knows a certain number of her husband's liaisons; she regards them as characteristic.

"How do you know, Mr. Cross, if your husband is happy?"

"You know or you know he is not. It is the middle ground that is challenging."

"We have been married seventeen years."

"You are too youthful and lovely for me to believe that. Now, if I were . . . seventy, you would be wise to get up after that audacious overture, and walk away."

"Oh, I think you're still quite dangerous."

"Thank you." Cross' head dips graciously towards his Caesar salad.

The plight that Betsy finds herself in is an odd one. She had married James Averill without much thought, or love: he was dashing, striking, rich and American. The early years are seldom hard and then there was the war—three years in which everything was put on ice. But after the war she fell in love with him, and she is now ready to be broken-hearted if he so much as mishandles an affair so that she *has* to notice it. She is of the opinion that love is most fierce when most at peril, or most interrupted by distance.

"You are far away," Cross observes. "It makes my dangerousness seem less probable."

The fish arrives and Cross himself pours the wine. She enjoys the traces of stone and grass in the dryness.

"That's very good," she says, and she knows hers is a voice that easily sounds expert on anything. That is the real imperialism: is it English class or the daring of American acting? She does revel in being between the two.

"Well," says Noah Cross. "I am ready." And, indeed, he has had enough of the salmon; he eats very little food. He eases his plate to one side so that he has a space of tablecloth in front of him on which he can draw spiral series with the tines of a fork.

"I work with the Boston Symphony," she begins. "They have their funding, of course, but we plan a very special event this Fourth of July. We want to do the Fourth Symphony of Ives. You know Ives?"

"I have only heard of him."

"He is an old man."

"Ah."

"Younger, I think, than you. He has not heard the piece played. It is on a very grand scale. Terrific. The orchestra has to be enlarged. A choir is called for."

Betsy does wonder why James has not answered the note she sent with Jim Jr. It is not a large amount, not for Averills, or Crosses.

"James has been very generous, already, through the Foundation. I don't like to ask for more."

"Aha."

"Ten thousand dollars."

He looks up. "That is ridiculous." He knows money is less critical than knowledge.

Her spirits falter, for when money is named, and dealt with, this old man's alive eyes become very gripping, even in the busy Waldorf restaurant.

"Ridiculously easy," he adds. "Mrs. Averill, we can go to dessert without another word. I am honored to be asked. I will attempt to be in Boston—though I fear that is unlikely. You are running things close, aren't you?"

"I know. I'd thought of canceling."

"Never cancel," he smiles. "That is a Selznick motto."

She has a bowl of raspberries, and he watches her eat them.

"Mrs. Averill, I have a great deal of money, and it came to me like fools going to a show. I could not beat it off. So, over the years, I have tried to put some of it back in the ground usefully. Without making a fool of myself. I sponsor. I encourage. I . . . take risks. I think that's important, don't you?"

She feels not just alone, or caught, with this titan who becomes more controlled the more he drinks; she feels lonely. For what if James is staying in New Mexico? She can never overcome the fear that every trip is an escape for him, a venturing from which he might not return. Then she sees how exposed she will be, on her own, able to come and go, well-off, still with that arrogant, charming English voice, yet all at sea, more lost than free.

"Tell me about the music," he asks.

"It's strange. Like a collection of musics—or several pieces played in different rooms, so that as the listener walks through the house he hears different fragments. Different emphases."

"The audience is asked to promenade?"

"Oh no, the movement is in the music. Though we will do it on Boston Common, so people may walk about."

"On July fourth?"

"Yes." She is proud of it all.

"Isn't that grand? You're very American."

"I feel so Shaftesbury and Harrods."

"I was thinking, listening to you," he makes that listening seem to make up for not eating, "that your voice has quite a twang now. I like it."

"Do you think so?" She is startled—offended even.

"More than you hear perhaps."

"I don't feel my voice has changed at all."

"Ah, but we never believe we change. I believe I am still capable of a younger man's excitement. Do you notice yourself fading? I mean, it isn't rapid—like a blush, like an erection. Is it?"

"Look at old snapshots of yourself."

"Yes, they are a curse. I would like to suggest we take a cab for coffee in my suite at the Pierre. I will write you out a check."

She has not anticipated that he has a base so close. But she can hardly send him there and back, not an old man. So, she smiles inwardly in a ghastly, panicky way, knowing she will have to trust his age. For Ives's sake. But she does see the danger; the city is more destroyed than she realized.

1921

When I went back to call on Miss Willa Cather, her apartment on Bank Street was quiet and cleared away for just the two of us— except for an English tea, with small sandwiches and mouthful cakes, and a bottle of Scotch evident not too far away if that was my preference.

I have noticed often when you see some people a second time, it is a different person. It takes us a little while in learning how to look at someone. Thus, with Miss Cather, what I had taken at first for a certain doughy kindness (fostered, too, by Miss Fleur Hickey's enthusiastic predictions of how we would get on) now proved to be a most forceful, penetrating intelligence all the more demanding for its restraint.

Miss Cather did not have to say too much, but her listening was draining. Not that she was unkind. Still, that rubicund maternal air she had had, or which I had seen, was replaced with an attentiveness that expected big things from me. Of course, she had been hostess to an occasion on that other evening, and I suppose that can make a blur of anyone, a small frenzy that wishes to please. But now, we were alone together, met by design: we had to be worthy. I had to live up to the deep-set, humorous but somehow quite ruthless gaze of this considerable writer. She seemed paler now, as if her proper task of thinking had swept away the bravado of the party.

So I lied. Now, I do not mean to excuse it by saying it was a complicated thing. But guilt can be confused, just as much as innocence. Hanging a man doesn't simplify him, however much you hoped for it. That may be why ridding ourselves of hangings and such is a measure of our readiness for difficulty.

Why did I lie? Well, I could propose that I was, by 1921, well aware how lying was in the U.S. air. I had seen that West gilded with artifice and invention; I had felt the helpless slide into pipe dream and so-called legend, which is often the word the liars employ when they are drunk. I could say a part of me was bitter that I could do nothing with my truths—the things I had truly seen or been present at. There was also the state I was in after meeting Bat Masterson— I had added a year to my age, certainly, and at least one more to the roll of my possible fathers. Without booze, I was drunk on the instability of the facts that most people take as their due.

I was in awe of Miss Cather and, like a small boy, anxious to impress her. I am one of those liars who says only what he would like to have as his truth—give voice to my hopes.

"I am very much moved, moved and influenced," she began, "by Mesa Verde. I was there several years ago, with my friend Edith Lewis. We explored for several days. And, ever since, I have thought I would write about it."

"Ma'am, you should," I told her. "Not enough people know of it."

"I am not sure that isn't its charm. We don't want to turn it into Niagara Falls. Mr. Blaylock, the thing is, I need a story, a construction, into which Mesa Verde could fit so naturally no reader hears it click into place. Do you see?"

"Well," I confessed, "I am not famous for my story sense. I wander some."

"A shape doesn't have to be a tidy sum of addition. You put an orange and a nickel on a table—there's a story straightaway, a likeness."

"They're both round?" I guessed.

"And you can get one with the other," she added. "There's a crossover, a bonding. Mr. Blaylock, I would enjoy hearing your sense of Mesa Verde. It moved you?"

There it was: my opening and my pit—they are so alike.

"Well, ma'am," I said quietly. "I would prefer you not to talk about this, or mention it in a book with my name attached, but I am, so to speak, the one in modern times who discovered Mesa Verde."

She looked through my head and said, "I will say nothing of it. Please explain."

"You see," I tried to shape my story. "There was a long time—"

"Centuries."

"Right. When Mesa Verde was unknown."

"Lost."

"That's it. Well, this would have been in 1891 or '92. I was just a humble cowboy, working on a big spread in northern New Mexico."

"Glorious country," she added.

"You bet. Now, we had some head that had strayed. North it was. And I rode up after them."

"You were alone?"

"I was. It was a small job. And I didn't know *where* they were at first. I was in that rough country at the foot of the plateau."

"No maps, I assume."

"Not a one. Not that I could have read a map much then."

"I still can't!"

"No, ma'am? Well, I began to follow a dry wash."

"You thought the cattle had taken it?"

"They might. After a bit it got into an area of boulders and thick scrub and it was hard to make a way. But I went on and then I came to the river."

"Ah. That was in flow?"

"It was a racing torrent. I lost my horse crossing it."

"Oh no!"

"Yes, I did. Good horse, too. Swept away. I very nearly thought I was done for. Crossing a river, you know, that is something."

"I can imagine."

"Well, on the other side—there it was."

"The mouth of one of the canyons?"

"That's exactly right!"

"What was the name of the river?"

"It didn't have no signs up!"

She laughed; she shook with the fun of it. "Oh, that's a good one!"

"But I learned later it was the Mancos River."

"Aha." Her blue eyes shone—she was a good, warm listener; I'm sure that's necessary in a writer. She had followed right along—I could feel her there.

"So you looked into the canyons and saw the ruins?"

"Enough," I admitted.

"What happened? Did you tell people?"

"I did," I allowed. "But quietly. I didn't want the fuss, you know?"

"I do, I do. Mr. Blaylock, tell me, did you find your cattle?"

"Never did."

"My," she murmured—she obviously had a lot of heart for animals.

"That any good?" I asked her.

"It's splendid. Listening to you, I did get a glimpse of how a place like Mesa Verde might stir a man, might mean a great deal to him."

I felt like she'd picked my pocket—very politely—stolen away a feeling of mine that I'd never quite known I possessed. But I felt good about it.

"Well," she said. "Don't *you* breathe a word of this—but I might see how to use it."

"Yeah?" I felt I couldn't wait.

"The place should be like music that someone living in a far grimmer spot—Niagara Falls, say—has never forgotten."

"That'd be O.K.," I said. What an idiot!

"Mr. Blaylock, you have been a stimulating breath of the West in this place. If I ever do it, I will make sure you have a copy."

"I'd appreciate that."

"And anything *you* do, I would want to see that."

"Me?"

"You have stories in you." She smiled. "Didn't you know?"

I went away, wondering about what she'd said. Maybe if I could pass stuff like that off on a top lady novelist, well maybe I could fool others. There was certainly a market for flimsy Western stuff, and others would meet it with less substance than I could muster.

So I went up to the offices of the New York *Morning Telegraph* where Bat was a sportswriter. We had talked about going to see Jack Dempsey fight the Frenchman, Carpentier. He had made it clear he wanted to see more of me, so we could talk. And he was an old man, troubled by his bad leg—maybe sadder at seeing me—but he didn't let it spoil him.

When I asked for him at the desk, I got a very wry look from the girl there, as if she'd overheard me telling the pack of lies to Miss Cather.

"He died. Today," she said. "Right at his desk."

She nodded at an unoccupied roll-top desk, and I saw no reason why I shouldn't go over to it. A gent at the next desk looked up at me.

"You the new man?"

"No, sir. I was a friend of Mr. Masterson."

The desk had not been tidied. There were circles where glasses or bottles had stood. There was a typewriter, books and papers. There was an old spur which the man had kept polished. There was a photograph of Mr. Wyatt Earp from away back. There was also an engraved plaque that said: "This is the desk and the abode of a tall story man, William Barclay Masterson."

I took that spur. Put it in my pocket.

1950, Santa Fe

"What do you want?" Nora Stoddard asks him. She has asked before, and the question now has taken on bluntness and fatigue. Why are strong women maneuvered into being bitches?

"It's not a question of that," says James Averill. He smiles and waves at the clear air, needing to dismiss some smoke or fog that is in the way of clarity.

"Of course, it is," she tells him. "It's always that. Or how much you want it. You may want it—but not enough."

"I don't think you begin to understand," he pauses, not sure whether to put a name to it.

"Understand what?"

"The Averill tradition."

They are in his hotel room in Santa Fe. It is after eleven at night, and Jim Jr. is in the next room, beyond the connecting door. They can believe he is asleep, for Averill carefully checked on his son before the conversation began, waiting for signs of subterfuge in the boy.

"You want to make love to me?" she supposes.

"Very much." He feels he won't get through the night without it.

"Just like that?" This is her most hostile moment yet.

"It's hardly so simple."

"Making love to me *isn't* simple."

"There's no need to shout." He never likes fighting.

"Why did you bring your son out here?"

"I wanted him to see the West, and to see you."

"To see if he approved of me?"

James Averill cannot decide how to answer this. He knows the answer, he tells himself, but he cannot arrange the words decently, without offense.

"It's not for him to decide, is it?" she probes.

"I will decide. Don't have any doubts about that."

"You brought him here to keep me off."

"That's nonsense!"

"Look at what happened. Isn't that what you wanted? You seem to me a most effective manager."

"Is that what you think?"

"I think you're playing with the idea now that you might fuck me. You won't. Not with your son next door. You wouldn't risk him waking up, coming in, discovering it."

"Would you?" he turns on her.

"Try me." She stands up and she starts to undress in a mechanically dissolute way that revolts him. His hand goes up again, waving to ward off the sight.

But she cannot maintain the tough act. And as her blouse comes off, she follows it to the floor. She kneels at James Averill's feet as he sits in an armchair.

"I love you," she says, "James Averill."

He looks at her and nods. He knows this much is so. He feels sure there is more capacity in women for love.

"And you?" she insists.

"I never know what 'love' is meant to mean."

"So you screw every woman you meet before the subject can come up?"

"What I want," he announces—he feels odd making the speech from an armchair, but she has him pinned there with her half-dressed warmth, and it is not without appeal. "What I want is to make my power count. When I am not here in the West I have a great urge to be riding alone across untouched, unmapped mesa country, knowing the land, making it fertile and prosperous, but keeping it beautiful. I want the Navajo to stay serene—"

"They're shit-face alcoholics. They're unhappy. They dream of killing us. They live in bleak land which they are expected to think is sacred or magical."

"I know!" cried James Averill. "And I want to help them. I want America to know its West, to see and feel this space."

"And you'll test bombs in that space, and you'll let your soldiers practice here. You're as bad as Jubal Valance—you want to be president."

"How did you know that?" He thinks it is his adroit secret.

"You look like a president," she laughs, as much a victim as any voter. "I assumed you had noticed."

"Is it absurd?" He is testing the water. "As stupid as your Jubal?"

"He's not mine. And it's certainly more likely than it is for him."

"My father," he begins, "my father was nearly killed in the Johnson County Cattle War. In Wyoming. He befriended the ordinary people, the immigrants who had come West and who just wanted to put up cities of commerce and tenements. Against the Association."

"What did he do?" She is afraid to submit to his story. She suspects it will undermine her.

"He went back East. Had bad dreams about it. Tried to put his money to good use."

"Took all the women he wanted?"

"I don't think so. But I don't know." He remembers the racing moods of joy and depression in his father.

"Why do you do it?"

"I like women. I feel the urge. And I believe if you want something you damage yourself—and the principle of desire—if you don't take it."

"That's exactly how men have treated the West. You *are* one of us."

"I wish," he says sullenly, but there is longing and ardor in his mind, "I wish I might just ride off and not be known again."

"A wanderer?"

"Exactly."

"With or without the Averill fortune?"

"I know, I *am* ridiculous."

"If you leave your wife, for me, I doubt," she has known this all along, "I doubt you will ever be president. But you might become famous."

"How so?" He is touched, alive for her answer.

"You are discreet now. You are known to the rich. In the right circles. The public doesn't know you. But with a great scandal, you *would* be known. Perhaps that's what you want? That's all Jubal wants. He's more likely to shoot at a president than be one. That's what the Navajo want. They want to be in movies."

"What would the scandal be like?" He only wants the specific information.

"Oh," she puts on her blouse and walks around the room, inventing. She steps back into the shoes she discarded, flipping them upright with her stockinged feet. "Millionaire Divorced by English Wife. Affair with Young Art Historian. Then you would marry me, and wait to be deceived—the cunning always suspect trickery."

"I would not!" He hates her set view of things, the loss of hope.

"You should. And your old friends will say, 'What ever happened to Averill?' You'll sink—from their world. You'll be in your fifties." She buttons herself up. "Stay with your wife. Run for some office. You'll no doubt win—you have a sad, romantic look when you talk about power. And you can have your mistresses. Play the game, James Averill."

"What if I prefer to do away with the game?"

"We can't."

"I think I can."

"You think there's an honest way, a true way, that you've not found? There's not. There's just a set of stories for you to follow. The line of them is all known."

"You're a lousy cynic."

"Aren't you more comfortable, inside, knowing you don't have to go on agonizing?"

"Over what?"

"Over thinking you might do the drastic thing."

"You make me sound like an ant."

"Now you know you're going back. It's easier, isn't it, damn you?"

She gets up and goes away without another word. James Averill looks in on the boy and reassures himself that he is sleeping. Jim looks younger than he is, his head tipped sideways on the pillow. Moonlight is creeping into the room toward his face. Averill draws the curtains to prevent the boy waking.

She is right. He is a manipulator, a user. He did feel comfort come back, like hot tea, when he saw how fully Nora had given him up. This relief overcame even the battery of her attack, and the spectacle of her lost love.

He knows he is on an edge, for he can hardly stand this compromise in himself, this submission to deceit, artifice and calculation. He has a frantic wish to go out after her, leaving the boy to wake alone, to catch her, to make love to her in the empty streets of Santa Fe. He could go where she lives, where she took him only a few days ago. He imagines himself with a gun, shooting the Jubal Valance he finds there, calmly pushing the body aside before he takes Nora. What does he want? How can he eclipse wanting in himself? How can he live with hope and energy still without these terrible, ruinous prospects, huge as drive-in movies, ghost riders in the Western night?

He wants to kill someone, just to escape the trap. He wants to be a great man, or find the merciful redemption in ordinariness. Perhaps he wants just to be dead, or to be the buzzard that looks down, guarding his corpse. To be a buzzard perched on a column in Monument Valley, or to be a canyon in one of Susan Garth's ancient photographs, to be cast in that glowing silver.

He will never sleep.

1923–24

McTeague looked from him out over the desert. Chaotic desolation stretched from them on either hand, flaming and glaring with the afternoon heat. There was the brazen sky and the leagues upon leagues of alkali, leper white. There was nothing more. They were in the heart of Death Valley.

The Von lowered the book from which he had read; it was a beaten and blanched volume, marked with blood and sand. He opposed his copper-colored blunt head to the vacuity of space. He inhaled deeply of the air so hot it had made a slow motion of life. He surveyed the perpetual, hallucinatory shimmy of the ochre distance.

"Great stuff," he growled.

This was the filming of the last pages of *Greed*, for which I had been employed as a guide, as someone acquainted with the furnace, an insurance against heatstroke, death or madness in the cast or crew. Except for the Von; he was far gone before he ever got there.

Hiring me—a job I regard still with bafflement and pride—was in truth a measure of his conviction that he was going to the ends of the earth, to the brink, so to speak, as close to hell as he could manage for the while. He did not much care to hear how I—an ordinary fellow, not half as bronzed from the sun as he was—had lived in Death Valley for years. It was established in his mind that there was no living there; this place was entirely the symbol of extinction and bitter conclusion to all human hopes. And so the Von bestrode the valley like someone in the *Pilgrim's Progress*, daring the hot blast of catastrophe and annihilation. I believe he could have found an odd, pious exultation if some of us had died there. Not that he was a cruel or malicious man, or wished harm to any individual; but he was all for death or glory in the lofty, poetical abstract. And a lot of laughs.

He'd come up to me, as brisk as a cadet, in his dazzling white singlet, with his pants rolled up to his knees. I could see drops of sweat in the harsh crop of his hair, like golf balls in a harvested field. And he'd say to me, "The world is a wilderness," nodding over his shoulder at the 130° F. infinity, "and even God is lonely in it." Then he'd wink at me and say, "That is a very ancient saying I made up today when I was taking a shit. You like it?"

I told him I thought it was grand—there you are, again, you see, that characteristic, obliging, good-natured lying of ours, without which no motion picture could ever be. Yes sir, I was getting accustomed to the lying.

We were a caravan of cars out in the valley, with GREED in slashing white paint on the hoods—it made us look more like prospectors. The cars were bulky with extra attachments of water. This was the Goldwyn Company taking over the desert in tribute to the eternal fallacy of gold. While it wasn't as grandiose maybe as Mr. Selznick years later building the old South in Culver City, still it was a small example of imperialist adventure, with the Von marveling as the film stock went to syrup and blithely introducing such modern conveniences as a portable piano to give "mood" to the scenes, and jars of caviar for dinner.

But I took them to the alkaline fields, choppy as sea but as hard as coral, to film the last scene, with Mr. Gowland and Mr. Hersholt handcuffed together, a hundred miles from water. The Von sat on the ground beneath a green-and-white-striped beach umbrella while Mr. Ben Reynolds worked the camera. The piano and a violin sawed away behind them so that the actors could lift their spirits to the last pitch of ironic doom.

"Play Wagner," the Von ordered, and then, when the whole thing was done, "Magnificent! Magnificent picture!"

Now, there had been talk out in the valley that the Von had shot so much film on *Greed*, and had so much detail in his story, there was no way the picture could come in under five hours. And there were those on the crew who didn't see the point in all the detail or all the days of ordeal in the valley when the movie was going to have to be cut down.

I asked the Von about this one night: he had noticed that I liked to listen to him, and I'd seen him watch me as he told me lies, seen my face expand with the pleasure of them, and made the next lie grander.

"Five hours?" he said in a pitying tone. "I tell you, old Bark, you are my pal. This is ten-hour picture. You grasp the full enormity?" And he put down his glass of claret (we kept the wine in the water to cool it!), so that he could hold up all ten fingers: they were like bones dipped in coffee, with rings as big as his knuckles.

"They're never gonna show a ten-hour movie," I said.

"Of course not!" he grinned. "I know what must happen. The wretched Thalberg is even now part of an alliance of Goldwyn and Metro. He will tame my lovely beast."

"How are you so cheerful about it?"

"I am not cheerful, Bark. I am magnificent! I am Ozymandias—'Look at my works, ye Mighty, and despair! Nothing else remains but the lone and level sands.' That's it, near enough. You see, Bark—Shelley, ignoramus—any fool can make a good picture: Griffith, Lang, Sjöström, Feuillade, Charlie, the Russians even. But I, the Von, I am making," his fierce, sultry buzzard's eye drew me closer, aswagger with his own drama, "I am making *ruined* film. Secret—don't breathe. Lost film! I am making a legend. It is like the great emperor who had done all on earth that any man could. And he saw there was one last, sublime achievement—he designed and built a ruined city."

"Who was that?" I was fascinated.

"No one!" he laughed. "The Von made it up!"

There was some con-man God to the Von—who else made so much up? Yet it helped you see how God might have escaped from somewhere.

I went back to Los Angeles with him after the filming: he was younger than I was, but he wouldn't let that deter him from continuing my education. He had to edit his picture, and he was estimating there might be a year's work in this—a year, incidentally, for which he would not be paid; for it was thought then a director would cut his own picture, the way you are supposed to wrap up a present.

"You're gonna work that long," I marveled, "cutting a film for nothing?"

"Sure," he said, "it make me famous." And he shot me that wink again, as if a crack in the sky suddenly opened and closed and you could see out there, beyond all our thinking and striving, it was just Turkish delight and siesta time.

Not long afterwards the Von told me I was to go along with him to a swank party. It was to celebrate the partnership of Goldwyn and Metro, and it was to be at a beach house on Ocean Front road. "Everyone" would be there.

"I can't go," I told him. "I'm not one of the swells."

"We say you are," the Von decided.

"Who do we say I am?"

"Who do you want to be? The last of the Romanoffs?"

"I don't speak no Russian, Von."

"Struck dumb by the hideous ordeal of the Bolsheviks!" He was an instant story man. "A living wreck!" He was in love with it. "You can do it, Bark."

Well, it was some party, and I wasn't the only invented character there. The house was filled with silk dresses and lingerie fantasies —the sort you change every day. The party spilled out over the terrace and down onto the beach. You could hear the boom of the Pacific, but it was beyond the floodlights. There was all manner of things to eat and drink; there was music, dancing, tennis, some cards for high stakes. And I was being pushed around as some new craze, a Russian prince who couldn't speak of all his horrors. The funny thing was, once I stopped cringing at what the Von was saying, once I accepted it, why it wasn't so bad, and I began to feel some ghost growing up inside me, some real, pained Romanoff, a brave fellow of rare nobility. I stopped laughing and took this ghost seriously.

There was a pair of slinky girls I'd seen, watching me in mirrors, a couple of sly-faced knockouts, sisters I decided, but sisters maybe who kept each other around as rivals. They had a dark-haired, Levantine look, a kind of stuffed-date allure, and there was the outgoing one and the one who just watched and waited. Well, I didn't have to say a word: it was like being at the movies, and in the picture, too. The Von built me up, and this time he threw in the fact that I was a chess master.

"You don't speak?" asked the quiet one, and I nodded vigorously. She put her head to one side to consider all the angles.

"We could play chess," she suggested, and in a minute she'd found a board with carved jade pieces. She set up the board on the staircase and there we sat, with her white silk stockings about five and a half inches out of my dumb face.

"Look," I said, in my Death Valley accent, "I don't quite play."

"But you talk?" She liked an honest fraud.

"It was Von's joke. I'm sorry."

"Don't be. I usually stammer."

I didn't get that one (I never heard her stammer once), but this was a smart set. The quiet girl—she told me her name was Gertrude Regina—she showed me around. Halfway through the party I thought why wouldn't Noah Cross be there, and I asked Gertrude Regina if she knew him.

"I know him," she said, as if to say who hasn't had pimples? "He's likely buying Ecuador, or Nebraska," she added.

So I relaxed and enjoyed myself, going in and out of my Romanoff

routine, with the Von and this deadpan, aloof Gertrude Regina oiling
the joke, and me wondering how the Von could be so exuberant
with the world waiting to fall in on him. But it was *his* trick, the
ceiling he was rigging so that it would fall. I realized that if I'd made
my film, I'd maybe be one of the big shots at the party, with Gertrude
Regina slinky and insinuating on my arm, and a house like that one
to call home.

"Tired?" she asked.

"How'd you know that?"

"Getting older while I watch."

"Hard graft being an actor."

"It's Hollywood," she said—and I could tell she hadn't thought
of quitting yet. "The real people died on the way here. In the desert."

So I reckoned I'd had my fill of the lobster tails and the interrupting
small talk, and I headed east—for the West again.

As I went out of the house, Gertrude Regina was there, leaning
in the doorway, watching me.

"That was dumb," she said. "About the desert." She watched me
as if I'd been hurt by it. Or as if she wondered whether I could get
her out of there. And for a moment, I considered it; long enough so
that I have never forgotten her and her look. The lost stick in your
mind—that's their home.

1950, A Silver Whip

It is before dawn, in Santa Fe, sometime in the last week of June—
which is to say, it is colder than James Averill anticipated. So he has
tried to wrap his light jacket around him, and he has pulled its flimsy,
tailored lapels up to his unshaved chin. He smiles in a defiant, shame-
less way, as if to encourage the notion in anyone seeing him, waiting,
prowling, pacing, that he might be a criminal or a killer pausing
before outrage. He is talking to himself, cursing and calculating in
an agony of uncertainty, whether to go in before light comes, or
whether that is allowing too much chance of Jim Jr. alone in the hotel
waking and finding nothing. He feels himself separating in this vicious, impossible whirl: so he stops and laughs out loud in the street,
trying to believe he has broken through the barriers of dilemma.

Finally, it is the helpless overflow of energy and the need to do anything that carries him, like water running downhill, to Nora Stoddard's apartment.

He knocks gently—so as not to disturb others in the vicinity? or is it a demented consideration for her sleep? He has to knock again: he can feel the roughness of the wood on his impatient knuckles. He knocks the top skin off his hand—he has lost his touch in this nervousness. There are bright pinpoints of scarlet. He licks them away and tastes the sour wood preserver.

She opens the door, torn, if not from bliss, then from some unconsciousness of comfort or consolation, some nocturnal feeding. There is an aggrieved look on her face, a face that is lovely still, but haggard and slipped off-center in the early light, not gathered or prepared; it is a face in which there has been an overnight tremor, or in which the culture of dreams is not yet dispersed or hidden. She has a robe on, threadbare toweling, and she is still knotting the sash. There is a mark on her chin, as if she has knocked into something, some demon, in her sleep. She is tough when she sees him; she licks her lips to shift the night's deposit, or to swallow the croak that has rested there. Still, her voice sounds broken:

"What do you want? At this hour?"

"I came to tell you that I love you," he says. "I'm going to do it. Give it all up." It sounds stilted, he has been over it so many times while waiting.

Nora Stoddard sighs—she would like everything to go away, and she wants aspirin for her face, not more demands for talk. She does not want a scene—does she? Well, why not, James Averill is the kind of man who maybe needs a few unbridled, blood-letting scenes to restore him to his senses and his role in this life.

"You're going to give it all up?" she says, and at this hour she makes no effort to disguise the mockery.

"I am." He is trying to edge into the apartment.

"So if you are giving all of it up," she argues, slow and heavy with fatigue, "that makes me nothing. Right?"

"Of course not." He winces at her dullness.

"I mean, a girl would like to be the 'it all' you are going *for*. You know?"

"You *are* that." He is pushing at a wall the exact location and strength of which remain mysteries.

"You didn't say that. You didn't say, 'I want you.' You say you're giving it all up. You're escaping. Starting again—that good old Western vacation."

"Why are you so hard?" he asks. It is the small boy in him she finds so appealing, so fit for rescue, so angelic even.

"Hard? Because I don't say, 'Oh, James, come in, sweetie. Come into my bed. Immediately. Now. Show me. And do it so fast you can *still* be home before Jim wakes'?"

He *could* kill her—there is something in fluent opposition, he has found before, that does delve down into what he suspects is an authentic, primitive violence in himself, an urge to overthrow.

But, "Please," he says. He is astonished. The actor in him, that rampant Hyde, is ready to break into heart-rending tears. So he says it all: "I can't live without you."

"Go away," she orders. "That's the only way you'll keep any love for me."

"I want *you*. I did say that!" He is in court!

She studies him: "Go away denied—you'll not forget that." She is smiling, crazily, with this gift. "I'll stay fresh. Young. Stop seeing me, you won't notice the aging." She is so vengeful. "I'll be an ideal for you. Why, when you're an old man—not too long to wait—you can tell yourself and anyone near you I was the lost love of your life."

He slaps her on the side of her face. His hand springs up—he is so stirred by the spontaneity. And as he strikes her, there, on the dark mark, he realizes that it must be some similar, prior, bruise, a target.

She reels away. She did not expect this. But she wants to laugh; she is so caught in the tracks of a "scene."

"Oh, boy," she says. "My lucky night."

The crack of the blow is startling. It seems more than was delivered, subtly enhanced. For effect? Perhaps it is just the passive air of the very early morning being detonated. But it brings Jubal Valance, quite naked, out of the bedroom, without any drowsiness. James reasons to himself as he sees the attack coming that Valance was in there, awake, listening, laughing in a pillow, waiting for her to be rid of him.

But then Jubal has him by the lapels and is pulling him bodily into the apartment. James hears the summery cloth ripping.

"Stop it," Nora is saying.

But then Jubal hits James in the stomach, and the older man, the man of power, is utterly exhausted. He scrutinizes the insane weave of the cheap carpet on the floor. It is so absurd, being there. Then there is a stinging pain as something hot falls on his back. Is it scalding water? He looks up and sees a comic harmony in the swing of Jubal's chunky penis, with another mercurial strand hanging from it, swinging aslant, and the falling curve of a splay of whips clasped in a silver stock. The lashes fall this time on his face.

"Fucking stop it!" Nora screams. And James Averill hears a shot. He sits up and sees Jubal retreating, panting, with Nora pointing an old revolver at him, holding it in front of her in two hands.

"You think I wouldn't?" she says. "You think a woman couldn't shoot Jubal Valance?"

"He hit you!" Jubal complains.

"So did you!" she yells.

"You liked that."

"That's my business," says Nora Stoddard, and then to James Averill, "Get up."

"She's mine," Jubal says to James quietly, cloyingly.

"I am not," Nora snarls.

"I say you are," he wants to argue.

"Jubal. Get dressed. Get out before I do kill you. Jubal. Listen. I fuck you. That's all."

"I can beat him," he points down at Averill with his whip.

"Just hope," she says—she notices she is out of breath, her beating heart has taken it all—"just hope he doesn't stick his lawyers on you." She doesn't think Averill will. "He'd make an American example of you. You know—the part the Valances play in this territory?"

"You shouldn't mess with me," Jubal Valance warns her.

"But I have. And I think I can handle you, Jubal. Now, you," she turns again on James. "Go away. Forgive me, and go."

Averill is weak on his feet. He needs some restorative. "We have business," he reminds her.

Her eyes flare; she is afraid of losing control.

"The photographs." He is out of breath still. "Susan Garth."

She shakes her head in fury and disbelief. "What? What of them?"

"They're very fine," he tells her, desperately.

Nora sighs: she always knew the photographs were a pretext.

"Go and see her." She tells him the address, the way there, how to proceed. She leaves the rest to him. "Susan would be pleased. Perhaps. Go see her. She might be good for you." She is so sure now about how much she prefers life.

"You won't come?"

"I won't."

"But you'll do the show?"

"If I don't have to see you."

Jubal laughs at this, and Nora groans at the tedium of dealing with him. Were the photographs an escape for Susan Garth? The thing left to do, away from the mess?

"Go, James. I'll keep him here ten minutes." She sneers at what she is saying. "Give you a getaway. As for you," she looks at Jubal, grotesquely hard on, strutting and whisking the air with his whip, "put your clothes on and get on with being president. And leave me alone. If you don't, I'll surely kill you."

Exhaustion returns. The passionate subside and withdraw. The eruption has passed, leaving alteration in the landscape that is not visible in the myriad cracks, flaws and canyons. The buzzard flying overhead has seen all this before.

1929

A story is leaving things out; it is a bird flying above the desert too old to remark on every grain of earth. When the bird knows it is flying, it must trust the ground being there, and it must abide by the spiraling churn of its wings, the feathering through time.

People would die—my mother, tired, sedately alcoholic, but free of Cherry Valance; Fleur Hickey, in headlines, on a train; Mrs. Frances Braxton Garth, chief beneficiary of the Garth fortune, patroness to several American museums, a touch cold to me at the end, as if I hadn't given her all she wanted. Mr. Wyatt Earp died, too, in January 1929, in a rented stucco cottage on the edge of Los Angeles. So I lost my several versions of a mother, and Bark Blaylock was rid of his last father. But by then there were glittering Wyatt Earps springing up on screens everywhere.

There was a period when Bark and I were doing our leisurely figure-eight journeys back and forth across the West. It wasn't by design, but I mapped it all out, where we had been, and it was a pretty shape, with intersections at the Canyon de Chelly, Carlsbad or at Furnace Creek. We didn't keep in touch, yet every now and then there we were, reunited, picking up some unsettled argument as if the pause had been no more than one of us having to take a leak.

"How old are you now?" Bark asked me one day.

We were riding on the floor of Chelly, silent by the hour, and we had just stopped at the White House Ruin where I planned to photograph the line of broken walls against the bare sweep of cliff face.

"Fifty-nine this year," I told him, unstrapping the tripod.

"You are?" He sounded thoroughly amazed at some spurt in my aging.

"Well, how old are you, damn it?"

"Fifty-four."

"There you are, then. There has always been five years between us. Still is. I don't see any cause for wonder then, if I'm fifty-nine."

"That," he said, very grand, "is not my point."

"You mean I'm growing old and you're not?"

"I don't want any argument," he said. "I just consider it's time you had somewhere settled where you could be."

"You think I'm not safe traveling around? Bark Blaylock, haven't you heard, this West has been tamed? The only lethal Indians are the drunks."

"Sight more dangerous, you ask me. Every tourist wants to be a desperado."

I took pictures all that day as the sun moved round. He just sat on a slab of slippery rock watching me until late afternoon and there were caves of shadow in the wall of the cliff.

"Get over by the house," I told him.

"Gonna take my picture? Thought you didn't like doing people."

"Get over there." He's so small in the picture you can't recognize him: he's those busy little modern times come to inspect the ruins. But I got him as he stood there, hands on hips, rocking backwards, like a city landlord.

"How was I?" he asked.

"Oh, you were outstanding," I said. "Close to perfect."

"Close?"

"I'd have liked it better if the bird shit had hit your head."

"What bird shit?" He looked up, like a fool in a cartoon.

"Oh, Bark Blaylock, is your eyesight going?"

We had a camp down there on the floor of the canyon, and a Navajo came by with some fresh corn for us. We baked it and ate it there by the fire, hunched up in our coats, listening to the wind up above.

"You mean that about a house?" I wondered.

"Why'd I mention it?"

"No need to get uppity. Would you build it?"

"Myself?"

"Yeah. I got the bit of cash from my father."

"You call it a bit?"

"It's all I have." He would not let dignity alone. Why shouldn't I have *something* in the end?

"I've got things to do, you know," he told me.

He had got into doing these books and kids' stories on the West, and though he didn't talk much about them I suspected they were doing well enough. Once we found a bleached-out comic by the roadside in Nevada, close to Tonopah, and he picked it up. It looked like the oldest thing around, that's what sun will do to cheap paper. But he scanned it, said, "One of mine," and put a match to it. It was too bright to see the flame. But, as the paper burned, the pictures came back into being and you could see cowboys doing quick draws with clouds of capital-letter talk blooming from their heads.

"Well, forget it then," I told him.

"I'll forget it when I want to," he said, and I knew he was going to do it, so long as the earth didn't split in half.

I spent that summer looking and thinking of a site that was a good place yet unlikely to be discovered in my lifetime. And I found the spot up above Window Rock. By the time I told him, he had found books on building and he had drawings.

"What's that?" I asked.

"Plans. You can't build a house without a construction in mind."

"I know that. But whose house is it?"

"It ain't mine!"

"So can I do the plans?"

He grumbled, but he consented to that whim of mine, and he showed me how to do a plan properly, with all the math and respect for the materials, so your house didn't collapse. He had a good tidy mind still, and we worked it out together.

"This is stone?" he wanted to know, pointing to sections in the plan.

"Keeps it cool," I said.

"I know, I know. We got to get that stone up there."

"Well, Lord, Bark, I want a house I can see out of." I know he thought I had been perverse in wanting to have it up on top of the cliff.

"You didn't think of Mount Whitney?" he asked.

"I knew you'd complain."

So he went down to Hubbell's Trading Post and he hired on some Navajo to help him—he was never what you'd call a big, strong man! And then in 1929 and 1930 we built the house, and we hurried on with it so there was some place to shelter in when that winter got hard. Every new idea I had he snarled and chewed his teeth, and got on and did it.

"You'd better be a builder now," I said to him one day when we were nearly done. "Always a call for that, if you do lose your money." There had been the Crash which did not have a very marked effect on the local Navajo—the poor handle slumps best, even if it means dying.

"Depression doesn't hurt comic books," he said. "You can't kill trash."

"Why'd you do them then?" I wanted to know.

And he cursed and studied a beam he was putting up, and he said, "If there's lies to be told, get a man who knows they're lies to do it. Otherwise, it's ruination."

"You should be on the radio," I said. "Selling cereals."

He nodded. "I wouldn't mind that."

You see what I mean—we just couldn't keep one idea straight between us, and it's a bleak life if your jokes go unnoticed.

The day came, in May 1930, when try as we might, the neither of us could find anything else that had to be done with the house. It was an odd dwelling, but it stood and I felt comfortable in it. For three days he had fussed around, checking things, and I knew he was wondering how to quit.

"Going to leave that old trunk in the middle of the room?" he asked.

"Where I can see it."

He sniffed. "Won't talk back to you," he allowed, smug, as if he'd seen through me.

"Where you going to go?" I asked him.

"Oh," he sighed, as if he hadn't thought about that one. "Maybe Nevada. I have to do a book about the rip-roaring silver-mining days." He had a despondent look.

"Do it here," I offered. "If you're going to make it up anyway."

"Want to get the feel of that country."

He went off down to his truck which he had got for carrying the materials. It was getting dark when he came back up the hill. He had to walk so slowly.

"Here," he puffed, and handed me a book. It was *The Professor's House* by Willa Cather. "You might like to look inside."

I opened the book and there was red writing on the first clear page:

> To Bark Blaylock:
>
> It takes a good man to tell
> a tall story and keep the
> height honest
>
> Willa Cather

"This is yours," I told him. Him and his lady friends.

"You hold on to it."

"I'm only looking after it for you."

"You said it."

I thought, I'll show the bastard. "Bark," I said. "I loved that Sharon. Did you ever think that?"

"Well," he reasoned, "everyone did. I still do, I reckon."

And he looked at me, trying to see what I had meant. But we both let it go, and I made him dinner and afterwards we sat in the big room with our chairs so turned he could hold my bad right hand, and we sat there all through the night grumbling at each other until the light came slinking in and he took off for Nevada.

1950, In Arizona

Coming up to the house—it is so strange, perched on the top of the cliff, like a bird settling its wings, or preparing to fly—Jim can see an old man and an old woman inside. They are sitting there in a patch of light, but at angles to each other, as if held in some abiding, comic fractiousness. He is loyal to his father's wish to come all the way to this house, yet he does not want to have to be polite with old people. He has felt growing uneasiness that they may not be back for Mummy's music and he cannot believe, what with the bruising and the tracery of slender wounds on his face, that his father is well.

"What happened, Dad?" he has asked—for it seems as if his father has woken up with the lace of blood on his face. Has he been battling in his sleep?

"Jim," says his father, studying the mirror. "I really don't know. I must have been bitten. In the night."

The blood is dry and very fine, the strands of it no thicker than thread. But it is so complete, and beneath its veil his father's face is so pale and so afflicted by surprise. Jim knows what he will not admit: that his father, James Averill, was awake, facing a pointed, absorbing attack, and that the damage to his inner strength was more than the abrasions on the surface. The boy knows they should be going home, before this damage gets out of hand.

"What happened to your face?" says Susan Garth, coming up out of her chair to greet them, gazing at the face and then at the boy with the same impassive, interested attention.

The old woman is too merciless for any claim of ignorance from Averill. He says he thinks there was a fight, and Jim marvels that his father cannot recollect the details, does not have an explanation —his father always knows what has happened.

"You're Bark Blaylock?" says James Averill. His pleasure is so evident it takes away the mystery of his own abused face.

"How d'you know that?" the old man asks.

"It seemed right," says Averill as he shakes the old man's hand.

"Well," says Susan Garth, looking down at the boy.

"We have to be back for the music," says Jim, conversationally.

"Time for fudge?" the old woman demands of him, heading off for the kitchen.

"Oh," says Jim. "Fudge! Well."

"There you are," says Susan, sure this will hold him. She has picked up a tray of the confection, a baking tin, cut into squares.

"Pecan and ginger," she says, pointing. "And vanilla there."

"I don't like ginger."

"You don't have to eat it."

"What's this one?" The boy's mouth is full.

"Pecan."

He swallows. "That's terrific." He loves the way she says "pecan."

"Take some with you, for the music."

Somehow, this matter-of-fact gift, this willingness to speed him on—and the sweet weight of the fudge itself—reassure Jim. He is patient through adult talk, of pictures and history, of a place Miss Garth calls "Los Ang-eles" with a hard "g." He lets Susan Garth show him her house and the canyon. He cannot believe how entirely and savagely the ground falls away, with the house left there, safe.

"Aren't you afraid of falling?" he wants to know.

She looks at him and sums him up. "All the time," she grumbles. And the child grins happily. "Yes," he sighs, trying to be kind to the poor old woman.

"May I see some pictures, Miss Garth?" Averill asks.

"You've come all the way," she tells him. "You'd better."

Without anything being said, it is accepted that James Averill and the old woman should look at the pictures together. Jim waits for Bark to occupy their vacancy.

"I ain't her husband, you know?"

"No, sir," Jim agrees.

"I just happened by. Of course, we're old friends."

"I see."

"You do?" The old man sounds intrigued.

"No, sir," Jim admits, and he gives the old man one of his cheery, confident smiles.

Bark Blaylock nods. "You a La Motta man or a Robinson?"

"Robinson!" says Jim. It is a matter of honor.

"Me too. Ever hear of Stanley Ketchel?"

"The Michigan Assassin!"

"Him. I was there the day he got killed."

The boy is fidgeting with eagerness, answers and questions.

"When Ketchel fought Johnson," says Bark. "It was like a boy, like you, in with a giant. Johnson would hit him—lift him off his feet. Ketchel never stopped. Never stopped attacking."

"For twelve rounds!" Jim marvels.

"Right. After the fight, they asked Ketchel, they said, 'Why'd you attack him all the time? He's so much bigger. Why didn't you move and tire the big man?' Know what Ketchel said?"

"No, sir."

" 'I didn't want to let him see how scared I was, or it would have been the worse for me.' And he was just battered blood and bones by then. How d'you like that?"

The boy nods greedily: it is so much wonder to digest, he feels tired.

"Hey," Bark shouts out. "We oughta give this boy some lunch. He's feeling faint." And he winks at the boy, as if to say, hang on, we can look after each other, even in this crazy world with this mad old woman.

"So, Bark, how are you?" asks Susan as they finish up their lunch of cornbread, beans and rabbit stew.

"Well, I'm here, aren't I?"

"Would you be up to a little drive around the West? Show these people."

"How little? I'm not going out for something if it's not respectable."

"You feel well enough?"

"I'm a lot younger than you!"

"What do you say?" Averill asks his son. "A tour on our way to the airport?"

"We could get you to Amarillo," says Susan Garth.

"With this boy?" asks Bark.

"Who else do I mean?" Susan tells him, cutting peach cobbler.

"This boy knows all about Stanley Ketchel," warns Bark, as if it is a scandal.

"You'll be company for one another, won't you?"

"You had great days in the fight business, Mr. Blaylock?" asks James Averill.

"Dempsey and Carpentier in '21," says Bark. "The summer I was in New York. My old pal Tex Rickard put it on. Gorgeous Georges, they called him," he confides in Jim. "Over in Jersey."

"Was Dempsey the best, sir?" asks Jim.

"Not sure Dempsey ever fought anyone good enough so we'd know."

"Gene Tunney?" This boy knows the facts.

"Tunney was a different kind of creature. I mean, a man can explain the weather to you. Tell you when it's gonna rain. Won't stop you getting wet. Doesn't mean the weather loses its power, does it?"

The old man turns to look out of the window. The glass is milky, silvered like an old mirror, until some ripple of wind or motion goes across it like a stroke, a ghost.

"When we gonna go, then?" Bark Blaylock has to know.

"We could see Chaco," says Susan. She is examining this old man's face, trying to preserve it.

"That would be fine," Averill tells her.

"And then, maybe," Susan Garth surmises, "we could go on over to Fort Sumner before we drop into Texas." She turns to Bark. "Be on our way, wouldn't it?"

"You want me to drive?" Bark assumes.

"I don't imagine we'll get the wheel out of your hands," says the old woman.

"How will you get back from Amarillo?" asks Averill.

"Oh, we'll find a way," Susan tells him.

"Ever seen the Pecos River?" Bark asks the boy.

"Never, sir."

"We'd best do it, then," he says, tight-lipped against one more burden of an old man's duty.

"Is that where Billy the Kid died?" asks Jim.

"Died?" asks Bark. "Don't know about died." But his tender bristling of perplexity only makes the child smile. The old man looks at the bright eyes and the upturned life, at the receptacle so open for filling. "Yes, sir," he admits. "That's the spot. You're a treat, I'll tell you."

"I've got an ointment," Susan says to Averill. "Put it on your face before you go out in the sun."

"Know what?" says Bark. "I'm just speculating." He is talking to the table. "But I'd reckon the guy your father had his to-do with, I'd guess he's a sorry sight."

"That's kind of you," says Averill. "But he went away not much marked."

"Jubal Valance," says Susan Garth, disappointed but not surprised.

"How did you know?"

"Seen the print of that whip before."

"Jubal's silly," says Jim.

"No one's free from that," his father tells him.

"Well," says Bark, stretching and a little uneasy at where this candor may lead, "wait till we get out there in the open on our excursion. Out there—Chaco, wherever—no foolishness there. I'll tell you. You walk that land and . . ."

"Yeah?" asks Susan.

"You know you're a great man," says Bark shyly. "A champion."

———————

1946

"This might be a last chance for seeing some of the old places," he had written to her.

"Meaning me," said Susan Garth, but she went just the same, so long as Bark would shut up about who she was. She would not have a scene.

So he came over from Nevada in his big new Packard—the GIs had been a soft market for quick Western stories—and he was full of reports of Bugsy Siegel and the new Las Vegas, about a shining saloon city plumbed into the desert, with rattlesnakes scraping their way across new marble floors and disappearing into the gold faucets.

"The gangsters are taking over," said Susan Garth as they drove on south.

"They're pretty poor for hoodlums," said Bark. "Only doing it for the attention."

They checked off the people who were dead, or gone away, somewhere, into some hole—Liberty Valance's religious daughter, Amantha; Mr. Roosevelt; Senator Ransom Stoddard; William S. Hart, only the other day.

The Packard took them across the Petrified Forest, and they stopped once to examine the silicate tree trunks strewn on the ground, the wood turned into a mosaic of burnished colors, the weight of the tree enormously, gravitationally increased.

"I would like to see a man like this," said Susan Garth.

"Entirely different structure," he told her, and she thought that pompous masquerade of raw ignorance was him at his worst.

They went on through the real Apache country where there were teams of small horses running along the roadside, and Indians for scowling jockeys. These were the ones to study if you wanted to believe how fierce the hostiles might have been. There was a flourish still to the Apache, a readiness for insolence, or staring you down, as he sat on his bristling pony and you sheltered in the Packard.

"How are we going to do it?" Susan Garth demanded.

"Do it?"

"We can't just go up to them, not if we're not saying who I am." She despaired of his refusal to understand common things. You couldn't talk to him without him turning his head in wonder, as if you'd just said the oddest thing he'd heard. He was growing old.

"There's a motel we can move into. That's where they're staying. Then I'll sort of bump into Howard."

"Oh, Howard! You know him?"

"We've talked."

She gave no sign of satisfaction; she found it hard to believe any Howard had enjoyed the experience.

"Looks like they've got a wet one," said Susan Garth. The clouds were down over the rolling pasture, and they made the ground look more like grass.

It was September 1946, and they found the motel, not far from

Willcox. Sure enough, the place was stiff with movie people on a weather wait, complaining about the food and how little there was to do, and whether it was worth going into Tucson for the evening.

"That's Howard," said Bark, when they took their place in the dining room.

"Trying to look like a gangster out of Abercrombie and Fitch," said Susan.

This Howard was silent, but in command of his table, a tall, slender, upright man in immaculately tailored Western clothes, letting his cold dandy's gaze rake the several pretty girls at the table. Occasionally, and out of the corner of his lizard mouth, he'd mutter some precious tough one-liner—the way some old-timers can hawk tobacco juice without looking—so that the girls howled with laughter and bounced their *Life* magazine necklines for him. At last Howard wearied of their adoration, stood up, scrutinized the room with immense but chipper disdain and began to stroll off towards some inscrutable and sinister liaison.

"Howard," called Bark, grabbing the fashion plate as he drawled past.

"I beg your pardon," hissed Howard.

"Bark Blaylock. Remember when you did *Viva Villa!*?"

"I don't talk about that."

"You remember me!" Bark was sure of it.

"Maybe I do. Maybe I don't," said Howard. "You seen John Ireland anywhere?"

"Can't say I know him," said Bark.

"Bastard's snaking after my girl," murmured Howard, clearly intending to slash the said Ireland on the creases in his shirt, if he ever found him.

"O.K., Howard, if we come and watch you shoot?" asked Bark.

"Bring some sun, you can come," said Howard bitterly.

"No problem," said Susan Garth.

"Oh, really," said Howard. "I'd have thought that was quite a problem."

"My father was an Apache medicine man," said Susan.

"Yeah, that's right," chuckled Bark.

"Madam," said Howard, "if I had a hat, I'd take it off to you."

So, a few days later, when the rain broke, they drove out to the *Red River* location, Susan with a casual, proprietorial smile on her cracked face. They were in a long, low-hilled valley with a couple of thousand cattle in pens, and wranglers pampering them so they'd do a good stampede on cue. There were trailers and there was a big marquee where everyone ate: it was like a limousine cattle drive, except all they were doing was going up and down the valley, letting the different angles serve for all the way to Kansas.

"You could have done it in the San Fernando," reasoned Susan Garth.

"Authenticity, madam," whispered Howard Hawks—who did have a hat on now, a moleskin Stetson, so firm it could have been petrified.

"Am I going to meet him?" Susan asked Bark quietly.

"Why not? There he is." He nodded at a gaunt, dark-haired stripling, weighed down by costume six-guns and a hat the size and shape of Cahuenga Peak. There was a delay, and in the course of it, like a good sheepdog, Bark managed to coax Susan, Howard and Mr. Montgomery Clift into a proximity sufficient to trigger the gentleman Howard's menacing manners.

"Miss . . . I don't believe I caught your name," he began.

"I didn't . . . Hickey," she decided.

"An Apache family?" asked the droll Howard.

"There was always Irish in the tribe," she told him, bare-faced and lunging closer.

"Miss Hickey . . . may I introduce Mr. Clift, our Matthew Garth?"

The spurious father and the unknown daughter shook hands, worlds and fifty years apart.

"Interesting role you've got," said Susan.

"Well, look," grinned Clift, tolerantly, "this is just a Western, you know."

"Still," she persevered, "the real Garth. He was an unusual fellow."

"Hey, Howard," whined Clift, "was Garth a real person? Is that right?"

Delicate and dangerous, Howard saunteringly rejoined them. "There are no real people," he told them. "See if they sue."

"Marvelous!" cried Clift, and he chuckled so his six-gun rattled.

And then Howard, always looking past the person he was talking to, asked, "Seen Ireland?"

"Where's Joanne?" giggled Clift.

"Watch it, sonny," the chilly Hawks scolded. "It's a man's world out here. We'll have to do the time-transition scene, then. Tell John!"

There was a stir of activity in which Susan Garth was able to say to Bark, "I may be sick to my stomach."

"Just watch," he urged her. "Howard's good. He's damn good."

"This is absurd."

"It's a movie, Susan! It's like a girl: it doesn't have to make sense if it's beautiful. Just watch."

John Wayne appeared, but it was a John Wayne with some sophisticated flour in his hair so that he looked nearly as old and disagreeable as Bark Blaylock.

"How are you?" Susan called out.

The swaying Wayne's progress faltered. He stopped. He started again. Now he really stopped. He did it like a dream—detached but eloquent.

"Don't I . . . ?" he asked, pointing at her.

"You'd better."

"Well, how *are* you?" asked Wayne.

"How's the weasel?" asked Susan Garth.

"He's the same," said Wayne. "You see him?"

"I talk to him," said Susan Garth. "Sometimes"—for Bark's benefit.

"Who's that?" asked Bark.

"Jack," said John Wayne.

"Oh, yeah?" said Bark, and then to Susan, "You see him?"

"Talk to him," she admitted. She asked Wayne, "What's this like, then?"

"How d'you like the look of me?"

"It's good. It suits you."

"Then maybe the picture's all right. Howard's snakebit about Ireland."

"Courting his girl?" asked Bark.

"I don't know courting. Howard's burning, I'll tell you."

"Maybe it's good for the picture," said Susan.

"Howard's all right," said Wayne. "If you don't laugh in his face. So long as he thinks he's checkmating you, and you don't say anything about the lies. Just let him frighten you to death. I gotta go!"

"I'd like to see a run-through," said Howard in a soft voice to still chaos. "Where are the fucking crosses?"

Property men quickly stuck rough wooden grave markers in the background of the shot.

"John," said Howard, "this is where we come out of the past on the voice-over about the war and the way the ranch grew."

"Got it," said Wayne, with a wave of the hand.

They tried it once, and Howard interrupted. He asked for Wayne's Dunson to be down on his haunches, so his back stiffened and Garth had to give him a hand up. They worked out a nice tidy little dolly so the shot started on Dunson and then filled out into the trio, Dunson, Garth and Groot.

"What do I do while they're talking?" asked Clift.

"Listen to 'em," said Howard, "and chew a piece of grass. Oh, and Monty, when Dunson interrupts you, just keep on talking. Don't yield."

So they rehearsed some more, and Groot's timing was settled in, until three actors in cowboy clothes had, in a moment or two, the travail and history of a family of men, always talking and thinking at odds.

"Let's go for a take," asked a world-weary Howard.

And there, on a September day, in Arizona in 1946, they filmed Texas in 1865, in front of Susan Garth, a tricky, subtle scene, with dust, crosses, pale grass and sun behind them and the eternal misunderstandings of people in the foreground. It was absurd, of course, a sign of sinking times; but it was perfect, too, and by the third take, the one printed, even Susan Garth was enjoying it and seeing the charm of a blind-side approach to her own buried childhood.

So she turned away, as abrupt as Wayne's Dunson. Yet she did it silently, so the take was not spoiled. And then she walked across that patch of ground, thinking it might as well be real. She looked back and Clift's gay smile shot out at her. He pointed his hand at her apparent boredom, as if the finger was a six-gun. And maybe Susan Garth did see a ghost of a resemblance.

July 1950, On the Common

It could be done in the studio: all the cross-talk, the stolen glances and the mingling moods of Susan, Bark, James and Jim could be obtained in the bouncing skin of an auto behind which Arizona and New Mexico slip by like water on glass. But they insist on the thing itself, the stops to refill the car, the haze of bugs on the windscreen, the fifty-mile straights through heat when maybe even the driver is dozing. It would be safer in the studio, with Bark driving.

"The music," says Jim when he sees from a newspaper that it is July already.

"We'll be there," James Averill assures him. Going home now for unspoken forgiveness.

They drive by way of Gallup, Standing Rock and Crownpoint until they reach the ruins of Chaco. They do feel then that the wash of the golden masonry is covering them, making them funerary, as grave as stone eagles guarding the hallowed city. They are speechless at Chaco, there is nothing to be said; only the going there will do, and its silence. Susan Garth takes one photograph, not of the city, but of the three men with her, Bark in the middle between two Averills, three figures with the indistinct blaze of desert behind them. It is not even one of her "pictures"; it is just a snap, and she will send them all copies, except that Bark will be dead.

They skirt Albuquerque and on 66 they make speed to Santa Rosa, dropping down to old Fort Sumner on a very hot, still day, playing Botticelli in the car.

The Pecos is not just dry, its bed has shifted, like a sleeper rolling over. As far as Bark can tell, it now runs over the ground where Pete Maxwell's house once stood. He tries to estimate the position of the fateful veranda, and he murmurs vaguely to Jim about the changes in a river.

"In Death Valley," he says, "there's only two inches of rain in a year, but people drown in floods."

"We must be getting on," says Susan, like a voice in their sleep.

"I had four fathers," Bark tells Jim, "and every one to be proud of."

The boy senses that the old man is disappearing, and he is sentimental enough to take care of him. Or watch him slip away. There is no fuss about salvation here, or help; it cannot be mustered amid the immemorial, baked-clay masses of that land. But passing will be observed.

They go into Texas and at some small crossroads on the way to Amarillo, in a movie theater grand enough for Lillie Langtry, but closing down in the deserted, windswept town, the old man and the boy go to see the last attraction, a revival of _Red River_, the print scarred with age, or use.

"This is Miss Garth's father," says Jim in the dark.

"Chalk and cheese," the old man answers. "Different breeds of people. The film is a pack of lies, don't you see?"

But Jim will not agree, not even with a weakening, fading man. "I like it fine," he says. "I like it very much."

"Oh, sure, I know," Bark allows. "If it comes to that, it's all right."

"The best I've seen," the boy insists, and takes the old man's hand to lead him out of the dusty cool of the theater.

The Averills leave the old people at Amarillo. They see them through the airport terminal window from the small plane that will take them to Dallas. They wave, all of them wondering if the others can see, if they know they are not alone.

Father and son fly into Boston. They are there on the third. James shows the hurrying Betsy the pictures he has bought from Susan Garth and Betsy says, Oh, lovely, but the music, take care of Sally. And James hugs his daughter and notices there is a new flinching in her. Time enough for that, time enough for all the trouble, do not be afraid of trouble. They are going to the Common, but it looks like rain. They are going for the Ives, the first performance, the wondrous groan and grind of all its ghostly voices of America, there on the Common on the Fourth, as the holiday ambles by. There is terror, there is destruction. But these are peaceful things, ordinaries.

The Common is crowded, and only the quick, living eye sees the fluctuations in the crowd as random, passionate and disordered. The other eye knows, without orders having been given, there is an inspired, demented regularity, like that of gnats in the air above a deep black pool in the Wyoming hinterland of 1879. Those gnats are dancing.

The music is beginning. Here comes the lovely rain. Gray drops falling, as if the heat is weeping.

"Let's get wet," cries Jim Jr., out ahead of their umbrella, capering, whirling, as brave as Chaplin.

The music is beginning.

A NOTE ON CHARACTERS

Matthew Garth (Montgomery Clift and Mickey Kuhn), Tom Dunson (John Wayne), Groot (Walter Brennan), Tess Millay (Joanne Dru), Cherry Valance (John Ireland) and Frank Melville (Harry Carey Sr.) are from *Red River* (1948), directed by Howard Hawks and written by Borden Chase and Charles Schnee from the *Saturday Evening Post* story "The Chisholm Trail," by Chase.

Ethan Edwards (John Wayne) and Debbie Edwards (Natalie Wood) are from *The Searchers* (1956), directed by John Ford and written by Frank S. Nugent from the novel by Alan LeMay.

Ransom Stoddard (James Stewart), Hallie Stoddard (Vera Miles), Liberty Valance (Lee Marvin) and Tom Doniphon (John Wayne) are from *The Man Who Shot Liberty Valance* (1962), directed by John Ford and written by Willis Goldbeck and James Warner Bellah from the story by Dorothy M. Johnson.

John McCabe (Warren Beatty) and Mrs. Miller (Julie Christie) are from *McCabe and Mrs. Miller* (1970), directed by Robert Altman and written by Altman and Brian McKay from the novel *McCabe*, by Edmund Naughton.

Mrs. John T. Chance (Angie Dickinson) is from *Rio Bravo* (1959), directed by Howard Hawks and written by Jules Furthman and Leigh Brackett from a story by B. H. McCampbell.

David Braxton (John McLiam) and Jane Braxton (Kathleen Lloyd) are from *The Missouri Breaks* (1976), directed by Arthur Penn and written by Thomas McGuane.

James Averill I (Kris Kristofferson) and Nate Champion (Christopher Walken) are from *Heaven's Gate* (1980), directed and written by Michael Cimino.

Travis Blue (Ben Johnson) and Denver (Joanne Dru) are from *Wagonmaster* (1950), directed by John Ford and written by Frank S. Nugent and Patrick Ford.

Noah Cross (John Huston) is from *Chinatown* (1974), directed by Roman Polanski and written by Robert Towne.

Roy Bean (1825?–1903) is a special American pioneer—a nonentity who propelled himself out of humdrum space into celebrity and legend. He seems to have done nothing except for effect and the colorful ways in which people might report it. His judicial reign west of the Pecos was all of the stage; his passion for Lillie Langtry was valiant, warm and moving only to the extent that it was impossible. The heavyweight battle at Langtry took place rather as described here. Still photographs of the occasion do show some primitive moving-film coverage. That the footage from it does not exist begins to suggest the film was never exposed. C. L. Sonnichsen's *Roy Bean: Law West of the Pecos* (Albuquerque, 1986) is a good introduction to Beanery.

Albert Bierstadt (1830–1902), born in Germany, came to America when he was two. But he returned to Germany as a young man to study painting. It was in the late 1850s that he came back to America and began to paint Western landscapes—large canvases full of exact, atmospheric detail—that became fashionable and expensive in the 1870s. The picture described in this book sounds like *Long's Peak*, which can be found in the Denver Public Library. Bierstadt often employed photography as a means to his art.

William Bonney (1859–1881) is the name commonly used to identify the figure known as Billy the Kid. But there are reasons for preferring the names Antrim or McCarty, and no evidence for the assertion that he was born in New York City. About the only reliably documented part of his life is the final five years, spent largely in New Mexico Territory, engaged in the Lincoln County cattle war and then moving towards that famous death which is every kid's starting point with the Kid. Walter Noble Burns wrote the first modern biography, *The Saga of Billy the Kid* (1926), but there is more use to be had in Ramon F. Adams's *A Fitting Death for Billy the Kid* (Norman, 1960) and Jon Tuska's *Billy the Kid: A Handbook* (Lincoln, Nebraska, 1983).

William Brocius can claim dates for neither birth nor death. But he *was* Curly Bill, a troublemaker or a pal in and around Tombstone in 1881. It is reckoned that he was killed by Wyatt Earp in 1882, but no body was ever found. There are also reports that Brocius went under other names, and that he had been involved in the Lincoln County cattle war, where he might have been known to the Kid.

Willa Cather (1873–1947) was a novelist much impressed by the prairies of Nebraska and the history of the Southwest. Her books include *O Pioneers!* (1913), *My Ántonia* (1918), *A Lost Lady* (1923), *Death Comes for the Archbishop* (1927), *Obscure Destinies* (1932) and *The Professor's House* (1925). This latter contains in Tom Outland's story a version of the discovery of a site like

Mesa Verde. Miss Cather had herself visited Mesa Verde in 1915 and had thoroughly researched the reports of how Dick Wetherill had found the place in the late 1880s. However, there had been earlier discoveries still— notably that by the photographer William H. Jackson in 1874. Thus, we can be sure of Miss Cather's politeness in listening to Bark Blaylock's story.

Edward Sheriff Curtis (1868–1952) was a photographer who devoted himself to recording the faces, the life and the ritual of various Indian tribes. His work is displayed in the twenty-volume *The North American Indian*. However, the anthropologist in Curtis was well mixed with the romantic—for he chose to remove all traces of the modern age from his pictures, and he liked to enhance the lights and darks of mood. Indeed, he sometimes carried Indian costumes with him as he traveled so that the subjects he found might have an authentic nobility.

Wyatt B. S. Earp (1848–1929) was born in Monmouth, Illinois. He drove a wagon on his family's 1864 journey to California and he later worked on the railroads as a grader, as a boxing promoter and as an all-round pro- spector, before settling to the career of lawman which led by way of Wichita and Dodge City to Tombstone. He had at least three wives, or common- law wives: Urilla Sutherland, Celia or Mattie Blaylock and Josephine Marcus, who was still his wife when he died in a Los Angeles tourist court. Shortly thereafter, Stuart N. Lake published *Wyatt Earp: Frontier Marshal* (1931), the most clear-cut version of the glorious legend. More interesting in its loyal but casual way is *I Married Wyatt Earp* by Josephine Marcus, edited by Glen G. Boyer (Tucson, 1976). Josephine Earp died in 1944, busily contesting the image of her husband that was beginning to appear on the screen.

Bob Fitzsimmons (1863–1917) was a boxer, born in Helston, Cornwall. Though never weighing more than 170 pounds, he took the Heavyweight Championship of the World on March 17, 1897, when he knocked out James J. Corbett in Carson City, Nevada. He lost the title two years later, to James J. Jeffries. His fights with Peter Maher and Tom Sharkey as described in this book are verifiable occurrences. He was disqualified by referee Earp in the San Francisco contest with Sharkey. Fitzsimmons died of pneumonia.

John, or Jack, Ford (1895–1973) was a film director. The most recent and complete work on Ford, Tag Gallagher's *John Ford: The Man and His Films* (Berkeley, 1985), admits that "Information on John Ford's work prior to *The Tornado* in 1917 is sketchy," but allows that Ford was in California from the summer of 1914 in a variety of assisting roles. So it is more than possible that he did work for Susan Garth as part of the camera crew on the lost *A Girl of the Hills*. Later, Ford became a reputable filmmaker, especially of Westerns. It was in making *Stagecoach* (1939) that he first employed Mon- ument Valley as a location and cultivated the lodge that had been opened

there, Goulding's. He would have been based there, in June and July of
1950, shooting *Rio Grande* with John Wayne. He also made parts of *My
Darling Clementine* (1946), *Fort Apache* (1948), *She Wore a Yellow Ribbon* (1949),
Wagonmaster (1950) and *The Searchers* (1956) in Monument Valley. But *The
Man Who Shot Liberty Valance* (1962) was filmed largely in Los Angeles.

John Nance Garner (1868–1967) was born in Red River County, Texas. After
a youth spent on the range, he practiced law from 1890 onwards in Uvalde,
where his clients came from the class of successful pioneers. He entered the
Texas legislature in 1898, and he was a congressman from 1903 to 1933,
being speaker of the House before he became Franklin Roosevelt's first vice
president, from 1933 to 1941. On his retirement, he went back to the Rio
Grande country.

Patrick Floyd Garrett (1850–1908) was born in Alabama, from where he
slipped gradually westwards, doing this and that. It is not recorded that he
ever sold trusses, but no "life" of Garrett dares claim completeness. He was
a cowboy, a sometime acquaintance of the Kid and not consistently on the
polite side of the law. But in 1880 he was elected sheriff of Lincoln County
in the Territory of New Mexico, an office that directed him towards re-
encounter with William Bonney and shots in the dark. After the events of
July 14, 1881, Garrett became a rancher, and in 1882 (with the considerable
help of Ash Upson) he published *The Authentic Life of Billy, the Kid, the Noted
Desperado of the Southwest*. Later still, Garrett was collector of Customs at El
Paso. He was a horse-rancher in the Organ Mountains when he was shot
and killed, on February 29, 1908, by a Wayne Brazel, who was duly acquitted.

Arnold Genthe (1869–1942) was a Berlin-born photographer who settled in
San Francisco in time to record the old Chinatown before the earthquake.
And when his camera was destroyed in the first damage on the April morn-
ing in 1906, Genthe borrowed another to make his famous images of the
disaster. In later life, he had success as a portraitist. His autobiography, *As
I Remember*, was published in 1942.

Geronimo (1829?–1909) was a chief of the Mimbres Apache whose tribal
name was Gokhlayeh. For over twenty years, he was variously at peace or
on roaming guerrilla campaigns against the American Army, retreating into
Mexico when it was convenient, surrendering if he was bored, killing a few
settlers and soldiers and enduring the stories of massacre. He submitted to
capture at last in 1886 and was deported to Florida where he became a public
attraction, having his picture taken and appearing at Theodore Roosevelt's
inauguration in 1901 and at the St. Louis World's Fair in 1904. He died at
Fort Sill in Oklahoma.

Wardell Gray (1921–1955) was born in Oklahoma City and raised in Detroit.
He played the alto sax for Earl Hines in 1943, and the tenor two years later

with the Billy Eckstine Orchestra. For the next decade, he was one of the leading figures in the bop movement, while also playing with Benny Goodman and Count Basie. He died of a drug overdose and his body was found in the desert outside Las Vegas. "Twisted" was his own composition. Subsequently, it was given lyrics by the singer Annie Ross.

Thomas Hardy (1840–1928), the author of *The Return of the Native* (1878) and *Tess of the d'Urbervilles* (1891), did live in Upper Tooting, a suburb in southwest London, in the early 1880s. Biographies do not list the names of all his house servants, but it is possible that the Mrs. Constance Miller on the loose in the Yukon in the late 1890s had been a young housemaid who glimpsed the master at work.

Howard Hawks (1896–1977) was a film director. He did location shooting for *Red River* in the area of Willcox, Arizona, in the summer of 1946. The allegation that the actor John Ireland earned Hawks's anger on that production comes from Jim Kitses' interview with the screenwriter, Borden Chase, published in *The Hollywood Screenwriter*, edited by Richard Corliss (1972). John Ireland was married to the actress Joanne Dru from 1949 to 1956. There is as yet no biography of Hawks.

Charles Ives (1874–1954) was born in Danbury, Connecticut. His success in life was in the insurance business. His finest failure was as a composer in the years before 1920. The piece "Three Places in New England" (which James Averill II hears played in Boston) was written just prior to the First World War, but it was not performed until 1948, in Boston. The poem that Averill reads is thought to be by Ives himself and it refers to the first of the three places—the St. Gaudens monument to Colonel Shaw and his colored regiment on Boston Common. Sadly, there was no performance of Ives' Fourth Symphony in his lifetime; and concerts are not given on the Common.

William Henry Jackson (1843–1942), born in Keeseville, New York, learned photography as a boy from his father. From about 1870 onwards, he traveled extensively in the West, carrying his wet collodion equipment as well as a darkroom. He was official photographer to the U.S. Geological and Geographical Survey of the Territories. Near the close of his prodigious life, he gave evidently ignored advice on the making of *Gone With the Wind*. His autobiography, *Time Exposure*, was published in 1940, and the best collection of his great work is at the Edison Institute, in Dearborn, Michigan.

Stanley Ketchel (1886–1910) was a boxer born in Grand Rapids, Michigan, of Polish descent—his original name was Stanislaus Kiecal. He won and lost the middleweight championship of the world twice in the years 1907–08, but despite his defeat by Jack Johnson in 1909, he was a contender still when he was murdered in 1910—as described in this book, though Susan Garth may have embroidered the circumstances to prove a point.

"Bat" Masterson (1856–1921) was born as William Barclay Masterson in Kansas. He had been a buffalo-hunter, an Indian-fighter and an Army scout, and he took a wound in a fight over a woman that left him with a limp. He won a reputation as a robust lawman in Dodge City in the late 1870s, but he declined into the running of saloons and the fostering of stories, and finally sank to the level of a New York City sportswriter.

George Lewis "Tex" Rickard (1871–1929) had been a cowboy and a Klondike gold prospector before he took up the promoting of boxing matches. He was the pioneer of "big" fights (Johnson vs. Jeffries; Dempsey vs. Willard; Dempsey vs. Carpentier), and it was with the fortune made from such events that he built the New Madison Square Garden on 8th Avenue between 49th and 50th streets.

Walter Scott (1872?–1954) was a Kentuckian who first saw Death Valley in about 1884 while working for a survey team. He then traveled with Buffalo Bill Cody's Wild West Show—more as a promoter than a performer. On his return to California, he engineered a modest gold fever for Death Valley and prospered for many years on the rumors of his good fortune. No one was more moved by these stories than Albert Johnson, a Chicago businessman in poor health, who came to Death Valley for convalescence and paid for the building of what became known as "Scotty's Castle," an enchanting and very habitable mélange of movie sets in the most unlikely setting imaginable. Scotty's Castle may now be visited by the public if one ventures as far as the northern end of Death Valley. Colorful legends still attach themselves to this implausible but romantic place.

Erich von Stroheim (1885–1957) was born as Erich Oswald Stroheim in Vienna. The "Von" came as he found work advising American movies on Prussian uniforms and manners in the years of the First World War. Stroheim began directing in 1918, with *Blind Husbands*. *Greed*—from Frank Norris' novel *McTeague*—was shot in 1923–24, but not released until 1925, perhaps a quarter of its director's first conception. Stroheim made other films—*The Merry Widow*, *The Wedding March*, *Queen Kelly*—but he never escaped his own reputation for extravagance or gave up the gloomy look of one who has known disaster. He had to turn to acting to survive and thus he found his swan song as the mortified but magnificent Max von Mayerling in *Sunset Boulevard*.

FAMILY TREES

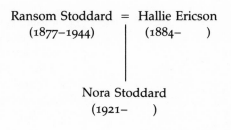

Ransom Stoddard = Hallie Ericson
(1877–1944)   (1884–   )

Nora Stoddard
(1921–   )

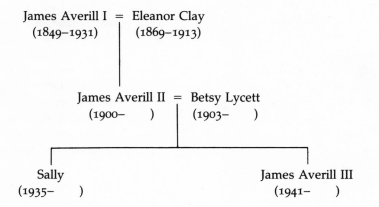

James Averill I = Eleanor Clay
(1849–1931)   (1869–1913)

James Averill II = Betsy Lycett
(1900–   )   (1903–   )

Sally   James Averill III
(1935–   )   (1941–   )

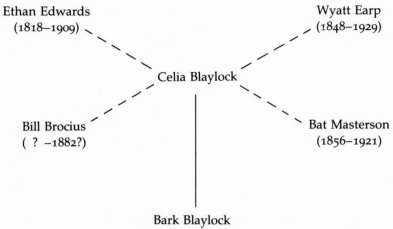

Ethan Edwards
(1818–1909)

Wyatt Earp
(1848–1929)

Celia Blaylock

Bill Brocius
(? –1882?)

Bat Masterson
(1856–1921)

Bark Blaylock
(1875?–1950)

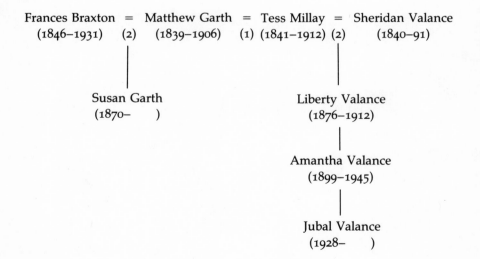

Frances Braxton = Matthew Garth = Tess Millay = Sheridan Valance
(1846–1931) (2)   (1839–1906)   (1) (1841–1912) (2)   (1840–91)

Susan Garth
(1870–   )

Liberty Valance
(1876–1912)

Amantha Valance
(1899–1945)

Jubal Valance
(1928–   )

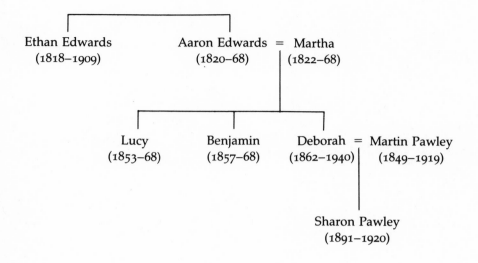

Ethan Edwards
(1818–1909)

Aaron Edwards = Martha
(1820–68)   (1822–68)

Lucy   Benjamin   Deborah = Martin Pawley
(1853–68)   (1857–68)   (1862–1940)   (1849–1919)

Sharon Pawley
(1891–1920)

A NOTE ON THE TYPE

The text of this book was composed in a film version of Palatino, a type face designed by the noted German typographer Hermann Zapf. Named after Giovanbattista Palatino, a writing master of Renaissance Italy, Palatino was the first of Zapf's type faces to be introduced in America. The first designs for the face were made in 1948, and the fonts for the complete face were issued between 1950 and 1952. Like all Zapf-designed type faces, Palatino is beautifully balanced and exceedingly readable.

Composed by Crane Typesetting Service, Inc.
Barnstable, Massachusetts

Printed and bound by Fairfield Graphics,
Fairfield, Pennsylvania

Typography and binding design by
Dorothy Schmiderer Baker